The Dream

David K Saunders

Published by Shadenet Publishing 2014
www.shadenetpublishing.co.uk

Cover design by Samantha Groom
magicat45degrees@googlemail.com

Cover picture by kind permission of the Guildhall Art Gallery, City of London. *'Sanctuary' (Edward IV and Lancastrian Fugitives at Tewkesbury Abbey)* by Richard Burchett

Maps by www.illustrativemaps.co.uk

ISBN-13: 978-1500196912

Also available as an e-book

For my wife, Maggie

Acknowledgements

Writing a novel is a solitary process but to finally cross the finishing line with a finished book requires the help, encouragement, expertise, and patience of others. So I would like to take this opportunity to say thank you to these special people who have made 'The Dreams of Kings' the book it is. Without them, this book would not be here for you to read.

Many thanks to June Polson for all her hard work in the typing of the early drafts, which gave me the encouragement to carry on.

To my golfing buddy, Mike Watson, for his tremendous effort in the reading of the early manuscript, not once, but twice. His constructive criticism, suggested changes, and enthusiasm, improved the book immensely.

To my lovely wife, Maggie-May, for her spell-checking skills, the reading and re-reading of endless chapters, and her never-ending patience in listening to her husband talk endlessly about characters, battles, and plots.

To my son, Luke, and his partner, Dawn, for their expertise in putting together the Yorkist and Lancastrian family trees, plus the website for the book.

Lastly, my most grateful thanks goes to Sue Shade, editor extraordinaire, who has corrected, amended, suggested, and checked, every word, line, page, and chapter. The book is a testament to the skill of a brilliant editor and I give my sincere thanks for her wonderful effort in making 'The Dreams of Kings' the book it has finally become.

David Saunders
21 April 2014

Contents

Map 1: British Historic Locations

Map 2: French Historic Locations

The Houses of York and Neville Family Tree

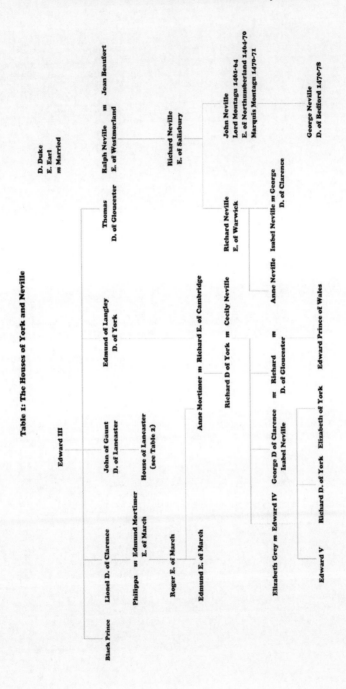

Table 1: The Houses of York and Neville

D. Duke
E. Earl
m Married

Edward III

Black Prince

Lionel D. of Clarence

John of Gaust
D. of Lancaster

House of Lancaster
(see Table 2)

Edmund of Langley
D. of York

Thomas
D. of Gloucester

Ralph Neville   m   Joan Beaufort
E. of Westmorland

Phillippa   m   Edmund Mortimer
E. of March

Roger E. of March

Edmund E. of March

Anne Mortimer   m   Richard E. of Cambridge

Richard Neville
E. of Salisbury

Richard D of York   m   Cecily Neville

Richard Neville
E. of Warwick

John Neville
Lord Montagu 1461-64
E. of Northumberland 1464-70
Marquis Montagu 1470-71

George Neville
D. of Bedford 1470-78

Anne Neville   Isabel Neville m George
D. of Clarence

Elizabeth Grey m Edward IV   George D of Clarence   m   Richard   Edward Prince of Wales
Isabel Neville   D. of Gloucester

Edward V   Richard D. of York   Elizabeth of York

The Houses of Lancaster, Tudor, and Beaufort Family Tree

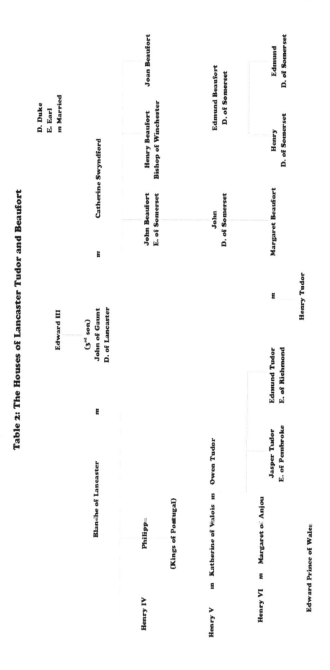

Table 2: The Houses of Lancaster Tudor and Beaufort

Prologue

The Manor House, Barton-le-Clay, Bedfordshire 23 May 1455

Fourteen-year-old Simon Langford heard the sound of many horsemen approaching, and assumed that it was his father returning from battle. Full of excitement, he had dashed from the house towards the approaching dust cloud. As the horsemen came into view, he realised it was not his father's party, for they wore the colours of an unknown knight. The group rode compact and fast – each horse moving in smooth, fluid unison with those around it as if they had become of one creature – each a component part of this swift, sinister force.

Simon stepped back into the treeline as they passed. He became fearful; his stomach turned over. He saw that they carried the blood of battle on their armour and weapons. There was a ruthless purpose in their movement and they were heading straight for the house. Fear entered Simon's body and he raced after them, his heart pounding.

He came upon the riders as they dismounted. Keeping his distance, he watched as two of his father's old servants came out of the house to confront this armed force. They each carried an old rusty sword, but due to their age, these were more for show than for action. Two of the dismounted horsemen walked slowly towards them, their swords drawn. Simon stood perfectly still. He was waiting to hear them speak, but no words were spoken. He watched with horror as their swords arched upwards – the move was sudden and swift. The two old servants staggered backwards dropping their rusty weapons. In that blur of movement, having been sliced open from crotch to chin, they started screaming.

Simon dropped to his knees and covered his ears. The two bloody swords that had disembowelled these old men flashed through the air in perfect, smooth, arcs. The screaming stopped abruptly as their heads parted from their bodies. The mutilated corpses fell forward into a lake of blood, followed by complete silence. The horsemen had witnessed an act of great savagery, but it seemed to Simon as if it were only a minor irritation, like swatting a fly. Their brutalised minds had extinguished all conscience.

Their captain started barking out orders. 'I want the house secured,' he ordered. 'If any resist, kill them.'

'What about the women?' asked one of the men.

'Do what is required to subdue them,' replied the captain.

The men knew exactly what he meant, and smiled. Lust glowed in their eyes.

The captain ordered half the men to sweep round to the left of the house and the other half to the right. He instructed that every member of the household be lined up in front of the house – be they dead or alive. He and two officers then strode through the front door and disappeared into the dark interior.

Simon sat on his haunches. Now alone, he stared at the bloody remains of the two servants. The speed of the killing had mesmerised him. Blood was flowing on to the flagstones, forming a circular sea of red around the grisly remains. His mind was stunned; his thoughts moved through a thick fog of disbelief. He was rooted to the spot.

A high-pitched scream chilled his heart. He turned his head and saw Anne, one of the kitchen maids, bolting from the house. She was caught halfway across the yard by three soldiers. They carried her, screaming, over to some large wooden barrels where they tied her, face down. Simon could hear her desperate sobs as they ripped and cut her clothes away. His mind whirled with despair. *They must be the forces of the Devil,* he thought. *Why has God deserted us?* He heard more despairing screams from around the house – what was happening to Anne was happening everywhere. The realisation made him start to sweat as he had just remembered where his mother and two younger sisters were. He launched himself from the ground and sprinted into the house. As he passed through the front door, he heard his mother scream.

The darkness of the hallway slowed Simon's pace enough for him to glimpse a small, sharp, hunting knife, lying beside a bowl of fruit on the hallway table. He smoothly picked it up as he passed, and slipped it through his belt in the small of his back. Raised voices emanated from the dining hall, and without a thought, he rushed in.

Simon's eyes flared with anger as he scanned the room. Standing to his right, stood his two younger sisters. They were tight up against the wall, their young faces cut and bruised. They stood in complete silence, their cheeks wet with tears. Each had the tip of a sword pressed against their young throats. The two henchmen, who had accompanied the captain into the house, held these swords and stood poised, awaiting the order to strike.

A large oak table stood in the centre of the room, and standing behind the chair at the far end was Simon's mother, her face showing loathing and disgust, her eyes ablaze with defiance.

On the left of the room, positioned halfway along the table, stood the unknown knight – the leader of the pack of savages. His sword was drawn and pointed towards Simon's mother. She hissed defiance at them.

'Oh…such brave soldiers…your mothers and wives would be so proud of you,' she said. 'Is this how you show your courage? By murdering old men? By raping young girls? By beating and then threatening to kill my young innocent daughters. I know you have murdered my husband!' Then, her voice rising in anger, she flung out her arm and pointed towards the leader. 'You scum would never have killed William in rightful combat. Such cowardly assassins like you have no honour, or God. May you all burn in Hell for eternity!'

Simon gasped – his father was dead?

The leader swung round and stared at Simon. 'So, this is your son,' he sneered. 'I will deal with him as I dealt with your husband.' With his hand, he made a cutting motion across his neck. The two henchmen sniggered.

The leader turned his back on Simon to address his mother. 'My name is Sir Thomas Raket, and I am now the master of this house and its chattels and lands. It has been granted to me by the Earl of Warwick as payment for my loyalty, and you, are now dispossessed of all you hold dear. You are destitute.' He took a step towards her. With narrowed eyes and malevolence in his voice, he hissed, 'If you do not reveal where the gold and coin are concealed, you will watch your children die.'

Lady Langford stared silently back, hatred in her eyes.

As Sir Thomas Raket whipped his sword through the air, it opened a small wound on Lady Langford's cheek. She gasped with shock as blood trickled down her face like a red tear.

'You will talk to me,' Sir Thomas Raket snarled, the sword hovering in front of her face.

Lady Langford stared unflinchingly at him. 'Death with honour is finer for me and my children, than to betray my husband to devils like you.'

Sir Thomas Raket raised his arm into the air. 'If you don't talk by the time I count to five, I will drop my arm, and your daughters will die, followed by your son.'

Simon stared at his mother. He saw the defiance radiating from her, but as she looked at him and his sisters, he saw the pain in her eyes, and her resolve starting to crumble. Simon knew she would reveal what the monster wanted to know – his mother would not stand there and watch her innocent lambs slaughtered – but her bravery right up to this moment had filled him with courage. He heard the monster start to count and with a Herculean effort, Simon vaulted on to the oak table.

As he landed, he smoothly pulled the knife from its hiding place in his belt. He darted along the table and launched himself on to the back of his father's murderer, his legs wrapped around the man's waist. As the blade of Simon's knife cut into Sir Thomas Raket's neck, the counting stopped. The man stood stock still. Simon whispered into his ear, 'Tell your men to lower their swords.'

Sir Thomas Raket did as he was bid.

'Mother, take the girls into the hallway!' urged Simon.

As Lady Langford gathered her daughters and ran from the room, Simon spoke to the two henchmen. 'Drop your swords and go down to the far end of the room.'

They both looked at their captain, who nodded vigorously. The two swords clattered on to the floor and the men moved to the far end of the room.

Simon told the captain to back up towards the other end of the room to where the door was situated. Once there, Simon, with all his young strength, sliced the knife deep across the captain's throat.

The captain made a gurgling sound, and fell to his knees, blood spurting from his neck.

Simon slipped off and cried, 'For my father!' before ramming the knife into the captain's back. Then, stepping through the doorway, he slammed the heavy oak door shut behind him and turned the key.

He turned away from the door to be met by his mother's embrace. He held her tightly; his heart was beating so fast he thought it would burst. His lungs were straining to gulp air into his body; his mind stunned by the terrifying events in the dining hall, and at what he had done. His two young sisters clung to him, their little hands forming tight fists as they held on to his jacket. Slowly, Simon's eyes focused on the blood that covered his hands, and the sight jolted him into action. Releasing his mother, he stepped back. 'We must leave now, if we are to live,' he said, with urgency in his voice.

'But how?' questioned his mother. 'These filthy savages are all around the house.'

'We will use the secret servants' passage,' said Simon. 'It is unlikely that they have discovered it; they have been too intent on satisfying their foul lust.'

The servants' passage ran through the centre of the house. They could move around unseen, going from the kitchens to the dining hall, or service rooms to bedrooms, without using the main halls. It also allowed access to the stables at the rear of the manor.

Simon, his mother, and sisters, were soon fleeing down the narrow passage. They reached the stables unseen. There, two estate workers, who had been hiding in the rafters, helped them quickly saddle up their horses. Simon, with one young sister sitting in front of him, and his mother, with the other in front of her, made good their escape. The two estate workers who had helped also now rode with them. They travelled swiftly, away from the manor house, their hearts heavy with sorrow for those left behind, knowing they were powerless to help them.

Simon felt the tears sting his eyes as thoughts of his father flooded into his mind. The rhythmic movement of his horse lulled him into a trance-like state where a wound of sorrow cut into his heart. The physical world around him disappeared and only the faces of his father, and Sir Thomas Raket, swirled around in his thoughts. The trauma of the last hour had fragmented his emotions; he wished he could feel numb inside, to escape the reality of this pain and despair. He knew his mother and sisters would be feeling the same – if only he could make it right for them and put everything back as it had been a few hours ago. It was then Simon saw the riders in the distance. He slowed his horse; his mother and the others did likewise.

The advancing horsemen split into three groups: the centre unit of thirty men headed straight towards Simon, whilst two smaller groups, comprising of ten men each, moved out from the main force. One group headed left, the other right, forming a pincer movement. Simon knew that there was no escape. His mind frantic, he looked towards his mother. She saw his bewildered look of confusion and pointed towards the advancing horsemen. 'They're our men returning from the battle!' she cried. 'Look, they're wearing your father's colours.'

The horsemen slowed as they recognised Lady Langford and her family. Simon closed his eyes. His body suddenly ached with weariness. They were safe.

Part One

1461–1464

Chapter 1

Friendship, Love, and Spies

Bamburgh Castle, Northumberland
28 June 1461

As Archbishop Bourchier lowered the crown on to the anointed head of Edward IV, proclaiming him King of England, Simon Langford stepped ashore at the port of Newcastle. He had taken passage on a trading ship, which had brought a cargo of pewter candleholders and drinking vessels from the port of London to Newcastle, for distribution throughout the north of Yorkshire.

He arrived at Bamburgh Castle as a glorious red sunset filled the evening sky. The castle was built on a rocky outcrop stretching out into the sea, and in the evening light it gave the illusion that it had been formed by God, straight out of the granite shoreline. It loomed high above Simon, dominating the countryside.

Margaret of Anjou's senior administrator, Sir John Fortescue, interviewed Simon before granting him an audience with her at eight of the clock that evening, in her private apartments. In the intervening time, he was given a private room with washing facilities and clean clothes. After his long journey, he was appreciative of these small courtesies. After washing off the sea salt, and the dust of the road, he dressed in the fresh clothes that were laid out for him. They smelled slightly of lavender. The luxury of these clean garments on his cleansed body relaxed him mentally and physically. He was now refreshed and keen to meet Margaret of Anjou, Queen consort of England, face to face. He had heard much about her – how she was a tigress in defending her royal crown. Her passionate and courageous French temperament could bewitch and enchant even the most flint-hearted of men, and the most soft-hearted could be driven mad with rage by her actions. Simon wondered if she would bewitch him or drive him mad.

He entered her private chambers at the appointed time with a feeling of apprehension. Margaret was sitting in a tall-backed chair close to the window. All Simon could see was her black silhouette framed by the last rays of the sun. He bowed low.

'Come closer,' Margaret said, in French.

As he moved across the room, she pointed to a spot in front of her.

'Stand there,' she commanded.

Simon did as he was bid. He was surprised that she was alone. Her hands went together as if in prayer. She leaned closer to him, and rested her chin on the tips of her fingers.

Simon could see her clearly, now. Her long blonde hair was tied back, tightly framing her face in a ring of gold. She was the most beautiful woman he had ever seen, but her alluring grey eyes were cold and they inspected him from the top of his head to the bottom of his feet, moving up and down his body as she evaluated his worth. Finally, she leaned back in the chair and rested her hands on the arms.

'Why have you come?' she asked.

'I have come to continue my father's service to you,' Simon replied, in fluent French.

'Your father was Sir William Langford, was he not?' she questioned.

'Yes, your Highness' replied Simon. 'He fell at the second battle of St Albans.'

'Ah! So you were the young boy who killed that toad, Sir Thomas Raket?' she said.

'That is correct, your Highness, and I have come here today to offer my services to you, to restore King Henry to his rightful throne and to see Warwick's head anchored on a spike.'

'That is one head we would all like to see on a spike,' Margaret replied, coldly. Then relaxing back into her chair, she smiled at Simon, her voice becoming warmer. 'Come, sit beside me,' she said, pointing to a chair.

Simon sat down. Margaret's eyes had softened towards him.

'The man – or should I say, boy – who eliminated that devil, Raket, will always be welcomed into the court of Queen Margaret of Anjou. Don't you agree, Pierre?'

Out of the shadows, as though conjured up by a magician, appeared a large man who Simon could only describe as a soldier. Startled, Simon stared at him. How stupid to think that the Queen would give an audience without protection close at hand.

The soldier, with his tall angular body, moved quickly to the Queen's side and gently rested his hand on her shoulder. She moved her hand up and affectionately covered his hand with hers. It was such a simple act, but to Simon seemed to signal more than just friendship. He had heard rumours about the Queen having lovers; some even said that Edmund Beaufort, 2nd Duke of Somerset – had sired her son, Prince Edward, because King Henry was celibate. Simon had always discounted such talk, but now doubt entered his mind. Luckily, for him, the room was now quite dark so his glancing look of astonishment had gone unnoticed.

Margaret removed her hand. 'Pierre, fetch a taper so we may light the candles.'

The man vanished into the shadows and reappeared with his long angular stride, moments later. The candles lit, he pulled up a chair for himself, and the three of them sat in a circle facing each other.

Margaret spoke. 'Simon, let me introduce you to Pierre de Brézé. The King of France, Louis XI, has kindly sent him to me with five hundred of his finest troops. Also, he has supplied money to finance our campaign against these contemptible traitors who have stolen my husband's crown and plundered his kingdom.'

As Margaret spoke, Simon watched her sitting proudly in her chair, her eyes sparkling as hard as diamonds. He saw that she was determined to annihilate King Edward, and Warwick's new reign in England. Her voice vibrated with strength, and he could see the tigress in her.

'We are raising troops in Scotland and the Welsh borders,' Margaret continued. 'More men, committed to our cause, are being mustered in the West Country, the Midlands, and the north. We will not go meekly from our kingdom – we will fight, and fight again, until we are victorious. My son will have his inheritance; he will sit on the throne of England.'

Simon realised that this struggle was not about King Henry; he was now a minor player – a pawn in the game. It was about Queen Margaret and her beloved son, Prince Edward. The French king had his own political reasons for assisting in the conflict; the Scots had territorial ambitions. It seemed everyone had their own agenda for being involved, and Simon's was the death of the Earl of Warwick.

Pierre de Brézé spoke. 'Simon, we have enough fighting men. I heard through your interviews that you are highly skilled in many tongues and accomplished with the pen. Also, you are quick of mind and your face is unknown. So, taking all this into account, the Queen and I feel your strength is not on the battlefield, but in our espionage network. With your skills, you would find employment at any of the great castles and we need someone at Middleham Castle right within the heart of Warwick's power base—'

'It is dangerous work,' Margaret interrupted, 'but we need information on Warwick's strategies, troop movements – anything that will assist us to victory. The risks are great. If you are caught, torture and a slow death will be the payment asked of you.' She paused and leant towards Simon, her eyes scrutinising his face.

Simon perceived the next question forming on her lips; his answer to her unspoken words was already formulated in his mind, his reply irrefutably bound to his oath of vengeance on Warwick.

Margaret sat upright, and Simon could feel the question hanging ominously in the air between them. Her face washed by flickering candlelight, she finally spoke. 'Simon, will you serve the cause?'

His spirit soared. To be at the centre of Warwick's web, to watch and plot his downfall – far better this, than to just be another sword on a battlefield. Simon did not hesitate. 'It will be an honour to serve.'

The firmness in his voice brought a smile to Margaret's face. She rose to her feet.

Simon did likewise. Taking hold of both of his hands, Margaret said, 'Thank you, my brave boy.' Her eyes were enchanting, her smile alluring. She leant forward and slowly kissed him on both cheeks. Her perfume was all at once intoxicating; her sweet breath brushed his skin as her soft lips lingered on his cheeks and in that moment, Queen Margaret of Anjou, stole Simon's heart. Like many before, he fell under her magical spell.

Middleham Castle, North Yorkshire
14 December 1463

Eleven-year-old John Tunstall waited nervously to see the Great Controller. He had been ordered to report to him at noon, sharp, but had no idea why he had been summoned. All morning, he had been dreading the midday bell striking the appointed hour, for the Earl of Warwick's Great Controller was a man to be feared. He was responsible for the smooth running of Middleham Castle and ruled it with a rod of iron. Nothing escaped him; if you stepped out of line, his punishment was swift.

John sat, outwardly calm, quietly watching the activity of the clerks, while desperately trying to suppress his rising anxiety. The six clerks, in this outer office, assisted the Great Controller with the administration of the castle and its estates. They drafted letters, managed the financial ledgers of expenditure and income, paid the wages to the castle's craftsmen, garrison, and general workers, and issued all the legal documents from death warrants and small fines, to eviction notices. They were the oil that greased the wheels and without them, chaos would reign. John was now a silent witness to the efficiency and orderliness of this complex domain of the Great Controller.

The large door that bore the royal seal of the Great Controller opened, and a thin reed-like man, wearing a black skullcap, emerged. He was dressed marginally finer than the other scribes were, and John assumed that he must be the senior clerk.

Black Skullcap beckoned; John felt the butterflies rise up in his stomach. He felt the eyes of the clerks on him as he walked towards the Great Controller's office. Black Skullcap held the door open, ushering him through.

Once inside, John heard the door close quietly behind him, and he stood still as his eyes slowly adjusted to the half-light. There was one, tall, very narrow window; it seemed to starve the room of light. All was quiet, except for the sound of quill on parchment – then it stopped. Out of the silence, a voice spoke. 'Come closer.'

John moved nervously across the room, his eyes searching out in the dimness. He stopped before an immense desk upon which he saw sheets of parchment arranged in tall neat piles. Behind this paper defence, gazing down on him, sat the Great Controller. John felt his apprehension rising and quickly bowed his head.

The Great Controller waved his hand towards a chair. 'Be seated,' he said sharply. 'We have much to discuss.'

The six clerks in the outer office had glanced up as John passed through the doorway into the Great Controller's office. They looked on as Black Skullcap closed the door and returned to his desk.

Simon Langford rose from his chair and made his way from the outer office. Walking quickly along the passage, he entered a room that backed on to the Great Controller's office, closing the door noiselessly. The room – a depository – had a number of wooden aisles running up and down its length, and reaching from floor to ceiling. On the wooden shelving were stored thousands of important documents. Each scroll was tied with a ribbon and its location recorded in a large ledger kept on a desk by the door. The room was dark and dry; a musty odour hung in the still air.

Simon walked slowly down the aisle furthest away from the door until he reached the wall that divided the depository from the Great Controller's office. There, he stopped, and listened for a moment before reaching out and soundlessly removing a small piece of wooden panelling from the dividing wall. Hanging on the other side of this wall, in the Great Controller's office, was a heavy tapestry. A small hole had been cut to match where the panelling had been removed. This allowed Simon to see the back of the Great Controller, and most of his office, but most importantly, he could hear all that was said.

John Tunstall and the Great Controller studied each other in silence. In this quiet moment, they collected their thoughts.

John had never been this close to the Great Controller before. His only previous contact being when the man had hastened past him, tall and lean, his black robes flapping behind him. If John saw this frightening figure first, he would hide; if not, he stood still and bowed as the other swished by. But now, sitting near him, John could see why the man was sometimes called the 'Old Owl'. His head was bald, except for a half circle of white hair that ran around the back of his head from ear to ear. His eyes were large and hooded; their colour hazel, a combination of green and yellow, the yellow being very pronounced. This made his eyes unusual, even startling. He had a small beak-like nose, and a thin tight-lipped mouth cut a scar across his lower face. He was very old: some said at least fifty-five years, which John thought made him very wise, and he had eyes in the back of his head. The nickname fitted him well.

The Great Controller examined the demeanour of the young boy in front of him. He took in the black hair and clear, blue eyes. There was no doubt that he was a little replica of his late father, Sir William Tunstall. He looked the boy up and down one last time, and with his thoughts now composed, and satisfied that he had chosen well, cleared his throat to signal the start of the interview.

From the accumulation of parchment stacked on his desk, the Great Controller produced a letter, which he carefully placed in front of himself. Then, looking intently at John he said, 'I have before me, a letter bearing the great seal of our King, Edward IV. It is confirmation that he is placing his youngest brother, Richard, Duke of Gloucester, under the protection of our Lord, the Earl of Warwick. He will be a ward in the earl's household for the next five years.' His yellow eyes flashed up, making John jump. 'Do you understand what this means?' he barked.

'I – I – do, sir,' replied John, fearfully, 'but – but I don't understand what it has to do with me.'

'It has everything to do with you!' exclaimed the Great Controller. 'You have been chosen. Out of all the boys in the castle, it is you who has been picked to become Duke Richard's companion, his best friend, and protector. It is a great honour; the earl himself has approved the appointment.'

John did not know what to say, and sat open-mouthed trying to grasp the implications of it all.

'You have nothing to fear,' said the Great Controller, sensing John's nervous confusion. 'You are aware,' he continued, 'that we live in unsettled times. Henry VI was a weak king who had inherited the madness of his maternal French grandfather, Charles VI. Henry's father, Henry V, was one of our greatest warrior kings so it was a great shame his son's head was too small to fill his crown. For a long time, the mystic illusion of royalty allowed the common people to believe in the divine right of their king, and I suppose people still want to believe, even after they are told the truth. But the barons and the royal court, on the other hand, knew the grim reality at first hand.'

John sat astounded; he had never heard anybody talk about royalty in such a disrespectful way.

The Great Controller, warming to his theme, continued. 'Because of King Henry's afflictions, his queen, Margaret of Anjou, was forced to rule for him. However, being a woman in a man's world, she was also seen as weak and was distrusted by the nobles, so rebellion spread amongst the principle dukes of the realm. Eventually, civil warfare broke out, which claimed the lives of many of the nobility. So...to sum up, we had a brave, lion-hearted queen trying to defend the crown of her husband who was more of a monk than a king. The situation was hopeless and could not be allowed to continue.

'It finally came to a head on a bitter snow-swept day at the Battle of Towton, in March 1461, when Edward, helped by our Lord, the Earl of Warwick, defeated Henry VI to claim the throne by force of arms to become King Edward IV. King Henry – as was, his Queen, and a few other surviving Lancastrian nobles, fled to the north of England where they are now desperately clinging on to the few loyal castles left to them.'

The Great Controller paused. He was pleased to see that young Tunstall was listening intently to his every word, but it was now time to explain to the boy his new duties.

'King Edwards's youngest brother, Duke Richard, is a child of this violent age. Unlike you and I, who have lived in the comfort and safety

16

of Middleham Castle, Duke Richard has lived through civil war, treachery, the violent deaths of his father and brother, and the distress of exile. So, King Edward and the earl have decided that he now requires stability, security, and friendship – I will provide the first two, and you, Master John, along with Lord Francis Lovell, will provide the last. Duke Richard will be arriving with a fast-moving armed escort tomorrow and you will be introduced to him the following day. From then on, you will be his companion.'

Now, it all made sense to John: the sudden activity he had seen in the castle kitchens – these were the preparations of the welcoming feast for Duke Richard. He was arriving on the Thursday because that was the only day of this Embertide week that was a non-fasting day.

'Do you have any questions?' queried the Great Controller.

John looked up. 'It's a big responsibility to look after a king's brother,' he said, 'and I don't even know how to address him.'

'In public, it will be "your Highness" or "my Lord", for he is a royal prince. In private, first names will suffice. But, I will offer you some advice, which you will do well to heed. Duke Richard is being trained for a life of privilege, great wealth, and immense power. You, Master John, on the other hand, are being trained for a life of service, loyalty and obedience to your Lord, so you must always remember that there is a line between you and Duke Richard. I am sure, over time, you will both decide where that line is, but remember, always be aware of it, and most important, do not step over it!'

Behind the tapestry hanging in the Great Controller's office, Simon Langford was about to replace the small piece of wooden panelling when he heard, in the distance, the sound of many chairs scraping backwards in unison as their occupants hurriedly stood up. The sound came from the outer office where he worked with the other clerks. He knew instantly that it signalled the arrival of the Earl of Warwick. With the hand that held the wood panelling now frozen in mid-air, Simon held his breath and looked back through the spy hole. The noise of the chairs had also alerted the Great Controller, who Simon saw had now risen from his seat, head turned to the door. He saw John Tunstall jump up, his head turning around, anxiously. The door into the Great Controller's office swung open.

Simon had been right, for there stood Richard Neville, the mighty Earl of Warwick. He was richly dressed, and around his neck hung the great gold chain of the office of Chamberlain of England. After King Edward, he was the most powerful man in the kingdom. Simon looked at him with loathing in his eyes, for there was the bastard who had allowed his father to be murdered, and his home violated.

He felt the old anger welling up inside him. The harrowing memories of that day, eight years ago, surged to the top of his consciousness. Then the anguish hit him; the pain that he had felt on that heartbreaking morning tightened in his chest. He nearly cried out in furious rage, but instead he slapped his hand over his mouth. His lips were dry, his hand damp with sweat. *Stay calm. Be still*, he told himself.

His mind slipped back to that harrowing May Day in 1455. It was the day after the battle of St Albans. His father had fought with Henry VI and the Queen, against the Earl of Warwick and his allies. King Henry lost the battle and fell into the hands of the earl. Simon's father, Sir William, had fought bravely and survived the fighting, only to be brutally stabbed to death – murdered – after he had surrendered to one of the earl's lieutenants, who had then claimed, and was granted by Warwick, Sir William's estate and manor house at Barton-le-Clay. That fateful morning, years ago now, seemed like only yesterday.

The following events, after that bloody morning, were driven by revenge. The manor house was retaken and secured. A few of Sir Thomas Raket's men escaped, but many more were cut down as they fled. Five were caught alive – these were quickly tried under the law and found guilty of their crimes. They were stripped and branded as rapists; their ears and noses sliced off and then they were put on public display before being hanged at Ravensburgh Castle.

Lady Langford petitioned King Henry VI to restore their estate back to them and when he heard of the atrocities committed by Warwick's men, he agreed with her request and sent her some beautiful gowns as way of an apology.

Although justice had been done, Simon still harboured within himself an implacable hatred for the Earl of Warwick. This arrogant man had condoned the murder of his father, rewarding his killer with his victim's estate, unleashing a band of murderous devils on to his family and their servants. Although Simon had killed his father's assassin, and most of his men had paid the ultimate price for their crimes, he knew his father's soul would never rest until he was avenged, and the Earl of Warwick was dead. His hatred for the earl had increased, and in moments of solitude, his mind dwelled deeply on revenge. He had thought that over the last eight years, this passion would dim, but the reverse had happened – he finally realised that to quell this fire within him, physical action was required. His mother tried hard to counsel him against this course of action, but eventually she conceded defeat. Not long after his eighteenth birthday, Simon took his leave from his mother and sisters, and with revenge in his heart, he headed for Bamburgh Castle to join the Lancastrian cause.

Simon was given a false identity, which only he, Queen Margaret, and Pierre de Brézé, knew. In his new existence, he was to be called Robert Furneys. He was then placed into the service of the spymaster whose name was John de Bothall, a travelling merchant who visited all the towns and castles in the north of England. It was the perfect cover to gather information useful to the Lancastrian cause. John de Bothall instructed Simon in the art of espionage. In his new life, he was the orphaned son of a clerk raised in a monastery – hence his skills in language and penmanship. All the necessary paperwork was acquired to support this story, and with the help of the spymaster, Simon was able to obtain employment at Middleham Castle.

During his time at Bamburgh Castle, Simon had been in the company of Queen Margaret many times. To begin with, she had taken to gently flirting with him, then later, when she had looked at him, her eyes had started to betray her longing. He, of course adored her and slowly over the weeks they became braver – a stolen kiss, a hand touched, a secret look. On the day he was leaving for Middleham Castle, she had entertained him in her private apartments, where she gave him a gold ring set with a small sapphire as a sign of her favour. Inside, were engraved the words 'To The Brave'.

'Come back safely to me', she had said, before kissing him with a passion that took his breath away.

Simon had hungrily returned her kiss, his hands caressing her body.

Finally, breathlessly, she had broken free. 'I will need you with me in years to come', she had whispered, huskily. Her eyes had shone with desire as Simon pulled her towards him...

Warwick's booming voice brought Simon's thoughts to a close. He looked with pride at the gold and sapphire ring that hung on a chain around his neck, then, once again, lowering the piece of wood panelling, listened intently.

In the Great Controller's office, John Tunstall bowed low, then after showing the required amount of acquiesce, drew himself up to his full height. He looked up at the earl who now loomed large in front of him.

The Earl of Warwick stood, feet apart, hands on hips. John swiftly scrutinised him. Fine velvets, silks and fur, clothed his hard, muscular body. Burnished gold glowed from his rings and buckles; around his neck, his gold chain of office – Chamberlain of England – gleamed with dominance. His whole countenance radiated authority; the rich royal blood that flowed through his veins bred the arrogance and ruthlessness of one who wielded absolute power. John could feel the energy and dynamism radiating from this man who was king in all but name.

Warwick's small eyes adjusted to the dimness of the room. 'Thomas, have you told the boy the identity of our new guest, and of his duties?' he enquired.

'Yes, my Lord,' replied the Great Controller.

John was astounded – it had never crossed his mind that the Great Controller had a name. He had always been this enigma, this tall, black manifestation that dispensed orderliness and discipline throughout the castle.

Warwick inspected John with an experienced eye – he had not

attained his high office without the ability to judge a man's character accurately. He could see through the complexities of any individual's nature and recognise their core attributes, their strengths and failings; if they carried courage and conviction within them or spineless impotence.

John returned the earl's inspection with a steady gaze.

'Young Tunstall,' barked Warwick. 'You are now aware of your new duties; I expect you to attend to them with due diligence at all times. Is that understood?'

'Yes, my Lord,' replied John.

The Earl of Warwick clapped his hands and dismissed John from the room.

As the door closed, Warwick turned to the Great Controller. 'I think young Tunstall will excel in his new role. He has the same character as his father.'

'I agree,' replied the Great Controller. 'I chose him with care; I only hope that Duke Richard will find him agreeable.'

'Oh, he will, Thomas, he will. Their characters will fit each other as a hand in a glove.' Warwick waved the Great Controller back to his seat and then made himself comfortable in the chair vacated by John. His face creased into a grin. 'I have excellent news, Thomas: the French are about to cease all financial aid to that French whore, Margaret, and at the same time that scrawny peacock, De Brézé, will be recalled to France by Louis, along with his troublesome mercenaries.'

'Excellent news,' replied the Great Controller. 'So the negotiations are now fully completed?'

'Yes, our diplomacy has finally surmounted all of the problems. They will formalise the treaty on the first of January then it's *adieu* to French Louis and his feckless meddling.'

'And the Scottish problem, my Lord?' asked the Great Controller.

Warwick's brow knotted slightly. 'That's not so cut and dried. They are aware that the French funding will cease, but not of the swiftness of it. We know from our agents that the Scottish Regency Council are becoming increasingly disheartened. Their will to continue support for

Henry and his French whore is cooling, so much so, that they have agreed to send emissaries to negotiate a truce with Edward on April 25 at York city.'

'So they are hedging their bets. They want to be sure that the French have finally withdrawn before committing their intent.'

'Exactly!' exclaimed Warwick. 'Once they know that the French have withdrawn, and along with them, their money, then those Scottish bastards will be more than ready to cease their hostilities and retire back across their border.'

'What then the fate of our royal Lancastrian foe?' queried the Great Controller.

'Ah...' Warwick sighed. 'This great game of kings and queens will be concluded. The ultimate manoeuvre – the *coup de grâce* – will finally be applied to Henry and his whore.'

Rising from his chair, Warwick leant across the desk until his face filled the Great Controller's vision. 'It's finally checkmate, Thomas!' he roared as he thumped the desk, scattering the 'Old Owl's' paper defence. 'It's checkmate!'

Behind him, Simon heard the door to the depository open and his heart quickened. He immediately went to replace the small piece of wood panelling, but in his urgency, he caught one side of the panel on the edge of the recess. As he pushed it home, it gave a loud audible click. His heart started to beat even faster, his mouth became instantly dry; he knew he had just possibly made a mortal error. He stood, and walked quickly up the aisle, away from the wall. Turning left at the end, he walked towards the door.

Bent low over the desk by the door, absorbed in his task, was one of Simon's fellow clerks. He was turning the pages of the great ledger as he sought the location of a stored document. Simon's sudden appearance made him jump. 'Oh, Robert, you startled me!' the clerk exclaimed.

'Sorry, my friend,' muttered Simon, a nervous smile on his face. He brushed past the clerk and walked quickly out of the depository.

The clerk cast an eye over Simon's retreating back. It had seemed to him that there was a curious awkwardness about this fleeting encounter.

A quizzical expression formed on the clerk's face, but he shook his head and returned to his task.

Black Skullcap observed Simon slipping quietly back behind his desk, and raised an eyebrow.

Simon knew his prolonged absence had been noted, and along with the other two mistakes he had made within the last five minutes, he felt the cold unforgiving creature of menace begin to stalk him. Intuition quickened his pulse. He could feel the beat of his heart filling his ears as he ran over the threatening signs: first, the noise of replacing the piece of wood panelling, which may or may not have been heard. Second, because of his agitated state, he had not handled the encounter with the clerk in the depository with his usual calmness, and third, Black Skullcap was now taking a more than passing interest in him. Glancing furtively around the outer office, Simon gathered his thoughts. He had two options: stay or go? He looked across at Black Skullcap, who was thankfully now fully absorbed at his desk, whilst the industry of the other clerks continued unabated.

His decision made, Simon rose from his desk for the last time. The information he had was priceless. It was imperative that Queen Margaret knew of this impending betrayal of her allies. If only he could communicate the news to her within the next two days, then there was a small chance that she could – maybe – change their minds. If not, then the Lancastrian cause was lost.

Simon did not look at Black Skullcap as he moved towards the exit, but felt his eyes fasten on to his back, following his every move. With great effort, he compelled his unwilling feet to walk slow and steady; his body tensed, waiting for that hand on his shoulder or the shouted command to stop. His breath came in short bursts as his courage tried to abandon him. He turned the corner and approached the stairwell.

Now, at last out of view, Simon sped down the steps two at a time. He checked his breakneck descent as the last of the steps disappeared from beneath his feet. Then, composing himself, he walked out into the castle courtyard. It seemed as if a hundred pairs of eyes were watching him. He suppressed the urge to run.

Smothering his foreboding, he unassumingly sought out the spymaster, John de Bothall, who had arrived the night before, during the first snows of winter. It was one of his regular visits, during which Simon would secretly furnish him with information that was helpful to the Lancastrian cause. When John de Bothall left the castle, Simon's intelligence would be dispatched to Queen Margaret, to be used in the fight against the Yorkist regime.

Simon found the spymaster laying out his wares for a viewing later that evening.

John de Bothall was surprised and alarmed to see Simon so early as their meeting was scheduled for much later that night. His stomach churned as he saw the anxiety on Simon's face. His young agent quickly informed him of the invaluable information he had just heard, and the danger he had generated acquiring it.

Simon took his leave with the spymaster's blessing to abandon the castle and ride with all speed to Queen Margaret. He had conceded that the situation within the castle was now uncertain; danger was uncurling from its slumber. This betrayal by their allies had to be relayed with all haste to the Lancastrian forces. As he walked towards the Great Keep, he realised that his time at the castle was now exhausted; his season of luck was over. The portcullis was raised, the drawbridge was down; safety beckoned. He sauntered out through the great, arched gate and turned left towards the stables. No one questioned him; clerks came and went on castle business at all times.

Picking the best mount from the general pool of horses, he rode away into the gathering dusk. The winter horizon merged into the land, the snow-laden sky threatened. It was going to be a long, hard, cold night.

The Great Controller watched as the door closed behind the Earl of Warwick. He slowly turned to his left, for just after the earl had thumped the desk, he had heard a slight noise – a click – that had emanated from behind his left ear. There was something sinister about it; something odd, he thought. He studied the tapestry hanging behind him; it depicted the four seasons. John de Bothall had given it as a gift to him on the last Embertide of Michaelmas, over two years ago, and he remembered the merchant had installed it personally.

He went to the edge of the tapestry and lifted it up. He looked at the wood panelling behind it. *Nothing untoward, there,* he thought. *Must be an old man's mind playing tricks.* He was about to release the tapestry when he saw a small area of light forming a small circle on the panelling. His face creased into a frown. Placing the tapestry back down, he studied the front of it intently. The area he was looking at depicted a harvest scene, carts laden with wheat, being pulled by oxen. He peered closer – he had an old man's eyesight as well as an old man's hearing. Maybe, he was imagining the whole thing, until…his mind filled with consternation; his eyes were incredulous as he saw the source of the light. He let out a gasp. A wheel on one of the carts had a hole at its centre, and it had been stitched ingeniously, so not there by accident. He studied the wood panelling, and finding what appeared to be a carved area, pressed his fingers against it. It moved.

The Great Controller stepped back from the tapestry, realisation spreading across his face. In the quiet stillness of his office, he collected his thoughts. Someone had been spying on him. He knew that once he raised the alarm, pandemonium would break out, but for now he could think – he needed to know who had done this, who had access to the room next door and for whom were they spying. Anger started to build within him. That poisonous click, he reasoned, was but a small key. *The smallest key,* he grimly thought, *can open the largest door, and by God, this door will be opened by the time I have finished.*

The Great Controller shouted for Black Skullcap. The cut panel in the depository was discovered and this confirmed a traitor had been at work. The clerk who had seen Simon in the depository told his story. Black Skullcap confirmed it and the order was given to seal the castle. The portcullis slammed down and the garrison began the search for Robert Furneys.

John de Bothall had decided to leave the castle at dawn the next morning. He too felt the danger closing in, but reasoned, because there had been no alarm sounded, the spyhole must still be undetected. Robert Furneys would be missed by morning, of course, but nobody would know the reason for his absence. But when he heard the shouts of 'seal the castle', he realised that he had made a grave mistake; he should have left with his young agent. Leaving all his wares behind, he made his way immediately towards the Great Keep. His horses were in the stables just outside the castle. If he could reach them, he could be away from the castle in a few moments.

He was approaching the gate when the portcullis rattled into place, trapping him inside. As it fell, so did his spirit. He realised it would not take them long to link him to the fugitive they were seeking. He had recommended Simon for the clerk's job, and he had supplied the tapestry. He also travelled to each of the earl's castles on a regular basis. Consternation settled on him; he tried to control the distraught, fearful impulse that was forcing panic into his body. He frantically looked around for another way of escape, then with a sinking heart, he saw Thomas and George – the Hallet twins – two of the finest fighting men-at-arms in the castle, walking quickly towards him. Their grim expressions instantly spelled his ruin. Suddenly, his arms were pinned to his sides.

'Going somewhere?' asked Thomas.

John de Bothall shook his head, but his eyes betrayed his anguish.

'The Great Controller would like a word with you because you've been a naughty boy,' continued Thomas.

'Oh, such a naughty boy,' said George. 'He's found a flaw in that lovely tapestry you gave him and he would, if you can spare the time, like to discuss it with you.'

The Great Controller looked down at John de Bothall kneeling in front of him. *This man*, he thought, *knows who all the agents are in the Lancastrian spy network. He is the one who places them in their positions, collects the information, and sends it back to Queen Margaret.* This, he was sure of, but for now he pitied this man. John de Bothall's dedication and bravery to the Lancastrian cause was to be admired. *But when, with dread, he watches the torturer slowly unwrap his tools of the trade, and sees them glinting by the light of the red-hot brazier...when he looks into the cold, detached emotionless faces of his persecutors, he will realise that he has just entered Hell and his courage will desert him – as it would any man.*

John de Bothall, noted the Great Controller as he studied him, was still a complete man; still whole, but not for much longer. Once the earl's tormentors had finished with him, he would be a bloody mess with limbs broken, flesh ripped, skin burnt to the bone – death would be a release for him, but not yet. First, he had to pay with blood. First, he would confess to all the information sent to the Queen – how it was sent, by whom, and then the names of other traitors hidden within the earl's many residences. Retribution would be swift and barbarous on all involved.

The Great Controller lent down and grabbed John de Bothall by the hair, roughly jerking his head back. 'Warwick wants blood for this outrage,' he snarled. 'Lots of it, and yours is only the first.' He stood back and watched as John de Bothall was dragged out to begin his ordeal of pain. Even if he revealed all that he knew before they even touched him, the torturers would still work on him for hours to make sure they had squeezed every piece of information out of him.

He looked over at Black Skullcap, who was nervously moving from foot to foot. Warwick had wanted his blood as well, for it was Black Skullcap's misfortune to have employed that traitorous clerk. He had let him escape, and he would have to pay the price. The Great Controller would do his best to save him, but the earl was in no mood to show mercy. He nodded. Two men-at-arms grabbed Black Skullcap, and he disappeared through the door, crying for mercy.

The Great Controller sat wearily at his desk. *Robert Furneys – who was Robert Furneys?* he pondered. He was a very brave young man who had escaped in the nick of time. Scourers had been dispatched to hunt him down, but it was now dark and snowing hard. He'd had a good start and the fresh snow would cover his tracks. The Great Controller assumed he must have gone north towards the Lancastrian strongholds, but he doubted they would find him. Anyway, it was too late for Queen

Margaret to change events now – the die was cast; her fate sealed. One small fish may have escaped, but a far bigger one had been caught in his net. John de Bothall would reveal the whole Lancastrian spy network. Not only were Holy Henry and his Queen finished politically and militarily, but their intelligence-gathering would be totally destroyed.

The Great Controller smiled to himself. *Every cloud has a silver lining*, he mused, but Duke Richard was arriving tomorrow. This embarrassment was the last thing he needed. It would be best to have the torturers complete their work tonight – he did not want John de Bothall's screams upsetting the duke when he arrived.

John Tunstall paused as he reached the bottom of the steps that led down from the Great Controller's office, his mind still racing with astonishment over the outcome of his interview he had just attended with the 'Old Owl'.

He could not wait to tell his mother that he was going to be the companion of Richard, the Duke of Gloucester and the King's youngest brother. He still could not believe it himself. He stopped at the entrance and looked out at the falling snow. It was the first snows of winter. He remembered waking that morning and his sudden excitement over the crisp and white altered landscape. One of his tutors had told him that there was an ancient significance to the first snows of the winter. No matter how old you were or how many times you had witnessed it, when it starts snowing, you stop whatever you are doing and rush to see it. It was one of life's magical moments.

John started walking across the outer keep towards the turret where he lived in a suite of private rooms with his mother, Lady Alice Tunstall. She was to serve the Earl of Warwick's wife – the Countess, Anne Neville – whilst John was being trained for knighthood.

John listened to the pleasant but unfamiliar sound of the snow crunching under his feet. He walked in ridiculous ways and smiled with delight at the comical effect his boots made in the snow. As he made his way towards his living quarters, he tried to protect his best clothes from the worst of the snowfall by hugging the wall of the Great Keep.

He was halfway around the outer keep when he saw the Hallet twins, guarding the Great Keep gate. They both looked frozen. He could hear them grumbling and cursing as they stamped their feet and rubbed their hands together. He knew them both well; the two of them were the best fighting men-at-arms in the castle and taught him the art of swordplay and unarmed combat. He realised they had not noticed him, so he quickly moved up against the castle wall out of their line of sight and with a playful look in his eyes, he quietly made two large snowballs and then stealthily crept towards the entrance. Carefully, he peered around the corner and awaited his chance. As the two brothers moved closer together, John stepped out and let fly. His two snowballs found their targets, and each twin received a direct hit to his head.

'Bloody donkey's arse!' cried George.

'Hell's teeth!' shouted Thomas.

John could not believe his luck – two bull's eyes! The master-at-arms suddenly appeared in the guardroom doorway. He was a giant of a man – six foot, six inches – and some said he was carved from solid oak. His face was battered and scarred, reflecting his profession.

'Tunstall!' he bellowed.

John laughed mischievously, and ran towards the entrance of his apartment with the master-at-arms threats of reprisals ringing in his ears. He looked back over his shoulder at them as he dashed through the archway into the base of the turret, where he collided with his mother's maid, Rose Thorne, who was carrying a tray of dirty dishes back to the castle's kitchens. Rose fell backwards on to the bottom steps of the spiralling staircase that disappeared up into the turret, while the tray shot up into the air scattering dishes that crashed with alarming loudness on to the cold, hard, stone floor.

Rose was twelve years old and had been John's mother's maid for only four weeks. She had beautiful dark hair and huge smiling brown eyes, and John thought she was the prettiest girl he had ever seen.

'Rose, are you all right?' cried John as he reached down to help her up.

She rose gingerly from the steps and smoothed her dress. 'Think so,' she said as she looked at him with amusement.

John felt himself blush. He always seemed to stumble over his words when he spoke to Rose, and now she was laughing at him, making him even more tongue-tied.

'I – I will find – pick up – get the plates,' he stammered.

Rose started to giggle, her beautiful brown eyes sparkling as she knelt down to help John as he scrabbled around on the floor picking up the dishes. Her hand suddenly rested on his, and John stopped, looking into her eyes. Rose looked down and then through her long eyelashes looked coyly up at him.

For the last few weeks, John had been trying to summon up the courage to tell Rose how he felt, but had always felt too stupid and tongue-tied until now.

'Rose, I think you are beautiful,' he blurted out, feeling himself blushing. 'I really, really like you.'

'I like you too,' she whispered, with smiling eyes.

John thought his heart was going to burst. 'You – you do?' he cried.

Suddenly, the castle's alarm bell sounded. John could hear men shouting. He looked at Rose, then dashed to the entrance of the turret and looked out. Men-at-arms were running towards the gates and battlements; shouts of 'seal the castle' rang out. He saw the portcullis being lowered and then the merchant, John de Bothall, being marched by the Hallet twins towards the Great Controller's office.

Lady Tunstall turned away from the window and looked at her son as he warmed himself by the fire. 'They are tearing the castle apart, searching for that young clerk,' she said.

'His name is Robert Furneys, although I doubt that is his real name,' replied John. 'According to some of the men-at-arms, he was spying on me and the Great Controller, when he was discovered. It would appear he has been spying for the Lancastrians for at least the last two years. Lord Warwick is furious.'

'And they say John de Bothall is the ring-leader?'

'Yes,' replied John.

'That's a shame.' Lady Tunstall sighed. 'I used to enjoy all the gossip he brought from the other castles.'

'Well, he's a dead man, now,' said John.

Lady Tunstall turned back to the window, and continued to watch all the activity within the castle.

John studied his mother. She was tall and slim, with long blonde hair and blue eyes, and now, without a husband, as lady-in-waiting and close friend of the Countess of Warwick. His father had been killed at the battle of St Albans, eight years ago, fighting alongside the earl. John had been three years old at the time and, of course, could not remember his father, but was told he was the image of him. His thoughts were broken by his mother, who had turned from the window to face him. 'So, you are to be the companion of the King's brother,' she said, proudly.

'Lord Warwick and the Great Controller picked me personally,' John replied, full of pride. 'Duke Richard arrives tomorrow, and I will be introduced to him the following day.'

'This is a wonderful opportunity for you. If you get on well with him, doors will open; your advancement in rank is assured...' She paused; a sad look filled her eyes. 'Your father would have been so proud of you, if he had lived.' She turned back towards the window to hide her sorrow.

Rose entered the room. 'Could you change out of your best clothes?' she asked John. 'I need to have them cleaned and ready. You must be looking your finest when you meet the King's brother.'

'Can Rose come with me tomorrow to watch Duke Richard arrive at the castle?' John suddenly asked his mother with a boldness that surprised them all, especially himself.

Lady Tunstall turned from the window and studied them both, a look of comprehension slowly settling on her face. Her little boy was growing up. This was his first infatuation; being captivated by a pretty smile was no sin. He was taking that first step over the line that divides childhood from manhood. She was pleased; a first love was always special, and Rose was an honest and virtuous girl, so no harm would come of it. She looked at Rose. 'Do you want to go?' she asked.

'Yes please,' replied Rose, as she looked thoughtfully at John.

John smiled at Rose. He went to change his clothes, feeling ten feet tall.

Chapter 2

The Arrival

Middleham Castle, North Yorkshire
15 December 1463

John Tunstall was standing on the top of the tallest turret at Middleham Castle, looking out to the horizon, his eyes searching out into the sun-dazzled snow.

'It's too bright,' John said, raising his hand over his eyes.

'Well, you'll not miss them against the snow,' replied Rose, 'unless their horses are all white, and Duke Richard and his men are wearing white clothes!' She giggled.

John loved her girlish laughter. It stirred a feeling of tenderness in him, something he had never felt for a girl before.

'Look, here they come!' cried a young boy, excitedly.

John could see them now; his excitement grew. They were still far in the distance – too far out to see any detail.

A biting winter wind suddenly spiralled around the turret, and Rose shivered. John removed his cloak and wrapped it around her shoulders. Rose looked up at him, and smiled as she gently leaned against him. John, not sure of what to do, gingerly placed his arm around her, and saw the young boy crinkle his nose up at them in disgust.

John looked down into the castle. Trumpeters were primed on top of the Great Keep to play a salutation. Two hundred garrison troops were drawn up in the castle yard, their helmets, breastplates, and weapons, gleaming in the winter sun. The master-at-arms was walking amongst them, making last-minute inspections.

God help any soldier who has a fleck of dirt or an unpolished piece of metal about his person, John thought.

Knights of the Earl of Warwick's retinue were positioned outside the castle, where they lined the route up to the great gate. They were mounted in full battle dress; the fusion of all their battle colours set against the white snow was magnificent in its brilliance.

John longed for the day when he could join them. He watched as a hundred scourers – light cavalry – were sent out to support the duke on his arrival to the castle.

The Earl and Countess of Warwick, surrounded by their close retainers and ladies-in-waiting, stood on the steps to the Great Hall. John could see his mother at the countess' side – all had their finest clothes on. Gold and jewels sparkled in the golden rays of this sharp winter's morning. He knew his mother would be frozen, no matter how many layers of clothes she wore. He hoped her ordeal would not last too long.

All the castle workers, except those who were detailed for last-minute chores, lined the inner walls in their best church clothes. Each had been given a small, brightly-coloured flag depicting the earl's and the duke's insignia, side by side. When Duke Richard entered the castle, these would be waved vigorously as they cheered their welcome.

Thomas, the Great Controller, hovered in the background. Against all the rich colours on display, he looked oddly out of place, dressed in his usual black – his face looked drawn and tired. It was obvious that he'd had a long night and, of course, the whole castle knew of yesterday's events. The rumour was that executions were scheduled for the following Saturday.

John watched all this splendid activity below him. He was glad he was just a spectator who could relax and enjoy the day, for tomorrow he would meet Duke Richard and then his life would be changed forever.

Richard, Duke of Gloucester, brought his horse to a halt as Middleham Castle came into view. He had beside him, two of his most trusted retainers: John Milewater and Thomas Parr. His third favourite retainer, Thomas Huddleston, was already at the castle. He had gone ahead the previous day with the baggage train, to supervise the unloading, and the preparation of his royal quarters.

Richard watched as scourers were disgorged from the castle, galloping over the crystal snow towards them. The mounted men-at-arms who formed his bodyguard instinctively moved slightly closer to him; they were dressed in their finest battle armour.

Last night, they had stayed at Fountains Abbey near the town of Rippon. There, they had prepared for their journey; weapons and armour had been polished and oiled, their number-one uniforms unpacked and made ready. Today, they looked supreme, each of them proudly wearing the *White Boar* of Duke Richard's standard. He had enjoyed his night at the abbey. The excitement of today had been stirring within him, so he had appreciated the quiet orderliness of this Cistercian Order. The 'white monks', known as such because their habits were made of coarse undyed sheep's wool, lived hard and active lives; they were also committed to long periods of silence for spiritual reflection and to honour God. Richard had attended Mass with the abbot and his brothers, where they had said prayers for him.

He looked into the distance towards the castle and saw bright flashes of light as the sun reflected off polished metal; the hazy colour of flags fluttering from towers broke the stillness of the morning horizon. Middleham Castle held no fears for him – he was looking forward to the extra freedom it would give him. To be away from the claustrophobic atmosphere of the royal court was a blessing, as was the great distance now between him and his brother, George. Since George had been made Duke of Clarence, he had become insufferable.

Richard knew that George had always sought attention, and since being made a duke, he could demand it. He had become even more spoilt and tiresome, and was forever tormenting Richard about his misshaped back. He would whisper the word 'hunchback', or 'crookback', as he passed him, with a caustic smile on his face. Because George was high born, and the brother of the king, Richard knew he could get away with the name-calling. No one else within the royal court would dare say such a thing to Richard's face, although he was sure they whispered it in the draughty hallways of the royal castles.

Richard's clothes had been specially tailored to hide the slight hump that raised his right shoulder higher than his left. The physicians had told him it was not noticeable at the moment, but would become worse, the older he became, unless he wore the special leather corset they had designed to straighten his spine as he slept. He was hoping that at Middleham Castle he would be accepted for who he was, and not for what he looked like, for his slight deformity did not affect his physical prowess at all. But best of all, it would be wonderful not to have to look on the spiteful face of George ever again.

He was, however, sad to be leaving his dashing elder brother, King Edward, but he would see him in the New Year when he came up to York on a Royal Progress. Edward had spent his youth at Middleham. *If it was good enough for Edward, it is most certainly good enough for me,* Richard thought.

Thomas Parr broke Richard's thoughts. 'We'd best be heading on, your Grace, or we'll be late for the welcoming party. We don't want them to freeze to death waiting for us.'

Richard smiled, and then spurring his horse, galloped towards the huge inspiring fortress of Middleham Castle.

The Earl of Warwick stood on the steps leading to the Great Hall, and surveyed the castle. All appeared to be in good order for Richard's arrival. He was disappointed that his three close retainers: John Conyers, James Strangways, and Thomas Metcalfe, as well as the others, were not beside him. He would miss their company during the grand welcoming feast. Without their humour, it could well turn into a tedious affair, but, at least, that traitor, John de Bothall, had named the agents in his the earl's other residences.

There were four in total, and the earl had dispatched his close retainers early that morning to arrest them. They would be brought back to Middleham to face the ordeal of torture – for who knew what other secrets may be squeezed out of them – followed by a slow traitor's death.

No wonder that French whore, Margaret of Anjou, had always been one step ahead of him; how she must have laughed at his efforts to catch her. Anger welled up inside him as he saw her self-righteous face taunting him, but he satisfied himself with the thought that when he caught her, he would have her confined to a Spartan convent with orders that she work in front of the hot kitchen ovens, dressed in a thick, wool habit, for the rest of her days. During his diplomacy, and much to his annoyance, the French king had stated that Queen Margaret was a French princess, and as such must be spared death if she was ever made a prisoner. If this was not agreed, then their support for her would continue. Warwick had no choice but to agree, although he would have enjoyed slowly impaling the scheming bitch on a long spike.

Warwick saw Duke Richard move into view; he had stopped outside the entrance to the castle as though waiting for the signal to enter. Warwick smiled.

Well…at least here is another asset arriving to add to my empire. It wasn't so long ago that his brother, King Edward, had arrived at Middleham at the same age, and look what I had achieved with him – he is now King, but still firmly in my pocket, thought Warwick, smugly.

I have great plans for Richard,. and his brother George, for they will marry my daughters Isabel and Anne. This will unite the two houses of York; then King Edward will marry a French princess of my choosing, which will unite the French and English thrones. With this new found power and influence, the whole world will listen when I speak, and heed the words of the great Warwick – for not only will I control England, my influence will extend to cover Burgundy, France and beyond.

Warwick smiled with satisfaction as he stepped forward to greet young Duke Richard.

Duke Richard sat quietly in his new bedchamber. The feasting was finished, the dancing steps now still, and the musician's tunes were silent. This grand day of welcome was done. He had taken off his elegant shoes that were covered with the finest cloth of gold and trimmed with pearls, the new scarlet leggings, and his deep-blue satin vest, trimmed with lace that sparkled with precious jewels. His beautiful mauve cloak, trimmed with the newest Italian velvet, had been conscientiously folded and put carefully away.

The castle was now in tranquil darkness, the draughty hallways now chilled and empty of life. All had retired to their rightful place of rest. Richard slowly climbed into bed and pulled the fur overlay up to his chin – it was another bitter cold night. In his thoughts, he entertained the day's events: Warwick had greeted him warmly as befitted a cousin and royal prince. Richard's gifts of two, fully trained hunting falcons, one for the earl, and one for his wife – for he knew the countess loved hunting with hawks – were genuinely received.

The welcoming feast had been long and a little boring, but Warwick had been attentive, liking Richard to an unpolished diamond that had been sent to Middleham to be burnished and smoothed, and over time, to sparkle and dazzle for all to see – just as he had polished and shaped Richard's brother, King Edward. Once the feast was over, the trestle tables had been cleared away and the music and dancing had commenced. Richard watched but declined the invitation to join in. His shyness had been put down to his young age, but Richard knew himself well. Music he loved; dancing he disliked, because it might draw attention to his deformity and, he sadly thought, would always be so.

Warwick had introduced his two daughters and it did not take Richard long to realise they were like chalk and cheese. Isabel, the eldest, was scatterbrained. Like a bee around summer flowers, she would flit from one subject to another, without intelligence or thought. It was the same with her emotions, one minute happy, and the next, sulky. She reminded Richard of his brother, George, both were self-centred and spoilt. *Maybe*, he mused, *all great families have to have one like that*.

Anne, on the other hand, who was only seven years old, was calm and serene; her wit was quick, her conversation thoughtful, and although she was very young, there was a maturity about her that Richard admired. Anne had made him welcome, and then had made him promise to play chess with her, once he had settled into his new life at Middleham…and what of this new life?

Warwick had explained how his education would continue as before, but his physical training would increase. He would now be taught how to fight in armour, when mounted, and on foot, with battleaxe and spear. Hunting would become more intense, for this was considered excellent training for war. Military strategy would be learnt and discussed daily. Richard looked forward to these lessons with excitement.

The only quandary of the evening that nagged at his mind was Warwick himself. Edward had warned Richard that Warwick was a great manipulator, and Richard had sensed that the words coming out of his cousin's mouth, although sounding fair to his ear, only disguised the thoughts and wily schemes going on in that brain of his. Those small, hard eyes stared at him just like a hunter taking his measure of his prey. Richard's last thoughts, before sleep darkened his mind, dwelled on the reality that he must treat his Warwick with caution.

Middleham Castle, North Yorkshire
16 December 1463

John Tunstall was dressed in his finest clothes, and now blazed with colour. His mother, and Rose, had been fussing over him as they helped him dress, and now he wore his best, crisp, white shirt, trimmed with lace, over which he wore a rich blue satin and velvet vest that ended at his knee. It was pleated into his waist by a narrow belt with a solid silver buckle and the sleeves were long and pointed. Around his shoulders, he wore a small, velvet cape, edged with fur. His legs were clothed in scarlet tights, and ended with narrow-pointed shoes.

When the Earl of Warwick and the Great Controller introduced Duke Richard, John felt a little overwhelmed by the presence of so many high-ranking people. He bowed low and called him 'your Grace'. Duke Richard greeted him with a smile and told him to call him Richard. John's instructions from Lord Warwick were to show Richard around the castle so he would know every corner and crevice before the day was out. Only the dungeons were off limits, because they now held the spies, arrested at the earl's other residences.

Finally, they had stood atop the castle's tallest turret, where John had stood the day before watching his companion's arrival. Both were looking out over the snow-swept terrain towards the River Ure. They had been exploring the battlements and towers for some time, and the bitter, north wind was now penetrating their thin clothes, rapidly numbing their feet and hands, the chill spreading slowly through their bodies. Outwardly, though, neither showed it, both waited for the other to seek the warmth of the turrets interior, as though to be first would be a sign of weakness.

The two boys were saved from freezing to death by their own stubbornness, with the arrival of young Lord Francis Lovell, also a ward of Middleham Castle. He called for them to change out of their best clothes, and to then attend the tilt-yard for their first lessons together in practising with sword and lance. They both walked thankfully towards the doorway leading to the interior of the tower. John stopped, and bowing low, waved Richard through. Richard did likewise and they both stood looking at each other; then suddenly they both rushed for the door. Pushing and jostling, they squeezed through together, laughing as they did; the first bonds of their friendship formed in that moment.

John Tunstall faced Duke Richard in the tilt-yard: the large enclosed arena where the arts of war were practised during the long, cold winter months. Large enough for jousting on horseback, the building was constructed entirely of wood, and the interior had within it a large fenced area, the floor of which was earth with fresh straw lain on top. The boys both wore protective padded jackets over which they wore chain mail for protection and added weight. The extra weight was to prepare them for the day when they would fight in full armour. They both wore gauntlets made from the latest lightweight copper alloy, and each held a blunted sword in one metal-encased hand, and a ten-inch wooden dagger in the other, in the style of swordplay called Florentine. Although they were the same age, and just under five feet tall, they held their weapons with calm awareness, for both had been training in horsemanship and weapons since the age of seven.

They now concentrated on being totally within themselves, centring their minds and bodies as they had both been taught – perception and anticipation, so important in sword fighting, could not be achieved unless the mind was centred. All outside distractions had to be banished as they had to be totally focused on their opponent.

The master-at-arms signalled for them to take up their stance. Both boys adopted an open posture with their daggers held vertically in front of them, and their swords over the shoulder of their sword arm, resting across their backs at about forty-five degrees from the horizontal, and their sword hand touching their ear. Their swords were now balanced for maximum efficiency. Both boys understood that a sword strike starts with the legs, and as the torso rotates, it is transferred and amplified as it moves up through the body into the sword arm.

A small audience had gathered to watch, some just out of curiosity, others were interested in the performance of the new boy, Duke Richard.

The Hallet twins leaned on the wooden fence surrounding the tilt-yard with intense interest on their faces. John was their protégée; they had helped to shape and train him. They felt nervous, an emotion that was alien to them, and they looked at each other with puzzled eyes.

'Are we going soft?' said Thomas. 'I haven't felt this nervous since big Sarah "wobbly arse" took me behind the cowshed to show me what the birds and the bees get up to.'

'Aye, she was a big 'un,' replied George. 'I've seen grown men take flight when those crossed eyes of hers took a fancy to them.'

'Well, some people are just too fussy,' replied Thomas. 'I, myself, likes 'em big! Anyway, nobody looks at the mantel when they're poking the fire.'

'Well, you're certainly not a man of refined taste when it comes to charming the fairer sex,' replied George. 'You'd poke anything if it moved and was faintly female!'

Thomas' hurt reply was cut short by the arrival of the Earl of Warwick and the Great Controller. All that were present bowed low.

Warwick clapped his hands. 'Continue,' he barked, as he leaned on the wooden fence, his small eyes taking in all who were present. 'I'll wager a silver penny that cousin Richard wins this joust. Who will wager for young Tunstall?' he enquired.

The Hallet twins raised their hands. 'We have a silver penny between us, my Lord, if you will accept it?' said Thomas.

'Done,' beamed Warwick, who liked a wager.

The Great Controller looked at the Hallet twins and raised his eyes to the heavens. *I hope they have the money*, he thought, *or a good flogging will be their payment, if young Tunstall loses.*

John studied his opponent, intently. With the arrival of Lord Warwick, the contest had suddenly gone from an enjoyable exercise, to a serious match, with the earl's money and their pride now at stake.

Both boys steadied themselves. The master-at-arms stood between them, his sword raised. When he stepped back, and lowered his sword, the contest would begin. Silence settled around the tilt-yard; tension strained to be released. The master-at-arms' sword flashed between them, and John immediately launched a 'snap' strike at his opponent. Transferring his weight on to his back leg, he threw the balance point of his sword from his shoulder so that it whipped around towards his target; at the same time stepping forward on to his front foot, he rotated his hips in line with his sword swing to increase the power of the blow.

Richard was taken by surprise at the speed of the attack, and the power of the strike; he instantly parried the blow with his Ballock dagger – but not completely. The force of the blow rode the sword up over the top of his dagger, and struck him a glancing blow high on his shoulder – the pain shot down his arm.

Now off balance, Richard was at a great disadvantage. He could not counter strike, as he would have to pass back through his centre of balance, making it slower and easier to read, thus allowing his opponent to step inside his blade's arc with a killer blow. He quickly closed his stance and moving backwards, he drew himself up to his tallest height and placed his sword and dagger in front of himself in a defensive position – his mind now painfully concentrated and astonished at the speed and power of his opponent.

John had already anticipated this defensive move from Richard, and launched a 'drop strike' – targeting the lower back leg by dropping his sword hand straight down from off his shoulder. He turned his palm over, and whipped his sword round towards its target.

Richard moved sideways and backwards, and watched with growing alarm as John's blade flashed passed his leg, glistening with menace. Noticing John was slightly off balance, Richard seized the moment; quickly raising his sword vertically in line with his face, he struck down at John's sword arm, but John had seen the blow coming and countered with a 'backhand reverse'. This stopped the downward path of Richard's sword, and the clash of metal rang painfully in their ears.

John whipped his dagger hand round, and thrust it up towards Richard's chest, who once again narrowed his stance to avoid the blow and moved backwards, snapping out a thrust to give him time to recover.

The watching men could see that the boys were well trained and skilful – John was the stronger and quicker – but Richard had natural rhythm, which had saved him from John's initial attacks.

Slowly, the two boys settled down into their own tempo and style, their swordplay becoming a single entity. Each of their movements were seen by the other and acted upon. It was as if the contest had become a sort of ritualised dance – one movement leading to another set of movements, with each trying to anticipate the motions of his opponent so that their sword would be drawn towards an opening in the other's defence. Each looked for subtle habits that would signal a certain blow, like a slight rotation of the sword hand before a swing, or a small step forward before a thrust – anything that would provide evidence of an impending strike – so that they could counter-attack with a killing blow before the other had completed their strike. But both had been trained not to have these fatal signs in their sword technique.

The boys were now tiring. With aching arms and sweat running off their bodies as they gasped for breath, the two of them grimly fought on with stubborn tenacity, searching for that small fatal weakness within the other.

John finally saw the opening he had been searching for. In one of his lessons with the Hallet twins, they had told him that when a man drops his shoulders it signals tiredness, and for a second he will not be able to react with speed. John had seen in a flash that Richard's shoulders had dropped a fraction, and he struck immediately. In a blur of movement, he stepped forward on to his sword foot, and thrust his sword through Richard's static defence – it was a killer blow – then moving his dagger arm down, and using an upward thrust, he hit Richard just under his rib cage. In real combat, it would have penetrated and ripped into his major organs.

The contest was finished, and both boys leaned on the wooden fence, exhausted.

The Hallet twins hurried to John's side to help him off with his chain mail and padded jacket, and to quietly congratulate him on his win. They kept their praise subdued, for they knew the earl hated to lose anything, especially money.

Richard's close retainers were assisting him in removing his protective clothing, when the earl strode towards them with the Great Controller in tow.

John watched the earl approach, wondering if he would be annoyed at him for having beaten his cousin, Richard. Would it be harsh words, or praise?

Warwick arrived in front of him, reached out, and put his hand gently on John's shoulder. 'Well fought, young Tunstall, you have done the castle proud. The master-at-arms, and those two scoundrels standing beside you, have taught you well – they must be well pleased with your performance today.'

The Hallet twins nodded vigorously.

'I am pleased that we are producing such excellent warriors for the future,' Warwick concluded. Seeing John look embarrassingly at the ground, Warwick put his hand under John's chin and lifted his face up. 'Your father, if he were here, would have been proud of you, John, as you should be proud of yourself with that fine display.' He ruffled John's hair and then turned to Richard. 'You fought well, cousin. I feel tiredness from your long journey may have lost you the joust, but next time, when you are fresh, it will be a more even contest.'

'It was a fair contest,' replied Richard. 'John won; I have no excuses. But next time – now I have the measure of him – hopefully, it may be a different story.'

The two boys looked at each other with tired smiles.

Warwick smiled to himself; both boys were very competitive, which was excellent. They would push each other to even greater efforts. He waved the master-at-arms towards him and turning to the Great Controller said, 'Come, we have executions to organise for tomorrow.'

The three of them started to walk away when Warwick suddenly stopped – pulling out his purse, he produced a silver penny, then looking at the Hallet twins, he flipped it high into the air.

Both twins rushed forward to catch it. The penny turned over and over, reflecting the light on its silver surface as it tantalisingly descended and the twins, their eyes mesmerised, reached up to catch it. As they did so, they collided violently, knocking their heads sharply together. 'God's Blood!' they cried in unison, as they tumbled to the ground. The penny landed in the straw between them.

Warwick roared with laughter, as did everybody else, except the Great Controller, who shook his head, sadly, and once again rolled his eyes towards the heavens.

Richard, John, and Francis, walked back to the castle still laughing at the Hallet twins.

John, with his impetuous free spirit, intrigued Richard, whose own upbringing had made him cautious and restrained. Francis, who was always smiling, and saw the best in everyone, walked in the middle. The three of them ran through the great gate into the castle, laughing and chattering to each other. They were on their way to Richard's first lesson with Friar Drynk. Both John and Francis were intrigued of what the very devout and pious Richard would make of their favourite priest.

Friar Drynk was a large, round-faced man of about forty years of age. The church had not been a spiritual calling for him; it was more the choice of an easier life. It was the priesthood or backbreaking toil of the fields. In the holy order he was guaranteed three meals a day, plus copious amounts of wine. Because of his eccentric personality, he had not fitted into the discipline of monastery life. They had tried many different paths for him within the monastery, but eventually he had ended up at Middleham Castle with the thankless task of instilling religion into the young men of the nobility. Friar Drynk loved his wine and for the most part was always pleasantly tipsy. Occasionally, he would disappear to the City of York where he could be found tasting the delights of its many brothels. He also had a small problem with gluttony. Apart from these minor faults, he was a fine example to his pupils; he knew the scriptures backwards, and would always win any theological argument.

Friar Drynk belched loudly as the three boys entered the room. He was walking slightly unsteadily towards his desk when he stopped abruptly in mid-stride. The boys stood still and waited, the room was silent, and then a low noted fart of extraordinary duration exploded from the back of Friar Drynk's habit.

'Ye Gods! There was a full charge in your rear gun,' gasped John, waving his hand briskly in front of his face.

'Aye, if you have two sniffs of that, you're a glutton,' replied Friar Drynk.

They all looked at Richard whose face was aghast; John and Francis started to giggle. 'Who's this new boy?' asked Friar Drynk as he wiped a greasy food-soaked sleeve across his mouth.

Francis controlled himself just enough to blurt out, 'He's Richard, Duke of Gloucester,' before collapsing into laughter.

Friar Drynk clasped his hands together and bowed. 'Your Grace, it is an honour to have you in my class,' he flattered, 'and may I say what a fine welcoming feast it was yesterday – the food was superb and the wine...' His eyes wandered off dreamily towards the window, '...was magnificent.' He then belched loudly again, and shaking his head, he tried to focus two bloodshot eyes on the boys. 'The lesson for today will be on the miracles of Moses—'

Before the friar could continue, John with his impetuous nature raised his hand.

'You have a question, already?' asked Friar Drynk.

'Yes,' John replied. He stood up, self-importantly cleared his throat and with a mischievous glint in his eye, he began. 'If God preaches charity and love, why does the church always strive to amass money and land?' John felt pleased with himself – the friar would not have an answer to that question.

'So, you question our Lord's workings?' asked Friar Drynk.

'Yes,' said John, triumphantly.

'Well, it would seem to me that you wish to put our Lord on trial, and to accomplish that you would have to be a lot wiser than him, so are you wiser?'

'Well, no, of course not,' replied John.

'So, you agree that you are not wiser. Well, if you are not wiser than

God, then you must be at least as clever, to judge him!' Friar Drynk waited for John's response.

Reluctantly, John admitted that he was not as wise, or as knowing, as God.

'So, you concede that God is infinitely more intelligent than you, his wonders cannot be comprehended or questioned by mere mortals?'

John reluctantly nodded in agreement.

'Excellent,' beamed Friar Drynk. 'I think its best that you just worship God and leave him to oversee the mysteries, wonders and workings of this world that he created, don't you agree?' he asked, his voice rising triumphantly.

'Yes,' said a chastened John with a defeated sigh. *Why is it that Friar Drynk always has an answer to every question?* John wondered. *One day, I will beat him*, he thought, without too much conviction.

Middleham Castle, North Yorkshire
17 December 1463

Saturday dawned. The still grey light unhurriedly revealed, in bleak sharpness, the sobering scaffold. It stood tall and menacing, intimidating all who gazed on it – the neat nooses hung silently awaiting their victims.

John de Botham lay on the floor of his cell listening to the slow beat of the executioner's drum. He did not fear death, only the manner in which it would claim him.

The senior gaoler had read out the Warrant of Execution with no emotion or judgement; he was just the official mouthpiece of the Earl of Warwick's authority. He now looked down on this ruined man, lying on the cold hard floor, knowing that his pain filled body was now broken and empty of information. He felt neither pity nor hate, for it had now come to the last act in this man's earthly play.

The words of the senior gaoler had anchored chillingly in John de Botham's mind from the moment he had heard them. 'You will be taken to a place of execution; there you will be hung by the neck until semi-conscious, then taken down. Your private parts will be sliced off and burnt on a brazier in front of your eyes; your stomach will be cut open and your entrails removed and burnt. Your arms and legs will be hacked off, and finally your head. You go to a traitor's death, make peace with your God, and may he have mercy on your soul'.

John de Botham had shuddered.

The inhabitants of Middleham Castle, and the surrounding countryside, went back about their business, the screams of agony from the five executed spies still ringing in their ears.

Warwick was satisfied as he looked down on the bloody, but now silent, scaffold; a traitorous canker had been cut out of his household.

Black Skullcap sat once again behind his desk. He was the most relieved man in the earl's employ, and most grateful to the Great

Controller for his deliverance from the earl's punishment. He had sat terrified in the dungeons for two days and nights, watching and listening to the screams of the five condemned men. Their pitiful pleas for mercy as the torturers went about their work, would stay with him until the day he died. *God willing*, he thought, *that will now be in my own bed*. He shivered at his narrow escape from the Grim Reaper. He would stay well clear of the earl's temper in the future.

The Great Controller sat behind his great desk, and pondered on the one spy who escaped. *I wonder who Robert Furneys really is*, he thought. *Where is he now?* For some reason, it was the only true identity John de Botham had not known. The Great Controller did not like loose ends, but their paths would cross again in the future, he was sure of that. *Patience*, he thought. *Patience*.

Bamburgh Castle, Northumberland
18 December 1463

Simon Langford stood in a large cavernous chamber, deep within Bamburgh Castle. Pillars and archways filled this spacious room; the thin winter sunlight that filled the narrow windows shot shafts of light through the dark shadows that crowded the corners and curved ceilings of this inner sanctum. Thick rugs covered the stone floor; tapestries coated the walls helping to keep in the warmth that blazed from a large log fire at the end of the room.

Margaret of Anjou sat beside this fire; the reflection of the flames shimmering over her rich bejewelled dress – her face, though, was set like stone.

Simon had just finished his report on the intentions of the French and Scots to abandon King Henry and the Lancastrian cause to its fate. The silence in the room stretched in tense disbelief, and he looked slowly around.

Margaret was immobile in her chair. Henry sat playing with his rosary beads and humming softly to himself. *No use to man or beast*, Simon thought.

Henry Beaufort, 3rd Duke of Somerset, leaned nonchalantly against a pillar. Half hidden by shadows, only his bejewelled hands occasionally glittering in the light of the fire reminded those present that he was still there.

Sir Ralph Percy, and Sir Ralph Grey – the commander of Bamburgh Castle – sat opposite Margaret. Their ears had heard this calamity unfolding; their faces showed painfully the disillusionment it brought.

Simon suppressed the urge to speak again, for it was best to let them digest this unpalatable news in quiet contemplation. He stepped out of the centre of attention, moved into the shadows, and waited.

Pierre de Brézé finally broke the disheartened silence, his voice emanating from a darkened archway. All eyes turned in his direction as they sought to discern him within the shadows, and just like the last time

Simon had met him, he suddenly appeared, as if by magic, in the centre of the room.

'Your Highness,' he said, addressing Margaret, 'it would seem that this chamber has turned into a crypt, for it would appear our spirit is dead.' Then, turning slowly around to look at everybody in the room, he challenged them. 'Where is your courage – your will to fight? Is that also dead?' He paused to let his words settle. All eyes followed him. 'We still have blood flowing through our veins!' he cried. 'We still live and breathe so can we not still change the course of events?' Turning back to Margaret, he said, 'Highness, we must sail for France immediately, and make King Louis see sense. I know he will not abandon you, his cousin, to the English. You will win him round and return with funds and more troops.'

Margaret slowly shook her head, but Pierre de Brézé was in full flow and did not notice her weary response. 'Somerset!' he cried. 'You must stop the Scots from meeting with that upstart, Edward. Once they know Louis is still sponsoring us, the Scots will continue their support.'

Henry Beaufort emerged from the shadows, his cruel eyes glinting in the firelight. 'I agree: Margaret must sail for France, and the Scots must be made to continue their support of us, but what of young Duke Richard?' he asked, shrewdly. 'He is arriving at Middleham Castle and will be ripe for the taking.'

'What? Kidnap him?' asked Sir Ralph Grey, alarm in his voice. 'He is only a boy.'

'I wouldn't care if he was still an infant in swaddling clothes,' came Henry's curt reply. 'If we had possession of him it would disgrace Warwick, and give us a strong lever of power over King Edward, who loves him dearly. We could send Richard's royal ring to him as proof that we held his younger brother.' Then, with a malicious laugh, he added, 'With his finger still in it!'

Margaret rose from her chair. 'Gentlemen!' she cried. 'We have no army left to fight with. Pierre, your own troops have been killed, or have deserted us. We are bankrupt of assets and ideas. I have nothing left to offer Louis in return for his support. With no money, the Scots will scuttle back to Scotland with their tails between their legs, like the mercenary savages they are. For the truth is, we are now too weak, and our enemies too strong – our struggle is at an end.'

Simon looked at Margaret, saddened by her words. Her dominant spirit had been crushed by his news. She had fought so long and so hard for her husband. They had all watched her struggle to uphold her son's right of succession, and her plucky resistance was admired by all, but now she was beaten. He wished he could go to her, put his arms around her. He ached to show her a tenderness of love, but knew he could not. He stayed quietly in the shadows, watching this final act play itself out.

Margaret drew herself up to her full height; her alluring eyes framed by her exquisite features. She scanned the room.

She may be defeated, thought Simon, *but she is still a French princess, who stands proudly in front of us.*

'I have listened to your words, Pierre, and agree with you that it would be best that I return to France, forthwith, to my father's court at St Mihiel-en-Bar. From there, my father, René of Anjou, will assist our cause with King Louis. While I am gone, Somerset will command.' Then turning to Henry, she said, 'You must formulate a strategy to prevent the Scots from deserting us; secondly, the kidnapping of King Edward's brother is not a cause for which I take pleasure from, but I will leave that decision to your conscience. Thirdly, rebellion must be stirred up in Wales and the West Country. If King Louis can see that we are not finished, then he may decide to still support us.'

Simon watched her speak, but saw by her eyes that she did not believe her own words – the sparkle had gone, there was no life or spirit in them.

Sir Ralph Grey stood up and faced Margaret. 'Your Highness,' he said, his voice subdued. 'I agree with all your plans except the kidnapping of Richard. He is but a boy, and it affronts my code of honour…'

Henry Beaufort strode across the room, his vicious eyes flashing; the sword that hung at his side was half out of its scabbard. 'You defy our Queen?' he growled.

Sir Ralph Grey's hand went to his sword as he spun around to face Henry. 'The taking of young boys is the Devil's work,' he snarled, 'and I will have no part of it.'

Two swords were swiftly drawn from their scabbards as their antagonism boiled over into open warfare.

Sir Ralph Percy stepped between them. Simon drew his sword and stood protectively in front of Margaret.

'Enough!' Margaret screamed. Everyone froze – all eyes turned to her. 'Enough! Enough!' she shrieked at them, as she crumpled into her chair. 'Why,' she beseeched, 'are you at each other's throats? Do we not have enough misery on our plates?' In despair, she covered her face with her hands.

The atmosphere in the chamber was now one of awkward discomfort. The two antagonists shifted their weight uncomfortably; their silent embarrassment was ended by Sir Ralph Percy suddenly taking charge of the situation.

'Grey, you will organise the defence of this castle. De Brézé, arrange safe conduct to France for her Highness. Somerset and I will devise a way of stopping the Scots from meeting with Edward and Warwick.'

Margaret, weary of their company, ordered them from her presence. They quickly left in subdued silence, taking King Henry with them. Only Simon was ordered to stay. She rose from her chair and walked slowly towards him.

Simon quickly sheathed his sword, but before he could speak, Margaret was in his arms. His hands slipped around her waist. She sighed, as her head nuzzled into his shoulder. He could feel the warmth of her body as it pressed against his. She was not a queen or a princess now, only a woman, whose world had just been torn apart.

Margaret raised her head and kissed him tenderly on his neck, her lips felt soft and gentle on his skin.

Instinctively, Simon's hands dropped down to her lower back where they gently caressed her slender buttocks; her hips started to sway rhythmically against him. 'What about the door?' he whispered.

'Do not worry,' she breathed sensually, into his ear. 'My ladies stand guard.'

Simon was surprised that he felt no fear for what was happening. He was committing treason and if caught, death would be swift, but he could not stop himself, such was the intoxication of her. Their bodies seemed to flow together, caught on a wave of desire. He closed his eyes, his early inhibitions gone, and let the passion possess him. Her lips found his, and they kissed hungrily. They undressed each other with a slow sensual urgency, and then Simon lowered Margaret on to a fur rug beside the glowing fire.

Night had fallen; the fire cast shadows over their bodies, creating dark shallow valleys and deep crevices, whose mysteries waited to be explored.

Margaret had stripped herself of her royal titles; her cares of state were no more. Her husband – simple, celibate, Henry – had vanished from this new world. She was no longer a royal wife; this was her rebirth, the beginning of a new life. She could feel Simon's young energy, his strong hands moving over her and she started moaning huskily, wrapping her warmth and softness around his hard body, holding on to him as he moved faster and faster. Her French passion overwhelmed her. Delirious with pleasure she cried out, then he shuddered, and moaned, and they were still.

For a while, they seemed to be floating within one another. Thoughts dreamily drifted around Margaret's head as she lay in Simon's arms; she was now just a woman being loved by a man. She would never fight for her husband's crown again. That final thought lifted a great weight from her. She rolled on top of Simon. When he put his hand behind her neck and pulled her lips on to his, she did not resist.

After they were spent, the cold slowly started to chill their entwined bodies. Simon placed more logs on to the fire, and then lay back down beside Margaret. He ran his fingers up and down her spine. 'What of Pierre?' he asked. 'Were you ever lovers?'

They both stared into the fire as the logs slowly crackled into life. Warmth washed over them.

Margaret smiled, and lifted her head to gently kiss Simon's shoulder.

'Oh, no,' she murmured. 'He is brave and loyal, and our love for each other is like brother and sister, unlike you, sweet Simon, who stirred something in me when I first met you those two long years ago. I would have taken you to my bed then, such was my desire for you, but time and circumstances were against us. I gave you that ring to make sure you would think of me as I have thought about you every day since. When you finally came back, I thanked God for your deliverance...Oh God,' she sighed, 'how my body ached for your touch.' Her face suddenly clouded over. 'You do love me?'

Simon did not reply.

Margaret rolled on to him, and once again, he could feel her nakedness.

'You do love me?' Margaret asked again, as she put her arms round his neck, and pretended to strangle him.

'Yes! Yes!' Simon cried. 'I will love you for ever; from our first meeting you captured my heart.'

Margaret snuggled into him, and tenderly kissed his neck.

'And the King, your husband?' Simon asked.

Margaret slid off him and rolled round until she lay on her back looking up at him. 'Ah...poor Henry,' she sighed. 'When I go back to France, I will not be returning.'

'But you said you would try and persuade King Louis to support your cause.'

'My cause is finished,' Margaret replied. 'I may give the illusion to the others that there is hope, for after all these years of fighting I cannot bring myself to suddenly dash their belief in this long undertaking. The reality is that winning the crown back is now unattainable; it will dawn on them all in good time. I just hope they will find a virtuous monastery for poor Henry – there, I pray, he will find contentment. And, myself, I just want to be a simple woman, to be what God intended me to be. I think I deserve that, after all my manly battles and the blood that has been shed in my name. It is now time for me to be loved.'

Margaret smiled up at Simon, her beautiful grey eyes studying his face. Her hand reached up, and pulled him down towards her. She kissed him hungrily.

As Simon's hand slid across her flat stomach; she arched her back. 'I think it's time for...' Margaret's words were lost, as a soft longing moan escaped from her lips.

Simon awoke in his own bed, and tried to clear his disordered thoughts. He wondered if he had been dreaming – his sore lips told him he had not – his sore muscles confirmed it! He closed his eyes, and let the sensuous memories of the night flood his mind. God, he was tired, but it was a wonderful tiredness; he was in love. He wanted to shout the news to the world, but knew he could not; their secret must stay a secret. He vaguely remembered leaving Margaret in the early hours of the morning. Love, he now realised, was a powerful affair; his heart was aching for her already. Margaret had told him that she would arrange for Henry to knight him today, to take his father's old title for his services and bravery whilst at Middleham Castle. He smiled to himself. He had made love to the most beautiful woman in the world and now he was to be knighted. How that wheel of fortune turns – he would be known as Sir Simon Langford.

His thoughts turned to his mother and sisters – they would be proud of him for winning his father's titles back. He vowed to himself that once his tender Queen was safely in France, he would return to England to see them. He swung his tired legs out of bed; he must be washed and dressed for the knighting ceremony and once it was finished, they would leave for the coast and board ship for Flanders.

Margaret awoke with her mind at ease for the first time in ten years. Her aching body was a reminder of her night of hungry passion; she put her arms around herself in a hug of sleepy satisfaction. *Sweet Simon*, she thought, as his smile and strong body filled her mind. *Today, we leave these old cares behind, no more fighting or scheming*. She was now no longer Queen. Tomorrow she would leave for France, to a life of freedom with the man she loved. She smiled with soft longing; she could still smell him on her.

Simon knelt in front of Henry of Windsor and felt the blade dub his shoulders. There was only a small gathering to witness the ceremony. Margaret stood beside Henry, helping him cope with the knighting. With his mind becoming more fragile, he would slip into one of his silent periods, and would no longer respond to the world around him.

The ceremony now over, Simon rose to his feet and acknowledged the polite applause from the attending nobles; his eyes looked longingly towards Margaret. She looked even more beautiful than ever. She wore a one-piece dress, woven with brown and gold thread, and fastened by a gold chain around her neck; it flowed tightly down to her waist showing off the roundness of her breasts. A circle of flowers had been embroidered into the dress around the waist; another circle was embroidered just above her knee and one more into the hem. The dress clung tightly to her body from her neck to her feet, showing off her tall, elegant beauty. Two long gold chains hung around her neck, and fell down to her waist, making her shimmer in the morning sun. Simon watched as she slowly led Henry away.

Margaret ushered Henry back to his chambers. She had, she knew, seen him perform his last act as a king. He would be staying at Bamburgh Castle as a figurehead for those who still wished to claim the throne in his name. *Poor Henry*, she thought, *only a pawn in this endless, but now, pointless struggle*. She held his hand and looked into his eyes. He looked back at her, but behind his eyes, he was somewhere else. She told him gently that she was going to France with their son and he nodded blankly. A tear unexpectedly came to her eye as memories of their wedding day sharpened into focus.

They had been married at Titchfield Abbey in the county of Hampshire on the 22 April 1445 – she was just sixteen. She remembered the joy she had felt, the sheer exuberance of the day, and the future had held so much for them. They had sailed from France two days earlier, and had landed at the great port of Portsmouth. She remembered the channel crossing had made her violently ill – so ill, in fact, that she could hardly wave to all those good people of the city who had lined their procession route. This had been her first ordeal on English soil. If only she had known then, the ordeal would continue for the next sixteen years, for soon after their marriage, she realised Henry was not fit to rule. He had not a kingly thought in his dear head so she had become not only Queen, but also King, and had fought and ruled for him. He, in his simple way, had loved her like a sister, but never like a wife. Their son was the secret result of her love for someone else, who was now long dead, killed fighting for her cause. She had never loved another man again, until now. Henry had accepted the child as his own. He thought in his simple way that it was some kind of divine conception. It did not change his life; he continued to live as a pious celibate monk and she had lived hers like a nun. But, no more – a new life beckoned with Simon, one that she longed for with all her heart.

Margaret leant down and kissed Henry on his forehead. He stroked her arm absent-mindedly, a vacant expression on his face. More tears ran down her cheeks for she knew this was their final parting, and she would never see him alive again. Sadness gathered in her chest. *The last sixteen years are but dust in the wind*, she thought.

'God bless you, sweet Harry,' she whispered. 'I tried so hard for you.' She squeezed his hand, and then walked slowly from the room, her eyes wet with tears for the life that could have been, but was now a future lost.

The small schooner slowly left the safe harbour of Berwick-on-Tweed, and headed out into the grey mist of the North Sea, carrying a small cargo of nervous souls from the court of Queen Margaret who were anxious for the future.

Margaret and Simon stood at the stern of the ship, and watched as England slipped away into the mist. They did not feel the cold wind that whipped off the December grey sea – their minds were lost in deep reflection.

Simon's thoughts turned to Warwick. Whilst the bastard still lived, his quest for vengeance was unfulfilled, but the world still turned and Simon would wait and watch. He knew his time would come.

Margaret dwelled deeply on the past that was now lost to her. That royal world she had inhabited had now expired. She slowly slipped her gold royal wedding ring from her finger. Holding on to the stern rail, she dropped the ring over the side.

The ring that Henry had placed on her finger all those years ago plummeted towards the sea, to plunge down into the icy depths, lost forever. It was Margaret's last symbolic act; her old life was finished, now consigned to a watery grave. A new and wonderful future beckoned.

Margaret and Simon looked at each other, as only lovers do; her ringless hand gently finding his.

Chapter 3

The Die is Cast

Bamburgh Castle, Northumberland
10 April 1464

The sounds of men making ready for war echoed around the castle. Red-hot sparks flew as blacksmiths hammered hot metal on their anvils; armourers sharpened steel; archers – their fingers raw from waxed strings – tested bows. Arrow makers, leather workers – these men, and more – were making ready the weapons of annihilation. The sounds and commotion of this rebel army resonated out into the countryside: the hammering and cursing, the shouts of command, horses being readied, and wagons loaded, announcing this ignoble art that man had honed, and tested, since the beginning of time. This bloody business of war was about to be unleashed, once again.

Sir Ralph Percy looked out from a high turret window and watched with satisfaction as the Lancastrian army took shape. The cold of the winter months had gone, and spring was now ushering in the warmth needed for their army to take to the field. The Duke of Somerset's voice from behind him, made him face back into the room.

'When will our forces be ready to attack?' Somerset asked.

Sir Ralph Percy looked at the duke. *God save us*, he thought. *The man's supposed to be in command and he doesn't even know if his army is ready or not!* He then caught the raised eyebrow of Sir Ralph Grey, who was clearly thinking the same.

'All will be ready in the morning, your Grace,' replied Sir Ralph Percy, disguising his annoyance.

Somerset did not reply. He walked towards a large table in the centre of the room that was covered with maps and battle plans. He spread both hands on the edge of the table and leaned against it, his menacing eyes slowly taking in everyone in the room. 'Gentlemen,' he began, 'we have agreed our strategy. Tomorrow, Sir Ralph Percy, and I, will leave with the army for Alnwick. Lord de Ros and Lord Hungerford will depart before us with a small detachment of scourers, who will head south for Newcastle to spy on Lord Montagu's force. We believe they are heading north to meet those Scottish turncoats in Norham Castle. We need to know their numbers and disposition, and, most crucially, their route. If they are taking the coast road, we will engage them just south of Alnwick; if they are on the old Roman road, which is the one Percy suspects they will be using, we will ambush them at Hedgeley Moor.

'Sir Ralph Grey, you will have command of Bamburgh, and responsibility for the King. As you all know, Sir Henry Billingham left us yesterday with a small force for Middleham. I have ordered him to kidnap young Duke Richard and bring him back to Bamburgh.'

Somerset paused and threw a menacing look at Sir Ralph Grey, whose body stiffened with silent indignation. He noted the silence with satisfaction, and continued. 'The Earl of Warwick, we are told, is also in the field with an army. He will be coming north to meet his brother as he returns with the Scottish emissaries, and then together, they plan to ride to the City of York to meet that bastard usurper, Edward. However, we are going to change their plans, for once we have dealt with Lord Montagu, we will head south and engage the Earl of Warwick in battle. I want to see both their heads on spikes! After our victories, our numbers will swell as more join our colours, and then we will march on the City of York, and confront Edward with our great army. With his younger brother at our mercy, I am sure he will negotiate surrender. If he doesn't,' Somerset's voice rose with harshness, 'then we will slice his brother up in front of the gates of York, and place his head alongside that of Warwick's and Montagu's. Then, when we have taken the City of York, we will add Edward's head to make a quartet of brothers.'

Somerset's brutal face shone with undisguised domination, his cold eyes full of yearning. 'England will be at our feet, and I will have control of the kingdom.' The last sentence hung in the air. Had he accidentally let slip his grandiose plans? That one word *I* instead of *we* had filled the room with a feeling of disquiet.

Sir Ralph Percy looked at him with growing disbelief. Did Somerset think that Henry's crown would sit better on his head?

Sir Ralph Percy and Sir Ralph Grey walked across the inner keep of the castle. Neither had spoken since leaving their meeting with the Duke of Somerset, but now cloaked by sounds of the hustle and bustle of the assembled army surrounding them, they now felt free to voice their inner thoughts.

'That bastard, Somerset, has disgraced our noble cause by sending Billingham to kidnap the boy,' growled Sir Ralph Grey. 'I pray to God that he fails, for I will have no part of it.'

'The man has also unmasked himself, for he thinks he can steal the crown,' cried Sir Ralph Percy, in disbelief. 'Our dear Queen Margaret always kept him on a short leash, but now she has gone, he is untethered. If we defeat Lord Montagu and the Earl of Warwick, then King Henry would not make London alive – Somerset would see to that. He would then declare Queen Margaret's son, Prince Edward, a bastard, and claim the throne for himself.'

'Aye, I agree with you, my old friend,' replied Sir Ralph Grey. 'But first, he has to win these battles and as we both know, Somerset and his two cronies, Hungerford and De Ros, couldn't fight their way out of an empty room.'

Sir Ralph Percy nodded his head in agreement. 'Promise me one thing,' he began. 'If we are victorious you must take King Henry with all speed to London, parade him before the people, and let them know he is alive and well. That way, we would spike Somerset's plans and allow Queen Margaret, and her son, to return in triumph. If we are defeated, then you must safeguard King Henry; he must go into hiding until fortune once again smiles on him.'

Sir Ralph Grey took Sir Ralph Percy's hands, and shook them warmly. 'Aye, it is agreed,' he said.

Middleham Castle, North Yorkshire
23 April 1464

From his room, John Tunstall looked out of the window. Nature was ushering in the spring. Tomorrow, he would go hunting with Duke Richard and Francis Lovell, and it would be the first time this year that they would go on their own, and on horseback. Up until now, they had been hunting in the butts where they stood stationary while the game was driven towards them. To hunt on horseback took real skill, and John was looking forward to comparing his own talents against those of Duke Richard's.

He watched as the sun slipped towards the horizon. A faint red glow appeared on the skyline, slowly moving upwards, encroaching on the blue-grey heavens. The first star of the night twinkled at him. *Excellent*, thought John. *Tomorrow will be a fine day*.

He heard his mother called out.

'John, I am going to the countess' rooms. I expect you there in one hour. Duke Richard, Lord Lovell, and the girls, will be there, so don't be late.'

John heard the door close. He waited for five minutes before rushing down the steps and out into the courtyard. He walked quickly across the yard and out through the gate of the Great Keep.

Unbeknownst to him, his mother watched from just inside the door of the Great Hall, a knowing look on her face.

John entered the tilt-yard. Over the last months, he, Duke Richard, and Francis, had practised there daily, honing their fighting skills. Now, it was empty and silent; quietness cloaked the building. The air smelt of fresh hay and wood.

Hearing a rustle behind him, John turned, and there stood Rose, her face alive with a smile just for him. She leant forward and kissed John lightly on his lips. He remembered the first time they had kissed…

It had been after the Christmas feasting and celebrations. The Earl of Warwick and his close friends, had been drinking heavily, and were becoming raucous and loud. As everybody knew, that sometimes ended in mischief-making and trouble. John's mother had signalled with her eyes for him to leave, and he had quietly slipped out from the Great Hall. His mother, he knew, would stay with the countess until she had been safely seen to her private rooms, for it was wise to keep out of the earl's way once he had a belly full of wine.

John recalled the next thirty minutes with a clarity that would stay with him forever. He had stepped outside, the cold December night greeting him, his lungs filling with clean, crisp air. It was a welcome relief from the thick, stale air of the Great Hall. He had drunk a few cups of wine that evening, so he leant against the castle wall to let the cold night air refresh him. He looked up at the heavens; it was a cloudless night and the stars in their multitude took his breath away, for they filled the sky and shone with a magnificent brilliance. It humbled him to look up at God's majestic creation. *Father Drynk was right,* he thought. *Man should never question the power of God.* His slightly drunken thoughts were interrupted by a soft feminine voice calling to him.

'Is that you, John?'

It was Rose. John quickly stood upright and unexpectedly felt slightly unsteady on his feet.

Rose's sweet giggle warmed the night. 'Methinks you've had a cup of wine too many,' she laughed. Then gently taking hold of John's arm, she guided him across the castle's inner courtyard. At the entrance to the tower, they stopped.

'I think I'm all right now, Rose.' As John said these words, the light from the torch, over the tower entrance, softly lit Rose's face, and he caught his breath at her beauty. His tongue stumbled over his words. 'Rose, thank...I'm drunk...I mean, not drunk—'

John's words were cut short as Rose leant across and kissed him full on the lips. It was the first time he had been kissed by a girl; this was his first real kiss. Her lips felt cold and wet. He pushed his lips hard against hers, and their teeth cracked together. *Oh God,* he thought, *this kissing is awful.* His inexperience made him feel foolish.

Rose broke off the kiss, and pulled John through the entrance and into the foot of the tower, where he stood immobile, like a scared rabbit. 'Let me show you,' she whispered.

John closed his eyes. This time, their lips were warmer and becoming hotter. Rose kissed him with a slow gentle caress; her lips were soft, like velvet. John's world disappeared – there was only Rose and nothing else. When she ended the kiss, he stood with his eyes still closed, his heart beating wildly.

'I must go,' Rose said, breathlessly.

John opened his eyes. 'Go?' he whispered, dreamily.

'Yes...go...it's late, and—'

Before Rose could finish the sentence, John stepped forward and embraced her. She lingered for a second, and then broke away.

'I must go, sweet John,' she murmured. 'If your mother comes back early, it will be the worse for us.' She kissed John quickly on the cheek, and then was gone, back into the darkness from which she had arrived.

John stood at the foot of the stairway, his mind dazed. In a moment, he reached the door to their quarters, not even noticing the four flights of steps he had just run up. His feelings were all jumbled up. His first kiss, what did it mean? What did he feel? Was it good or bad that they had kissed? What would his mother say, if she knew? Did he feel love? What did love feel like? Did it feel like this? He had no idea, for he was young and unpractised in these matters, but there was one definite certainty amongst all his confused thoughts, and that was his desire to kiss Rose again...

They lay in the fresh, soft straw of the tilt-yard. Rose was telling John about her forthcoming visit home. She was looking forward to seeing her mother, father, and her two younger sisters. She had not seen them for six months or more. She chattered excitedly about the clothes she would wear, the gifts she would take, and her feelings for them all. She told him about the small hamlet of Newton-le-Willows, where she was born, and their family's small, thatched cottage.

John listened and watched Rose's eyes sparkle, the emotions rippling across her pretty face. She told him everything, hiding nothing. He knew most people always held their guard up, never revealing their inner selves to anybody, not even to the people they loved, but he and Rose told each other everything they thought or felt – no secrets were kept. He confided all his opinions, ideas, fears, and dreams, to her, and she, to him. He could not imagine his life without Rose. He leant over and kissed her.

'What was that for?' she asked.

'It's a leaving kiss. I must go. It's becoming dark and I think I am already late.'

They walked towards the exit of the tilt-yard.

'I will not be here tomorrow morning,' John said. 'We are going hunting early; it's our first time this year on horseback.'

'Please be careful,' said Rose.

'Don't worry, I'll be fine. See you tomorrow evening?'

'Of course.'

They walked back through the gate of the Great Keep together, and into the castle, each turning their separate ways.

The two guards on the gate smiled as they watched John and Rose walk by; there was no need for words. Young love, they thought, and they looked at each other with a knowing expression.

Richard, Duke of Gloucester, sat quietly engrossed in a game of chess with Anne Neville. Isabel Neville, the Earl of Warwick's other daughter, sat chattering to Francis as they played a game of dice. Lady Tunstall stood with the countess at a large table, which was covered with different coloured fabrics and laces, discussing the design on a complicated new headdress.

A few servants fussed around, but generally, all was calm. This was the scene that greeted John as he entered the room. As he looked around, he saw Anne and Isabel raise their hands to their mouths and start to giggle. Richard and Francis smiled broadly, and John wondered what the joke was about, but remembering his courtly etiquette, he walked towards the countess, and bowed low. 'Greetings, my Lady. I trust you are well today,' he said.

'I am very well, today, young John, and pleased to see that you are also looking well.' The countess smiled at him, her eyes twinkling with mirth.

John turned to his mother and bowed low.

'Why are you late?' Lady Tunstall enquired.

'I went for a walk around the battlements, and forgot the time,' John replied.

His mother did not reply, for she knew exactly where John had been, and with whom. She realised that with young love came secrets. Before Rose, there had never been secrets between her and John, and she did not want them now. She would talk to him about Rose tomorrow.

As John turned to go, the countess called to him. 'I didn't realise that the battlements were covered in straw.'

'More like the tilt-yard,' shouted Richard, for they all knew about John and Rose.

John looked behind him. To his embarrassment, the back of his woollen jerkin and tights had straw caught in the threads. It had been dark when he left the tilt-yard, so he had not noticed, and now his secret was revealed. He could feel his face becoming hot, he knew that in seconds he was going to blush bright red with embarrassment. Oh, how he hated that, for there was nothing on God's earth that would stop it. He walked to the farthest end of the room, and leant against the wall to hide the evidence. Richard and Anne left their game of chess and quickly walked towards him.

'Come, let me brush you down,' said Richard, concerned for his friend's embarrassment. Then, he whispered, 'You should know there are no secrets in this castle.'

John glumly nodded in agreement.

'Cheer up,' said Anne. 'Rose is the prettiest girl in the castle; all the boys would like to be in your shoes.'

John nodded once again, but this time with a proud smile on his face.

'You had better come and help Richard with this game of chess; he's not doing too well,' laughed Anne.

The three of them returned to the chessboard.

As John's face cooled down, he watched Richard and Anne, and realised that over the last few months, the two of them had become very close. It was obvious that they enjoyed each other's company. He wondered that in time, when Anne was old enough, maybe, she and Richard would become more than just friends. He reached over the chessboard to move Richard's queen.

Yorkshire Dales
24 April 1464

Richard, Francis, and John, left Middleham Castle an hour after sunrise. Entering the forest, they followed the River Ure upstream. Their instructions were to go no further than Wensley, but because the river turned west there, they had decided they would follow the river towards its source at the base of the Dales. They were going to enjoy their day's hunting, and with no superiors to accompany them, they would enjoy their freedom even more.

As they entered the wood, the morning air became colder. The sun shot rays of light through gaps in the canopy, but they carried no warmth to drive away the mist that hugged the damp forest floor. The sounds of birds and mammals filtered through the trees.

John loved the early morning forest; he always sensed a spiritual feeling as though they were in God's real cathedral – a holy place. He felt the Lord's presence was nearer to them here, in this natural world, than in any of God's man-made houses. He sometimes thought that God preferred to spend his time with the innocent animals of the forest, than the company of man. It could be that the natural world was far more important to him then the wickedness and stupidity of mankind. *Another good question for Friar Drynk*, he thought.

John reined in his horse beside a large oak tree, deep within the wood. He examined it closely. Richard and Francis pulled up behind him. High up from the ground, the bark was deeply flayed. John pointed towards the marks so that Richard and Francis could examine them as well. 'It's a large buck that's made those boundary markings,' he said, 'and they are fresh. He'll be laying his scent all around here to warn off other males.'

Francis dismounted from his horse and crouched down on the ground. 'His tracks move off in the direction we have been travelling in,' he said, standing up. 'The marks are close together and not too deep, so he's not in any hurry.'

'Well, of course he's in no hurry,' said Richard, with impatience. 'The rutting season doesn't start till late July, so he's obviously conserving his energy!'

'John must be doing the same for Rose,' laughed Francis, 'because he seems to be slowing down lately.'

John slipped from his horse and chased Francis around the oak tree in mock anger.

'While you two are playing games, I'm off to catch me a deer,' said Richard. He spurred his horse into a slow trot.

John and Francis quickly mounted their horses and followed him.

The solitary mature stag stood on the far side of the small clearing, with the three boys now dismounted, on the other side. They stood perfectly still, taking cover just inside the treeline, and downwind. They studied their prey in silence. The animal's antlers were a six-pointer. They knew that most mature bucks had two or possibly four pointers – so six was very rare. He was a beautiful specimen. The boys could see its head already mounted and hanging in the Great Hall – but first they had to kill it.

The warmth of the weakened April sun had finally burnt off the early morning haze. Far out to the horizon, the sky was a pale white-blue, but it gathered in strength to a solid blue as it loomed overhead. John looked up in wonder, and thought it must be touching the angels. The sky was so high it seemed to go up forever, dwarfing all that lay beneath it. His attention was brought back to matters in hand, as the buck started to move with a God-given elegance and grace; its thick brown winter coat had all but moulted, replaced with a beautiful, sleek, summer coat of chestnut red.

Richard whispered for Francis to go left, and for John to go right. Keeping inside the treeline for cover, they would slowly circle around behind their prey, and drive him across the clearing towards Richard, who would be waiting with his hunting bow. But, before they could move, the buck suddenly halted, and its regal head rose to full height. Its ears twitched, and its tongue licked his nose – a sign that it had detected a scent. Then, without further hesitation, it took flight for cover. It had distinguished a physical movement that signalled danger.

The boys looked at each other in frustration, then without a word, they quickly mounted their horses, and spurred them out into the clearing towards where the deer had been. They scanned the area to find the cause of their prey's flight. They had just reached the centre of the clearing when bloodcurdling war cries shattered the serenity of the morning. Their horses reared up in startled fright, and the sound of hooves filled the air as ten, heavily-armoured men, broke cover from the treeline, and charged towards them.

In unison, the boys spurred their mounts towards the woods, their minds totally confused, but one thing they did know: this sudden terrifying menace meant them harm. These men were not playing games.

The arrow that thudded into Francis' left shoulder instantly lifted him off his horse, sending him in a backwards somersault. He felt a sharp pain, and was then spinning through the air. Powerless to save himself, he hit the ground hard, and at speed, like a spinning pebble that skips across the water. Each time he landed, it knocked more air out of his lungs, and when he came to rest, he saw the arrow protruding from his shoulder. On each of his heartbeats, blood rhythmically spurted from the wound; his lungs felt empty. Badly winded, he gulped like a landed fish. He felt a coldness slowly moving up his legs, and then his hands started to shake – he could not stop them. Darkness began to force itself upon him.

Richard wheeled his horse tight round to the left as Francis hit the ground the first time. John wheeled to the right, and as they turned about, they realised that they were caught between two bands of soldiers. Confusion defeated their thoughts, for they understood nothing of this sudden violent madness, and they were acting on instinct alone. They reached Francis as he came to a crumpled stop. Quickly dismounting, they stood protectively over their wounded friend, back-to-back, swords drawn.

The troops that had fired the arrow were on foot, and as they walked slowly out into the clearing, they knew these boys were going nowhere.

The mounted men-at-arms formed a circle around the boys. This ring of containment stood silently watching, their weapons glinting with menace. Richard and John slowly took in this sight, their minds still reeling with shock and disbelief at the violent rampage of the last five minutes.

John looked down at Francis, who a few minutes ago had been laughing and full of life, but now was still and bloodied. Anger tightened in him. 'Come on, you sons of whores,' he shouted. 'Finish this bloody business for I swear by almighty God some of you will die with me.'

The watching men-at-arms smiled at each other; the little cub had courage.

Richard saw them smile. He lowered his sword and stuck it point first into the ground.

John turned around, a look of horror on his face.

'Lower your sword,' said Richard.

John's look of horror turned to one of confusion.

'If their intent was to kill us, they would have done so by now,' Richard whispered. 'I imagine they have another purpose for us. Come, we must tend to Francis.'

John reluctantly lowered his sword.

Sir Henry Billingham dismounted, and walked towards them. 'Duke Richard?' he barked.

Richard stepped forward.

'By the authority of King Henry,' barked Sir Henry, 'and on the orders of the Duke of Somerset, I have been commanded to take you to Bamburgh Castle.'

The two boys now knew that they had fallen into the hands of Lancastrian troops.

Richard spoke, his voice full of controlled anger. 'And have you orders to shoot a young boy, not yet thirteen years?'

'He has God's good fortune not to be dead, for I aimed for his heart,' shouted the archer, who had just arrived on foot.

Richard looked at the archer with a steady gaze. 'Tell me your name,' he demanded.

'My name is James Dam, and what son of a whore wants to know?' he replied, with a sneer.

Richard held his gaze on the archer, then in a loud voice so that all could hear, he said, 'So they haven't told you whom you have been hunting, today?'

The archer shrugged his shoulders with indifference.

'My name is Richard, Duke of Gloucester; my brother is King Edward.' Richard said no more; his words struck them all.

John could see the royal blood in Richard that had come from his father, Richard, Duke of York, and his mother, the Duchess, Cecily Neville. His royal breeding seemed to touch every man present; his composure assured. John marvelled at how Richard was so in control of the situation.

The archer stood astounded; the mounted men-at-arms shifted uneasily in their saddles.

'Your Grace, I had no idea of your royal status,' cried the archer, and then looking at Sir Henry, he shouted: 'Sir, you should have told us.'

Sir Henry cast a withering glance at the archer. 'Be silent, you fool,' he growled. 'Did you think we had travelled all this way just to hunt a squire's son?'

The men looked at the ground, their faces now heavy with shame.

Sir Henry looked at them all. 'Aye,' he finally admitted, with resignation in his voice, 'I agree. It's a bad business, but his Grace, the Duke of Somerset, has ordered it be done, so done it will be.'

John realising the die was cast, thought only of saving Francis. 'If we comply,' he said, 'you must return our wounded friend to Middleham Castle alive, and with all God's speed.'

'You are in no position to make demands,' replied Sir Henry.

Richard drew his sword from the ground. 'If this is not agreed,' he shouted, 'then you will take me to Bamburgh, dead.'

John moved to Richard's side, sword raised.

Sir Henry was impressed with the courage of the two boys; it rekindled his honour. He felt ashamed of his actions as he looked down at the crumpled form of the young boy. There was no dignity in this brutal act, he did not want this death on his conscious. Duke Richard was right; he had no orders to kill someone so young. He motioned for two of his men to dress Francis' wound. They broke off the shaft of the arrow leaving four inches protruding at the front. The arrowhead had just broken through the back of the shoulder. A trained surgeon could pull the shaft through, leaving a clean wound, but if they removed it now, he could bleed to death on the ride back to Middleham Castle. The two men bandaged the wound tightly and lifted Francis to his feet where he became semi-conscious. His face was white and bloody; his hands started shaking again.

'John…Richard…' Francis mumbled, as the pain took hold.

John went to him. 'Francis, it's all right, they are taking you back to Middleham.' As he spoke, he could see the pain rip into Francis' body. Tears of frustration suddenly stung John's eyes; he felt so helpless watching his friend suffer.

'Take good care of him,' John pleaded to the two soldiers.

They nodded grimly. 'We will see him safely back to Middleham,' they said.

Richard put his arm around John's shoulder and gently moved him away. Then turning to Francis, his whispered into his ear, 'They are taking us to Bamburgh, Francis. Remember, Bamburgh Castle.'

The two men-at-arms gently lifted Francis on to his horse. Sir Henry gave them instructions: once near to Middleham they were to tie Francis to his horse, and send it the last half a mile on its own; the horse would know its way home. They were then to head north and rendezvous at Hexham in two days' time. To throw off any pursuing party, Sir Henry and the rest would travel northwest to Stainmore Forest; there they would turn north-east skirting Barnard Castle, and then on to Hexham. From Hexham, they would travel north to Rothbury Forest, and then on to Bamburgh Castle.

The two men-at-arms mounted their horses, then one tightly either side of Francis, they slowly moved off in the direction of Middleham Castle.

Richard watched them depart. He bowed his head and prayed for Francis' safe return.

John was about to silently curse God, when he remembered what Friar Drynk had said about questioning the workings of the Lord. Instead, he cursed the men around him because men had planned what had happened to Francis. God had given men free will and this was the result of their actions, not of God's.

With their feet tied to the stirrups of their horses, Richard and John moved out with Sir Henry and his men towards Stainmore Forest. John thought of his mother and Rose. He felt despondent but he swore to himself that no matter if he should die or live, he would make them proud. *No more tears*, he thought, *it's time to act like a man.*

Richard thought of his brother, Edward, and the Earl of Warwick. He knew that they would leave no stone unturned to rescue him – the whole of England would be roused with their anger. He looked at the men around him, and thought how little they knew. Their actions today would unleash a whirlwind of vengeance. *They had better pray for a quick death in battle*, thought Richard, *for if captured, they will die cruelly on the scaffold for their treason.*

April rain swept in across the Dales towards them, with thick, black, heavy clouds carried on gusting winds. The sky had earlier been a perfect blue, but now with their capture, it had turned an ominous black. Richard wondered if it was an omen, and if so, for whom.

The same wind swept up behind the Duke of Somerset as he marched his army towards Hedgeley Moor, which lay just north-west of Alnwick, there to lay ambush for Lord Montagu's forces as they travelled north to meet the Scottish emissaries.

Two sentries patrolled the entrance to Middleham Castle's Great Keep. It was nearly lunchtime and they were starving. They had both missed breakfast due to an overindulgence in ale the night before. If they had been late on parade, the master-at-arms would have overindulged them in extra duties and maybe a flogging; it was better just to be hungry. The boredom of their morning's guard duty was weighing heavily on them, and with rumbling stomachs, the conversation had finally come round to food.

'I'm going to have a large plate of beef stew and bread when we come off duty,' said one, licking his lips.

The other, with a smile on his face, placed two hands on his stomach. 'Well, I fancy a nice...' his gaze wandered over his companion's shoulder. The other sentry's head slowly turned round in the direction of his gaze. There in the distance, approaching the castle, was a horse, with what looked like a small body tied to it. They stared in disbelief and narrowing their eyes, strained for more information.

'That's young Francis, if I'm not mistaken,' said one, concern rising in his voice.

'Francis?' queried his companion.

'You know...Francis...Lord Lovell. It's him!' he shouted. 'Fetch the master-at-arms.'

As one sentry ran to the guardroom, the other ran across the drawbridge to take charge of the incoming horse. He gripped the reins. 'By the Holy Virgin,' he whispered, as he saw the arrow stump protruding from the boy's shoulder, and his blood-drenched clothes.

The boy was unconscious, but still the sentry spoke softly to him. 'You're going to be all right now, my Lord,' he said. 'You're going to be all right.' He slowly and gently guided the horse towards the entrance to the castle.

The Great Controller sat forward in his chair, his forearms folded on his desk. He was scanning an order from Lord Warwick when he finished reading, and looked up at Black Skullcap who was seated in front of him. 'The earl's only been gone for one week and already he requires more victuals, all of them luxuries for himself. It's hard enough keeping his army of two thousand men fed, and in the field.' A trace of exasperation had crept into his voice.

Black Skullcap nodded in sombre agreement. 'Where is our Lord, now?' he asked.

'He's camped near Rievaulx Abbey, which is on the River Rye in the

Hambleton Hills – it's north of York. They are waiting to join up with Lord Montagu's forces as they head south with the Scottish emissaries. It will be a show of force to impress the Scots, and welcome King Edward to York.' Then turning back to the earl's list, the Great Controller said, 'We will have to send to the other castles for some of these supplies—' He was cut short by the ringing of the alarm bell that summoned the duty guards to their stations. Dropping the already forgotten order back on his desk, he turned towards the window. 'What can possibly be the meaning of that?' he asked.

Black Skullcap rose from his chair and headed towards the door. 'I'll find out,' he said, and sped from the room.

The Great Controller marvelled at the quickness of his senior clerk – he wondered how, with such skinny legs, he could be so swift and nimble. He slowly rose from his chair, and made his way to the door. For the life of him, he could not think of any reason why the guard would be called out. The earl was away with most of the men. All of the Lancastrian supporters were bottled up in the north. All was peace and quiet around Middleham...maybe it was just a practice exercise that he had not been informed of.

He walked past the now standing clerks in the outer office, and as he reached the main door, he heard the sound of fast approaching footsteps. He stopped and waited.

Black Skullcap appeared, his face red and breath laboured; a thin line of sweat upon his forehead and eyes wide with shock. 'Sir,' he gasped, 'it's Francis – Lord Lovell. He's just returned to the castle, unconscious and badly wounded. Duke Richard and John Tunstall are missing.'

The Great Controller was speechless. He stared at Black Skullcap, watching him suck air into his laboured lungs. Suddenly, he was past him, and running down the stairwell. It was either a hunting accident – which he prayed it was – or something he did not even want to contemplate. He reached the bottom of the steps, and ran out into the castle courtyard towards the guardhouse. He could see a lot of activity around the entrance. *Let it just be an accident*, he prayed, but a dark thought kept forcing itself into his mind: if it was not an accident, then it must be what he had always dreaded.

A throng of people parted in front of him, as he reached the guardhouse, and entering the building he was met by the master-at-arms, his face grim with worry. Behind him, lying on a table, was the still body of the young boy – the tip of the arrow protruding from his back. The Great Controller knew this was not a hunting arrow; the tip was a long slim Bodkin arrowhead designed for war. His worst fear was confirmed.

Lady Tunstall heard the alarm bell ring. She hurried to the window of her room, and looked out. Down below, all looked normal, but looking across to the Great Keep, she noticed a small commotion taking place, although she could not see the reason for it. The master-at-arms was taking charge of the situation. *Maybe*, she thought, *it's a fight between a few of the soldiers.* The castle had been so quiet and still this last week, with Lord Warwick and most of the men gone, maybe the boredom and drink was beginning to tell.

She saw the Great Controller hurrying across the courtyard, his black robes fluttering like some giant crow. Her brow knitted together; it must be more serious than she had thought. She then saw Rose dash from the small knot of people surrounding the keep, and her stomach flipped. Rose appeared to be crying; her body movements were full of disjointed panic as she headed towards their quarters. It was then that Lady Tunstall saw the horse in the shadow of the keep gate; blood covering the saddle, neck, and chest of the animal.

'No, no,' she murmured, and then she understood. 'Oh God!' she screamed. 'John!' She turned towards the door; her legs were slow, and dizziness made her head spin. She gripped the chair in front of her; then the door burst open.

Rose rushed in and fell at Lady Tunstall's feet. 'Lord Francis has been gravely wounded!' she cried. 'They think the boys have been taken.' Sobbing, she looked up, her face wet with tears. 'John's gone, my Lady. Sweet John is taken.'

Lady Tunstall fell to her knees beside Rose, and held her tenderly as tears fell gently from their eyes. The emotions she felt were straining to break free. Holding them tightly in check, she whispered to Rose, 'Come, we must go to the countess and find out what's to be done. We must be strong for John.'

Rose stopped crying and nodded her head in firm agreement; a look of resolve settling on her pretty features.

The Great Controller stood in the castle infirmary.

Francis had been laid on the large, oak table used by the castle's surgeon to perform his amputations, bone-setting and other painful operations. A small soft mattress had been placed between his body and the hard, solid, surface; he lay on his side unconscious.

Gathered with the Great Controller was the master-at-arms and the barber surgeon – the senior surgeon who normally tended the castle's hierarchy had accompanied Lord Warwick, as Master Surgeon General to the army, as was always the case when the earl took to the field. The young barber surgeon normally only pulled teeth or lanced the occasional boil. He had never treated combat wounds, although, he had watched the senior surgeon perform many operations.

The Great Controller stared at the barber surgeon with unblinking eyes. 'I need you to do this, James,' he said, gently, trying to put the young man at his ease. 'That arrow must be removed immediately, before the wound turns bad. We have no time to summon help from the monastery at Rippon; the boy will die before they arrive. The master-at-arms will assist you; he knows a thing or two about arrow wounds.'

The young surgeon nodded. 'I will do all I can to save him.'

The master-at-arms clapped him on the shoulder. 'Good, now let's get to work,' he said. 'We have no more time to waste.'

The young surgeon prepared his tools: pincers to draw the shaft through the shoulder, wine to cleanse the wound, and a button-shaped cauterising iron to seal it. The red-hot charcoal brazier was brought in, and he placed the iron deep within the heat. Then, removing the arrowhead, he cleaned the broken-off shaft at the front of the shoulder with wine. He inspected it closely as he did not want any pieces breaking off and being left in the wound as he drew the shaft through.

Satisfied all was well, he motioned for the master-at-arms to hold the boy tightly, and gripping the shaft, he pulled it through the shoulder in one smooth fluid movement.

Francis screamed out; the pain making him conscious.

The master-at-arms was about to place an opium-soaked sponge over Francis' face to induce a deep sleep before they cauterised the wound, when the Great Controller stepped between him and Francis, placing his hand gently on the boy's brow. Francis groaned loudly.

'Francis…' The Great Controller quietly soothed into his ear. 'You must tell me: were the boys taken?'

Francis nodded his head, and let out a low moan.

The master-at-arms tried to push past to administer the sponge, but the Great Controller held him back with his hand.

'You're a brave lad,' The Great Controller whispered to Francis. 'Where were they being taken, Francis? Do you know where?'

Francis nodded his head again.

'Tell me, just one word, my lad,' said the Great Controller, his voice rising.

Francis started moaning louder, and once again, the master-at-arms tried to push past. 'Enough,' he said. 'The boy's had enough.'

The Great Controller's yellow eyes flashed at him. 'I'll decide that.'

Then, Francis, through gritted teeth, whispered the word. 'Bamburgh.'

The Great Controller smiled grimly, and moved out of the way. As he left the room, the master-at-arms administered the opium sponge. Within seconds, Francis was in a deep sleep.

The young surgeon pulled the heated iron from the brazier and cauterised the wound. Next, with the help of a local healing woman, he applied a dressing that had been soaked in a special mixture of herbs. A clean, dry bandage was wrapped tightly around it, to hold it in place.

The master-at-arms left the infirmary, satisfied all had been done correctly, and rushed after the Great Controller. He caught up with him on the steps to the Great Hall. 'You could have killed the boy!' he cried.

'Trying to force that information out of him.'

The Great Controller's yellow eyes filled with anger. 'I had to have the information on Duke Richard,' he bellowed. 'Do you think I could face Lord Warwick and King Edward, and just shrug my shoulders when they ask me where he is being held captive?'

The master-at-arms stepped back; he had not thought that far ahead.

'I had to ask the question even if it meant losing young Francis. Sometimes, hard choices have to be made – don't ever forget that the King's brother comes before all others. Is that clear?'

The master-at-arms nodded.

'In future, never dare to question my actions. Now go, and organise a detachment of six of the best men-at-arms we have left in the castle. I ride for Lord Warwick in one hour!'

Lady Tunstall and the Countess of Warwick watched from the battlements as the Great Controller rode out from the castle. Behind him, looking distinctly uncomfortable was Friar Drynk, Duke Richard's three close retainers, and a detachment of soldiers bringing up the rear.

Before his departure, The Great Controller had explained to them his plan of action, and promised that he would do all in his power to return the boys safely to Middleham Castle. Where there had only been despair, he had given them hope, and shortly, they would go to the castle church to say prayers.

Rose, also on the battlements, watched the Great Controller depart. She felt as though she was detached from the world. She had chores to do, but no desire to do them. She wanted comfort, but had no family here to comfort her. She felt empty; lost. *Oh, John*, she thought, *I told you to be careful*. Tears filled her eyes again.

A comforting arm went around Rose's shoulder. It was Lady Tunstall. 'Rose, you must come and pray that the boys are returned to us safe and sound; that is all we can do now.'

As they turned to go, Rose looked for one last time as the Great Controller and his party disappeared into the distance. How she longed to be going with them.

Chapter 4

Life or Death

Hedgeley Moor
25 April 1464

Sir Ralph Percy looked up at the heavy, grey, sky. The wind and rain were unrelenting, having driven steadily into their faces since they had arrived on the moor early that morning. Three thousand men were soaked to the skin – horses, equipment, and weapons, ran with water. They had no shelter to hide from the unrelenting rain as they waited for the enemy.

God, this is madness, thought Sir Ralph as the bleak and desolate landscape tested his spirit. He could not believe Somerset's simple battle plan – if it could be called a plan. His strategy was a full-frontal assault on Lord Montagu's small force as soon as they were in sight. He recalled how the Duke of Somerset and his close retainers had turned on him when he had urged for caution. 'Montagu is no fool', he had counselled. 'The man has proved himself an able general and would never confront us unprepared'. They had laughed with arrogance at him.

He looked along the battle lines. They were drawn up in close order formation, and they were too tight. If Lord Montagu had cavalry, they would be out-flanked. His archers would also have an advantage with the wind behind them. Sir Ralph cursed the Duke of Somerset. *The man's a fool. This is not an ambush; it's bloody suicide.*

He looked at the men under his command – they were in no fit state to fight. Exhausted from their long march, they were soaked and hungry, their spirits low. Wind and rain battered their faces, and half their supply of weapons was on the carts stuck in the mud, two miles behind. Sir

Ralph knew they should pull back, regroup, dry out, reorganise, and engage Lord Montagu later. He decided to try one more time to make the Duke of Somerset see sense.

Spurring his horse, Sir Ralph Percy rode to the only tent that had been pitched and located centrally behind the army. As he strode in, the sudden warmth and dryness of the interior felt like a blanket of indulgence wrapping itself around him, and he basked for a moment in its luxurious comfort.

The Duke of Somerset sat with Lord Hungerford and Lord de Ros, sipping wine, whilst Sir Thomas Finderne and Sir Thomas Wentworth stood behind them.

'What is it, Percy?' snapped Somerset. 'Weather not to your liking?'

The others laughed and Sir Ralph felt the anger tighten within him. 'Your Grace, you would do well to share its discomfort with your troops if you wish them to fight bravely for you. If you cannot walk amongst them and stiffen their resolve then we should delay engaging Montagu.'

Somerset's arrogant eyes looked Sir Ralph up and down. 'This is not a pitched battle!' he shouted. 'It's a skirmish; we outnumber them two to one. Hungerford and De Ros confirmed their strength to me two days ago. We will crush them within an hour, no matter if nature, or you, thinks otherwise.'

'Your Grace, you must reconsider.'

The urgent tone in Sir Ralph's voice annoyed Somerset even more. 'Enough!' he shouted. 'Today, we fight.'

Sir Ralph's frustration finally boiled over. 'This is our last chance to salvage the Lancastrian crown,' he roared, 'and you,' he pointed at Somerset, 'are ill-advised. Your strategy is irresponsible, your conduct as a leader is inept.' Sir Ralph could feel the blood rushing to his face as his anger took hold of him. 'The last Lancastrian army that will ever take to the field is paraded outside waiting for a worthy leader to win them a glorious victory. But I see no leaders here, only fools sipping wine with not a care for those brave men outside!'

Somerset rose from his chair. Shaking with anger, he hurled his goblet of wine across the tent. 'You will die for those words, Percy,' he snarled.

Fingers curled around swords. Rain sounded an executioner's drum roll as it beat heavily on the canvas roof above their heads. Two swords flashed through the air colliding in a metallic roar.

Sir Ralph stepped quickly forward with a two-handed thrust, forcing Somerset off balance, the blade inches from his neck.

Somerset stumbled backwards, but as Sir Ralph swung his sword up over his head ready for a downward strike, two scouts rushed into the tent. Sir Ralph's blade stopped frozen in mid-air.

'My Lord Somerset,' shouted one of the scouts with panic in his voice. 'The enemy is upon us with a force that will overwhelm us.'

Somerset regained his balance and looked at the startled faces of Lords Hungerford and De Ros. 'By the Holy Mary,' he whispered, 'you have given me false information.'

'They must have gathered reinforcements as they marched,' stammered Lord Hungerford.

Somerset turned his sword towards him with disbelief in his eyes. 'You idiots have led me into a trap,' he snarled, as he drew back his sword to strike.

Sir Ralph stepped between them. 'Queen Margaret was right,' he said, angrily. 'We are now too weak and our enemies too strong. We must pray that God looks kindly on us.' Then striding towards the entrance of the tent, he cried, 'Come, we must join our men, immediately!'

They rushed out. Lords Hungerford and De Ros headed for the left flank, their faces white with fear. Somerset rode to command the centre, his face red as he raged at the two men.

Sir Ralph Percy returned to the right flank, his face grim with foreboding.

The arrow slowly rotated as it sped through the air towards the Lancastrian army. Its target, a young soldier just to the left of Sir Ralph Percy. The large, broad, metal tip penetrated through the soldier's neck, damaging his spinal cord. His legs instantly collapsed, and he crashed to the ground, paralysed. No one had seen this arrow approaching through the driving rain, but its effect was instantaneous. The men around the mortally wounded soldier shifted nervously on their feet. The dying youth looked up at them with pleading eyes, his nose, and mouth filling with blood that would slowly drown him. Nobody looked at him.

Lord Montagu's master archer had loosened eight arrows in less than sixty seconds, all aimed along the Lancastrian front line. Eight men lay dead or dying.

The Duke of Somerset's archers knew they could not reply. If they fired into the wind, their arrows would fall ineffectively short. A ripple of fear went through the duke's men. The lone archer had shown the advantage.

Lord Montagu had five hundred archers on each of his flanks now firing in unison. In less than thirty seconds, three thousand arrows rained down on the Lancastrian lines. Men fell wounded or dead on to the now blood red, sodden ground.

Sir Ralph Percy knew that they should have charged the enemy when the first arrows hit, but sadly, he knew the order would never come. He watched with dismay, but with no surprise as Lords Hungerford, and De Ros, broke ranks and fled the field, closely followed by their men. Finally, he saw, as he knew he would, the Duke of Somerset and his men take to their heels as the enemy onslaught rushed towards them. His disillusionment and sadness at the final defeat of the Lancastrian cause was complete.

The Yorkist cavalry now arched out to the right and left, with the Duke of Somerset just escaping the enclosing force, but for Sir Ralph Percy there was no escape. The time for running was over; his cause was finished. He watched as his men fled as best they could; the battle had finally come down to him and a few of his close retainers.

He looked out over the moor and remembered it, not in this wet bleakness, but in high summer when its glorious landscape filled with beauty. He smiled as he recalled the joy and freedom of those summer days, when they rode and hunted with free spirits and light hearts.

The noise of the battle seemed to fade around him and he sensed his warrior ancestors gathering close by, to accompany him on his final ride.

Time for one more illustrious gallop over this magnificent estate, he thought. Drawing his sword, Sir Ralph Percy rode towards the advancing enemy.

Rothbury Forest, Northumberland
26 April 1464

With their feet still tied to the stirrups, John Tunstall and Duke Richard trotted along a small, forest path, deep within the woods. They had soldiers to the front and rear of them, and John had long given up any hope of escape. Sir Henry Billingham still rode up front, leading as he had done since their abduction.

John, now starving and exhausted, glanced at Richard, who was half asleep on his horse. They had been travelling continually for three days with only short rest breaks. His mind had wandered from complete acceptance of their fate, to one of raging anger at the bastards for what they had done to them. His thoughts dwelled on poor Francis, and whether he had made it back to Middleham. Or, perhaps he had died a lonely death, abandoned in the forest. John had no way of knowing. The two soldiers who had been detailed to accompany Francis back to the castle had never arrived at Hexham to join up with Sir Henry's force as they had been ordered to do. They had either been captured, which was highly unlikely, or they had deserted. Were they ashamed and fearful of what had happened in that clearing? To be associated with such a wicked act was dangerous for them and their families. Had they just melted back, vanished, evaporated into the safety of some quiet part of the kingdom?

John's pensive thoughts turned to his mother. He could see her loving smile, and his weary body ached for the security of their warm quarters. How he longed to be home with her. His spirit sank lower. The anxiety of never seeing his mother, or Rose, again, put alarm into his heart. He forced back the tears that threatened his tired eyes; he had sworn that he would never cry again. He would never complain or show any weakness to these Lancastrian bastards.

John's melancholy thoughts dissipated as Sir Henry halted their column. In the gloom of the forest, he just caught the outline of undefined shapes moving in the murky shadows. As he looked around, he saw there were hundreds of these ghostly phantoms slowly slipping past them. As more came closer into view, he realised that these spectral apparitions were soldiers. All were on foot, their faces white, eyes fixed to the ground. The world around them did not intrude on their shocked minds. Their clothes were wet and muddied, and many had bloody bandages around their heads or arms.

Richard moved up beside John. 'These are Somerset's men,' he whispered. 'Look: many wear his battle colours. There's been some sort of skirmish and I'd wager he's lost.'

For the first time in three days, the boys smiled at each other.

Sir Henry called out to a group of soldiers near to him. 'How go you?'

Two soldiers, one wounded in the leg, his arm around his comrade's shoulder for support, stopped. 'Lord Montagu has won the day on Hedgeley Moor!' he cried. 'Our Lord Somerset is defeated.'

Sir Henry shook his head. 'This cannot be!' he cried, in disbelief.

'It can be and is be,' said the wounded soldier. 'The Lancastrian cause is finished.' Then with frustration in his voice, he cried, 'Good King Henry has lost his crown; he is no more a king than I am!'

'Where do you head for?' asked Sir Henry.

'Hexham,' replied the soldier. 'We have been told that food, and our fighting wages, await us. Lord Somerset, it is said, will be there with fresh troops, but if you believe that, you'll believe the earth is round!' He gave a hollow laugh. 'Most men are heading home, thankful that their body and soul are still together. We will make for Hexham, but will only dally a day or so to see our wages, and then we will slip away. There's no more fighting for us; our cause is done.'

Before Sir Henry could reply, the two men limped away, quickly swallowed up in the gloom.

The men that were shuffling slowly past them began to thin out and Sir Henry's group moved off. Shortly afterwards, they came across the dead and dying.

These men have succumbed to their last breath, thought Sir Henry. *They lay where they have taken their last mortal steps, their muddy tracks showing from whence they came, but where they have gone now, only God knows the answer to that.*

Other men lay with their backs against tree trunks, their life's blood seeping away. Their thin cries for help sent shivers down John's spine. He looked at Duke Richard and saw that his eyes were cold and unconcerned by these sights.

Duke Richard saw John's troubled glance and moved up beside him. 'Do not be concerned for these bastards, they deserve their deaths,' he whispered. 'If they had won, they would have had our heads on spikes by now.'

John knew that Richard spoke the truth. He pondered how the duke could always cut out any feelings or emotions and just summed up a situation with coldness. It seemed to freeze John's heart, for whilst he felt compassion for these dying men, Richard would have them all dead.

The evening shadows were growing long when Sir Henry Billingham finally called a halt to their journey. 'We will rest here for the night,' he said, wearily. 'Tomorrow we arrive at Bamburgh.' He could find no excitement or enthusiasm in his voice; the shock of the Duke of Somerset's defeat weighed heavy on his mind. The unthinkable slowly began to dominate his thoughts. He fought these unpalatable images with all his mental strength, trying to find reasons to still believe in their cause, imagining grand plans that would provide a great victory. But slowly, the reality of the situation defeated all his hopes, and his dreams faded away. He finally admitted to himself that the wounded soldier who had spoken to him in the forest was right; they had no king or queen to fight for, and now no army to fight with – the Lancastrian cause was finished.

He slowly sat down at the edge of the forest and looked out over Northumberland's rolling dales. His eyes were moist as he thought of all the good men who had given their lives in this great struggle; all the widows and orphans it had created. Now, it was ended, all purpose to his life was suddenly gone – a feeling of quiet despair settled on him. Then a hand gently shook his shoulder.

'Sir, the men would like to speak to you,' said a senior man-at-arms.

'What on earth is there to talk about? Those soldiers in the forest spoke plainly enough,' Somerset replied, tersely.

The senior man-at-arms looked embarrassed. 'It's about the boys, Sir.'

Sir Henry rose reluctantly to his feet, and walked towards his men.

Richard nudged John in the ribs and pointed to Sir Henry. 'Looks like trouble,' he said.

Both boys were chained by an ankle to a tree, their horses grazing contentedly on the edge of the forest. They watched as the men gathered around Sir Henry. Voices became excited, arms were raised, fingers pointed in their direction. The boys knew this was about them. They watched, but could not hear what was being said. It developed into a heated argument with Sir Henry drawing his sword. They heard him shout above the chorus of voices. 'Those boys will be delivered to Bamburgh, alive!'

Richard and John knew their lives hung in the balance. The sixteen other men reluctantly dispersed into the woods around them. They gathered in groups of three or four as they settled down for the night. The boys could hear their low mutterings. As hard eyes glanced over at them, they instinctively moved closer together.

John knew that whilst they were important to Sir Henry, who was honour-bound to deliver them alive to Bamburgh Castle, they had become a liability to these other men. There was nothing left for them to fight for except their own lives. To be caught holding the two of them would mean a certain death sentence, and he could think of no good reason why these men would let them live. He understood what the argument had been about. 'We had better pray that we see the dawn,' said John, darkly.

Rievaulx Abbey – Earl of Warwick's Encampment 26 April 1464

The Earl of Warwick sat in his tent and gazed out over the sodden landscape of the early dawn, watching as his army unfolded itself from a night of peaceful slumber. It had been a cold night. He looked out as the heavy showers and the quick, cold wind of the morning slowed the start of the day. It was well that his men had ample tents and accommodation within the abbey, for none needed to be wet or cold.

His small eyes focused back on to the Great Controller who stood before him. He felt the cold leave his body only to be replaced with rippling hot sweats. He wanted to erupt into a rage at the news the Great Controller had just brought him, but could not, for it was on his authority that the boys had been allowed to go hunting on their own – there was nobody else to blame, but himself.

Sweat started to run down his back, and he looked out again at the teeming rain, wishing it could wash this bad news away. His mouth felt as if it had burnt dry.

He motioned for one of the servants to bring him wine. All about him waited and watched as he gulped the cool drink with anger and frustration. Lady Tunstall penetrated his thoughts: his good friend Sir William, Lady Tunstall's husband, had died, fighting with him at St Albans, and now her only child had been taken, along with Duke Richard, a royal prince, who had been placed under his protection by King Edward. The humiliation that this terrible news brought, stung his spirit, and his rage at last erupted. Rising from his seat, his small eyes hardened with anger.

'When I find the devils that committed this heinous act, they will be roasted over hot coals!' he roared.

All in his presence drew back from the force of his temper, except the Great Controller, who moved not an inch.

Warwick's hard eyes swung towards him; the Great Controller held his hand up. Warwick looked at the hand in front of him. It seemed to possess some magic force for he became still and silent.

The Great Controller spoke quietly to him. 'My Lord, now is the time for cool thought and quick actions, for if we are to save the boys, we have no time to lose.'

Warwick, his face red with anger, nodded in agreement, and slowly composing himself, he slumped back into his chair. 'How is Alice?' he asked. 'Is she bearing up?'

The Great Controller shook his head, sadly. 'She stands proud, as her heritage says she must, but her sorrow is as any mother's – it runs deep and sharp within her. I promised to bring her son home to her.'

Warwick thumped the arm of his chair. 'And by God, we will!' he shouted. 'By God we will, so now tell me your plan.'

The Great Controller produced a detailed map of Northumberland and spread it out over a large table in the centre of the room. He silently studied the map as he gathered his thoughts.

Warwick's impatience broke through the silence. 'Come on man!' he cried. 'You said quick action was required, so spit out this plan of yours.' He saw the Great Controller's yellow eyes flash up, and the effect startled him, as it always did. Ever since he was a young boy, those eyes had that impact on him. After all these years, he should have been immune to their power, but he still was not, and most probably, never would be. He stood in silence and waited.

'My Lord,' began the Great Controller, 'the information on the kidnapping of Duke Richard and John Tunstall is sparse. We know they were taken by Lancastrian forces on the morning of the twenty-fourth. They were abducted near the village of Wensley, and are being taken to Bamburgh Castle as we speak.' He paused and looked around him. 'Before I continue, the room must be cleared of all men who will not be involved in this operation, for loose tongues, no matter how innocent, may give a key to the enemy with which to unlock our plans. We cannot be too careful; the lives of Duke Richard and John Tunstall depend on us.'

Warwick nodded in agreement. 'Tell us who stays,' he said, a half-smile forming on his lips as he looked around the tent. He was beginning to warm to the intrigue of the situation.

The Great Controller reeled off the men who were to stay. 'Duke Richard's close retainers: John Milewater, Thomas Parr, and Thomas Huddleston. For your Lordship: Sir Conyers and Sir Metcalfe. I require the twins: Thomas and George Hallet, and Friar Drynk.'

Warwick looked around him and saw that the twins and Friar Drynk were absent. He ordered a messenger to bring them forth. 'All that are not named may go,' he commanded, and with a clap of his hands, the tent emptied. 'Francis will survive the arrow' he said, as they waited for the twins and Friar Drynk.

The Great Controller was not sure if it was a question or a statement, but replied none the less. 'It was a clean wound. He will live, although his left arm will not be as flexible as it used to be. He may have to adapt his fighting style in the future. Only time will tell.'

'All three boys are my responsibility,' growled Warwick. 'It would seem those Lancastrian bastards still have a sting in their tail, but I will have the heads of those who ordered this outrage, and the heads of those who carried it out. Somerset will be the first, for he must be behind this evil deed.'

The twins and Friar Drynk entered the tent and bowed low before joining the small audience of the Great Controller.

The Earl of Warwick looked at the Great Controller. 'Now then, Thomas,' he said, rubbing his hands together with anticipation, 'tell us your plan.'

Rothbury Forest, Northumberland
27 April 1464

The cold, half-light settled its weak strength on Duke Richard and John Tunstall as dawn crept silently into the forest – a welcome friend awakening them from a fitful slumber. The thin light meant life. The blackness of the night had threatened death, but daybreak had arrived and they still breathed. They looked at each other with nervous smiles on their tired faces.

The silence of the morning was abruptly broken by Sir Henry Billingham, who strode around cursing loudly to himself. 'Those cowardly bastards!' he shouted. 'They're like rats deserting a ship!'

Richard and John sat up straight and looked around them. They could only see Sir Henry and three of his senior men, but no more – the rest had obviously slipped silently away during the night.

John reasoned that if the evidence to their crime could not be killed then they had decided it was best to abandon the evidence that linked them to the crime. With nothing left to fight for, and with no possibility of wages, the men's decision had been an easy one.

Sir Henry dropped down on to his haunches in front of them, his face tired and angry.

The two boys looked at him. They saw before them a man at the end of his tether. Richard spoke first.

'Leave us,' he urged, 'and go with your loyal retainers; save yourselves. John and I will be—'

'My orders were to deliver you to Bamburgh Castle,' interrupted Sir Henry.

'But you could save yourself,' Richard quietly reasoned.

'I will deliver you to Bamburgh as ordered!' Sir Henry shouted, the frustration in him mounting. 'Then I will head for France, and when the time is right, I will return to take the crown from your brother's head and place it back where it rightfully belongs: on a royal Lancastrian brow!'

'But this is madness,' said Richard, also becoming frustrated. 'This war must stop. It cannot continue forever.'

'It will continue until the last noble Lancastrian is dead,' replied Sir Henry.

'And that will be soon,' retorted John. 'You will all be hunted down like the dogs you are. We will not forget your actions against us and what you did to Lord Lovell. You're all murdering—'

Richard put his arm across John's chest. 'Enough,' he said, quietly.

Sir Henry rose to his feet and looked down at them. The boys' thin, tired faces looked up at him. He had made them face death more than once. How had it come to this? His distinguished career had ended with the abduction of boys, and then fleeing like a frightened dog to France. He realised his shame, what he had done was wrong. Words – no matter how repentant – would never be enough to put it right. There was no point in continuing the conversation. The sooner this mission was completed, the better.

Sir Henry turned and walked away. 'Put the prisoners on their horses,' he commanded sharply. 'We ride for Bamburgh.'

The boys had been in the saddle for over three hours when Duke Richard smelt the sea. The salty aroma inflated his lungs; its sharp freshness filled his body. That first indulgent breath cleared his tired mind.

They were on the brow of a hill, looking down, as the land flattened out to the sea, and there, dominating the shoreline stood Bamburgh Castle. The wind and the sea threw stinging spray against its solid granite, walls. It was a futile gesture; the great rolling ocean with its white-tipped, running waves would never claim that majesty of stone. He remembered the first time he had breathed the sweet tang of the sea – he had been eight years old – fleeing with his mother, and brother, George, from Queen Margaret's army.

They had boarded ship at Dover one cold January morning four years ago, and fled to Burgundy. His father, brother, and uncle, had just been killed at the battle of Wakefield. Now, his world had turned full circle, for once again as he smelt the sea, his life was in danger.

They entered Bamburgh Castle with its Lancastrian banners flying high above their heads from the ramparts. They were a small, bedraggled group, who raised not a stir at their entry. A few curious eyes watched them dismount outside the Great Hall, but the news of the Duke of Somerset's defeat had roused the castle into a hornets' nest. Men and weapons bustled everywhere. Wagons were arriving with fresh supplies of food and drink as the castle readied itself for siege.

John looked around with hungry eyes, taking in every detail. He had never seen a castle prepare for war. Middleham Castle had never been threatened during his short lifetime. It had always been solid and sedate, a comfortable home, but here, armourers sweated as every blade was sharpened. Arrows were being stacked in huge bundles around the battlements. Large vats with which to boil oil were being placed at strategic sites. Women with young children headed out of the castle towards the safety of the north. The air pulsed with excitement.

Duke Richard watched the frantic activity. 'This will be,' he said quietly to John, 'the Lancastrian last stand.'

John nodded in agreement, his eyes wide as this mighty castle readied itself for battle.

They were led through the Great Hall, their eyes quickly adjusting to the dim and smoky light. Healing women lay out trestle tables, not for feasting upon, but to receive the wounded. Barber surgeons, recruited from surrounding towns and villages, laid out their instruments – all was quiet efficiency. Duke Richard knew its sombre atmosphere reflected a new purpose.

They were ushered into a large office situated off the Great Hall – it overlooked the castle's inner courtyards and the gate of the Great Keep. A man, short and solid, rose from behind a desk. As he did so, he handed a letter to a messenger and ushered him from the room.

A young serving maid entered as the messenger left, bearing a flagon of honeyed mead and one leather cup. She was startled to see Richard,

John, and Sir Henry, who were muddy, dishevelled, and unwashed. She stood by the door, unsure of herself.

John, seeing her nervousness, stepped across and took the tray from her. Dark hair cascaded down and framed the prettiest face he had seen for many a long day. The maid smiled at John's kindness, and he felt some of the tensions of the last few days ease as he gazed at her, but she reminded him of Rose and his heart ached. 'What is your name?' he asked.

'Lindsay,' she replied, nervously.

'Ah,' John said, 'a beautiful Celtic name. It matches your prettiness.' He noticed the girl blush. He did not want her to go. After all the madness of the last days, her soft innocence reminded him of a different world.

'How old are you?' asked Richard.

'I'm thirteen,' she proudly said, 'and it is my birthday today.'

Richard reached into his doublet and produced a silver penny. 'For you,' he said, 'for bringing light into our day.'

The girl blushed even more and looked at Sir Ralph Grey. He nodded to her. Her hand closed around the coin, and with a dazzling smile, she was gone.

Sir Ralph walked to the door and ordered the guard who stood outside to let no one pass. He then closed the solid oak door shut. They all studied one another.

The boys saw a man with cropped, fair hair turning white-grey at the temples; his hard rugged features and straight bearing indicated a man who had been soldiering all his life. A brave man, Richard thought; a man who had seen his fair share of battles, but was he an honourable man?

Sir Ralph studied the two boys before him. Although tired and hungry, they stood proud. Both had dark hair and blue eyes. *Who is who?* he thought. One had eyes that flashed around the room in anger – he could see the belligerence in him – whilst the other stood quietly, his features calm and thoughtful, unwavering eyes never leaving his own. *I'll wager he's Duke Richard*, Sir Ralph thought. He turned to Sir Henry.

'Well, Henry, you seem to have completed your sordid little mission. I presume one of these boys is Duke Richard.'

Sir Henry nodded. 'The one with the hump,' he said, pointing to Richard.

Richard's eyes glittered icy cold as he heard the words leave Sir Henry's lips. 'You will die for that,' he hissed. 'Your torturous death will begin with your tongue being ripped from your foul mouth.'

Sir Ralph took a sharp intake of breath as he saw the hatred ripple through Richard's body. 'So, why in God's name do we have an extra one?' he shouted.

'I had to bring him or kill him,' replied Sir Henry.

'Just as you tried to kill Lord Francis!' cried John. 'For all we know, you may have succeeded.'

Sir Ralph's eyes hardened. 'In God's name, Henry, what have you done?'

Sir Henry's face turned red. 'We shot Lord Lovell with an arrow to stop them escaping.' He sighed with distress. 'I swear we didn't know it was him at the time, all we knew was that Duke Richard had dark hair, so the one with light hair took the arrow.' His eyes fell to the ground.

'By the Virgin Mary!' exclaimed Sir Ralph, his voice full of disbelief. 'You couldn't capture three small boys with a force of twenty experienced troops?'

Sir Henry shook his head.

'You could have abandoned the other two boys in the forest. By the time they had reached Middleham to raise the alarm, you would have been long gone...' Sir Ralph shook his head sadly as his words trailed off into silent frustration. 'Where are your troops, now?'

'The cowardly dogs deserted last night,' replied Sir Henry, his voice quiet after his moment of shame. 'We heard of Somerset's defeat as we travelled up through Rothbury Forest. We passed many of his men. They said they were making their way to Hexham to regroup. Somerset had promised to bring fresh troops, although many, it would appear, are finished with fighting.'

'Aye, we heard that was the plan,' said Sir Ralph. 'My orders are to hold Bamburgh until Somerset's great victory.' Then with a caustic laugh, he added, 'The one that he keeps on promising us.' Sir Ralph stopped laughing; his eyes looked tiredly around the room, and then with a quiet voice, he said, 'I lost my good friend, Sir Ralph Percy, at Hedgeley Moor – abandoned, aye, deserted by Somerset, De Ros and Hungerford. I am told he died a good death along with his brave retainers, so with our best men gone I hold out small hope of Somerset winning. Most will not follow a leader who cuts and runs, but as I am duty bound to do, I will wait for this mythical victory. I will not run from this final battle.'

Sir Ralph studied Sir Henry and saw a man that had lost heart in their cause. The air of defeat that surrounded him could easily rub off on to his own troops. He made a decision. 'I want you and your men out of the castle by nightfall,' he barked, his voice stern enough to deny any argument. 'I do not want you here when the Yorkist army arrives. If they breach our walls and know of your dishonourable actions they would put every one of my men to the sword.'

Sir Henry was silent

Sir Ralph looked at him, knowingly. 'I believe that you desire to go?'

Sir Henry nodded. 'I head for France and—'

'Good, that's settled then,' said Sir Ralph, pulling open the door. He stared with silent distaste as Sir Henry strode from the room with no backwards glance or farewell, and then shut the door behind him.

Turning to the two boys, Sir Ralph said, 'I will organise fresh clothes and washing facilities to be provided, and food. You will not be in the castle dungeons. I have made arrangements for you to be held in a comfortable room high within a tower, with good views and fresh air, but your door will be well guarded, so no thoughts of escape!' He stopped talking; looking at the two boys his eyes softened.

Richard instantly saw this and quietly thanked God. *At least the man has some mercy in him*, he thought.

Sir Ralph continued. 'This is not a situation I wished for, but it is one I have to resolve along with the future of our good King Henry. You are in no danger, but until I find a way to set you free, you will remain here as my prisoners.'

'I thank you for your kindness,' said Richard. 'It would seem we are all here under difficult circumstances that are not of our making.'

Sir Ralph Grey nodded in agreement as he opened the door.

Hartlepool Bay, North-East England
27 April 1464

The straight, sleek lines of the merchant ship cut through the dark sea as she raced north. She was a single mast, square-rigged cog, of six hundred tons. Every inch of sail was uncovered as she hastened past the headland of Hartlepool Bay. She had been constructed during one warm summer, on the banks of the River Hamble in the New Forest, Hampshire, and named *The Sparrow Hawk*. She had a standard clinker-built hull and a modern integral stern castle.

The Hallet twins and Friar Drynk stood in the middle of the lower deck, their arms resting on the side as they watched the headland disappear into the sea mist behind them. They had started their journey late the previous evening from Stockton, on the River Tees. They had raced from the Earl of Warwick's camp at Rievaulx Abbey along with the Great Controller and Duke Richard's three retainers, and requisitioned the ship using the authority of King Edward through the earl's office of Chamberlain of England.

The captain and crew had accepted the order with good grace; in fact, this unexpected adventure had been a welcome change from their normal trading routes, and the prospect of a small bounty, if they made the journey within two days, only added to the excitement.

Thomas Hallet looked at Friar Drynk and felt a small pang of pity for him. His large body was not used to hard riding, sleeping under canvas and the privations and hunger of army life. He had blisters on his body where blisters should not have been and a hunger in his belly that was slow torture to him.

Thomas slowly removed a large piece of cheese and some sweet oatmeal biscuits from inside his padded jacket. He watched Friar Drynk's head whip round, his eyes fastening on to the banquet that had just been produced. He watched as the friar's hand tightened on the handrail, his body becoming taut, his eyes greedily consuming the food that Thomas held in his hand. 'The trouble with you, friar,' he said, 'is that your mind is dominated with food and wine, when it should be full of God!'

'I know,' Friar Drynk sighed, his eyes never leaving the food. 'It is a small weakness I have, but some men's minds are full of women, or money, or power.'

'And Warwick's,' laughed George, 'is full of gunpowder, for he seems to explode all the time.'

As all three laughed, united by the humour, Thomas divided the food and Friar Drynk devoured his share in seconds. The ferocity of his eating amazed the twins.

Friar Drynk licked his lips.

'If only we had some wine,' said George, teasingly, as he reached into his padded jacket, a half-smile on his lips.

Friar Drynk's body tautened again as his eyes followed George's hand. 'You haven't?' he questioned.

George nodded. 'I have.'

'May God bless you, my son,' said Friar Drynk.

George produced a bottle of wine and held it just out of the friar's reach. 'You will have to pray for me,' George said, waving the bottle around in the air. 'For I will need all the help I can muster to get me through the gates of Heaven.'

'I will pray for you for ever,' said Friar Drynk, taking hold of the bottle with holy reverence.

The Great Controller watched the three men, from the raised stern deck. There was no food or drink on the vessel. They had sailed as soon as they had taken command on the evening tide and there had been no time to load any provisions. Urgency was all that mattered; food and drink could wait. It amazed him how the twins always seemed to produce whatever they needed, when they needed it. He smiled to himself. *They are artful magicians*, he thought, *and by God, we will need some magic to rescue those boys from Bamburgh Castle.*

Rievaulx Abbey – Earl of Warwick's Encampment 27 April 1464

The Earl of Warwick raised his richly gloved hand above his head, and threw it forward. Gently spurring his horse, he slowly started the great march to Bamburgh Castle. Trumpets silenced the early morning chorus as the signal to move off was given.

He twisted around in his saddle and looked at the two thousand troops paraded behind him. It always filled him with pride to see his army on the march; banners flying, outriders protecting their flanks, heavy wagons bringing up the rear. It was a powerful sight and he grunted to himself with satisfaction. This was the second part of the Great Controller's plan: the first had been to take ship to Holy Island. They had a long, hard, four-day march in front of them and he had made sure that every man under his command knew that Duke Richard and John Tunstall had been taken by Lancastrian forces. This outrage had filled his men with righteous anger. There would be no slacking or complaining on the long road ahead.

They moved off on to the old Roman road and headed north. Warwick thought of the journey stretching out in front of them. They had two days to reach Newcastle. There, they would pick up fresh provisions, and the great siege guns: *London*, *Newcastle*, and *Dijon*, so costly and treasured that they had their own names. The use of cannon had never been utilised to break a siege during this civil war; that is, until now. He had sent out envoys to the Lancastrian garrisons at the fortresses of Alnwick and Dunstanburgh, offering a full pardon if they surrendered, but there was no such offer to the garrison of Bamburgh. Their walls would feel the full force of his cannons. They would be smashed open, breached, retribution would be swift – an example would be made. The world would learn that no one could hold the King's brother to ransom and live.

The marching army settled into a steady rhythm and this lifted Warwick's spirits as he listened to his men singing bawdy marching songs – they were in good humour. Satisfied all was well, his mind turned once again to matters of state. He had sent messengers south to King Edward. The news they carried was both good and bad, for after much discussion with the Great Controller, he had decided that it was best to tell Edward the truth about the abduction of his dearly beloved younger brother. As the Great Controller had pointed out: by the time Edward received the news and made the journey north, Richard would be either dead or rescued. Whatever the outcome, the truth could not be hidden. This distressing news would be tempered with the report Edward would receive of the destruction of the Duke of Somerset's forces by Warwick's brother – Lord Montagu – who had routed the Lancastrian army on Hedgeley Moor. Warwick knew Edward would be delighted; he would try to squeeze an earldom out of him as just reward for his brother's service.

Warwick had also sent orders for Lord Montagu to rendezvous with him, and both their armies, at Alnwick Castle in three days' time, to finalise the strategy for the capture and execution of the Duke of Somerset and his Lancastrian allies. Once that was completed and his brother's elevation to an earl had been achieved, Warwick would then be able to turn his attention to the future Queen of England.

Warwick pondered on whom he would chose as a bride for young Edward. Any pretty French princess would put a bulge in his young trousers. France was the favourite – an alliance with them made sound strategic sense. With the rear door of England closed to the Scots, and a powerful alliance with France, England – indeed, himself – would have a powerful voice amongst the nations of Europe. He would write to King Louis, shortly, and begin negotiations.

Then, there was the question of Edward's brother, George, and Warwick's own daughter, Isabel. A marriage between these two would unite the two houses of York, or maybe, Warwick considered, with a shiver of excitement, Isabel as Edward's wife. *God, dare me thinks such an intrigue, for I would be father-in-law to the King and my grandson would be the future King of England.* His mind filled with ferment at the audacity of the proposal. George could then marry a French princess and still unite the two countries.

Thoughts of young Duke Richard suddenly filled Warwick's mind, and poured cold water on all his plans. These sobering thoughts brought him back to the present. If all his schemes were to come to fruition, then saving Richard was now his priority, for if Richard died, King Edward would blame him, and then all his plans would be left hanging in the balance.

The Earl of Warwick rode on, devilishly plotting for every eventuality like the foxy manipulator he knew he was.

Chapter 5

The Game's Afoot

North Sea, off the Coast of Northumberland 29 April 1464

The Sparrow Hawk skirted north around the Farne Islands, which lay four miles off the coast of Northumberland. During the night, the crew had left the squally showers well behind and now they sailed under a cloudless blue sky. The warmth of the sun had chased off the early morning sea mist as the ship turned towards the shoreline.

The Great Controller stood on the deck of the stern castle, gazing back as the vast mudflats of Budle Bay receded into the distance. Far off, he could just make out the hazy outline of Bamburgh Castle before it too faded from sight. This brief glimpse of the fortress formed an image of Duke Richard and John Tunstall being held captive within its great walls. He offered up a silent prayer for the success of this mission, and then hurried forward to the bow, mounting the steps to the raised forecastle. He knew that they must now be close. Straining his eyes over the distant sea, he searched impatiently for land. The flatness of the horizon was finally broken, as Holy Island hove into view.

Two birds swooped low across the bow of the ship, dipping their enormous white wings in salute. This act seemed, to the Great Controller, to be a courteous acknowledgement from one marine voyager to another. He smiled to himself. *Albatross on the wing,* he thought. *Now, that is a good omen.*

He watched, as the island slowly came closer, the sounds of the ship filling his ears. The large sail strained against the mast, its fastenings creaking in protest as the wind sought to free it from its labours and send the ship, zigzag, across the sea. The steady thump of waves on the hull, shouts of command, the cursing of sailors – this salty commotion resonated around him.

His mind turned to the men he had brought with him; all excellent soldiers who had proved their worth many times over. The only one with a question mark over him was the friar. Would he be the weak link? The one who cracked under danger? Now that their mission was upon them, it was time to talk to him, to judge the measure of the man.

Suddenly, he heard shouts and cheers, for at last his destination was before him. Lindisfarne Priory filled his vision; the sailors had won their bounty. He saw the neat stone buildings, the small figures of the Benedictine Monks as they went about their tasks. Some stopped and pointed nervously towards *The Sparrow Hawk*.

There, finally, the Great Controller supposed, was the key that would unlock the gates of Bamburgh Castle. Excitement crept into him; energy that he had not felt in years flowed through his veins. Surprised by this sudden surge of life, he shouted for his small band of men to gather round.

'Presently, we will land on Holy Island,' he said. 'It would be wise to assume that the surrounding lands are still hostile with Lancastrian forces, so be vigilant. Eyes and ears open, weapons ready; you all know the drill.'

Heads nodded and the Great Controller paused, satisfied he had their attention. 'As you all know, our objective is to rescue Duke Richard and John Tunstall from Bamburgh Castle. When we arrive there, it will be the Hallet twins and Friar Drynk who will accompany me into the castle.' Looking at Duke Richard's retainers, he said, 'You three will keep watch outside the castle and assist us in our escape.'

'With all respect,' interrupted Thomas Parr, 'it should be us, Duke Richard's close retainers, who should enter the castle, for we are charged by the King with the duke's safety.'

'Aye, he is right,' urged John Milewater.

The Great Controller raised his hand. 'I realise your concerns, but Friar Drynk must go in because he can talk for us on religious matters.

108

The twins, because they are the finest fighting men I have ever known, and lastly, Lord Warwick had a greater responsibility to the King than you did. Do not forget: Duke Richard was under his protection, a ward within his household.'

Thomas Huddleston pushed forward. 'I would never argue with your authority, but I urge you to allow one of us to accompany you into the castle. Our honour dictates that.'

Thomas Parr stepped forward. 'If we wait outside the castle walls, our courage will be questioned, and we can fight as good as any man here!'

The Great Controller silently weighed up their request. Duke Richard's retainers watched him anxiously. To refuse their request would drive a wedge between them all. Finally, he spoke. 'Decide which one of you will enter the castle with us.'

Smiles broke out around him.

Friar Drynk spoke and all eyes turned towards him. 'The gates to Bamburgh Castle will be shut tighter than a duck's arse by the time we arrive. Are you sure we will gain entry?'

The Great Controller studied Friar Drynk. The man was losing weight. His robe hung loosely off his once corpulent frame; cheekbones, even a chin, were emerging from his fat, podgy face. Bloodshot eyes were now clear. He noted that the friar's gaze was steady, confident, and most significantly, there was no fear in them.

'Do not worry about entry into the castle,' the Great Controller replied, 'but remember, once inside we will have to think on our feet. Circumstances will dictate our strategy.' He looked at the circle of heads around him. Satisfied he had men of honour and courage around him, he said, 'We disembark shortly.'

The men gathered their equipment. The waiting was over, and this bold undertaking was at last under way.

The abbot of Lindisfarne Priory received them with good grace. He read the Letter of Authority handed to him by the Great Controller.

As the abbot scanned the letter, the Great Controller gauged his character: he was old and slim, his face lined but bright, and wispy, white hair crowned his head. He could see that he was a man who would do what was right – at least as far as the priory was concerned. He hoped the abbot would agree to assist them. He did not wish to use the Hallet twins to enforce his authority with blood, but if required, he would not hesitate.

The abbot looked up from the letter. 'How can we be of service?' he asked.

The Great Controller relaxed.

The abbot was shrewd and perceptive. He had known for a long time that the old order under King Henry was finished. Edward, the new king, was now the future, the protection and the well-being of the priory was his first responsibility. It had been destroyed, and the monks driven off many years ago, by Viking raiders. Since then, they had worked hard to re-establish it, so to help these men in their cause would mean security. There was no need to oppose them. Kings came and went, for they were mortal men, but God was eternal.

The abbot motioned the Great Controller to a chair. 'Shall we start?' he said, with a gentle smile.

Bamburgh Castle, Northumberland
30 April 1464

The whisper was earnest; it demanded an answer. The five men looked at each other, and two shifted uneasily in their seats.

The man who had whispered the unthinkable stared at them. 'Well,' he hissed, 'are you bastards with me, or not?'

A shocked silence filled the room. At last, one of them replied.

'It is a cowardly deed you are asking us to engage in, and I, for one, do not know if I have the stomach for it.'

Another voice spoke. 'To murder innocent boys in cold blood is villainous work.'

'You weak bastards,' mocked the whisperer. 'Warwick and his puppet – that whoring bastard, Edward – have killed and murdered our closest kin. All of us around this table have lost loved ones: brothers, sons, uncles, and fathers. This is our last chance to have revenge and to let them taste the salt of their tears, to let them mourn for a brother or cousin.'

'Aye, he is right,' spoke another. 'For even if they find the boys alive, Warwick will still show us no mercy.'

An older, deeper voice silenced them. 'My brother was killed, fleeing from the Battle of Towton, murdered by Warwick's barbarous army, so now is the time for cold retribution. I will swear on my mother's grave that my knife will draw me some royal Yorkist blood before I die.'

The whisperer, his face flushed with excitement, challenged the two with misgivings: 'Three of us are in,' he said. 'Are you two doubters with us, or against us?'

The two men nodded reluctantly. 'Aye, we are in,' spoke one. 'We agree revenge is called for but it just doesn't sit right that those two boys in the tower have to be the sacrifice.'

'To Hell with them,' said the whisperer. 'The twenty thousand who fell at Towton wouldn't agree with you.'

'Enough,' said the older voice. 'The deed is to be done and that's the end of it. We will kill the little bastards tonight, just before dawn; our action will be swift and silent. We will be like ghosts in the night.' His chilling words grew in the silence as the enormity of them filled the room. When the old voice spoke again, he murmured deep and low; the others leant forward to catch his words.

'We have been good and loyal archers to Sir Ralph Grey for many years now, and have fought bravely for him, but we will not stand quietly aside while he hands these boys back and then leads us to the executioner's block. For as the sun goes down on our brave Lancastrian resistance, we will strike a final blow, a blow for all the common soldiers who have fought and died for King Henry and our brave Queen Margaret. Warwick and Edward will remember the sting in our tail long after we are dead.'

Road to Bamburgh Castle, Northumberland 1 May 1464

The old cart rattled and bumped its way along the crumbling road towards Bamburgh Castle; the one occupant cursing and moaning at every jarring jolt. The riders around him smiled as they listened in amazement to his vast vocabulary of profanities.

Friar Drynk found that swearing took his mind away from the recurring image of wine bottles floating in front of him. The fantasising about food had slowly dimmed, but wine was still a problem, although he was pleasantly surprised at how good he felt. His thinner frame was filled with unexpected energy. His once slow and watery eyes were now clear, his vision sharp. He felt younger. The release from the boredom of castle life suited him. As they approached their final destination, he felt something strange stirring within him. *This is what they must call excitement*, he thought. He decided that he quite liked this feeling – this sense of purpose. Cracking the reins, he urged the horses on.

'George, Thomas, scout ahead,' ordered the Great Controller. 'When you see Bamburgh, alert us immediately.'

The twins spurred their horses and cantered off into the distance, whilst the cart and the other riders continued their slow progress.

'We must be nearly there,' said John Milewater.

'I pray we are,' replied Friar Drynk. 'My arse could not be more sore or bruised from this ponderous journey.'

When the twins reappeared, the Great Controller raised his hand and brought the party to a halt. They reported that Bamburgh was less than half a mile away.

Bamburgh Castle, Northumberland
1 May 1464

Sir Ralph Grey inspected the party in front of him. King Henry, wearing plain clothes, and a humble green cloak around his shoulders, was mounted on a nondescript horse. He sat smiling at everyone around him.

Sir Ralph addressed the captain of this escape party. 'Head west for Dumfries,' he instructed. 'It's nearly dusk; the darkness will be your friend. Remember to rest during the day. Travel only at night until you have reached friends and safety.' He stepped back and cried, 'God be with you!'

Other soldiers saluted Henry as he passed, and shouts of 'God save the King' rolled around the castle walls.

Sir Ralph watched as they made their way to the great gate; he was glad to see them go. Knowing that King Henry was leaving for safety took a burden off his shoulders, for his scouts had told him that Warwick's army would arrive outside the castle walls tomorrow.

His mind turned to the boys in the tower: they were a further problem he wished he did not have – a death warrant hanging over the castle. *Damn Somerset, and Billingham!* he thought. But what to do with the boys? The whole garrison knew they were in the tower and the groundswell of opinion was that they should be used in the defence of the castle. Some said, hung over the battlements by their wrists to stop any assault by cannon on the castle walls. He realised that he could not just set them free, which was what he would like to have done, for it would cause unrest, and sap moral. To let them go would not change anything; the mere fact that they were here meant the die was cast; Warwick would have his blood. Sir Ralph knew without doubt he was a dead man, but he hoped to barter the life of Duke Richard in exchange for the lives of the garrison. He prayed Warwick would grant them all a pardon.

The Great Controller, and his band of counterfeit monks, pulled up outside the castle gates. They were now all wearing the monks' habits supplied by the abbot of Lindisfarne Priory.

The guards on the ramparts relayed their presence to the master-at-arms, who was busy supervising the departure of King Henry. The great gates opened. Men-at-arms rushed out and formed two lines either side of the drawbridge. King Henry rode out; a knight on both his flanks. Behind him were assorted gentlemen and mounted men-at-arms. The party numbered fifteen in total.

The Great Controller whispered to his companions, 'If I'm not mistaken, here comes old King Henry.'

All eyes on the cart stared at the ordinary figure heading towards them. As Henry drew level with the monks, his eyes turned on them. He raised his hand and said with a smile, 'God be with you, my brothers.' His stare lingered on the Great Controller, his expression changing to that of a man trying to remember a distant memory.

The Great Controller shrunk within his habit, whipping his face away from Henry's stare. The realisation that he may have been recognised from their meeting many years ago when he had accompanied the Earl of Warwick to court, hit him like a thunderbolt. What a fool he was, for the possibility of it had never crossed his mind. The whole operation was in danger before it had started. He held his breath.

As Henry's party rode past, the Great Controller looked nervously after them. The distance between them lengthened and he breathed a sigh of relief. Then, faintly, the words, 'Nice to see you, Thomas,' floated musically over the evening twilight.

All eyes on the cart turned to the Great Controller, but the party kept on moving. Nobody had paid any heed, for Henry was always muttering to himself. The Great Controller shrugged his shoulders and smiled, a look of relief on his face.

Quietly, Friar Drynk said, 'Who else may know you, sir?'

The look of relief faded from the Great Controller's eyes. He pulled his hood up over his head, and slunk down in the back of the cart.

The master-at-arms approached the cart. 'What have we here?' he demanded, as his eyes investigated them. 'A gaggle of monks who are either lost or stupid, or both. Have you not heard that Warwick's army marches against us, and you pious idiots will be of no help to us when he arrives, so if you know what's good for you, then you best be on your way.'

'Do not mock us, my friend, for we are men of the Lord,' replied Friar Drynk, sternly. 'We have come to save your souls, not your lives. We journey from Lindisfarne to our mother priory at Durham, but our most holy abbot instructed us to break our journey to offer spiritual salvation to your men. I have a Letter of Authority confirming this.'

Friar Drynk produced the letter and handed it to the master-at-arms who read the contents then handed it back, embarrassment now silencing his tongue.

Seeing the man's discomfort, Friar Drynk seized the moment, and continued. 'We have brought with us the holy relics of St Cuthbert, our founding father, and with their holy powers your men may be blessed to save their souls. Do you wish us to take them away?'

The master-at-arms shook his head. 'No. No, Father,' he said, apologetically.

John Milewater passed a box to Friar Drynk.

The friar gasped. 'Ah, the holy relics,' and then theatrically rolled his eyes towards the heavens as though he was holding the bones of Christ himself. He reverently lifted up the casket for all to see. It was made from a rich, dark, mahogany wood, inlaid with fake precious jewels.

The master-at-arms and his men stepped closer. Whispers of awe left their lips.

Friar Drynk knew he had them in the palm of his hand. *Just the final thrust*, he thought, *and we will be welcomed into the castle like saints who have just descended from Heaven*. 'As you all know, the ceremony of Mass before a battle is crucial to all solders. For if sudden death befalls you, and you are not purged of all your sins, then only Purgatory or Hell awaits your souls, but these holy relics will guarantee you your place in Heaven.' He looked at the faces in front of him. All had a desire in their eyes, a need of reassurance for their souls. Triumphantly, he challenged, 'Do you grant us entry or not?'

The master-at-arms stood back and waved them towards the gate, bowing with holy reverence.

Friar Drynk smiled to himself and the twins just managed to contain their laughter.

'Well done,' said the Great Controller, allowing himself a smile. His decision to bring the friar had been right. *Shame*, he thought, *that the bones in that fake holy box had come from pigs*.

As the cart trundled through the great gates and into Bamburgh Castle, all smiles and subdued laughter were forgotten. The castle was bristling with weapons and men, all of them sworn enemies. If their disguise slipped, they would be dead within seconds. Their hearts beat faster, their minds concentrated, and the 'Old Owl' pulled his hood further over his face.

John Tunstall and Duke Richard watched the departure of old King Henry from their window high up in the tower.

Lindsay, who brought their meals, had told them that he was leaving for the 'safety of his person'. They had deduced from this information, and the fact that the castle was now prepared for siege, that a Yorkist army must be nearby.

Butterflies stirred within John's stomach, for once the Yorkist forces laid siege, their lives would become negotiable, and life or death would once again become their close companion.

Duke Richard turned away from the window. 'Well, Sir Ralph Grey has resolved the future of old King Henry,' he said. 'Let's just hope he now resolves ours.' Receiving no reply from John, he continued. 'His options will be very limited. I do not think he intends to kill us, but on the other hand, he will not just set us free. Therefore, the time has come for us to plan our own destiny, for if events go badly for the castle then the mob will come looking for us. They will desire our blood as desperately as a drowning man craves air.'

John was only half listening to Richard. He was watching a cart with a group of monks enter the castle. They all had their hoods up except for the one who held the reins. John's eyes were drawn to his face. *My God,* he thought, *he looks like Friar Drynk, but at least ten years younger.* He narrowed his eyes to take in more detail, but they disappeared from his view as the cart rounded the tower. This image of a younger Friar Drynk reminded him of home. He felt anger rise within him. He realised that Richard was right; they had to take charge of their own destinies. It would be better to die fighting than timidly going to their deaths like sheep. He walked over to the small table and sat down opposite Richard, noting the dark shadows under the young duke's eyes. The paleness of his skin and the strain of the last few days were etched on his face. *I must look the same to him,* John mused. It was time for action.

'We will make our escape at dawn,' whispered Richard.

'But how?' asked John.

'When Lindsay comes at first light with our breakfast, you will feign sickness,' replied Richard. 'This will draw the guard into the room. I will then strike him down, and then we will lock them both in this room while we make our escape.'

'But we have no weapons, and if we manage to escape, how do we reach safety?' asked John.

'We will strip the heavy support poles from those,' he said, pointing to three tapestries hanging on the walls. 'We will make two short stabbing spears and one club to strike down the guard. I have kept a knife from our last meal; we have all night to fashion these weapons.'

John looked at the tapestries and the blunt eating knife that Richard now held in his hand; it was not a lot, but as he had said, they had all night. 'Do you think we will fight our way out of the main gate with these sticks?' laughed John.

'No, no,' said Richard, his face deadly serious. 'I have noticed that just after dawn, a patrol of scourers leaves the castle through the main gate. I imagine they are scouting for my brother's army or Warwick's.'

'And you think,' said John, excitement in his voice, 'that we could escape at the same time?'

'Yes,' replied Richard, his voice rising. 'If we can find a couple of horses – which I don't think will be too difficult – we could ride out right behind the scourers.'

'And if we trust in God,' said John, quietly, 'then we may make it out alive.'

'Exactly,' said Richard triumphantly. 'And if we don't make it, then at least we will have died bravely, in action…' His voice trailed off. They looked at each other, both suddenly realising the enormity of what they were planning. The cost of failure would be their lives.

Richard slid to his knees. 'Come, we must pray for our deliverance,' he said trying to disguise the fear in his voice.

John joined him and although he did not believe as strongly as Richard did, he would pray just as hard.

While they were praying, John studied Richard's back through half-closed eyes. He had heard what Sir Henry Billingham had said, and had seen Richard's angry reaction. There was a very slight curving of his spine, from the bottom of his neck and down over his shoulder, but it was hardly noticeable.

'Richard,' John said, softly.

Richard stopped praying, and opening his eyes looked enquiringly at John.

'Your…your back looks fine to me.'

Richard's eyes flashed like diamonds, and then softened. 'I have a slight curvature of the spine,' he said, matter-of-factly. 'It will apparently become worse, the older and taller I become, but at the moment, with careful tailoring, I can disguise it.'

'Does it hurt you?' asked John.

'Sometimes, at the end of a day's training in the tilt-yard or in cold or damp weather, it aches, but it is a curse I have to bear. My brother, George, tormented me daily about it; called me the runt of the litter…I am glad to be free of him.'

'I will never mention it again,' said John, solemnly.

'And I will always be your trusted friend,' replied Richard, 'even if I turn into an evil, hunchbacked warlock,' he added, with a hollow laugh.

The soft leather-clad foot silently mounted the first step. Dawn was a thin strip of light on the horizon – a rich azure blue. A birdcall broke the night's silence. The five assassins moved smoothly up the steps of the tower, each silent footstep taking them closer to their target.

The guard outside of the boys' room was woken from his light slumber by the points of two daggers pricking his throat. With sleep and panic muddled within him, he jumped up from his chair. It crashed to the stone floor and he froze in fear.

'Hell's fires!' whispered a hoarse voice. 'Let's wake the whole damn castle!'

Within the locked room, Richard and John were instantly awoken from their light sleep. They could hear whispered voices outside, then the jangle of keys. They knew this was not Lindsay with their breakfast; whoever was outside of their room meant them harm.

They heard the key enter the lock, and rushed to the corner at the far end of the room. They stood with their backs to it, the short wooden stabbing spears they had fashioned late into the night, at the ready.

As the key slowly turned in the lock, the boys' eyes stared at the handle. Their mouths were dry, their hands clammy, their hearts drummed in their ears. Slowly, the door swung open, and four men entered without a sound. Their eyes fastened on to the boys. Unspoken, the men moved swiftly towards them; this deed was to be done quick and fast.

Richard and John saw that the men wore the leather jerkins of archers, and the colours of Sir Ralph Grey. John was stunned to think that he would have ordered their deaths. As the men raised their double-edged daggers, the boys stepped forward, and thrust out their short spears.

The men advanced. 'Those sticks won't save you,' sneered one.

The boys stepped back, assuming their defensive positions, when a low moan cut through the room.

The fifth archer, who had been guarding the door, staggered towards them, holding his neck, blood spurting out from between his fingers. A high-pitched gargle rumbled up from his throat and he fell to his knees in the doorway. A short stabbing sword was thrust into his back. His eyes bulged from his head as he wriggled in pain, like a speared fish.

120

The four archers whipped round towards their comrade, just as a foot came through the door and smashed into the kneeling archer's head, sending him to the floor and ripping the sword from his stomach. Blood sprayed from the gaping wound, and he lay quivering on the floor in his dying agony.

Two monks entered the room; each had a twelve-inch dagger in one hand, and a short stabbing sword in the other.

The archers stared at them with uncomprehending eyes, but there were only two of them and they were four. They looked at each other with smug smiles. The odds were in their favour, but as the archers moved towards them, the two monks pulled their hoods back.

Richard and John stared in quiet disbelief, for before them stood the Hallet twins: Thomas and George. Momentarily stunned, the boys stood watching as the twins moved in on the archers.

The twins were quick and ruthless. They fought as one, each knowing exactly the movements of the other, possessing some inbred intuition that only twins have. As one thrust, the other would parry; if one feinted, the other would attack. The four archers were cut to pieces in seconds; two lay dead, two badly wounded.

George knelt beside one of the wounded perpetrators, feeling for the gap between his ribs. He placed his dagger over the man's heart and pushed slowly downwards.

The archer raised his head, and watched as the blade slowly entered his chest. Tears filled his eyes. 'Please no,' he moaned. 'Oh God, please, no, no...'

George slapped his hand tight over the man's mouth before ramming the dagger home. The man's scream froze in his throat; his arms and legs trembled and were then still.

Thomas Hallet moved to the other wounded man, whose eyes widened in terror. He expertly found the gap between his ribs and positioned his dagger.

Richard moved across, staying Thomas' hand. He gripped the dying man's hair, and pulling his head up to within inches of his own, he demanded, 'Who sent you? Was it Sir Ralph Grey? Tell me the truth, for you cannot enter Heaven with a lie on your lips.'

The man shook his head. 'No one sent us,' he whispered.

Richard stood up and nodded at Thomas who slowly slid his dagger into the man's chest. He wriggled frantically on his back and died silently.

John stood rooted to the spot, dumbfounded at the events unfolding before him. Watching Richard's icy ruthlessness with the last man had stuck in his mind. It confirmed that Richard was merciless against his enemies, something John had to learn for himself, for these assassins deserved their deaths. If the twins had not arrived just in time, it would have been him and Richard lying dead on the cold, stone floor. Just when John thought there could be no more shocks, the Great Controller strode into the room, whispering orders.

'Thomas; George; bring the guard into the room; make sure he is gagged.' He walked over to Richard and John, his face smiling. 'Come, we must go with all haste. Dawn is breaking, and we must leave before the castle awakes.' He put his arms around the boys and ushered them from the blood-soaked room. Locking the door behind them, they swiftly made their way down from the tower.

Waiting at the bottom was the cart that John had seen entering the castle the previous evening, and sitting at the front holding the reins was the monk he had seen. 'Is that you, Friar Drynk?' John asked, with a quizzical look on his face.

Friar Drynk laughed. 'Well, I'm definitely not a ghost!' Then ruffling John's hair, he whispered, 'Thank God and all the saints in Christendom that we found you safe and well.'

The Great Controller's eyes flashed at the friar to silence him, and then motioning to the two boys, he murmured urgently, 'Quick, hide under these blankets.'

Richard and John slipped under them in the back of the cart, their tension and fear of the last days vanished. They were amongst friends, surrounded, at last, by capable hands.

Friar Drynk cracked the reins, and swung the cart towards the great gate. As they approached it, ten scourers cantered past them.

The master-at-arms came out from the guardhouse. 'Leaving so early?' he asked.

Friar Drynk kept the cart moving. 'God's work never stops,' he said, raising his eyes to the heavens.

'Well, thank you for your blessings,' cried the master-at-arms, as they trundled passed him.

From the back of the cart, the Great Controller made the sign of the cross, and then they were through the gate and away.

Lindsay climbed the steps to the tower, carrying a tray of breakfast for the two boys. Dawn had broken and it was going to be a fine day. As she placed her small feminine foot on to the last step, she stopped – her gentle face frowned. The guard was absent and his chair was lying on its side. *If he's been drinking again, I'm going to have to report him*, she thought, annoyance hardening her girlish features. She approached the door and noticed that it was splattered with red-brown marks. Something was wrong. An ill omen shivered down her spine. Her heart beat faster. She placed the tray on the floor and knocking on the door, heard a muffled cry in response. Taking the key from her pocket, she unlocked the door. It swung slowly on its hinges.

In front of her, was the guard, tied to a chair and gagged; his eyes red and wild as though he had been locked in this room all night with the devil. Lindsay stepped towards him and then froze: the blood-splattered walls and the butchered corpses rushed into her eyes. She tried to close them, but they would not respond. Against her will, her head moved from side to side taking in the horror of it all. Her head swam, and she gripped the door frame to keep her balance, feeling wetness on her hands. 'Oh God, please no,' she murmured, realising what it was. With revulsion, she slowly looked down, and saw with horror, her red, bloodied hands. Her scream split the silence of the dawn.

Men stopped in their tracks. The second scream galvanised them into an automatic primeval response as they all rushed for the tower.

Bamburgh Castle, Northumberland
3 May 1464

The Earl of Warwick arrayed his army outside Bamburgh Castle. It was mid-morning and he watched the swallows dipping and diving around the castle walls, searching for nest sites amongst the nooks and crevices. The sun was shining, it was a fine spring day, and he was in good spirits. Everything had dovetailed together nicely: he had just received news that the Great Controller had bravely rescued Duke Richard and John Tunstall. The garrisons of Alnwick and Dunstanburgh had accepted his offer of a pardon and had surrendered peaceably, their forces now disbursed. His brother, John – Lord Montagu – had captured the Duke of Somerset and his close lieutenants at Hexham and shortly he would have Sir Ralph Grey's, and his cronies', heads on spikes around Bamburgh Castle.

He had a list as long as his arm of Lancastrian sympathisers who would not live the week out. He rubbed his hands together with satisfaction. 'Where are the guns?' he bellowed.

'Being positioned now,' replied the quartermaster.' Would you like to inspect them, my Lord?'

Warwick ignored the question. 'And the gunpowder?' he asked.

'Half a mile away,' came the reply.

Warwick knew that gunpowder became very unstable over prolonged periods of travel. The ingredients saltpetre, sulphur, and carbon, had to be mixed evenly to manufacture a stable powder, but in transit, the heaviest of the three would sink to the bottom of the barrel and if not remixed carefully, this volatile powder could cause the guns to explode prematurely. He remembered how King James II of Scotland had been killed in this way while besieging Roxburgh Castle in 1460.

'I will inspect them now,' he barked, and then said quietly to himself, 'before that dammed powder arrives.'

Warwick grunted with pleasure as he watched the great guns, *London,*

Newcastle, and *Dijon*, being levelled and ranged. They could fire a ball weighing forty-two pounds over several hundred yards with great accuracy; no wall could withstand their power. His inspection was cut short by the news that the Great Controller had arrived with the boys and was receiving hospitality within his tent.

'Excellent news,' he beamed, and strode past him, smiling, towards the tent.

The messenger was taken aback by Warwick's rare good cheer.

Sir Ralph Grey looked out from the battlements at the powerful army drawn up outside his walls. He watched with morbid fascination at the three great siege guns being deployed. He knew their power, and realised that this would be no long siege – Warwick wanted blood. There had been no offer of surrender or pardon, and after the escape of the boys earlier that morning, he knew none would be forthcoming.

The news and the manner of their escape had gone around the castle like wildfire and the bloody deaths of five of his archers had shocked everyone. What had they been thinking of, to attempt such a vile deed?

The guard who survived had told of the events: the archers, the monks escape, and all within the heart of his castle. It was said that the guard should have been punished, along with the master-at-arms, for letting the monks enter and leave, but Sir Ralph Grey knew there was no need, for as he watched Warwick's guns being prepared, he knew their punishment would be swift enough. He turned and left the battlements. It was time to write a farewell letter to his dear wife, and with it, his last will and testament, for he knew his fate: he would not out live the day.

The Earl of Warwick strode into his tent, bristling with energy. 'Well done, Thomas!' he cried, to the Great Controller. 'Well done. Your plan worked. Are the boys in good health?'

'Aye, they are, my Lord, but only by God's grace.'

Warwick raised an eyebrow. 'Explain,' he barked.

The Great Controller quickly told him of the subterfuge they had used to gain entry to the castle; how they had located the boys, and their surprise at finding Sir Ralph Grey's archers in the boys' quarters with the evil intent to murder them; how the Hallet twins had cut them to pieces and finally, their escape.

Warwick listened intently to the Great Controller's report. 'Well,' he said, looking at the boys, 'it was a damn close thing for you two. Thank God the twins are a formidable pair of swordsmen.' He sat down in a large padded chair and made himself comfortable. He then motioned for the boys to approach closer.

Leaning forward, he said quietly, 'You have now seen the evil of men at first hand, and I know you have both stared death in the eye and have acted with courage. We are all proud of you. This experience has made you men, but you must also realise that you are both still young and have much to learn so I will look to your futures once we have taken care of the evil bastards who did this to you.'

He rose from his chair and put a hand on each of the boys' shoulders, his voice rising as he gave his command. 'Richard, you will ride south, shortly, to meet your brother, the King. John, you will ride for Middleham, but first you both go to the City of York to witness the executions of the men who ordered your kidnapping. I have ordered that they be treated as common criminals, and kept in chains, with no high privileges.'

'The twins should be rewarded for saving our lives,' said Richard.

Warwick turned his head towards Richard, with a look of surprise at this sudden request. 'Aye, they will be,' he said, thoughtfully. 'Shortly, I sail for France. I have business to attend to with King Louis. I shall take them with me. I'm sure a few days in a French whore house will be a novel reward for them.'

Warwick's gaze stayed on the two boys. 'I will take you two as well. It will do you good to see France and its great royal court. It would broaden your horizons, and be part of your education.' Then with a playful laugh, he said, 'Maybe we will find a couple of pretty French maids to entertain you both.'

The Great Controller looked at Warwick. He did not need to speak; his yellow half-hooded eyes said it all as they flashed with an unspoken question.

Warwick recognised the look. 'Thomas!' he cried, with a mischievous glint in his eye, 'I'll tell you my plans later.'

Richard and John, full of excitement, accompanied Warwick to watch the firing of the great guns. They stuffed their ears with wool, and stood well back. Once they had witnessed the power of the cannons, they were to ride with the Great Controller, as ordered, to the City of York, to witness the executions.

Chapter 6

The King's Great Secret

Parish Church, Grafton Regis, Northamptonshire 3 May 1464

The priest, whose threadbare and crumpled black gown matched his advancing years, looked up from under his large bushy eyebrows at the young couple standing before him.

The man was well dressed in rich hunting clothes, but none the less, only hunting clothes. The woman stood in a plain green dress; she wore no jewellery, or elaborate headwear.

He felt nervous; there was sweat on his top lip, which he could feel cooling under his nose. He had been the priest in this parish for over thirty years, and never in all that time had he been asked to perform such a ceremony. They had warned him that if word of this marriage became public, his fortunes would take a turn for the worse, but he still could not believe that the man standing in front of him was who they said he was, and for him to be married in this small village church with only a few witnesses present was unthinkable.

The priest shook his head to confirm he was not dreaming; his tired red eyes with their failing sight peered nervously at the couple and he took a deep breath.

'I declare, by our Lord God, and in the eyes of all men, that you are now man and wife.'

Lord Hastings looked around at the small congregation as the priest and his young assistant launched themselves into a final wedding hymn. Gathered around the young couple were the bride's mother – Jacquetta, the Duchess of Bedford – two gentlewomen, and himself. The rest of the church was empty. All were smiling broadly at the newly married couple, but their eyes, including his own, held a look of disbelief as the ceremony reached its conclusion.

He watched his friend, Edward, King of England, look at his new royal wife with eyes full of lust. She, the widowed Lady Elizabeth Grey, returned Edward's look, her eyes reflecting her triumph.

She will be no King's whore, Lord Hastings thought. *Her cool resistance has finally been rewarded with a Queen's crown.*

He could see why Edward had desired her virtue. She was truly a beauty, and would even have put a bulge in the Pope's cassock if he had laid his eyes upon her; but for Edward to marry the widow of a Lancastrian knight was wanton madness.

They had met while Edward was hunting in Whittlebury Forest, near to her family home. She had appeared, standing under a large oak tree when Edward had first seen her. Dismounting, he had stared at her for several minutes before asking her name. Lord Hastings knew that within those few minutes, Elizabeth had bewitched him with sorcery, for Edward fell hopelessly in love with her. In his many subsequent secret visits to her family home, the spell had grown stronger until he had finally agreed to marry her.

It was after the Garter Service on 23 April, Saint George's Day, they had journeyed leisurely northwards using the excuse of a hunting trip, from Windsor up through Leicestershire to Grafton Regis, and finally arriving at this small parish church.

On their journey, Lord Hastings had tried hard to dissuade Edward of the unsuitability of the match, but arguing was hopeless, for Edward was intoxicated by her – smitten. Lady Grey had befuddled his brain with some secret love potion. To break this bewitching spell – to rid himself of this all-consuming desire – Edward would, he had cried, 'Have to bed her!', but such was the stubbornness of the woman towards his advances, the only way was to either rape her, or marry her, and even kings had to obey God's laws – so marriage it was. Edward had then added, as an afterthought, 'but I am the King, so can always undo what is done'; then with a sly smile, 'I will rearrange matters at a future date'.

The priest motioned for the Duchess of Bedford, and Lord Hastings, to step forward and sign the marriage certificate. Lord Hastings realised that once it had been witnessed there would be no undoing of this madness, no rearranging at a future date. He looked at Edward, who waved him urgently towards the priest, and that fatal pen, knowing that Warwick and most of the nobles would be stunned and shocked by these events. Stepping forward with a heavy heart, Lord Hastings signed the document. He knew that trouble lay ahead.

Once the formalities had been completed, Edward, with indecent haste, rushed with his new wife, towards the royal hunting lodge to consummate the marriage.

That's Edward, thought Lord Hastings. At twenty-two, he was young, impetuous, and reckless with women. Elizabeth was four years older and far more experienced, having already been married, and the mother of two young children. *Maybe she will tame him*, Lord Hastings thought, and then shook his head, quickly dismissing the thought. *Pigs might fly!*

The Duchess of Bedford clutched the marriage certificate; the evidence tightly held to her chest; her eyes shining with triumph. Her sorcery had worked. She hurriedly departed the church for Grafton Manor. Her husband, Richard Woodville, with the help of her magic potions, had done well under old King Henry, and her close friendship with his Queen, Margaret of Anjou, had advanced him from being a lowly knight to become the first Earl Rivers, a privy counsellor, and a Knight of the Garter. Now that Henry and his Queen were exiled to the barren lands of the north, they had decided to jump ship and nail their colours to King Edward's mast. They could not have done it any better. It was a triumph for Jacquetta's black art, to have her eldest daughter marry the Yorkist King. Now, lands and titles would be harvested for their family. As long as Elizabeth kept King Edward satisfied in bed – for all knew his brains hung between his legs – all would be well. Warwick and the others could whine and shout, but the deed was done and she had the marriage certificate to prove it.

Behind the doors of the royal hunting lodge, Edward and Elizabeth tarried in their wedding bed.

Elizabeth found Edward tall and handsome, so it was no chore for a royal bride. In fact, it was a joy. Many times, she had nearly weakened under his advances, but the thought of her mother's anger, if her plans were destroyed, had kept Elizabeth chaste. Now, she could love with abandon. Since her first husband had died, she had endured over three years of chastity. With womanly needs, her empty bed had made those years hard to bear, but now, at last, she held a man whom she had grown to love, finally feeling his touch, his lips, his desire. She was naked, longing in her passion for him, but still the silent image of her mother floated around the bed reminding her of the power they now held over him. She quickly pushed it from her thoughts; there would be time enough later for artful scheming – the advancement of her family could wait – this moment was hers, and hers alone; she was going to enjoy every caress and kiss.

Edward, for his part was overjoyed with his new bride. How elated he felt, for in bed she was like a harlot, kissing and holding him in ways he had never experienced before. Finally, he lay spent until she again slowly rekindled his desire. As he slipped once again, helpless under her seductive spell, he thanked God that he had found such a wanton bride – he was in love.

Lord Hastings took the letter bearing Warwick's great seal from the messenger.

'To be opened by the King,' said the man. 'My Lord Warwick instructs it be read immediately – I am to wait and return forthwith with our Sovereign Lord's reply.'

Lord Hastings studied the messenger; there was no point in asking about the contents – even if the man knew, it was his duty to remain silent. He could not open it, for 'the King's eyes only' was the instruction. He turned the letter over in his hand, studying it for some invisible clue as to its contents. *What to do?* he thought. Should he disturb Edward at this moment, of all moments, or wait until his passion had cooled? Lord

Hastings hesitated, unsure, and then he remembered what his father had said to him years ago. 'Only fools dither', he had boomed. 'Men act'. Stung by the memory, he strode into the royal hunting lodge and knocked on the door.

'Who disturbs the King?' shouted Edward.

'Hastings, my Lord,' came the reply.

Edward held the letter, his hands shaking, his eyes reading in disbelief. Elizabeth and Lord Hastings stared at him, concern already in their eyes.

'Ye Gods,' whispered Edward. 'Warwick sends me news of the destruction of the Lancastrian army at Hedgeley Moor and then dashes all celebration...' He stopped and looked at Lord Hastings, and Elizabeth, tears of anger forming in his eyes. 'Richard, my brother, has been taken. Those Lancastrian bastards have given me an evil present, on this my blessed wedding day.'

Elizabeth sat in bed, a fur overlay wrapped around her shoulders to protect her modesty. Lord Hastings stood in the doorway. Neither went to aid Edward, because of the presence of the other. Both were silent, not certain who should speak first – new wife or old friend.

'We must ride north with all speed,' said Lord Hastings, decisively. 'Where are they holding him?'

Edward passed the letter to Lord Hastings who read it hungrily. 'Bamburgh...Warwick should be there now. Richard may even be free, as we speak.'

'Or dead,' replied Edward, with anger. 'Send the messenger back to Warwick. Tell him we ride for York tonight, and will meet him there in two days. You will ride to Stony Stratford and return with our hunting party, but no word of what happened here today. I will take Elizabeth to her mother's. In three hours' time, we ride north.'

Lord Hastings turned to go, but Edward called him back. 'William, when you arrive at Stony Stratford, send messengers to my nearest and most loyal retainers, to meet us on the road to York tonight with their knights. I require three hundred to enforce my authority when we arrive in the north.'

Lord Hastings strode purposely from the room

Elizabeth knelt on the bed, the fur overlay slipped from her shoulders. She knelt there naked.

Edward took in her well-rounded bosom, slim waist, and gentle curving hips, and gasped at her beauty.

Elizabeth leant forward, allowing her breasts to swing tantalisingly before Edward's eyes. Her hand slipped behind his neck, and she pulled him down towards her, gently brushing her lips against his – she wanted him to carry this image, to remember her softness and beauty. When Edward returned, it would be to her arms, to her bed.

Lord Hastings galloped along the dusty roads towards Stony Stratford, his face grim with worry. The look of triumph he had seen on Jacquetta and Elizabeth's faces proved that sorcery was behind this marriage. Something dark and powerful had been used to snare the King. He knew Edward would never have married of his own free will; he had dozens of beautiful women at court who were honoured to share his bed, so why wed this one? It did not make any sense. He vowed that he would not rest until he had the evidence to charge the Duchess of Bedford, and her daughter, with witchcraft, and to have this dangerous marriage annulled.

Bamburgh Castle, Northumberland
4 May 1464

Bamburgh Castle stood mortally wounded; her great walls breached by Warwick's powerful artillery. His first wave of shock troops had entered with little resistance. Small fires flickered from the battlements; flames licked up from turret windows; smoke drifted lazily inland, like a charcoal wave slipping in off the ocean.

Warwick looked on with satisfaction. *No more swallows dipping and diving around the castle walls*, he thought. *I've ruined their summer, and the same applies to those Lancastrian rebels, but their cause is ruined for good.* He watched the second wave of troops charge through the breached walls, their bloodcurdling shrieks splitting the air. Sunlight glinted on their blades. Hooks and ferocious spikes protruded from their ten-foot bills. The troops behind them carried swords, daggers, or short axes – more deadly in the crush of close-quarter combat.

Warwick had ordered that no quarter be given; only senior officers were to be taken alive. He was relieved that King Edward was not with him, for he would grant pardons to all and sundry, and what was required now was a steel fist to smash these Lancastrian bastards into submission, once and for all.

Hopefully, Warwick mused, *the kidnapping of his younger brother will toughen him up; put some vengeance into his heart.* Duke Richard had asked that all the women within the castle be spared. What was it he had said? Something about a serving girl – Lindsay. She was to be treated well, for she had been kind to him during his captivity. *He's as soft as his brother is*, Warwick thought, but he had issued the order anyway, in the vain hope that his men obeyed it.

The screams of Lancastrian defenders being thrown from the battlements interrupted his thoughts – he decided it was time to dispense his justice!

From his mount, Warwick surveyed the scene within the castle: smashed rocks littered the interior, bodies lay cut to pieces by shards of granite, or the steel of his troops; smoke wafted and spiralled skywards. The sickly stench of burnt human flesh filled his nostrils. He raised his hand and bellowed, 'Cease fighting!'

The frantic movements within the castle froze instantly as though an ice maiden had blown her frosty breath over them.

Warwick pushed himself up in his stirrups. 'All surviving defenders are to be spared,' he shouted. He wanted a few defeated men left to tell the tale, to bear witness to the end of the Lancastrian cause. Turning to his close retainers, he growled, 'Bring me all surviving officers, and that bastard, Grey, if he still lives.'

They found Sir Ralph Grey amongst the rubble of his office. A cannon ball had gone through its wall bringing down part of the roof. He laid badly injured, legs broken, head smashed. They dragged him out and laid him down in front of Warwick, who dismounted. Drawing his sword, he rammed the tip in under Sir Ralph's chin and forced his head up.

Sir Ralph howled in pain; blood oozing through his clenched teeth.

Warwick twisted his sword, his malicious eyes examining his victim.

Sir Ralph screeched in agony.

'You held the King's brother, you snake of the Devil!' Warwick shouted. 'You dared to threaten royal blood.'

Sir Ralph stared back with his one good eye, showing no fear.

Warwick saw the life fading from it; in his heart, he knew Sir Ralph was a brave soldier, one he would have been proud of if he had served him, but he was Lancastrian through and through, and would now pay the price. He wanted Sir Ralph to feel the steel he held in his hand, and quickly, before his spirit slipped away.

Warwick raised his sword high above his head.

Sir Ralph Grey looked up and seeing the sword flash in the early May sunshine, he calmly closed his eye as the sword descended, and prayed his old friend, Sir Ralph Percy, would be waiting to greet him.

City of York
5 May 1464

John Tunstall entered the great walled City of York as the mid-morning sun warmed his back. He had smelled the city a few miles away, and now the overwhelming stench gagged his breath. His companions, Duke Richard, the Great Controller, the Hallet twins, and Friar Drynk, also reeled from the foul smell.

The sweet air of the countryside was now a memory as they rode towards the Great Minster. John watched the hustle and bustle of this influential city. It was rich from the vast wool trade it controlled; wealthy merchants, traders, landowners, and farmers, rushed with busy intent. Drinking houses and bordellos overflowed with drunken patrons; harlots patrolled their territory; street hawkers shouted their trade. As they neared the Great Minster, the city changed its rich vibrant colours to a more sombre shade. York was the religious centre of the north; the great cathedral and numerous churches dominated the city. The immensely rich archbishop owned half of it; King Edward owned the rest.

Around the Minster, were gathered troops wearing the colours of John Neville – Warwick's brother, Lord Montagu. From their midst, strode a well built man with fair hair and blue eyes; a smile stretched his features. They halted their horses and the Great Controller dismounted as the man reached him.

'Thomas, you old fox!' cried Lord Montagu. 'You did it; you have the boys with you?'

The Great Controller smiled back. 'Aye, John, by God's grace we do.'

The two men embraced.

John and Richard dismounted and Lord Montagu turned his beaming face towards them, a look of genuine relief settling on his rugged features.

'Cousin Richard; young John; you've had some adventures I'm told, and some scares, no doubt.' Then placing a hand on their shoulders, he said, 'But, by our Lord, you are safe enough now. Tonight, we will celebrate your freedom, and tomorrow…' he continued with a sudden harshness, 'we will execute the men who committed these crimes against you. But come, you must be tired and in need of refreshment. I will tell you the order of things once you have rested.'

King Edward approached the city as the midday cannon was fired. Around him were his close retainers, and their indentured knights followed close behind. Three hundred in all, rode with the king, their brilliant colours glorious in the May sun. Trumpets sounded a royal welcome as they entered the city.

Its citizens bowed in deference as they passed, many wondering how this Yorkist King would treat their Lancastrian city.

Rich merchants were preparing their eloquent speeches of excuses, and counting gold coin to grease the palms for royal pardons, but Edward had only one thought: news of Duke Richard.

As he approached the Great Minster, he saw Lord Montagu standing on its steps, waiting to greet him. Dismounting, before his horse had even stopped, he rushed urgently up the steps.

Lord Montagu stepped back, but before he could bow, Edward clasped his arms.

'Cousin John!' Edward cried. ''Tis good to see you. I hear excellent news that you have cracked the nut of the Lancastrian resistance for me.'

Lord Montagu grinned. 'Aye, your Majesty, you are well informed.'

Edward's smile faded, his expression clouding over. Putting his arm around Lord Montagu's shoulder, he guided him into the privacy of the entrance.

'Good cousin, John, I have a chest full of honours to bestow on you for your brave victories, but before any celebration is allowed I must have news of Richard; his fate will decide if there is to be gaiety or sadness.' His shoulders slumped at the thought of his young brother; it was easy to say those two words, but if sadness it was then he knew his heart would break. He spoke with forced hope. 'Have you heard from Warwick? Is Bamburgh taken? Has Richard…?' Edward's voice trailed off, but Lord Montagu's eyes were smiling, and a grin hovered over his face.

Edward's eyes hardened. 'This is no laughing matter,' he hissed.

Lord Montagu threw his head back and laughed. 'Oh, I believe it is, dear cousin,' he chortled, as his eyes looked over Edward's shoulder.

Edward looked around. There, standing on the steps of the Great Minster, was Richard. Edward froze; he thought his heart had stopped.

Richard ran towards Edward, shouting his name with delight.

Edward scooped him up and held him tightly, tears in his eyes.

Warwick arrived that evening as the long shadows of the northern night crept in over the day. The town's people hid from his hard stare as he made his way through the narrow streets with a detachment of his close retainers. They knew he was seeking retribution against Lancastrian supporters, and none wished to catch his attention or displeasure.

As he passed, they noted the bloody sacks slung over the horses that were bringing up the rear; the severed heads of Warwick's enemies dripping blood over the cobbled streets.

Warwick entered the Great Hall. The loud babble of voices dropped to a whisper as his presence was detected. The throng moved quickly out of his way as he strode towards the king.

Edward, standing on the dais, watched him approach. *As if Moses is parting the Red Sea*, he thought.

Warwick bowed at the foot of the dais as etiquette demanded.

Edward stepped down and embraced him warmly. 'Cousin Warwick,' he cried, 'there is no need for ceremony. You and Montagu have exceeded your duty. No sovereign could wish for finer commanders. It is I who should be bowing to you.'

Warwick smiled, his eyes full of guile. 'It was Thomas, my Great Controller, who planned and executed the daring rescue of Richard and young Tunstall. My brother, John, defeated the Lancastrians at Hedgeley Moor and Hexham. I have been but a poor player in these matters, sadly only arranging affairs from afar.'

Edward smiled, noticing that Warwick was being unusually chivalrous with his portrayal of events. *What is he scheming for, now?* he thought.

'You are too gracious,' replied Edward. 'I have arranged that we dine in private tonight with Montagu, Thomas, brother Richard, young Tunstall and Lord Hastings. I wish to hear all the brave accounts of battles and rescues from the horses' mouths!'

John sat at the king's table with Warwick, Montagu, and the others, listening as Richard told them how courageous John had been during their ordeal: how they had stood back-to-back, swords drawn for Francis, committed together to fight to the death, standing side by side in Bamburgh Castle with their wooden spears against their would-be murderers. John could feel his face redden.

Edward leant over and ruffled his hair. 'You are too young for me to make you an earl,' he laughed, 'but your courage will not be forgotten. I'm sure cousin Warwick will enlarge the Tunstall estates in our gratitude.'

'Aye, gladly,' replied Warwick. 'Thomas will arrange it with Lady Tunstall when he returns.'

John glowed with pride.

The conversation turned to Lord Montagu, who told them the details of Hedgeley Moor, and how the Duke of Somerset had turned and run, and then his capture at the battle of Hexham.

John listened to it all, hardly daring to breathe in case he missed some detail. He heard Lord Montagu explain his tactics, the brave and daring acts of his men. John looked at him with awe – Lord Montagu was a hero.

Richard asked, 'Why do the nobility fight each other? Can they not live in peace?'

Warwick cast his knowing eye at him. 'Richard,' he said, 'there is one thing that you must learn: the strong always fight the strong, and the victor always takes from the meek. That we live in splendour is because they toil in our fields from dawn to dusk, obey our laws, pay us taxes, and then quietly die, and when they are gone, their sons and daughters take their place. It is the way of nature: the strong rule; the weak obey.'

'But, in the Bible, it says the meek will inherit the earth,' ventured John.

Warwick threw his head back and laughed. 'All they inherit is a plot of land four feet by six feet in their local graveyard!'

Edward and Lord Montagu joined in the laughter.

Richard's face remained serious. 'So, if we must fight each other, then he who strikes first wins the day.'

'Aye, that is so', said Edward, joining in the conversation, 'but not only who strikes first – courage, planning and momentum are also required and Lord Montagu has just proved it.' Then, looking across at Lord Montagu, Edward grinned slyly. 'Or should I say, the Earl of Northumberland has just proved it!'

Lord Montagu rose slowly from the table, disbelief on his face. 'My Lord cousin,' he spluttered, 'I am honoured, I did not expect…'

Edward rose and waved him to his seat. 'It is well deserved,' he said. 'I now have two earls who are brothers to rule the north for me, to end hostilities and bring prosperity to the region. I, at last, can rule in peace; we will formalise matters tomorrow.'

Warwick sat back in his chair, a satisfied look in his eyes.

Edward turned to the Great Controller. 'And what for you, Thomas? For rescuing a royal prince, you must be rewarded.'

'Your Majesty, I have all I require. My gracious Lord Warwick provides for all my simple needs.'

'But there must be some dream you desire,' demanded King Edward. 'A knighthood? An estate? A beautiful woman? What do you wish for? Come, man, I require an answer.'

The Great Controller looked into his cup of wine. 'Well…there is one dream I have, and that is to travel to a foreign land.'

The table was silent as they listened to the rich voice of the Great Controller.

The great log fire had burnt low, candles were slowly dying, and warmth and shadows filled the room.

John and Richard were straining to keep their eyes open; wine, food and heat, had dulled their brains.

'And what foreign land would that be?' asked Warwick, a knowing look in his eyes.

A mischievous demeanour came over the Great Controller's face. 'France,' he said, 'to see the opulence of their royal court, to taste the refined richness of their cuisine, to see the wonder of their art, the beauty of their women.' Then casting a sly glance at Warwick, he said softly, 'I believe you are going there shortly, my Lord. It would be an ideal opportunity…' His voice trailed off as Edward shot a questioning look at Warwick.

Warwick glared at his Great Controller, who was now staring innocently back into his cup of wine.

'Yes, yes,' Warwick mumbled, 'I'm going, shortly.'

Edward cocked his head to one side. 'Why?' he asked, as he took a sip of wine.

Warwick sighed and looked up at the ceiling. Then, taking a deep breath, said, 'It is time you thought of marriage.'

Edward spluttered into his wine.

Lord Hastings put his elbows on the table, and rested his chin in his hands. A look of concern shimmered across his face as he stared at the king.

Edward stared back at Lord Hastings, guilt in his eyes. 'I'm young and becoming rich,' he quickly stammered, regaining his composure. 'Why would I want to marry when I have many beautiful women clamouring to enter my bed chamber?'

'Because,' cried Warwick, 'you are the King and your marriage is an affair of state, not your heart or what between your legs fancies. It is a serious business. You can still have mistresses, but kingdoms can expand, be strengthened by royal marriage.'

'And you think, France?' questioned Edward, trying to calm himself.

'Yes. An alliance with France makes perfect sense. With their support we would become the most powerful partnership in Europe, Spain, Burgundy, and the others would bend to our wishes.'

'And when do you leave on this royal quest?' asked Edward, now trying to look unconcerned.

'I travel shortly,' replied Warwick.

Edward's face creased into a frown.

Warwick laughed and slapped him on the back. 'Do not worry, cousin, only the most beautiful will be selected for you to choose from, and there is always my daughter, Isabel, if none are to your liking,' he said, with a sly wink. 'Oh, and by the way, I'm taking Richard and young Tunstall. It will be good for their education, and now it seems, Thomas, my Great Controller, has invited himself along as well.'

'Will you be gone long, my Lord?' asked Lord Hastings.

'Four to six weeks,' replied Warwick.

'Excellent!' smiled Lord Hastings, shooting a knowing glance towards Edward. 'It is time for our King to get used to the idea of marriage, and to brush up on his bedroom French!'

Laughter resounded around the table.

Edward smiled thinly as he caught Lord Hastings' eye.

The sound of steel parting muscle and bone carried to the ears of the silent spectators as the executioner's axe chopped down for the final time.

The last headless body was wrapped in a rough blanket, and carried from the scaffold to join the other ten awaiting burial; their heads impaled on wooden stakes.

The Duke of Somerset died bravely. He tried to make a speech, but the Yorkist soldiers had jeered him down.

Lord Hungerford's face was frozen in the petrified scream of his death, as was Lord de Ros's.

Joining them, was Sir Thomas Finderne, Sir Edmund Fish, Sir William Tailboys, Lord Hungerford's brother – Robert, and four of his gentlemen friends who had all been captured along with the Duke of Somerset at the battle of Hexham.

It was a beautiful May morning; nature was free and fresh. *Not a good day to die,* thought John Tunstall. He had winced at the first two executions, but after them, it had been bearable. He looked up at the blue sky and shuddered; no matter how fair this day promised, this bloody yard was grim. He watched morbidly as blood dripped in congealing slowness from the scaffold. Revenge had gorged itself and was now satiated. He was about to leave his seat, to be away from the dead eyes that stared at him from the row of heads impaled on wooden stakes, when Duke Richard put his hand on John's shoulder. 'There is more,' he whispered, with a thin smile.

John slowly lowered himself back into his seat as a man was dragged from the edge of the square, struggling and screaming for mercy. He was roughly manhandled on to the scaffold.

'Sweet Jesus, sweet Jesus,' he wailed, as he frantically looked around with wild eyes at the silent crowd who watched him.

Their cold-hearted eyes stared back at him with detached curiosity.

Realising there was no escaping his fate, no miracle by the hand of God to save him, he fell to his knees, crying and whimpering as a dark wet stain appeared around his crotch.

John suddenly recognised the wretch; he turned his surprised face towards Richard.

'That's right,' said Richard. 'It's the archer who shot Francis on the day we were kidnapped. Remember: he made the mistake of telling us his name.'

'James Dam,' whispered John.

'Aye, James Dam,' repeated Richard. 'I sent word to our army just before the battle of Hexham to hunt him down. They checked every archer taken prisoner, and as luck would have it, they found him.'

'So, now he pays the price,' said John, his stomach churning as he watched the executioner slip the noose over the condemned man's head.

'This is retribution for Francis,' replied Richard, coldly, as the man was yanked to his feet and then hoisted a foot off the scaffold.

The man's whimpering and screaming stopped abruptly as he gasped for air, his feet danced frantically as they tried to find solid support. Finally, he lost consciousness, and was lowered back down on to the scaffold.

The executioner's assistants quickly strapped him to a long oak table.

The crowd watched in silent anticipation as he slowly regained consciousness, and began frantically sucking air into his lungs. Then, his terror retuned as he became aware of the executioner standing over him with a nine-inch butcher's knife, slowly cutting his clothes away until he lay there naked.

James Dam, his eyes blazing with terror, screamed.

Slowly, and with delicate precision, the executioner disembowelled the man. Richard had promised him gold coin if he could keep the man alive and conscious throughout the process. He unhurriedly burned James' entrails before his very eyes, and then paused to wipe the blood off his hands, and arms, while he pondered what organ to remove next. *Maybe his penis and testicles should be sliced off and fed to him*, he pondered. *It will certainly keep the screaming down.*

The executioner reached down and pulled them up taut, his knife expertly going to work.

King Edward, The Earl of Warwick, Lord Montagu, and their close retainers, sat picking at their meal of cold meats, bread, and sweet pastries.

An elaborate, iced cake had been prepared, depicting the executions. It was meant to be a celebration, a tribute to their victory, but now it reminded them of the grisly events of the morning. The cake sat ignored; nobody had the stomach to taste it.

Warwick thumped the table to emphasise his point. 'Cannon are the future!' he cried. 'They have rendered castles extinct. I made short shrift of Bamburgh, which proves my point.' Turning to Edward, he whispered, 'The Crown should have a monopoly on all artillery; it would make your grip on the kingdom stronger. Rebellious nobles who retreat to their castles would no longer be safe when your royal cannon arrived.'

'You speak true,' replied Edward. 'We will talk at length on this subject, later. For if I didn't have to build castles then my exchequer would be the richer for it; but now I leave for London. Richard will accompany me to Baynard's Castle to visit our mother. After the events of the last weeks, it will do the young man good to be with his family for a while.'

'Aye, and young Tunstall will depart for Middleham shortly,' replied Warwick. 'Lady Tunstall will be reunited with her son as promised by my Great Controller.'

'And what of my two lords?' enquired Edward.

'We ride north again; there are still Lancastrian sympathisers to be dealt with,' replied Lord Montagu.

'I will return to Middleham in a few weeks to rest and reorganise,' said Warwick, 'and then to France. I will collect Richard from his mother at Baynard's Castle.'

Edward and Lord Hastings glanced at each other; time enough to undo his marriage before Warwick returned from France.

Richard leant forward and addressed Warwick. 'My Lord, did your men find the serving girl, Lindsay? Was she unharmed?'

'Aye, she is safe' replied Warwick. 'She stays with my men outside the city walls.'

'Good. I will take her to Baynard's Castle with me. My mother will find employment for her and there she will be safe.'

Warwick's hard eyes studied Richard. 'Why are you bothering with a serving wench?' he asked.

Richard stayed silent for a moment, and then as if talking to himself, muttered, 'She has a good spirit and deserves a better life for her kindness.' His words sent a hush around the room and he rose from his chair and walked to the centre of the table. He leant forward and picked up the iced cake depicting the executions, which nobody had the stomach to eat, and carried it towards the fire at the end of the room. All watched in silent fascination.

Standing in front of the fire, Richard slowly studied the cake – the little headless figures, the executioner with his black mask, the red icing running off its sides. In a clear voice, he announced, 'The men this cake depicts committed great crimes against John Tunstall, Francis Lovell, and myself, and they will pay for their sins in the eyes of God.' Turning towards the fire, he raised the cake above his head and threw it on to the burning logs. As the flames devoured it, he cried, 'May you all burn in Hell!' He turned around slowly, to face the table.

A chill went through the men sitting around it as they saw the cold hatred that masked a face so young.

Warwick raised an eyebrow. Richard had gone from kind concern to loathing within the wink of an eye. He would have to watch this young pup, for when he found his teeth he would make a ruthless enemy.

Middleham Castle, North Yorkshire
8 May 1464

Rose stood on the battlements searching out into the countryside. She had stood in the same spot every evening since John had been taken, foolishly hoping to see him ride over the hill towards her, sitting tall in his saddle, handsome and smiling his special smile for her.

She leant against the cold stone and said a prayer for his safe return as she had done every day. She prayed for Lady Tunstall, who had hardly eaten since he had been taken; her clothes now hung off her. She said a prayer for Francis, who was making a good recovery. Then, the anger came into her again; that feeling of abandonment by God. Her small fist hit the castle battlements in frustration. A tear ran down her cheek, chilled in the cool evening breeze.

As she rubbed it away with the outside of her hand, she caught a slight movement in the far distance. She froze, her hands gripping the edge of the stone in front of her. The air that she breathed refused to enter her lungs, and she gasped in short quick breaths. Unknown intuition made her heart race. It was John!

Dashing to the end of the battlements, Rose leaned out, trying to be nearer to him, waiting for her eyes to confirm what she already knew. The black robes of the Great Controller, then the brown habit of Friar Drynk, filled her vision, and at last, the flowing black hair of John filled her heart. She smiled and sobbed at the same time as she raced from the battlements towards Lady Tunstall's apartment, crying out all the way: 'John is back! John is back!' She had no care in the world; God had answered her prayers. John, her love, was home.

Chapter 7

The Best Laid Plans

*Royal Court, Nogent-le-Roi, Loire Valley, France
5 June 1464*

Two greyhounds loped across the hall towards their master. As they moved through the shadow and light, their bejewelled collars reflected a kaleidoscope of colour.

King Louis XI of France knelt down and greeted them, a look of pure delight on his face. He made them sit, their tails, in unison, furiously swishing the cold stone floor. He fed them a few morsels of cold meat, not too much, for the master-of-the-kennels kept them on a strict diet – they needed to be sleek and fast for hunting.

Turning to his two old friends, Georges Havart, and Pierre de Brézé, the king complained, 'If only all my subjects were as loyal.'

'Then a king's life would be tedious and dull for a man as yourself,' replied Georges Havart.

'Aye,' joined in Pierre de Brézé. 'The cut and thrust of government, and the intrigues of power, is food and drink to you, as sun and rain is to a flower. Without it, you would wither and die.'

'But, you must have some respite from the cares of state,' murmured Georges Havart.

'Hunting with dogs is my weakness,' replied King Louis, 'so tomorrow, we will hunt with bow and hounds, and then later we will stalk the crown of England with a pretty maiden, for Warwick arrives at Rouen in two days, time.' He dismissed the hounds back into the care of his kennel master. Too much domestication would make their lives even shorter than the five or six years they had before arthritis – the curse of hunting dogs – set in, for then a quick death was the royal reward for their slowness.

'Right gentlemen, to business!' exclaimed King Louis. 'Before we start; Pierre, how is my cousin, Margaret of Anjou?'

'She is well, your Majesty. She resides on her father's estate, with a small court.'

'Is she at peace?' the king asked.

'Yes, she accepts her fate with good grace. She has found contentment,' replied Pierre de Brézé.

'I hear rumours,' laughed Georges Havart, 'that she has also found a young lover to fill her days and keep her awake at night; maybe her contentment comes from tiredness.'

'That I do not know,' replied King Louis, 'but I do know that Warwick has many enemies in France who will be plotting his demise, and Margaret of Anjou is his bitterest. It would be best to keep a close eye on her until Warwick has returned to England.'

'I will instruct Etienne de Loup to carry out your wishes and place her under surveillance, your Majesty,' replied Georges Havart.

King Louis sat back in his chair. His black hair flopped over his forehead, his close, deep-set eyes shut momentarily as he gathered his thoughts. 'Duke Francis of Breton…' he said, as he opened his eyes. The great intelligence within looked at his two companions to confirm they were listening, '…has dispatched letters to every duke or prince in France informing them that I am offering the whole of Normandy to the Earl of Warwick, if he helps me subdue them all. He has even included my brother Charles, Duke of Berry, in his traitorous circle, and, as you know, Pierre, for your brave services in England, I have just confirmed you as the great Seneschal of Normandy, and Captain of Rouen. It is you who will rule Normandy for me. No other Frenchman will, and certainly no Englishman, for Normandy is the jewel of France.'

Pierre de Brézé thumped the table with his fist. 'If you order it, your Majesty, I will bring the treacherous Duke of Breton before you. I will drag him here with a bull's ring through his nose.'

'I know you would', smiled the king, 'but the problem goes back to my grandfather, mad Charles VI, who gave his crown and his youngest daughter, Catherine, away to the English after his humiliating defeat at Agincourt in 1415. Catherine married Henry V and their son, the future Henry VI, my cousin, was cursed with his grandfather's madness, which later, as Pierre knows at first hand, plunged England into fifteen years of bloody civil war. I suppose one could say that my grandfather eventually had his revenge, but during this period, the dukes and princes of France ruled their lands as kings. My father, Charles VII, was also a puppet to these French nobles. He was weak and shallow and allowed them to control him and that is now my problem, for they resent, or even hate, me for trying to unite France. They yearn for the old days when they answered to no one. That is why there are plots afoot to challenge my authority. They would like their King put back into his box and for them all to sit on its lid!'

'The Duke of Burgundy is the key to this problem,' said Georges Havart, 'for not only does he rule Burgundy, but also Flanders, Holland, Luxembourg and more.'

'I agree he rules too much,' said King Louis. 'If I subdue him, then the rest will have to bend their knee to me, but to subdue him I will need the help of the English and that is my dilemma. My people say I should seek no friendship with them, but to unite France it is vitally important that Warwick arranges the marriage of my wife's sister, Bona of Savoy, to King Edward, for then he would have to support me and not that upstart, Burgundy.'

'But why fight them, your Majesty, when it would be easier to let sleeping dogs lie? Enjoy your lands and let the dukes and princes pay homage to you, although it would only be lip service as they would still have to contribute to your treasury. You could then pursue your pleasures – hunting, travelling and whatever you desired.'

King Louis jumped to his feet. 'Georges!' he cried. 'Do you not see that France is at a crossroads? I could take the easy road that you have just described, but France would cease to exist, and it would become a land of little kingdoms, which would eventually turn on each other. On the other hand, I can take the road of total war, and spend a lifetime fighting these dukes and princes. Then, the English, Italians, even the Spanish, seeing that we were weak would invade us, and France would once again be laid to waste. But if I take the road which unites the French and English thrones, I could destroy Burgundy, and bring the rest of these rebellious princes to heel, and then I could make France the greatest power in Europe.'

King Louis' eyes were sparkling with excitement as he paced the room. He stopped and faced the two men seated at the table. 'Remember Joan, our beautiful, courageous Joan of Arc?' he cried. 'I saw this vision in armour when I was but six years old. She came to that dank, grim, castle of Loches where my father and mother had left me for the first ten years of my life. I remember she was like a heavenly vision with the words of God on her lips; her armour shimmered in the sunlight as she bathed in the cheers of the crowd. It was just after her first great victory over the English at Orleans. She plucked me from the boredom of castle life and took me on a pilgrimage to the Our Lady of Clery, that small church just south-west of Orleans. The English had destroyed the interior of the church during the battle, but we still worshipped at the broken but beautiful shrine devoted to the Blessed Virgin that had been brought from Gaul all those hundreds of years ago. Finally, she left me, and the sadness of my young years, as I watched her ride away, still haunts me – that vision of what France could have been even now burns in my heart.

'This hero of France went on to destroy the English at Jargeau, and Patay, and then her crowning glory, her triumphant entry into Rheims on 17 July 1429. There, she had my spineless father crowned Charles VII of France – this maid of Orleans had set the whole of Europe ablaze. The hearts of Frenchmen, from Marseilles to Dieppe were filled with pride; she was uniting France.'

The king paused, savouring the memory, and then picking up his cup of wine, he walked to the window. As he sipped, he looked out over the small town towards the wooded hillsides that surrounded it. In the far distance, he saw a colourful procession. *That will be Warwick's ambassadors*, he thought. He turned from the window and walked back to the table. Placing his cup down, he resumed his seat.

Pierre de Brézé and Georges Havart sat silently, watching him.

King Louis continued. 'After our Maiden of Orleans' great victories, the dukes and princes started plotting against her – a united France was not what they desired. The foremost amongst them was that bastard, La Trémoille. He betrayed her to the Duke of Burgundy who captured her at Compiègne and sold her to the English. My father could have and should have, ransomed her, saved her, but the French lords controlled him so he did not speak for her freedom, he did not act for her freedom – he sat on his cowardly hands and did nothing. To the shame of France, the English burnt her at the stake in the market place at Rouen, on 31 May 1431.'

The king rose from his seat. 'And that, gentlemen, is why I will unite France at any cost to make amends for my father's sin; to bring justice down on Burgundy and the others for what they did to her. Remember the old saying, "Punishment and retribution are the wages of evil."? Those bastards have earned their wages and the time has come for me to pay them!'

Pierre de Brézé and Georges Havart saw the fire that burned within King Louis – they realised that France, at last, had a worthy king.

The king's first secretary knocked on the door and entered, bowing, his hands clasped in front of him. He announced the arrival of Warwick's ambassadors, Lord Wenlock and Richard Whetehill.

King Louis' eyes glinted with intent. 'Today the hunt begins!' he exclaimed, as he raised his cup of wine. 'Our quarry is a united France.'

'Aye, a united France!' cried his companions, as they raised their cups in unison.

St Mihiel-en-Bar, Lorraine, France
5 June 1464

Simon Langford felt the warmth of the sun on his eyelids as he drifted from light dreams to consciousness. He could feel the soft beauty of the woman beside him, smell her perfume, and enjoy her closeness. He kept his eyes shut so that he could prolong the moment. After the passion of the night, the quietness of the early morning held them in its spell, their souls as one. He moved closer to her, knowing that the day was about to intrude on their intimacy.

He opened his eyes, slowly. The sky was a perfect blue, and through the open window, a gentle warming breeze brought the smell of the vine and the relaxing scents of lavender and honeysuckle into the room. He propped himself up on to his elbow and looked at the beautiful woman beside him, this woman who had been a Queen; this Lady of Anjou who had stolen his heart. As he studied her face, her eyes slowly opened. They did not squint or open one before the other in a jumbled sort of way, they just opened in perfect unison – two exquisite eyes, full of love, looked at him.

'So you are real,' she murmured. 'You've been away so long I thought I was dreaming.' Margaret moved her arms and legs around Simon's naked body, and gently kissed him. A contented sigh slipped from her throat. 'Don't leave me so long, again, my love,' she whispered. 'When you are here, there is music and laughter as though the angels have descended from Heaven, but when you are gone, my days are deserted, and my heart waits in sad solitude for your return.'

Simon ran his hand up her soft thigh until it reached the gentle curve of her waist. His lips slipped over her smooth skin and caressed the smooth slope of her neck. He found her lips, and her silken body moved rhythmically against him, a simple feminine sign of desire.

'I must return to my estates in England by the autumn,' he murmured, as his hand slid over her stomach.

'You must stay until Christmas,' Margaret pleaded.

'We will have all summer…'

Her fingers touched his lips, staying his words, and Simon saw the tigress rise in her eyes as she untangled herself from him.

'You have been gone for four weeks to your estates in England,' she cried. 'When you returned last night, you told me your mother and sisters were in fine health and your estates are in surplus, so, next time, we can send a messenger with your requests. He will return with news of your family, letters, reports; it is so easy.' She knelt beside him. 'Simon, my love, I've missed you so much…' small tears formed in her eyes, 'say you—'

Simon's finger now touched her lips, silencing her words. He leaned towards her, kissing away the tears that slipped from her eyes. 'I will not leave your side until Christmas.'

Margaret's eyes flashed at him.

'I promise; I promise!' he cried.

A look of triumph filled her face as she threw him back on to the bed, her legs straddling his waist.

'That's if I survive that long,' he laughed.'

They lay by the river, the two of them alone, their picnic awaiting their hunger. Simon lay on his back, looking at the blue sky; Margaret laid at right angles to him, her head resting on his stomach. The silence was broken by the sound of water over stone; they could hear the shrill 'chee-chee' of a pair of kingfishers as they swooped and dived over the river. *They will be starting their second brood of the season, by now*, thought Simon. He raised himself on to his elbows and watched as one of the birds, its emerald-blue feathers flashing, dived beneath the surface. It landed back on its perch over the river, a large stickleback held firmly in its beak. The kingfisher repeatedly struck the fish against the perch to kill it, and only when it was dead, would the spines in the fins relax, allowing the bird to swallow it head first. Simon marvelled that something so small and beautiful could be so deadly at hunting – *only God could create such an elegant assassin*, he thought.

His lover stirred; her head turned towards him.

'Were they all executed?' Margaret asked.

Simon could tell by her sad eyes that she feared the worst. 'Yes,' he replied. 'Somerset, Hungerford, De Ros, plus many more, were executed at York. Sir Ralph Percy died bravely at Hedgeley Moor; Sir Ralph Grey died defending Bamburgh, and those that haven't been killed by that butcher, Warwick, and his brother, have fled the realm. As you know, many seek asylum at the court of Burgundy.'

'And Henry?' Margaret whispered, as though by uttering his name, all the sad memories of the past would come alive and this new life would be taken from her.

Simon could see the memory of her husband still wounded her. Gently, he said, 'Henry is still free, hiding between the borders of England and Scotland.'

'If he had fought as well as he hides then his crown would never have been lost,' Margaret said, bitterly. 'We know his cause is finished, but it would seem many still don't, for while you were away I had representations from the court of Spain, and the German Emperor. Even King Afonso of Portugal sent an ambassador – a Monsieur Silva – with his beautiful daughter, Ana Paula neto Silva, to offer assistance in reclaiming the throne, but they only volunteered to further their own causes. As Queen, I commanded in name only, the power I possessed was through the nobles who only showed me loyalty to feather their own nests. I believed I ruled, but the truth was our cause was always doomed because I was a woman, and not a king.'

'Pierre de Brézé, Sir Ralph Percy, and Sir Ralph Grey; they all loved and supported you. I still love and support you,' said Simon.

Margaret lent across and kissed him. 'I thank God every day that you do,' she whispered, 'but the truth is, I could count my true supporters on one hand and that is why we lost the crown.' She said it with a finality that ended the discussion.

Simon rose and walked to the edge of the riverbank; the sun was warm, the sound of the flowing water relaxed his mind. It was a good day, and optimism for the future filled him. His family and estates were flourishing, the small château here in France was perfect, and the woman he loved filled his life. The only black cloud on this otherwise perfect horizon was that bastard, Warwick; the man stopped him from leaving his past behind, tormented his dreams, and burst into his thoughts at the strangest of times.

Simon closed his eyes and prayed. He decided to give the problem of Warwick to God; if vengeance was to be his then the Lord would show him the way. If not, then he would leave it be, and he would embrace this new life.

After praying, he watched the kingfishers skim low over the water, gathering aquatic insects in their beaks; the sight of them feeding brought his mind back to more mundane matters. *Food – time for that picnic*, he thought.

Margaret studied Simon as he walked towards the river. She loved him without doubt. Just to be near him filled her with a beautiful strange energy – her heart would sometimes beat faster or she would become a little breathless when he walked into the room. Whatever it was, she had never felt the like before. He had golden hair and blue eyes, that was true, and his features were rugged, not handsome, but it was his smile that captivated her. The first time he had looked at her with those piercing blue eyes and smiled, her heart had melted, and had done so ever since. She was happy, but deep down she felt sadness, for she was growing older and knew her beauty would fade. Would he eventually, like most men, leave her for some pretty, young girl like that Portuguese beauty, Ana Paula, who had visited her with her father Monsieur Silva? She closed her eyes and prayed that they may grow old together. As she opened them, Simon knelt down in front of her.

'Time for food!' he cried.

She leant forward and kissed him. 'First, you have to earn it,' she smiled, as her arms wrapped around his neck.

The sun was low as Margaret and Simon returned to the château; dusk was slowly merging into the coolness of the night. As their mounts trotted into the courtyard, Margaret's son, Prince Edward, rushed from the entrance and down the steps to meet them, his face flushed with excitement. Two of her ladies-in-waiting laboured to keep up with him.

'Mother,' he cried, full of youthful enthusiasm, 'we have visitors. My father's loyal lieutenants have arrived with news from the Duke of Burgundy.'

Margaret's heart sank – it was Simon's first day home – she had wanted it to be special. The picnic had been perfect and tonight there was to be a celebration meal for his safe return. She had organised actors to stage a small play. Poets and writers had been invited. Minstrels would play and there would be dancing, but her old life, the one she had left behind in England, still clung to her like an old heavy cloak. She suddenly shivered. 'And who are our new guests?' she asked, trying to keep her voice relaxed.

'Sir Henry Billingham and Sir John Woollaston,' Prince Edward replied proudly.

Margaret's ladies-in-waiting rushed to assist her as she dismounted, and as she climbed the steps, she suddenly stopped. Turning to Simon, she said with mock haughtiness. 'Come, Sir Simon Langford, your Queen desires your presence.'

As Simon followed Margaret into the château, he could see her spine stiffen. His beloved was once again the Queen of England, and a different stage now awaited her.

Margaret of Anjou swished into the antechamber. Both Sir Henry Billingham and Sir John Woollaston bowed low, and Margaret offered her bejewelled hand to them, which they both lightly kissed.

'Well, gentlemen, what brings you to my small court with such urgency?' she asked as she sat down in a large, tall-backed chair at the end of the room. Her ladies-in-waiting brought up smaller chairs for her guests.

Simon stood beside the Queen, his hand resting on the back of her chair.

'The Duke of Burgundy – Philip the Good,' replied Sir John Woollaston, 'has sent us to inform you, my Lady, that the Earl of Warwick arrives in the port of Rouen in two days' time, to negotiate the marriage of the Queen's sister, the Bona of Savoy, to Edward, that false King of England.'

Margaret sensed the excitement that suddenly filled Simon's body. She shot a quick glance at him; his eyes were sparkling with anticipation. She decided it was time to end this charade. The Lancastrian cause was finished and it was time these gentlemen were told so.

'Firstly,' she replied, 'Edward is no false King of England.' As this simple sentence left her lips she felt a weight had been lifted from her – she had finally stated the truth. She watched the two men in front of her ripple with indignation. This, she knew, was not what they wished to hear, but hear it they would – the genie was, at last, out of the bottle. 'Edward has been anointed with the holy oil and crowned in Westminster Abbey and commands the respect of the nobility and the people, while my husband, poor Henry, wanders the barren lands of northern England like some lowly vagabond; he is no more a king than you.'

'Your Highness…' protested Sir Henry.

She held her hand up to silence him. 'King Henry was never a king. He was an illusion that the people wished to believe in, but he stood small in the shadow of his father. As a husband, he was an illusion, but one that I tried to believe in. Sadly, every year, the illusion dissipated until it was no more.' She fixed her diamond stare on the men in front of her. They sat opened-mouthed at her words. She threw her head back and laughed. 'And now they demand another French bride for another English king!' she exclaimed. 'Henry V married a French princess. His son married me, and now they desire the beautiful Bona of Savoy. Do men never learn?' she cried, raising an eyebrow, and extending her hands in an upward motion.

A flustered Sir Henry rose from his chair. 'Your – your Highness,' he stuttered, 'the Duke of Burgundy wishes the marriage stopped.'

'And we know why,' Margaret cried. 'If France and England form a powerful alliance, they would turn their attentions on him, his own continental ambitions would be stopped, and he may even be deposed.'

Sir John Woollaston suddenly rose from his chair, pushing it back and sending it clattering across the floor. The tension thickened. 'He wants Warwick dead!' he shouted. Silence filled the room.

Margaret sat in her chair, her face filled with excitement. 'Now that would be a fine undertaking; his death would be greatly pleasing,' she cried, her personal hatred for the man rising to the surface, but as her words circled the room, she suddenly, desperately, wanted to stop them. It was too late; Simon had heard them and her plea to God to keep him by her side, now undone by her own stupid words.

'When do we leave to exact vengeance on the bastard?' Simon cried.

'Dawn,' replied Sir Henry.

Margaret rose from her chair. 'Simon…' she pleaded, but her words tailed off as she saw the determination on his face. Slumping back on to her chair, she stared at the floor. She would rather Warwick lived for a thousand years than lose Simon, but it was too late she realised, bitterly, and it was her own selfish fault.

Royal Court, Nogent-Le-Roi, Loire Valley, France
6 June 1464

King Louis watched as the backs of Warwick's ambassadors disappeared though the doorway. All arrangements for his arrival and stay had been agreed; the chief citizens and the senior clergy of Rouen would receive him with full pomp and ceremony. He himself would stay at the village of La Bouille and enter Rouen the following day, dressed in splendour to act out his part as a sovereign king.

'Honours and festivities must be showered on our guest,' King Louis said. 'Lord Warwick must return to England our firm ally.'

Etienne de Loup, his shadowy spymaster spoke. 'I hear rumours of a plot,' he whispered in his hoarse way, his head slowly looking up, engaging the eyes of the king.

'Plot? Plot? What treason do you speak of?' cried King Louis.

'I have only heard slippery phantoms of deceit,' Etienne de Loup growled. 'No solid fact, but Burgundy is mentioned, and English men loyal to Margaret of Anjou have been seen meeting at her château. I will, of course, have them followed, but I fear for Warwick.'

'By all the saints in Heaven, you must unravel this mystery!' shouted the king. 'No harm must befall Lord Warwick, for if it does then France will also suffer.'

'As we speak, the spies of our enemies are suffering the ordeal of torture,' replied Etienne de Loup, his reptile eyes narrowing in pleasure at the thought of it. 'If any knows, they will speak; our agents are also seeking the answers.'

King Louis rose from his chair and paced the room; he always thought better on his feet. 'Pierre, as Captain of Rouen, you must check the arrangements for the safety of the Lord Warwick. Order whatever you require: men, weapons, equipment.'

Pierre de Brézé nodded.

'Georges,' instructed the king, 'secure the surrounding countryside. I want men in all the villages. They must report any movements of armed men or suspicious gatherings.'

'It will be done, your Majesty,' replied Georges Havart.

'Etienne, time is our enemy; we rely on your talent for loosening tongues. You must double your efforts, so request whatever you need.'

Etienne de Loup stood up, his lizard eyes slowly looking around the room. His face broke into a satisfied smile showing his sharpened yellow teeth, and his tongue flicked around his lips. As the men in the room tried not to recoil in disgust, a hoarse cackle left his lips. 'I'll away to double the pain,' he whispered. 'You will have answers shortly, your Majesty.' He bowed and was gone.

The room was silent but Etienne de Loup's malevolence lingered. The six remaining men quietly thanked God that they were not the subjects of his interrogation.

Rouen, France
7 June 1464

The securing lines curled out from the fore and aft of the ship towards St Eloi wharf. John Tunstall watched from the stern castle as brawny stevedores wearing sleeveless leather jerkins, their muscular arms bulging, secured the heavy lines.

Along the jetty and around the docks stood richly dressed dignitaries, soldiers of rank and elevated clergy, their opulent robes and glittering jewels contrasting starkly with the grimy streets and the poor that walked them.

Etiquette demanded that royal blood be greeted by royal blood, so the Duke of Bourbon stood at the front of the jetty, resplendent in his ceremonial robes and gold chains of office, waiting to offer a regal greeting to the mighty Earl of Warwick.

John looked with hungry eyes at the hustle and bustle of excitement below him; the sounds and smells of France assailed his senses. He could not believe that he was actually here. He looked at his two friends, Richard, and Francis. Their faces shone with wonder, their eyes wide.

Warwick appeared from the stern cabin, his body richly clothed in blues and gold, his back straighter than a pikestaff. Supreme confidence and authority showed in his every move. He walked to the top of the gangway.

The musicians on the wharf below instantly brought life to their instruments, their playing nearly drowned out by the cheering and clapping of the crowd.

Warwick stood and basked in the welcome, his eyes drinking in the moment. At the bottom of the gangway, stood his two ambassadors: Lord Wenlock, and Richard Whetehill; they half bowed, each an arm outstretched towards the Duke of Bourbon. Warwick slowly descended, waving to the crowd as he did so. Following behind were his household officers, chosen knights, and an honorary guard of archers as befitted his rank.

The earl and duke embraced warmly, and after exchanging gifts of gold and diamonds, they marched from the wharf followed by the exuberant crowd.

The music and noise slowly dimmed into the distance. The three boys watched until the celebration was swallowed up by the city. St Eloi wharf now stood deserted. The ship was hushed. All of those aboard were left spellbound by the events that had unfolded before them. Only the soft singing of the wind through the rigging, and the gentle rolling creaks of the ship broke the silence.

'Thank Satan's hairy arse that's over with,' said Thomas Hallet to his twin brother. 'These Frenchies always get excited.'

'Aye,' replied George, 'they do love a bit of bowing and scraping.'

'Whoring arse lickers,' concluded Thomas, then lowering his voice to a whisper, 'but now we can slip ashore and sample the delights...'

'You two will be sampling nothing,' barked the Great Controller.

The twins raised their eyebrows at each other and then turned to face the Great Controller who had appeared behind them as silent as a ghost. 'We are in a foreign port and your duty is to protect the boys. Remember, the Devil's work may be afoot; they were taken once, it will not happen again.'

'Yes, sir. No, sir, I mean—' started Thomas.

The Great Controller cut him short. 'Enough,' he said. 'Stay close to them. Tomorrow, we sail up the Seine, to Paris. Once there, you will be free to sample the delights of the city. Lord Warwick, in his wisdom, has left a purse of money for your reward in rescuing the boys so until we arrive in Paris do not let them out of your sight; understood?'

The Hallet twins nodded vigorously.

Broad smiles filled the Great Controller's vision. 'And God help Paris,' he cried, as he walked away.

The three boys looked at each other. 'Paris!' they exclaimed in unison, their faces breaking out into wide grins.

'We will be there tomorrow,' cried John, his feet starting to dance a circular jig in excitement.

'It's the greatest city in Europe,' cried Francis, joining in the dance.

'But it's only a city,' shouted Richard, embarrassed by his friends' carefree dancing.

'It might be only a city,' replied John, as his jig brought him round to face Richard.

'But it's four times the size of London,' Francis joined in.

'And full of wonders,' cried John, as he came round again.

Both boys seized an arm each and spun Richard around with them. He resisted at first, but then finally admitting defeat he shed his inhibitions and shouted, 'To Paris; we're going to Paris.'

Spinning faster and faster, they all finally collapsed, laughing in a heap on the deck.

Rouen, France
8 June 1464

The Earl of Warwick left the 'Cathedral of our Lady' where he had made an offering to the success of his mission. It was a short walk back to the Franciscan Friary, where he lodged with his small court. The time was seven of the clock, and the city was awake and bustling. In thirty minutes, King Louis would arrive, and negotiations on an Anglo-French alliance would begin.

First on the agenda, was a bride for Edward, and then his own military support in defeating the Duke of Burgundy, and then what reward for assisting the King of France to secure his throne? The earl's mind fell eagerly to the possibilities. *Maybe a yearly pension of say, four thousand marks, or when the Duke of Burgundy is defeated, all the spoils of the Low Countries.* He knew what he craved the most – the idea filled his thoughts in the early mornings when sleep and consciousness parted: to be ruler of his own kingdom, to be Prince of Holland.

King Louis paused on the outskirts to the city; he wanted this to be a powerful, rich, entrance; one that would dazzle Lord Warwick. He had with him trumpeters, heralds, knights, guards from his standing army, and squires and grooms by the plenty. His eyes examined them all. Satisfied, he spurred his horse and entered the city. His trumpeters sounded a royal salute.

Warwick heard the notes; his squires quickly checked his rich attire and then stood ready to open the large wooden doors. As the king approached, they would swing them open to reveal the earl as a vision of power who would then walk out, followed by his entourage to greet the king.

Dieppe, France
9 June 1464

Philip de Chastle spoke in a voice hushed with secrecy. This royal officer had been sent by the Duke of Brittany to outline the plan of attack against the Earl of Warwick. Sir Simon Langford, Sir Henry Billingham, and Sir John Woollaston, sat in the shadowy corner of a dockside tavern and suffered its hot sultry atmosphere. Sipping cool, watered, wine, they listened intently to his words.

'Etienne de Loup, King Louis' enforcer, knows something is afoot,' whispered Philip. 'His eyes and ears are everywhere; our agents and sympathisers are disappearing into his dungeons daily as he seeks to unravel our intentions.'

'So, he could discover our strategy at any moment,' said Sir Henry, alarm in his voice.

'Only if he gathers me in his net,' replied Philip, 'for I am the only one within his grasp who knows the plan.'

'You mean there is not a single person here who knows, apart from you?' asked Simon, his voice incredulous.

'That is correct,' confirmed Philip. 'The less who know, the less chance of discovery.' Then changing the subject, he asked, 'Are your men dispersed safely around the town?'

'Aye,' replied Simon. 'They are in small groups of two or three so as not to draw attention to themselves.'

'What are your numbers?'

'Thirty,' replied Sir Henry. 'Mostly English exiles, but a few brave French, Spanish, and Dutch.'

'Excellent,' beamed Philip. 'We have the same number from the Duke of Brittany, a mixture of French, English, and Dutch – it would seem Warwick's enemies come in many nationalities.'

'There is much blood on his hands,' said Simon with venom as thoughts of his father filled his mind.

'Enough of all this talk,' Sir John Woollaston butted in. 'We need to know what is required of us so we can brief our men and discuss the merits of your strategy.'

His blunt statement seemed to focus the others' minds.

Philip leant closer to them. 'The walls and gateways into Rouen are well guarded. The villages and surrounding countryside are also brimming with the King's men.'

'So, how do we enter?' whispered Simon, dismay in his voice.

'We don't,' replied Philip. 'Over land, the town is impregnable.'

The three men looked at each other and then stared at Philip, confusion in their eyes.

'But, it does have a soft underbelly,' Philip said, a small smile playing at the corners of his mouth. He watched the anticipation grow within the men. 'The harbour is unguarded!' he finally cried, triumphantly.

Eyes within the room glanced towards their table; Philip looked embarrassed at his companions. They fell into silence until the attention on them had ceased. Cautiously, he continued. 'The Duke of Burgundy is sending a ship here to Dieppe.' He watched the excitement creep into the others' eyes, then continued.

'Warwick will spend his last night aboard his ship before sailing for England on the morning tide. During that night, we will sail silently into Rouen harbour, berth against the seaward side of his vessel, board her, and then dispatch the bastard to the demons of Hell. We will then sail silently away.' Philip sat back and awaited questions.

'If the alarm is raised as we berth alongside, then their numbers may be too great for us to overcome,' said Simon.

Philip waved his finger from side to side. 'No, no,' he said. 'All the King's troops are facing outwards; they are stationed on the city walls or far out in the surrounding countryside. We will have more than enough time to complete the mission and make good our escape.'

'How will we know when it is Warwick's last night?' whispered Sir Henry.

'That monster, De Loup, may know some of our agents, but he doesn't know them all,' replied Philip. 'I have some trusted men who will inform us when the time is right.'

'And the ship?' asked Sir John Woollaston.

'She arrives in two days' time under the cover of darkness. She will anchor outside of the harbour. I have longboats organised to ferry you and the men out to her then we will disappear from Dieppe unseen, silently, in the blackness of the night. It will be as though we had never been here.'

The four conspirators sat back, with satisfied smiles on their faces.

Simon raised his glass. 'To the silence of the night,' he whispered.

Two men hidden by the shadows of the bar also raised their glasses; a knowing look passing between them. Finishing their drinks, they slipped out of the tavern to report to their master.

Rouen, France
11 June 1464

The Earl of Warwick stood staring out of the window of the Franciscan Friary, and awaited his guest. It was early morning, and he admired the beautiful gardens that sloped gently away from him towards the forest.

Monks like orderliness, he thought. *Be it a row of carrots or a trimmed hedge, all has to be laid out precisely, just like their lives, governed by prayers and rituals.* He smiled to himself. King Louis was the opposite of orderliness – he travelled France constantly, his court struggling to keep up with him. He was not concerned with luxury or fine food; he was driven by his dream to unite his kingdom. Warwick admired him; he was clever, resourceful, and full of energy – a man he could do business with.

Feeling jaded, he slumped down in a chair. The long journey from his estates, and then crossing the English Channel, had sapped his energy. Since his arrival in Rouen, King Louis had provided the best entertainment his court could devise as well as showering him and his negotiators with gifts. The king's personal gift to him was a gold cup encrusted with gems. His negotiators had received gold coins specially minted for the occasion.

The truth is, Warwick thought, wearily, *I don't need gifts, or lavish entertainment. What I desire is for these negotiations to be successful. I need Edward married to a French princess and myself made Prince of Holland and Zeeland, then I can have all the gold cups I need, all the feasting and dancing a man could require, for power is the richest possession of all, power makes any dream come true!*

He heard footsteps in the hallway outside, and sitting upright in his chair, he forced these half-dreamlike thoughts from his mind.

There was a sharp knock on the door. Two men-at-arms entered and they stood either side of the entrance, in through which swished King Louis, smiling and bustling with purpose.

Warwick and King Louis walked slowly through the gardens. The king had dismissed his close advisors but the guards kept a respectable distance behind them.

'We will have no eavesdroppers out here,' King Louis said, 'and, because your French is excellent, we do not have to worry about the formalities of interpreters either.'

Warwick nodded to acknowledge the compliment.

King Louis continued. 'My Ambassadors are negotiating greater privileges and trade opportunities for your merchants. I have arranged for our famous silks and satins to be shown to them – they may take whatever they require back to England as samples. Hopefully, it will tempt both our merchants to cross the channel – increased commerce will strengthen the ties between our two countries.'

'If nothing else, it will enrich their wardrobes,' laughed Warwick.

'Then they will all become walking announcements for the beautiful wares of France,' retorted a smiling King Louis.

The two men walked in silence, gathering their thoughts on the questions they needed answering.

King Louis raised the back of his hand to his mouth and gave a refined cough – a starting point for his first question. 'My Lord Warwick, is your influence still strong over young King Edward?'

'He is reliant on my counsel,' replied Warwick.

'Is he reliant enough to accept a bride of your choice?'

Warwick nodded. 'Yes, he would accept my choice.'

'Excellent,' beamed King Louis. 'My officials will negotiate the size of the dowry with your ambassadors. I will agree to pay Edward as soon as he marries my sister-in-law, and then, of course, there is the matter of a settlement for yourself, a reward for your efforts.'

'But you require more than a marriage to solve the dilemma of uniting your kingdom,' replied Warwick, bluntly.

King Louis appreciated from Warwick's short statement that he was well informed. Gently touching Warwick's arm, he guided him to a wooden bench, cut into one of the tall, neatly trimmed hedges. They sat down.

King Louis' deep, close-set eyes stared at his own simple, green hunting shoes. He knew it was crucial that Warwick returned to England his firm ally and friend. He reasoned that if they were going to collaborate, their alliance had to be built on honesty and trust – which he knew to be very rare within the nobility. Now the dice were about to be thrown, he had no choice but to believe in Warwick, who he hoped was one of those exceptional men that respected and returned honesty when it was presented to them. Only time would tell.

'Richard, I will be frank with you,' King Louis said, addressing Warwick by his Christian name. 'I have many problems, all inherited from my father and grandfather. Both were weak, and a weak king only rules anarchy.'

'And a strong king can inherit rebellion,' replied Warwick.

'You are very perceptive,' smiled King Louis.

'So who are your main antagonists, besides Burgundy?' asked Warwick.

'The Duke of Brittany, Duke of Orleans, Count of Charolais and more,' replied King Louis, instantly. 'Their names are forever on my mind. They whisper treason to my brother, Charles, promise him the throne; they know he is weak and shallow, one they could control.'

'The second son born into a royal family always seeks what the first born has inherited,' said Warwick. 'It is as though they feel cheated. That sense of almost being a king makes it easy for others to influence them. The prize is tempting – alluring; it stands glittering before them. They are swayed by traitors who murmur honeyed words in their ear and tell them that all they have to do is just reach out and take the crown for themselves.'

'Yes,' agreed King Louis, 'it is a lesson repeated throughout history, but with your help, my friend, it will not be repeated here.'

Warwick knew that now was the time to strike his bargain, to offer his assistance and ask for his reward. 'Burgundy must be deposed if you wish to save your crown,' he said in his forthright way. 'I will furnish you with men, archers, and weapons to achieve this end.'

'But what of King Edward?' interrupted King Louis. 'Will he not have to agree to this?'

Warwick laughed. 'Once he has married a pretty French princess he will have thoughts of only one course of foreign policy and that will be between the sheets. No, it is me who decides our foreign strategy.'

King Louis rubbed his hands together with excitement. 'This course of action that is opening up through our collaboration will secure my throne, and you, my dear Warwick, are the key!'

Warwick suppressed the urge to ask for his reward.

King Louis stood up and resumed walking; now taking longer, quicker strides as his mind raced with many thoughts. 'We must confirm the wedding, no detail will be too small, trade will commence, and the sharing of foreign policy must be discussed.'

Warwick, having been racing to keep up, almost collided with the king when he suddenly stopped.

King Louis grabbed both of Warwick's arms. 'My friend!' he cried. 'You must think me a man of no grace. Forgive me. All that is laid out before me is only possible through you; what honour or riches can I bestow to show my gratitude?'

Warwick felt the satisfaction swell within his chest. Here, at last, was his great chance to be a king in his own right, to stand as an equal to all the royalty of Europe. 'I wish to be Prince of Holland and Zeeland,' he said. 'I cannot dress it up or add frills to this request. They are simple words and I have said them plainly enough.'

King Louis threw his head back and laughed. 'Only an Englishman could be so direct,' he spluttered through his laughter, and then throwing his arm around Warwick's shoulder, he turned him towards the friary. 'Come, we have much to discuss. If you are to rule Holland and Zeeland, then first we must plan the demise of Burgundy.'

They set off at a fast pace, talking and scheming as they went.

Etienne de Loup watched as King Louis and Warwick approached him. His face betrayed no emotion, his reptile eyes were cold, but the answer the king needed waited on his lips.

Baynard's Castle, London
11 June 1464

Cecily Neville, the Duchess of York, sat in her chair, dumbstruck by the statement that had just assailed her ears.

Her son, King Edward, was still speaking, his mouth opening and closing in an agitated way but the words were silent. She heard not a sound. There were but two words spinning inside her head that kept repeating themselves over and over. This mighty statement that had nearly stopped her heart. She stared at her eldest surviving son and replayed the moment, again. 'I'm married'. He had blurted it out like a five-year-old, full of apprehension, but there was a wilful stubbornness behind his words.

She rose from her chair and walked to the window. The River Thames flowed past; a great artery of water that was the essence of London – its heartbeat, bestowing vitality and life on this great city. Watching the activity of the boatmen as they plied their trade calmed her spirit. Her mind slowed, her thoughts became crystal clear. She turned from the window and faced her son.

'Who knows of this marriage?' Cecily demanded.

'No one,' replied Edward. 'It is my great secret.'

'Warwick certainly doesn't know!' Cecily shouted. 'The man is in France negotiating new trade agreements, diplomatic alliances that all hinge on you marrying the Bona of Savoy.' She strode from the window bristling with anger and stood in front of Edward. 'You are making a fool out of the greatest magnate within your kingdom, a man who is not only your cousin but also a good and loyal friend. Together, with his brother, they have ended all Lancastrian resistance to your throne and how do you repay him? How do you show your gratitude? By sending him on a fool's errand to France. You will make him the laughing stock of Europe.'

Edward looked up at his mother. Known as 'proud Cis' because of her royal pride, and the temper that went with it, he was now feeling the hot blast of it. 'The marriage must be annulled,' he spluttered.

'Annulled? Annulled?' Cecily screeched.

Edward slunk lower in his chair, as the heat of his mother's anger started to roast him.

Cecily raised her hands in the air. 'God preserve us!' she cried. She walked back to the window and rested her hands on the cool stone. She looked out over the river with her back to Edward. Calmly, she said, 'You say this marriage is a great secret?'

'Yes, it is,' replied Edward, glad that her voice was calmer.

'So, were you the only one there?'

'No,' Edward replied, confused.

'So, I presume that as you married this Lancastrian widow, Elizabeth Grey, she was also present, and of course there must have been a priest and his assistant, so that's four of you who know this great secret, and who were the witnesses? Who signed the marriage certificate?'

'Hastings,' said Edward.

'Well, he can no more keep a secret than you can keep your manhood under control. And the other one?' Edward was silent, but Cecily heard him fidgeting in his chair. 'And the other one?' she asked again, her voice rising.

'The bride's mother,' Edward finally said.

Cecily spun around from the window and faced Edward. 'Jacquetta, Duchess of Bedford?' she cried.

Edward nodded, glumly.

'I knew her when she was called "Jacquetta of Luxembourg". I was there thirty years ago when she married her first husband, John, Duke of Bedford. She was a scheming witch then and she is a scheming witch now. She has used her daughter to bewitch you with potions and charms, to snare you like a stupid dull rabbit.'

Cecily walked across to Edward and lent down, her face red with temper. 'For sixteen years she was the best friend and confidant of Margaret of Anjou. She used her position to have her lowly second husband made a lord, and Knight of the Garter. She was the second most important Lancastrian in the country. She plotted with that Bitch of

174

Anjou against your father. Along with her, she was responsible for his death and you have married her daughter!'

Cecily straightened up and backed away from Edward. 'Shame on you!' she cried. 'Shame on you!' Her eyes filled with tears. 'If only your father were here,' she said, as tears flowed down her cheeks.

Edward rose from his chair. 'That is why the marriage must be annulled,' he whispered.

'Who has the marriage certificate?' Cecily asked. There was silence. Her eyes turned on Edward, understanding now fuelling the fire that burned in them. 'She has, hasn't she?' she screamed.

Edward turned away from her. 'Yes,' he replied.

'Then there is no undoing of what has been done. You are married and that is the end of it. You are a fool and have been played as a fool.'

There was silence as they both stared at each other.

'Warwick is your problem now,' Cecily said, quietly. 'You best plan how to deal with him, for I fear this marriage will rip your kingdom apart.' She stood back and looked at Edward, wiping tears from her face. 'How could you be so stupid when we have finally achieved peace after all those years of bloody, civil war? I fear you have started it all over again; you have squandered the trust of the people. You are not fit to be King!' She walked towards the door, anxious to be away from the wretchedness of the room. Before leaving, she stopped and looked at her son. 'And this is all because you could not keep your reckless lust under control.'

Edward took his hunting jacket off and tossed it across the room where it landed untidily across the table. Sitting down, he wearily placed his head in his hands. An air of frustration surrounded him, and his mother's words still rang in his ears. 'You are not fit to be King', she had said.

Lord Hastings entered the room and sat down opposite Edward with an 'I told you so' look on his face.

'My mother is displeased with my marriage,' grumbled Edward, as he kicked his boots off and slumped back into his chair.

Lord Hastings rose and walked to the table where he poured two cups of wine. Handing one to Edward, he resumed his seat.

Edward took a gulp of wine and stared up at the ceiling. 'I cannot give her up,' he said, the image of Elizabeth stirring his loins. 'I think of her all the time, nay, desire her all the time.'

Lord Hastings glanced secretly around the room, even though he knew they were alone. 'They have cast a strong spell over you,' he said, shaking his head, sadly.

'Spell? Spell?' cried Edward, suddenly sitting up straight. 'What spell?'

Lord Hastings stared at him, his eyes wide with conviction.

Edward slowly slipped back down into his chair as he awaited a lecture.

'The night before your marriage,' Lord Hastings began, 'was the eve of St Walpurga's, one of the four grand Sabbaths of the witches' year. It is the night when God-fearing people bolt their doors and sleep with holy artefacts around them, because on that night, witches worship Bacchus and practise their unholy rituals with coarse orgies and sacrifices.'

Edward sat up, his face alive with interest. 'What are you implying?' he whispered.

'Only what I have said before: that you were bewitched by your wife and her mother.'

Edward laughed nervously. 'You are imagining all this,' he cried, shaking his head in disbelief. 'Where do you get all these wild theories from?'

'They are not wild theories,' Lord Hastings shot back. 'You remember Eleanor Cobham? She married Humphrey, the old Duke of Gloucester in 1431. Well, ten years later, she was convicted of using potions supplied by Margery Jourdemayne, the "Witch of Eye", to make the duke fall in love with her. Two unfrocked priests, Roger Bolingbroke and Thomas Southwell, used the black arts to perform the ceremony. They were all convicted of witchcraft and of using wax images to snare the duke into marring her. Jourdemayne was burnt at Smithfield and the two men were hung, drawn, and quartered.'

'And what of Eleanor?' asked Edward.

'The marriage was dissolved by the Archbishop of Canterbury, two cardinals, and three bishops who had conducted the trial. Eleanor had to do public penance through the streets of London, barefoot and bareheaded. Nearly naked, she had to carry a two-pound candle in each hand while the men and woman of London threw rotten vegetables at her. She was then imprisoned in a wretched dungeon for the rest of her life.'

'Ah, I remember the case now,' sneered Edward, with disbelief in his voice. 'Some say the charges were trumped up by the duke's enemies because he was the main stumbling block in the final negotiations for peace with France. He was so disgraced by the trial that he lost all his influence at court, and in the end, could not even save his wife from her fate.'

'After your marriage,' continued Lord Hastings, undaunted by Edward's cynicism, 'I sent agents secretly to Grafton Regis and the surrounding villages to try and discover if there was any truth in these rumours, that they practised the black arts there. I have found witnesses who have heard strange sounds, screeches and chanting coming from the cellar late at night especially on nights when the moon was waning.'

Edward's eyes widened with scepticism. 'You are foolish to believe in such nonsense. Bring these accusers before me, so I can judge them.'

'None will testify in public, for fear of their lives,' replied Lord Hastings.

'I thought that may be the case,' laughed Edward.

'But they all say it is a common occurrence,' Lord Hastings ploughed on, determined to finish his argument. 'I will gather more evidence, and as was the case with Eleanor Cobham, will have your marriage annulled.'

'If any other man had made these accusations against my wife, I would have had them executed,' hissed Edward, his face turning red with anger. 'You must keep these mad ideas to yourself. I do not want my court full of sly whisperings about spells and potions. These fanciful theories are to be kept between you and me.'

'You are so bewitched by your mother-in-law, methinks I could show you all the evidence in the world and you would still not believe me,' cried Lord Hastings, with frustration.

An ill-tempered silence hung between them. Finally, Lord Hastings heaved himself from his chair and refilled their wine cups. He passed one to Edward who had slumped back into his chair, suddenly exhausted by all this talk of Warwick and witchcraft.

'If what you say is true, then may God protect you in your quest,' Edward said quietly, a smile playing around his mouth. 'But be very careful, my old friend, for if they suspect you, they may turn you into a frog.' He chuckled to himself as he took another gulp of wine.

Dieppe, France
13 June 1464

The oars silently dipped into the silky, black water; five longboats slipped from the shoreline, quickly swallowed up by the moonless night.

Simon Langford watched the lights on the great harbour walls grow distant, finally twinkling weakly and then, one by one, extinguishing. They were surrounded by blackness; only the soft creaking of the boat, and the gentle rhythm of the oars as they moved in unison through the water could be heard.

Simon looked ahead into the darkness, his eyes straining to see the vessel that awaited them. He listened to the boats as they cut through the water. Every pull on the oars left the frustrations of the last few days further behind. Now, he had a purpose; his quest for vengeance had begun.

'Light on the starboard bow,' came the muffled cry from the lead boat.

Simon's eyes moved to the right. In the distance, he saw a pinprick of light flashing out their destination. The boats swung towards it.

Rouen, France
14 June 1464

John Tunstall watched once again as the great harbour of Rouen opened up before him.

It had been five days since they had sailed up the Seine to Paris; five days that had turned their world upside down. They had left on the morning tide as heavy drizzle had tried to dampen their spirits, but the excitement of Paris could not be dampened. They had departed that wet, grey morning as inexperienced innocents, young boys ignorant of the charms of the fairer sex, and returned with no mysteries left to puzzle them.

John looked at his companions. Outwardly, they looked the same, there were no marks or signs to say what had happened to them, but inwardly they changed forever. His mind drifted back to his first sight of Paris…

'Have you ever seen the like?' shouted Duke Richard, as Paris hove into view.

The great city spread out before them, four times the size of London. Majestic cathedral spires filled the sky exalting the glory of God. Grand, imposing, municipal buildings lined the wide avenues that led away from the harbour, a thousand narrow streets like a tangled spider's web spread out as far as the eye could see. Lofty town houses, rowdy taverns, and bulging shops crowded their sides, some straight, others leaning at impossible angles. The buildings of Paris looked down on their colourful citizens as they jabbered and shouted, rushed or dawdled. They watched, impartial, as tragedy and comedy, life or death, played out under their permanent gaze. The boys gaped at its bewildering vastness; this city set down on the banks of the Seine, this melting pot of human existence.

The Hallet twins smiled at each other as the Great Controller approached, a leather purse in his hand. 'You have three days and two nights to explore the city,' he said. 'Be back aboard on the evening of the third. Understood?'

The twins nodded in unison, and then taking the purse, they shook it to savour the sound of clinking coin. 'God bless our Lord Warwick,' they cried.

'Remember,' said the Great Controller, 'we are not well liked by the French, so go peaceably about your business, and do not bring attention to yourselves.'

'Not speaking French will attract attention,' shouted Richard. 'I wager a silver penny you are back before nightfall.'

'Done,' replied Thomas Hallet. Smiling broadly, he held the purse up and shouted, 'You will learn that money talks in any language, my Lord.' With that, both twins were down the gangplank and gone.

The Great Controller shook his head and muttered a prayer to the saints for their safety.

Jean Jouffroy, Cardinal of Arras, sat in a small stateroom within Hôtel Saint-Pol, the royal palace. He had sailed from Rouen on the Earl of Warwick's ship, acting as chaperone to Duke Richard, and his companions. It was a duty he was pleased to undertake, for it confirmed King Louis' trust in him, but now his patience was beginning to wear thin.

He glanced around the royal room; his eyes saw, but did not convey, the richness of it to his brain. His mind was elsewhere. He rose from his chair and instructed one of the royal pages to search for Jean Bourré, King Louis' chief financial secretary, as he was late for their meeting, as usual.

The arrangement was that he would oversee the activities of the boys during the day and Bourré would look after their evening's entertainment. He smiled to himself at the irony of the arrangement – he had taken them to the church called Saint-Germain l'Auxerrois. It was nicknamed the 'parish of the Kings', for many kings – including King Louis – had worshipped there. It was famous for its stunning stained-glass windows – the boys had marvelled at the splendour of them, and tonight they would be sampling the delights of young ladies. He pondered how strange the world turned, but King Louis and Warwick had ordered it so and the matter had fallen to Bourré to organise.

Jean Bourré rushed into the room. A tall man, broad chested with a ruddy face, he looked younger than his forty years. 'Sorry, your Grace,' he cried, 'so much to organise, so little time, but I have hired some pretty courtesans, young and fresh for the English boys...'

Cardinal Jouffroy held up his hand. 'Enough,' he said. 'My ears are closed to your duties but make sure it is done discreetly. They are not to know the matter has been organised for them. It must seem to be a natural order of events – a pleasant surprise at the end of a pleasant evening.'

Jean Bourré nodded in agreement, and a smile lingered on his face.

Cardinal Jouffroy looked at him, and then a broad grin broke across his features. 'Jean,' he laughed, 'this is a strange duty we have to perform: me showing them God during the day, and you showing them the sins of the flesh during the night!'

'Aye,' laughed Jean Bourré, 'they won't know if they're coming or going by the time they leave us.'

'But one fact is for certain: they will never forget us, or their time here,' replied Cardinal Jouffroy...

John Tunstall looked on absent-mindedly as their ship docked at St Eloi wharf. The sights of Rouen did not disturb his thoughts. His mind was still back in Paris filled with the girl who had slipped into his bed two nights running, lain naked with him, and guided him through the soft pleasures of her body. She had no inhibitions in her seduction of him, for two nights he had hardly slept.

Her name was Marie and he had first laid eyes on her at Richard's welcoming banquet in Paris, hosted by King Louis' treasurer, Jean Bourré. Her eyes had found him many times during the meal. He danced with her, then talked with her, and even stole a kiss from her as they walked in the royal gardens with only the moon as a witness. She came secretly to his room that night and the next. He did not know where she came from or who she was – she would press a finger to his lips every time he asked a question. On the second morning, John had woken to find her gone.

'Penny for those thoughts, Master John,' said a voice, softly, behind him. He turned and saw Thomas Hallet.

'They're worth more than a penny,' John replied.

'Methinks you were thinking of a girl, and it wasn't Rose.'

John's face started to redden.

'Was it your first time? I mean you and Rose haven't...?' His sentence trailed off as he saw the anger spring into John's eyes.

'Rose must never know,' said John, his face even redder with guilt and embarrassment.

'She will know, Master John, as soon as you kiss her, she will sense the difference.'

'But how?' asked John.

'Saints' shite, if I know!' replied Thomas. 'It's all a whore-sucking mystery to me, but she will know.'

John turned around and looked down on the harbour, his face despondent.

Thomas leant beside him. 'Don't worry, Master John, serving girls like Rose expect young gentlemen to be experienced in these matters, and thankfully, our Lord Warwick has arranged that you now are.'

'Our Lord Warwick had nothing to do with it,' replied John, stiffly. 'She was a merchant's daughter who fell in love with me.'

Thomas smothered a laugh. 'She was no more a merchant's daughter than I am King of England,' he said. 'Why is it that Duke Richard and Lord Francis are walking around with grins as big as half-moons on their faces? I think one of you may have struck lucky with a merchant's daughter, but not all three of you.'

John turned to look at him, understanding slowly filling his eyes. 'You mean...?'

'That's right,' butted in Thomas. 'Me and that brother of mine had to find our own whores, so you can think yourself bleeding lucky our Lord Warwick provided yours.'

John turned and looked down into the harbour, again. He now felt foolish. How stupid of him to think that it had all happened by chance. Thankfully, Thomas had put him right before he made even a bigger fool of himself.

Richard and Francis bounded up the steps to the quarterdeck.

'Thomas, there you are!' cried Richard. 'Have you sobered up from your adventures in Paris?'

'Aye, my Lord, and I hear you had some adventures yourself.'

'I had a wonderful time,' replied Richard.

'The girls were beautiful,' chimed in Francis with a grin from ear to ear.

'We have our Lord Warwick to thank for that,' said John, with sober authority.

'What do you mean?' said Francis.

'What I mean is that the girls didn't happen by chance.'

Francis and Richard looked at each other as John's words settled on them.

'By all the saints in Christendom!' cried Richard. 'You say our Lord Warwick planned it all...?'

John looked at Thomas, who winked at John as he walked away.

Trumpets and drums announced the serving of the grand feast.

John Tunstall took his place in the orderly queue that wound itself into the Great Hall from the adjoining chambers. He had just sat through an hour-long Mass in the Franciscan chapel. There, the monks had prayed that God would bless the enterprise of King Louis and the Earl of Warwick. The chapel was full, for none wished to offend these great men. John was glad to be out of its stifling hot confines. As he entered the grand hall, musicians played bright popular tunes. Jesters or court fools danced and juggled and to everyone's delight, they mimicked the great and small. The nobles sat at the top table and then by rank, the guests carried on down the hall. Servers and pantry maids rushed around placing gold salt cellars, wooden flagons of white or red wine, finger bowls of scented rose water and long thin sticks of French bread on each table. The trumpets sounded, announcing the serving of the first course of thick-spiced broth. The hall was full of chattering noise, laughter, and the smell of wonderful food.

John sat back and watched the ceremony of it all unfold before him. This was their last night in France and because the banquet would stretch well into the night, it had been organised for them to sleep in the friary. *But tonight, no Marie,* he thought, guiltily, and looked across at the Earl of Warwick. When the earl had met them off the ship, he had asked, 'How was Paris, cousin Gloucester?'

'Interesting', Richard had replied, his face like a mask.

Then there had been much smiling and winking from the older men who accompanied him.

John watched as the earl talked to those around him, King Louis listening to his every word. Warwick's small, hard eyes darted everywhere; his ears, John was sure, heard everything. He suddenly felt a yawn coming on, which he tried unsuccessfully to stifle.

Warwick's eyes focused on John, his face breaking out into a rueful smile. 'Too much bed and not enough sleep, Master John,' he shouted down the table. He talked quickly to the men around him. They all started laughing, their eyes turning towards John.

John felt his face go red for he knew what they were all laughing at. Suddenly, a squat ugly man with yellow, sharpened teeth appeared at King Louis' side and whispered urgently into his ear. The king, Warwick, and their close retainers, exchanged tense whispers.

John leant over to Francis. 'Who is that man?' he said.

Francis leant closer to him and whispered, 'Apparently, his name is Etienne de Loup. He is King Louis' cold-hearted butcher.'

'Every king needs one,' whispered Richard. 'My brother has Tiptoft, the Earl of Worcester, to do his dirty work.'

Suddenly, King Louis, Warwick and their senior men, rose from their chairs and followed Etienne de Loup from the hall. A ripple of silence followed them as they strode away.

The guests looked around, unsure of what to do.

King Louis' senior household man walked to the dais. 'Honoured guests,' he said. 'Our lords have been called away on urgent state business, and they have ordered that the festivities continue.'

Within minutes, the Great Hall was abuzz with rumours.

River Seine Estuary, France
15 June 1464

The light flashed in rhythmic intervals from the top of the cliff. Cutting through the darkness it signalled to the ship below.

Philip de Chastle's voice softly broke the silence. 'Time to go, my brave boys; Warwick is aboard his ship.'

Simon Langford felt his stomach muscles tighten. He heard the anchor chains being reeled aboard, the flap of canvas as sails unfurled; the cool night breeze found resistance to its freedom, and the ship slowly moved from its concealment within a small cove, and headed out into the estuary towards the mouth of the Seine.

Simon felt his heart beating harder, and a slight pounding filled his ears. It was a sensation he had felt before when as a young boy his father's murderers had arrived at his manor house, and later during his narrow escape from Middleham Castle. Now, again, excitement and fear mingled within him.

'Simon, gather your men,' said Philip. 'You have the honour of boarding Warwick's ship first.'

As Simon began to move forward, he felt Philip's hand on his shoulder. 'Remember, my friend,' Philip whispered, 'Warwick is a formidable fighter. You must catch him while sleep slows his actions.'

Simon felt the anger at his father's murder fill him. 'I will show him the same mercy showed to my father,' he hissed, coldly.

It was a couple of hours before dawn when they slipped silently into Rouen harbour. Ships' lanterns glowed ghost-white through the thick, sea mist, while their crews slept unaware of this deadly intruder. Slowly, the dark shape of Warwick's ship condensed before them. Nervous mouths tried to swallow their dryness. Weapons that had been checked many times were checked once again. Bodies, taut as bowstrings, stood motionless on the deck as the two ships closed.

'Make ready my lads; look lively,' whispered Philip, as he walked down the length of the deck.

Sailors tensed as they readied themselves, the glint of grappling hooks in their hands. Finally, the silence was broken, and the command came. The grappling hooks flashed out. Sailors grunted with effort as they drew the two ships together.

Simon leaped the gap, and men swarmed aboard after him. A soft ripple, like thunder, sounded as their leather-clad feet landed on the deck. He headed for Warwick's cabin situated in the aft castle, soft light glowing from its windows. As he raced along the deck, he slowed. Something was wrong; a nagging sensation in the pit of his stomach fed his concern. Why had there been no resistance to their boarding? No shouts of warning? He burst into Warwick's cabin, his sword, and dagger ready to strike. There was the answer to his questions, for it was empty, bare of life.

A large candle burned brightly on the table, and a piece of parchment had been placed beside it. The message read, *To my assassins, death my reward.* It was signed, *Warwick.*

Simon looked at the faces crammed into the doorway behind him. Frightened eyes stared back at him as understanding seeped into them. He looked at the message again, then back to the faces now as white as corpses. 'We are betrayed!' he cried.

His men joined in this chorus of despair. 'We are done for!' shouted one. 'We are dead men!' cried another. Other shouts of anger and bewilderment joined in from around the ship as they discovered it was deserted.

Simon picked up the parchment and studied the words in disbelief. 'God, you have deceived me!' he shouted, his anger filling the cabin. He screwed the parchment into a tight ball and hurled it into the corner, and then he heard the hiss of arrows, like an angry wind, rushing over the ship.

Screams of pain rent the air. The tramp of disciplined feet could be heard marching along the wharf towards them.

Simon reached over and extinguished the candle with his fingers. He stood in the darkness, burning with anger. Thoughts raced through his mind with such swiftness he could not catch them.

Slow down, slow down, he told himself. *You must think calmly.*

In the darkness, Simon closed his eyes and reined in his thoughts. He knew they were undone – of that, there was no doubt – but how? Who had betrayed them? Was it the torturer's skill, or had a Judas sold their secret for a purse of silver? How naive to have planned this attack, and not foresee this betrayal; to not have even thought that Warwick would not be here with his men.

Sudden shouts of command from the wharf filled the cabin, and Simon knew that Warwick and his men were making ready their attack. Spurred into action, he raced to a gun port. Thrusting his head out, he saw with horror that their ship, *The Marie*, had gone. 'The bastards have double-crossed us!' he cried to his men.

There was now no escape on the seaward side, and the dockside was bristling with King Louis' and Warwick's men. Simon knew the bastard would be strutting about the wharf enjoying the spectacle unfolding before him. The thought of dying by the hand of one of Warwick's men, using Warwick's steel, as they had done to his father, filled Simon with anger.

The bastards will not kill me so easily, he vowed. Making the sign of the cross, he moved towards the cabin door.

Simon heard the moans of the wounded as he knelt on the deck, his eyes adjusting to the shadowy scene around him. Men were crouched tight up against the side, sheltering from Warwick's archers. He moved up beside them. Looking down on to the wharf, he saw the enemy forming their attack positions, their weapons glinting under the flaming torches that illuminated the wharf.

The man beside Simon cursed loudly. 'Damned whoresons have us trapped like rats. It's only a matter of time before we are food for the fish.'

'Aye, the scaling ladders will be brought up shortly,' joined in another voice. 'Then a quick death is all we can pray for.'

Simon turned around and sat with his back against the wooden side. The situation was hopeless. *Have we come all this way just to die?* he mused. *A pointless journey to extinction, with that bastard, Warwick, standing on our bloody corpses, piled high, the victor once again!* He wondered how things had changed so quickly. He had boarded Warwick's ship with fire in his belly, swift revenge in his heart, and now he was trapped, caught in Warwick's deadly web.

He frantically tried to conjure up a plan of escape, for if things stayed as they were, by dawn, he would be dead, and that was the truth of it. God, he knew, had deserted him. His 'rose of Anjou' slipped into his mind. She had been right when she had warned him of the danger of such a risky mission, and now he would give all he possessed just to hold her for one last moment. He felt his temper rising in frustration. He swore an oath that their lives would not come cheap; it was time to organise their last stand.

Reaching out into the darkness to pull himself up, Simon felt the coolness of metal. He moved his hand around the shape – it was circular. He felt the smooth curve of iron around wood – a wheel. He sat upright.

By all the Saints! he thought. *I am sitting next to a cannon!*

He moved quickly along the deck, keeping his body low as he sought out Sir Henry Billingham and Philip de Chastle. Quickly finding them, he crouched down.

'We are done for,' said Sir Henry, resignation in his voice.

'Aye,' joined in Philip. 'That bastard of a sea captain who brought us here was the one who betrayed us. As soon as we had left his ship, he cut the grappling hooks and high-tailed it away. The bastard's delivered us to our enemies wrapped and packed as neat as a trussed turkey.'

Simon sat on his haunches. 'I have a plan that will save us,' he said, gently.

'There is no plan in Heaven or earth that can save us,' growled Philip, 'apart from growing angel's wings, and flying away.'

'Philip is right,' whispered Sir Henry. 'For none of us can swim, so we are trapped; our retreat is cut off by the black waters of the harbour.'

Simon put a hand on each of their shoulders. 'Listen; they have left the cannons on board. There will be a line of them on a lower deck pointing straight at the wharf.'

'Cannons are no good without cannon balls,' said Philip sharply, 'and they certainly didn't leave any of them behind.'

Simon shook their shoulders. 'It's not hopeless, you fools. Cannon will fire anything as long as its metal and we have the barrel of gunpowder that we brought with us to scuttle the ship once we had dealt with Warwick.'

'Simon's right,' said Sir Henry, slowly. 'We have cannon and gunpowder. All we need is something to fire at the bastards.'

'So if we find some sort of ammunition and fire the guns, what is your plan after that?' asked Philip.

'This is what we need to do,' replied Simon, with urgency in his voice. 'You must find, amongst the men, any with knowledge of cannon or the handling of ships. My strategy is simple: once the cannons are primed, the ropes binding us to the wharf are cut. Immediately afterwards, we will fire the cannon. The force of the recoil will push the ship out into the harbour. The men who can handle the ship will lower the sails. Luckily, the tide is in our favour so Warwick cannot bring up a ship to attack us on our seaward side, but with the tide going out, our escape from the harbour will be possible. Once clear, we will then be in God's hands.'

There was a hushed silence between them. Simon could not discern their faces in the darkness.

A slow chuckle came from Philip. 'It could work,' he said, excitement growing in his voice.

'Aye, we will make it work,' joined in Sir Henry.

'Simon, you clever dog!' exclaimed Philip. 'It's your plan, so tell us our orders.'

Simon stood back from the cannons and watched as the men with experience worked around them. They had found nails and tacks in the ship's carpentry store. The gunpowder charges had been rammed down the barrels, the nails or tacks had been poured in, and the guns were primed and ready for action. The men now stood ready around the ten primed cannons, their bodies bathed in sweat, awaiting the order to fire.

Simon climbed the ladder on to the upper deck, a slim line of pale gold glowed along the horizon, and he knew Warwick would wait for the full dawn before starting his assault. He could just make out the scaling ladders waiting to be slammed against the ship as the prelude to their attack.

Philip de Chastle, bending low, came across the deck towards him. 'It is time,' he said. 'Are the guns primed?'

'Aye,' replied Simon. 'My men know their duty, and yours?'

'Aye, the same,' replied Philip. 'I have fifteen men up the masts waiting to unfold the sails. The others are waiting with axes to cut the securing ropes. Remember, I will blow the whistle once to signal for the lines to be cut; when I blow it the second time, you fire the cannon.'

Simon nodded, and stepped on to the ladder to the lower decks. 'I will await your signal, my friend.'

'And may God be with us,' replied Philip.

Simon arrived on the gun deck as the last of the gun ports were opened.

'Roll out the guns,' shouted the senior man.

The men crammed on the wharf, who were preparing for the assault, heard the guns slam forward. Their movements froze as they saw the barrels protruding from the side of the ship. A voice suddenly shouted in panic, 'Holy Mother, save us.'

Men turned and ran, striving to escape from the guns. Many slipped on the wet wood of the jetty, their screams filling the air as they were trampled. Others were pushed into the black, silent water, their chain mail, and heavy breastplates, dragging them down to a watery grave.

Warwick stood at the end of the wharf, finalising last-minute details for the attack, when he heard the screams. He turned and saw a wall of men rushing towards him and went towards them, his arms outstretched. 'Stop!' he shouted. 'I command you to stop!' It was hopeless; the force of their panic drove them onward. Then he heard a thin whistle. He turned his head towards the ship, and then another whistle rang out. Warwick's brow furrowed in puzzlement.

Glowing tapers touched the firing holes, and flames flashed from the barrels. The thunder of the cannon deafened all. Nails and tacks sped towards the wharf spreading out into a wall of metal fragments a hundred yards wide. It ripped artery from muscle, and muscle from bone. Men exploded, streams of blood sprayed like fountains – the wharf had become a butcher's block. The ship keeled steeply over seawards from the recoil, the swirling smoke from the cannons suddenly hiding her from sight.

Warwick's hard eyes stared at the carnage on the wharf. He stood like a statue, rooted to the spot, his mind unable to grasp the reality of what lay before him.

The thick smoke from the guns slowly started to clear, and he looked for his ship, anger slowly building with him.

Every single bastard on that ship will suffer a slow death for this, he vowed. His eyes strained to make out her shape. At last, the smoke thinned, and Warwick's face changed from anger to bewilderment. 'By the Holy Mary,' he whispered. 'She's gone!'

Admiral Jean de Montauban was a solid, square-shaped man of medium height, highly intelligent, who had started life as a fisherman's son. He was now a close confidant of King Louis, and admiral of his fleet – a man who had risen by capability alone. King Louis promoted and admired ability, not titles, or wealth. Nicknamed 'Hard Fist' by his sailors for the no-nonsense and disciplined way he ran his ships, the admiral had no time for adventurers or pirates within his ranks. He was building a navy that would surpass that of both England and Burgundy.

Standing on the stern castle of his flagship, *St Malo*, Jean de Montauban felt immense pride. She had been built at his instigation, and was the newest ship in King Louis' navy – her design fused the latest revolutionary Mediterranean and European ideas. Her sleek lines, and shallow hull, gave her stability, making her a perfect gun platform. Unlike the old ships, which were bulky, top heavy, and would roll and sway like clumsy barrels, even in a calm sea. An extra mast and sails had been added near the forecastle, making her large, fast, and highly manoeuvrable. Jean de Montauban smiled. *Just how I like my women,* he thought.

They had left Le Havre on the dawn tide. Their orders were to arrive in Rouen harbour mid-morning with the *St Malo* and her sister ship, *St Nazaire*, to escort the Earl of Warwick out through the estuary and into the English Channel; to bid him farewell and a safe journey with a gun salute. The earl, Jean knew, would be astounded at the size and design of these ships. It would make his own little wooden tub look antiquated – outdated. He rubbed his hands together with glee as he anticipated the looks on the faces of the English sailors. He ran his eye over the ship one last time and then gazed over to admire the sleek lines of *St Nazaire* as she sailed alongside.

'Ship on the starboard bow,' shouted the lookout in the crow's nest.

Jean de Montauban brought his spyglass up to his eye. The vessel, he imagined, was probably a large trading cog from Rouen, running silk and lace to Santander, or Bilbao, in northern Spain. 'What do you make of her, captain?' he asked, as he passed the instrument to his second-in-command.

'Well, she's a...' the captain paused in his reply.

'Come on, man,' urged Jean de Montauban. 'You have younger eyes than me.'

'She's a warship,' replied the captain. He lowered the spyglass. 'We need to close for another five minutes before identifying her.'

'Set a course to intersect her,' barked the admiral. 'Signal the *St Nazaire* to follow us.' He stood stock still on the deck, his face set as he waited.

The captain walked to the ship's rail and raised the spyglass. 'She's a warship, all right, and flying English colours. Wait...' he paused, 'there's something odd about her; her sails are set wrong, and she's trying to turn away.'

Jean de Montauban was instantly beside him. Grabbing the spyglass, he hurriedly placed it to his own eye. 'She's flying Warwick's colours!' he exclaimed.

'Something's amiss,' he whispered to himself. 'Something is badly amiss.' He lowered the spyglass, and then straightening his back and squaring his shoulders, he ordered, 'Prepare the ship for action.'

Philip de Chastle's voice sounded across the deck. 'Ships on the starboard bow.'

Simon was in conversation on the lower deck when he heard the shout. He raced up on to the aft castle, his eyes following Philip's raised arm.

Other men joined them. More raced to the forecastle trying to identify the danger.

'They're French,' shouted a voice from the bow.

'But what are they?' questioned another. 'I've never seen so much sail; they must be a new design.'

Philip ordered a change of course. He knew they could not outrun the other ships, but if they could reach land – any land – there was still a chance of escape.

Simon watched the men clumsily try to alter the mizzen sail; others struggled with the main sail. He knew, at that moment, they were condemned; there would be no escape.

Philip shouted for attention, and the men gathered round.

Simon stood at the back of the aft castle alone, and watched the ships racing towards them. Was it only a few hours ago that they had been full of jubilation? Laughing and slapping each other on the back at the wondrous escape? Now, the Grim Reaper was speeding towards them. It mattered little what Philip said; none on this ship had a future. Today, death awaited them all

Admiral Jean de Montauban studied Warwick's ship as they pulled alongside her. There were obviously no professional sailors aboard; her rigging was all to cock. The men on her decks were soldiers, mercenaries, and, he noticed, there were wounded amongst them. His eyes took in a number of bodies laid out neatly. The arrows embedded in the hull, and masts, told him the ship had been taken with force. He turned to his captain. 'It appears these pirates have stolen Warwick's ship.'

'Aye, sir,' replied the captain. 'The mystery is how and why?'

'We are about to find out,' replied Jean de Montauban. 'Prepare to board her.'

Orders flashed around the ship; she moved up along the starboard side and the *St Nazaire* moved in on the port side.

Simon watched the two ships manoeuvre themselves alongside. They dwarfed Warwick's vessel. He looked up and saw archers, their weapons trained on them. Sailors stood ready with grappling hooks and cutlasses – a clear voice ordered them to lay down their weapons. The decision after Philip's speech was to fight to the death, to end this failed mission in glory but now looking at the massed archers, they knew there would be no brave fight, just execution.

Indecision took hold; a single arrow hit the deck in front of the crew. They heard its hiss, and the thump as its barbed head penetrated the deck. As its feathered flights quivered before them, so their courage slowly drained away, and they laid their weapons down.

Simon closed his eyes, his heart heavy. He thought of his 'rose of Anjou', and wondered if he would ever see her again.

St Mihiel-en-Bar, Lorraine, France
1 July 1464

Margaret of Anjou walked silently through the gardens of her château, alone. The garden sloped gently down to the banks of the River Meuse. She paused there and looked across at the City of Verdun. Her father had told her its Celtic name meant 'Fortress that watches the River'. There had been settlements there for thousands of years: Gauls, Romans, and Germanic, and now it was a major point of transit for goods moving north from the Mediterranean and that mysterious dark continent of Africa. Merchandise arrived from the wild, frozen east of Russia; cargoes headed south from England, France or Burgundy. It was a prosperous city bustling with merchants. Church spires crowded the skyline. It was overflowing with men of the cloth who swarmed like flies feeding off her riches; even the Pope had his greedy hand in her wealthy carcass.

Margaret sat down on a small stone seat where she had sat many times with Simon, talking of their plans for the future. Now, while he was gone, she would come down alone. It was here that she felt close to him. She sat silently, watching the muddy, green water rush past. The mid-morning sun reflected silver ripples that danced and glistened on its silky surface. She sat entranced by them, lost in her thoughts.

The hurried footsteps went unheard, but a gentle touch on Margaret's shoulder and a voice she had known all her life broke her melancholy thoughts. She turned around in her seat. 'Oh Papa!' she cried, as she rose to her feet. 'I thought you were in Paris,' She smiled and reached out to give him a welcoming embrace.

Duke René of Anjou stood silent and still, worried lines furrowed his brow, and he nervously bit his bottom lip.

Margaret checked herself. 'What is wrong, Papa?' she asked.

René gently took his daughter's hand, and motioned her to sit down again. Still holding her hand, he sat beside her, his gentle face full of concern. 'I have news of Warwick,' he said.

Margaret's eyes met his; she saw the sadness in them. 'He still lives?'

she whispered.

'Aye,' he replied with a sigh. He saw her face drain of blood.

'And Simon?' she whispered, searching his face, pleading for relief.

God, how he wished her mother, his Isabel, was still alive. This was a hard task for one to do alone. 'They were betrayed,' René said, shaking his head. 'All betrayed; my agent has told me—'

'No!' Margaret cried, putting her hands over her ears. 'Do not say it.'

Duke René took his daughter's hands and pulled them slowly from her ears. A great sob heaved from her, as her head fell on to his chest. He put his arms tightly around her, steeling himself to force out the words he knew would fracture her heart. 'My agent has told me, they were all executed. There are no survivors.'

Middleham Castle, North Yorkshire
20 August 1464

The huge red sphere dominated the evening sky. John Tunstall watched as it balanced on the horizon, its dark centre dissipating a hue of colours that set the heavens ablaze. He felt its warmth waning. This glorious summer's day was now spent, and his hot, tired body welcomed the cool evening air.

He slowed his horse, and looked down the valley. The lengthening shadows seemed to reach out around him, drawing him towards a familiar shape, a huge black silhouette framed by the setting sun.

Middleham Castle loomed before him. Tiny lights blinked out from the village that huddled around its great walls. As he watched these twinkling lights, his mind reflected on the last four months. He had seen violent death and the treachery of men, learnt the tender touch of the fairer sex, and discovered there were more secrets kept on earth than stars in the heavens. Those young, laughing boys, taken that day in the forest, were no more; they had gathered secrets of their own – now that they were young men.

Trumpets sounded out around John. In the distance, great torches of oil and wax flared into life, illuminating the Great Keep. Trumpets replied from its battlements. He saw the Earl of Warwick and his close retainers form up into a tight formation, with the earl at the front, sitting tall and proud in his saddle.

John dug his heels into the sides of his mount and moved up beside Richard and Francis. All three looked at each other and grinned, excitement fluttered within them. They watched as Warwick entered the gate to the Great Keep, to a huge cheer.

As they entered, John's eyes took in the cheering crowd. Over their heads, he saw his mother, standing on the steps of the Great Hall, smiling and waving at him. His eyes anxiously searched for Rose; then with relief, he saw her, standing away from the steps, half hidden by shadows. Throwing his head back, he looked at the heavens and crossed himself; he was home at last!

John sat with Richard and Francis, in the Countess of Warwick's chamber. Rose, Lady Tunstall, the countess' daughters: Isabel and Anne, other ladies of rank, and servants, crowded around them.

Rose was more finely dressed than the last time he had seen her; she had been promoted and was now maid to the countess.

John had just recounted their departure to France from that great city of Portsmouth – its citizens, a brave and hardy lot, who over the years had fought off the Vikings and the French. The Spanish had also tried raiding, along with the Dutch – all had received a bloody nose for their trouble. He told them of Spice Island, the oldest part of the port, where sailors and harlots danced in the street to tunes he had never heard before – sea shanties they called them – and they drank dark, sweet-smelling liquids. It was a place where no one slept and godly people did not go.

Francis recounted their sea voyage to Rouen. Richard told of the wonders of Paris and then the attempt on Warwick's life. All the listeners were spellbound.

Lady Tunstall and the Countess of Warwick glanced at each other and smiled; both had their loved ones back. The castle was alive again – it had been quiet without the earl and his men – with visitors few and far between. Boredom had been their enemy, but now the castle bustled with activity; the garrison was back in their barracks.

Nobles arrived to pay homage to the earl. The Great Controller was ensconced in his office, his clerks working overtime as warrants and orders flew from their quills. Those who had been lax with rent or tax now queued to pay their dues before they were ordered to pay them at the whipping post. The kitchens were busy; the countess and her ladies now had menus to plan, new dresses and elaborate headpieces to design, and gossip from far and wide to discuss.

John looked at Rose as she listened intently to their tales. Her beautiful dark eyes shone with excitement. He had forgotten just how lovely and vibrant she was. He longed to be alone with her. She glanced at him as if she knew what he was thinking. Their eyes met, and a silent message that only loved ones knew, moved between them.

The Earl of Warwick had been in residence for only one week before he departed for Reading. A meeting of the Privy Council had been called to discuss the issue of new coinage, but the earl would use this gathering to announce that his negotiations with the French had been successful. He would say that trade and defence treaties had been signed, and then with a grand flourish he would name King Louis' sister-in-law, the Bona of Savoy, as King Edward's new bride.

John stood on the battlements and watched the earl and his retinue, ride into the distance. He felt slightly envious not to be going with them. The travel and adventure of the last few months would make it hard to settle back into the routine of castle life. He also had not seen Rose for days. Maybe she knew what had happened to him in Paris during those two long nights. He wondered if there was some womanly way she could tell; perhaps there was some special mark on him that only girls could see. Or, maybe, it was simply because she was now maid to the countess, and her time was not her own.

'John,' whispered a female voice, softly.

John spun around, the earl forgotten. 'Rose...you managed to slip away,' he said, with delight in his eyes.

Chapter 8

Witchcraft and Betrayal

Grafton Manor, Northampton
15 September 1464

Elizabeth stared at her mother, her face showing a mixture of temper and disappointment. Her voice hissed out like a whip. 'You swore it was finished, no more sorcery.'

Jacquetta, the Duchess of Bedford, sat in a large oak chair inlaid with red velvet cushions, a present she remembered from Queen Margaret of Anjou when she had been first lady of the land. She shivered; this September evening had turned chilly. A fire had been lit, and leaning towards its heat, she stared intently at the angry young flames as they licked hungrily at the logs. The warmth slowly penetrated her thick clothing. Finally, she sat back and returned her daughter's stare. 'It would have been finished if Edward had announced your marriage, had told the people that you were now Queen of England, but he didn't, did he? It has been four long months since he took you to bed as his wife, and still he keeps you hidden. The longer this great secret continues, the easier for him to cast doubt on its legality.'

'But he loves me!' cried Elizabeth. 'He would never deny me; never betray my love.'

Jacquetta threw her head back and laughed. 'When he grows tired of bedding you; when he suddenly has other more pressing business to attend to, then, my girl, your days will be numbered. Remember, the longer you are apart, the weaker our spell grows.'

'We must have patience,' pleaded Elizabeth. 'Your powers will never be strong enough to control him.'

Jacquetta rose from her chair and stood over her daughter. 'My powers were strong enough to rid myself of my first husband. He may have been a duke and the son of a king, but he treated me as a serving wench. He died on the night of 14 September 1435, at Rouen. As I slipped his wax image into the fire, I could hear his screams; the louder they became, the more tears of joy I cried at my release from him. My powers were strong enough to have King Henry make my second husband – your father – the first Earl Rivers, a Knight of the Garter and a privy counsellor. My potions were strong enough to bewitch Edward to marry you, and so will be strong enough to have him announce to the people that you are his queen.'

Elizabeth leaped from her chair and faced her mother. 'If it is found that we are using the black arts then queen, or no queen, we will be burnt,' whispered Elizabeth, anger in her eyes.

'And if we don't, then ruin awaits our family. If Warwick prevails and wins Edward over, then they will declare your marriage illegal and he will marry the French bride whose name is on Warwick's lips.'

'They cannot undo what is done!' cried Elizabeth.

'They can, and will,' sneered Jacquetta softly, as though addressing a child. 'You will be sent to a convent and forced to become a nun. Your father will be arrested on some trumped up charges, stripped of his titles, and quietly executed in some dark cell within the Tower, and I will be tried as a witch. Already, Hastings is trying to gather evidence against me. God knows what they would do to your brothers and sisters; our family will be erased from the pages of history. So, you see, Edward must announce your marriage. Then, and only then, will Warwick's power over Edward be broken and our family safe.'

Elizabeth slowly sat down in her chair. She studied the fire, and nodding her head, she quietly whispered, 'You are right, there is no other way, but once I am crowned Queen, then no more spell making.'

'Once you are Queen we will have all the power we need, there will be no need of such magic.'

'Is that a promise?' questioned Elizabeth, turning her full stare on her mother.

'Yes, I promise; now come,' ordered Jacquetta, a smile of triumph on her face, 'we must change for the ceremony. The moon is waning; it is a perfect night for witchcraft!'

Reading Abbey
15 September 1464

'Welcome, my Lord,' said the monk, bowing low.

Warwick slipped from his horse and passed the reins to the monk. 'Who is in charge of quartering?' he barked.

A tall, thin, angular monk appeared from the shadows.

'My Lord,' the monk answered, his body bent, his eyes fixed firmly on Warwick's boots.

'See to my men and horses,' commanded Warwick, his eyes as hard as flint. 'Come for me when they are settled.'

'As it pleases my Lord,' said the monk, bowing lower.

Warwick stood alone in front of the high altar within the abbey church. Evening vespers had finished long ago; monks and guests had retired for the night. He knelt before the altar and crossed himself. Looking down, he studied the grave of Henry I, the youngest son of William the Conqueror, who had founded the abbey, and who was buried there in 1136.

He was a wise king, thought Warwick; *a good judge of men and a skilled diplomat who had ruled England well but fought with France. We are very similar, for I rule England through Edward but we differ towards France. I will not fight the French, but will use them as a stepping stone. Tomorrow, when I announce the King's marriage and the alliance between England and France, it will be the start of my quest to wear my own crown, to rule my own realm, for although I own vast lands here in England, they are Edward's lands, and he can give or take them away, for he governs this realm.*

Warwick said his prayers and then took a seat to the side of the altar. He sat, enjoying the peace and solitude. Tomorrow was the beginning of his grand plan to rule his own dominion. Once he was Prince of Holland and Zeeland, and with King Louis already in his pocket, they would carve up Burgundy between them. Then, he would build an empire on the weak rump of Europe. He looked forward to the dawn.

Royal Chambers, Reading
15 September 1464

'Well,' said Lord Hastings, 'Warwick's arrived; lucky for you it's late. You don't have to give him an audience now, but you will have to face him tomorrow.'

King Edward frowned. 'You have the plans in place to expunge my marriage?'

Lord Hastings nodded.

'It is a bad business,' continued Edward. 'Warwick must never know. If he did, his loss of face would be too great to smooth away with more titles and lands.'

'Aye, war would be the result. He would take your throne, of that there is no doubt, and England would have a new king.'

'Better that I should have a new wife, then,' said Edward.

'An easier price to pay,' said Lord Hastings, wryly.

Edward picked up his large wine goblet and drank long from it. Placing it back on the table, he wiped his mouth with the back of his hand. Looking at Lord Hastings, he spoke softly as though he was a condemned man. 'Lord Rivers is to be arrested tomorrow morning?'

Lord Hastings nodded

'The charges for treason are ready?'

Lord Hastings nodded again, and then to spare Edward further distress, said, 'Elizabeth will be taken into confinement. No harm will befall her, although you will never see her again.'

'And the rest of her family?' asked Edward, quietly.

'They will be dealt with in time, your Majesty. The evidence of witchcraft against Jacquetta and the rest of them is still incomplete, but I am nearly ready to bring charges. Their end will be swift and bloody.'

Edward walked to the window, and looked out at the darkness. The stars shone brighter under the waning moon. 'Could we not just banish them from the kingdom?' he asked.

'Death is more final,' replied Lord Hastings.

Edward sighed. It was going to be a long night; he would not welcome the dawn.

Grafton Manor, Northampton
15 September 1464

Gusts of driving wind surged down the deep valley that had been carved out over the millennium by the River Tove. It rattled and shook the windows and doors of the old manor house that stood high up on its southern ridge. Its deserted rooms and hallways vibrated to the sound of the howling tempest.

Elizabeth heard the bolts on the solid oak door slide shut. They were all locked deep within its cellar; safe from prying eyes.

Black candles burned in holders on the wet slimy walls. In the centre, stood a large long table covered in a black cloth. In the front of this, a charcoal fire burned within a brazier. A small cage stood beside it; inside, a black cockerel dozed, from the heat of the fire.

A young woman stood to the side of the altar. She was naked, except for a thin black cloak fastened loosely around her shoulders.

Elizabeth had never learnt the woman's name, or where she came from – only her mother knew that. She looked at her two sisters, Anne and Margaret. They too were naked, as she was herself, except for the thin black cloaks they wore. Nakedness was always part of the ritual. Her mother wore a white gown tied with a golden belt, and a tall straight hat on her head, on which a magic eye was embroidered on the front and the back.

Elizabeth heard sounds from the dark, shadowy corner of the cellar as the unfrocked priest and his assistant were preparing themselves.

Jacquetta began chanting softly in Latin as she marked out the sacred circle around the altar. This circle would be their protection against the forces of darkness. As long as they stayed within it, they would be safe. Satisfied it was complete; she stood by the brazier, perfectly still.

Elizabeth felt the excitement stirring within her. Before these rituals, she hated the thought of taking part, and after, she hated herself even more, but once it started, it was like a drug. Some force within her loved the thrill of the ceremony, the nakedness, the lewdness, the turning of the world on its head – she found it irresistible.

From the corner, a drum started beating out a soft regular rhythm. Jacquetta held her hands out over the brazier; a small white pouch fell and it fizzled in the heat. Suddenly, a green flame rose three feet high, filling the cellar with a wonderful fragrance. As it engulfed everyone, their inhibitions fell away.

Elizabeth loved this feeling of freedom; the green flame was always powerful magic.

The young woman with no name climbed on to the altar and knelt in the middle of it. Her eyes were closed as she gently swayed to the rhythm of the drum.

Elizabeth watched her mother move to the centre of the sacred circle to start the ceremony.

'I call on the foul spirits, evil demons and the fallen angels of the earth,' Jacquetta cried. 'You that feed on murder, incest, torture and all the unclean acts of the word, come to me you evil ones, be obedient to me, you foul apparitions, in the name of Satan, I call on thee.'

The drum became louder; another white pouch fell on to the brazier and a red flame danced on its surface.

Elizabeth and her sisters began moving around the inside edge of the sacred circle chanting:

Air, fire, water, earth; elements of astral birth,
I call on you now – attend to me in this circle,
Rightly cast, safe from curse and safe from blast,
I call on you attend to me.

As the sisters chanted, Jacquetta reached out to the young woman on the altar and slipped the cloak from her shoulders.

It was the signal for Elizabeth and her sisters to do the same. Their thin cloaks fell to the ground and they moved naked through the flickering candlelight, their eyes bright with excitement as they chanted for the demons. Round and round, faster and faster, they danced, the heat making sweat run down their bodies.

Suddenly, Jacquetta shouted, 'It is time; they are coming!'

The defrocked priest appeared within the circle, a gold mask with

209

horns, concealing his face. He stood in front of the young woman on the altar, fully aroused.

Elizabeth and her sisters started chanting louder.

The young woman lay back, and wrapped her legs around the priest's waist. They copulated with a slow rhythm. The black cockerel appeared, a knife flashed and blood cascaded over her breasts and stomach.

The sisters chanted: *Birth to death and death to birth, day to night and night to day.* They chanted faster and faster, smearing the cockerel's hot blood over the priest and themselves. More potions were thrown on the fire.

'I summon you demons of the deep!' cried Jacquetta. 'You spirits of the dark, I command you to obey me!'

The young woman and the priest shuddered, and stopped their fornicating.

'They are here,' whispered Jacquetta.

Elizabeth and her sisters rubbed themselves slowly up against the priest as they peered out into the shadows. Beyond the sacred circle, they could not see, but could feel the presence of green-winged phantoms, snaked-tailed demons, and razor-clawed monsters. They sensed red eyes studying them and heard the echo of infernal laughter.

'May the circle be open and remain unbroken. May the circle be open to the power of Hell; mine to use!' cried Jacquetta. Staring into the shadows, she went to the edge of the circle.

A face was slowly forming by the cellar door. At first, it appeared as just smoke entwined with glowing light. As it slowly moved towards them, the sisters fell to their knees in homage to the Lord of Evil. The presence glided to the edge of the circle, the smoke, and light now formed into a hideous face. Large malevolent eyes, burning red, looked at them. Acrid streams of smoke flowed from the back of its head giving the appearance of writhing snakes. The gargoyle from hell floated downwards until it faced opposite Elizabeth. Flames licked from its mouth. 'I want her,' it hissed. The demon turned towards the priest. 'Take her now,' it commanded.

Looking at the priest, Jacquetta pointed to Elizabeth. 'They want her; they know she wants the crown. Take her!' she cried, as the demon slowly faded into dark acrid swirling smoke.

Elizabeth lay back on the altar, and wrapped her legs around the priest. His strong hands moved over her body, sending shock waves of pleasure through her. She felt their sweat and the hot blood of the sacrificed cockerel mingle as the priest moved against her. She heard the rhythmic chants of her sisters rising to a crescendo. She felt the heat of the brazier as more offerings flashed upwards. She panted for breath as the priest increased his rhythm, her head swimming, her heart pounding.

'They will obey! They will obey!' shouted Jacquetta.

The priest moaned and shuddered violently.

Elizabeth heard her mother's voice again.

'Oh, force of all forces that can penetrate the rocks of the earth, the depths of the oceans, the stars of the skies, whose power will overcome all things, my will is created through you. I command you to make King Edward acknowledge his Queen, who has fornicated as sacrifice to you.'

Jacquetta bent low over a green crystal ball, running her hands over it. 'Look!' she cried. 'The King slumbers; his mind is weak, the time is right. Demons of the underworld begone; your forces of the night, my will to obey.'

A raging wind flew around the cellar extinguishing the flames of the candles. Cackles and screeches echoed into the night, and then suddenly all was still. Only the light from the brazier lit the circle.

Jacquetta slipped to the floor exhausted.

Elizabeth untangled her legs from around the priest's waist, a satisfied smile playing around her mouth. Now, at last, she would be Queen. After tonight, nothing on earth could stop her being crowned. She lay back on the altar, rubbing hot sweat into the cockerel's blood. Slowly mixing it over her body, she watched in a trance-like state, as her sisters, intoxicated with witchery, fornicated wildly with the unfrocked priest and his assistant.

Royal Chambers, Reading
15 September 1464

She came to Edward in his dreams: Elizabeth, naked, lying on a long black table, her legs around him. She was moaning. He felt her soft flesh, smelt her perfume; he was intoxicated by her. He heard chanting, a drum beat, bodies moving in the shadows. She reached up, and pulled his lips on to hers. As she exhaled into his mouth, a force entered his body. He felt its will fill him. Suddenly, she was panting, swooning; sweat glistened on her. He trembled, and then closed his eyes. The ecstasy rolled over him in waves, and then he was falling, hurtling down into a black pit until he hit the bottom.

Edward awoke with a start; hot, sweating, and alone. He ran his hands over his face. He was real enough but Elizabeth was not. It should have been just a dream but it was more, much more; it was touched with a sharp reality.

The royal bedchamber was pitch black. Edward's heart slowed down, and he felt calmer. *Just a dream*, he thought. He turned over and pulled the fur overlay tightly up to his neck. It was then that he heard a sharp cutting sound to the left of the bed, and then another to the right, followed by the scraping of claws, or talons, over stone. There sounded a sinister swishing and rustling.

Almighty God! Edward thought, his stomach churning. *It sounds of leathered wings or tails.* He pushed himself upright, pulling the overlay up to his chin. He thought he saw small, red eyes winking all around in the darkness. He tried to shout but his throat felt as if it was full of sand. He heard a rushing noise, becoming louder and louder.

A wind spiralled around his bed. Stronger and stronger it blew, and the fur overlay flew away. Edward held on to the bedpost for dear life. He knew if he fell, he would hurtle down the black pit into hell.

Hideous screeching filled the chamber, and then a voice of cold evil hissed around the room. Edward saw the creature slowly forming at the foot of the bed, its great, clawed, talons reaching out towards him; its eyes like red, burning coals staring with a malignant evil towards him. He shrunk down into the bed,

'To save yourself, you must acknowledge Elizabeth as your Queen. She must be crowned within the month,' it screeched, its command filling the room.

'I will! I will!' cried Edward, his eyes wide with terror.

'So be it,' hissed the creature. 'If not, you will be mine for eternity.'

A noise, like air rushing out from bellows, filled his ears, as the creature evaporated before his eyes. Then, silence. All was calm.

Edward's arms ached from gripping the bedpost. He stared wildly into the darkness, and then he screamed.

Henry Bourchier, steward of the royal household, stepped out of the royal bedchamber. 'Where is Hastings?' he shouted.

'He is on his way, sir,' replied the master-at-arms. 'I have sent men to fetch him.'

'I need him now; the King is badly distressed.'

The master-at-arms heard the sound of running feet, and turned around. Lord Hastings appeared, half-dressed, sleep still leaving his eyes, scabbard and sword held loose in his hand.

Henry Bourchier beckoned him towards the door. 'Come, William,' he said. 'We have sore need of you.'

As the door opened, the men-at-arms gathered outside silently moved forward, straining to glimpse into the royal bedchamber. The master-at-arms, who had his back to them, whispered tensely, 'Back in line, you nosey bastards.'

Lord Hastings gasped as he entered the room. Velvet cushions, chairs, candleholders, books, and sheets of parchment, lay scattered. The whole room was in chaos, as though a whirlwind had passed through it. Edward was crouched at the top of the bed, his wild eyes continually searching all around.

Sir John Howard stood at the end of the bed, his sword drawn. He saw the question in Lord Hastings's eyes. 'I was checking the changing of the guard with the master-at-arms,' he said, quietly. 'The time was early morning, four of the clock, when we heard our Majesty scream out. We arrived within seconds and found the room as you see it now.'

'What did the King say when you arrived?' asked Lord Hastings.

'He was shouting, "Light, light, for the love of God, bring candles". He has not uttered a word since.'

Lord Hastings moved across to Edward and knelt beside him. 'Your Majesty,' he whispered, gently; 'it is Hastings.'

Wild eyes slowly focused on him, a hand shot out and gripped his shoulder. 'William, thank God you are here!' Edward cried, then pulling him closer, whispered, 'Your ears only, William, your ears only.'

Lord Hastings turned and looked at the two men. 'The King orders the room be emptied.'

Henry Bourchier and Sir John Howard bowed their heads and left, closing the doors softly behind them.

'I dreamt of Elizabeth. She was real; I felt her flesh!' Edward exclaimed. 'And then they came – the princes of darkness – they filled this room, pulling at my very being, my very essence. Where you kneel now was a black pit. I could hear the tormented souls screaming for mercy, trapped in its very depths.'

Lord Hastings stared wide-eyed at Edward. 'You were dreaming, your Majesty, a nightmare that seemed real, you—'

Edward cut him short. 'It was no nightmare!' he cried, through trembling lips. 'Look. Look!' he said, pointing to the floor. 'Look. Cuts and scratches, talons and claws,' he whispered. 'I tell you they were here. The Devil himself spoke to me, ordered me to acknowledge Elizabeth, make her my Queen. My very soul depends on it. She must be crowned…' His voice tailed off.

'This is her mother's doing!' cried Lord Hastings. 'She summoned up these creatures from Hell. She must be stopped, executed…'

Edward gripped Lord Hastings tighter. 'No. No!' Edward beseeched him, his face bloodless.

'Then, what are your wishes?' demanded Lord Hastings.

'You were right, all along,' Edward whispered. 'My wife and her mother do have the dark powers. I now know and believe that to be true, as sure as the sun rises. We must not carry out our plan. You must stop the arrests of her family, not a hair to be harmed on any of them,' he said, his voice trembling with fright. 'I fear for our souls if we go against them. Tell them, outside, that I sleepwalked through a nightmare, and not a word of this to a soul.'

'My lips are sealed,' replied Lord Hastings, 'but I will have to be quick to stop the arrests.' He stood up and hurried for the door. Pausing briefly, he asked, 'What's to be done about Warwick?'

'Better to face Warwick than the Devil,' whispered Edward, as he slumped back on the bed.

Great Hall, Reading Abbey
16 September 1464

The Earl of Warwick had been up before dawn, his excitement for the day cutting short his slumber. With a few of his close retainers, he had walked the banks of the River Kennet, that ceaseless highway that brought raw materials into the town, and then the strong guilds of vintners, fullers, shoemakers and weavers sent their finished goods out on barges that plied their trade to London and beyond. He had bantered with some of the river men, who were relieved that the earl was in such a light-hearted mood. Next, he attended Mass in the abbey church and afterwards had been shown a most holy relic: the hand of St James.

Now, he stood outside the Great Hall, the clerk to the council's secretary standing ready to announce him. Warwick nodded, the huge doors swung open, and he stood looking at the throng of nobility within.

'His Lordship, the Earl of Warwick,' shouted the clerk.

All eyes turned towards the door. The earl was dressed splendidly in rich reds and golds – a vision of power and wealth.

Smiling the smile of the cat that had stolen the cream, Warwick strode into the Great Hall.

King Edward watched with a heavy heart as Warwick took his place of honour, opposite. Glancing around the Great Hall, he noted that all of England's great families were represented there: the Stanleys, Veres, and the Staffords. The Earl of Salisbury was present, as was the Duke of Norfolk, and Edward's own brother, George – the Duke of Clarence.

He felt the sweat on the palms of his hand, and his heart beat a little faster. Although he breathed, the air seemed not to reach his lungs. Had it all been just a dream? Were there no demons or dark pits waiting for him? His mind thought desperately of an escape from uttering the words that sat like bile in his stomach.

Warwick stood up and surveyed the chamber with satisfaction. All the great men of England were assembled to hear his triumph. 'My great

Lords of England,' he began. 'My negotiations with the King of France have been successful. Trade agreements have been signed to allow free movement of goods between our two countries. Our merchandise will also travel through France to Italy, or other countries free of French tax. This opens up a new era of commerce for our merchants that will enrich the treasury,' he bowed to Edward, 'and of course, ourselves. We will rid the country of this pox of a recession.'

The chamber erupted in applause. Warwick held his hand up and the lords settled down. Some leant forward in anticipation to hear the earl's next announcement.

'I have agreed a new foreign policy with King Louis,' Warwick continued. 'We will be sending a thousand of our finest archers and teams of men with our latest cannon, to help him bring the dukes of Burgundy and Brittany under control, thus uniting his kingdom. For this, he will pay the sum of fifty-thousand gold crowns to our Majesty, King Edward.'

Warwick winked at Edward and theatrically whispered from the corner of his mouth, 'That should pay for the upkeep of your mistresses, my Lord.'

The chamber filled with good-natured laughter.

'A strong France,' shouted Warwick, 'united with a strong England, will dominate. Europe, Holland, Spain, or any other country, will not dare challenge us.'

Cheering broke out.

'With no threat from Europe, our navy will sail the seas further than ever before, searching out new lands. We will build an empire that will surpass the Greeks or Romans.'

Those within the chamber rose to their feet, erupting in applause. The great lords thumped the table in delight.

Warwick basked in the tumultuous cheers until they slowly subsided. 'And now, my friends, we come to the hub of my speech.'

The chamber became deathly quiet as the men within listened in anticipation for Warwick's next words.

'I have agreed a marriage alliance between England and France. It

217

will cement all that I have just described to you. The bride for our illustrious King Edward is...'

Warwick paused – always the showman – and the lords, dukes, and earls in the packed hall lent forward in their seats to catch his final words.

Edward looked on in horror. He felt his skin crawl under his clothes. He sat frozen, and then he felt a stirring within him as he remembered his dream: Elizabeth kissing him, the force that entered his body, taking hold, controlling him. He lurched to his feet, his mouth opened. With dread, he felt the words bubbling up. He tried to stop them but could not. 'There will be no French marriage,' he blurted out.

Every head in the great chamber swivelled towards Edward as he felt more words rushing from his mouth. 'I am already married!' he cried.

The chamber froze; nothing moved. The clerks' quills stopped their writing. Servers, suspended in mid-stride, stop their duties. Wine stopped flowing from bottle to cup.

Warwick's world stopped turning. He stood staring at Edward, his body unable to move. The blood in his veins seemed to still, and he thought his heart would stop. Only his thoughts still functioned, three words dominated them: *I am married*. They had destroyed his plans in seconds. His mind raced. *King Louis will think me a fool. The whole world will know of this humiliation*. His heart started beating faster; blood rushed to his face, and he glared at Edward. 'You cannot be married!' he shouted at him. 'Your marriage is an affair of state; we decide!' he gesticulated, swinging his arm around the room. 'Who you marry is for the good of England, not you.'

'I have married Elizabeth Grey,' blurted out Edward, a look of sheer surprise on his face.

'Elizabeth Grey?' exploded Warwick. 'Elizabeth Grey? Who in God's name is she?'

'She is a Lancastrian widow with two children,' joined in Lord Hastings, trying to deflect some of the earl's anger away from Edward. 'It is rumoured that her mother, Jacquetta, Duchess of Bedford, has bewitched our King with—'

Edward reached up and dragged Lord Hastings back into his seat. 'Enough,' he hissed, his eyes wide with bewilderment.

'I know of her; she is a Lancastrian witch!' shouted Warwick. 'Bring her before us; we will have this marriage annulled on the grounds of sorcery.'

Lord Rivers rose to his feet; Warwick's hard eyes swung towards him.

'Sir, you slander my wife and daughter,' cried Lord Rivers, 'and you, Hastings, will pay for those words. You have no evidence to support this ridiculous claim of witchcraft.' Then reaching into his coat pocket, he produced a piece of paper. 'Look. Look!' he cried, waving it about in triumph. 'I have evidence to support mine, for here is the marriage certificate.' His face glowed with smug satisfaction as he shoved it under Warwick's nose.

Warwick stared at Lord Rivers with loathing in his eyes. *That bastard's father has been little more than a squire,* he reasoned, *and Rivers, a greedy, self-seeking weasel. Along with his witch of a wife, they manipulated King Henry to elevate Rivers to a position where he did not belong, and now they have Edward in their grasp.*

'I will have your head for this!' Warwick bellowed at Rivers, 'and...' he pointed a shaking finger at Edward, 'I will have your crown.' As he turned to go, he noticed hands covering mouths. Stifled laughter reached his ears; anger and humiliation flowed through him.

'The King doesn't like riding French whores,' someone shouted, to loud laughter.

They will all pay for this, Warwick vowed. His hard eyes took in all who mocked him, he would remember whom his enemies were.

As the Great Hall erupted with disbelief at what had just taken place, Lord Hastings sat quietly and watched as Warwick strode from the chamber, cutting a giant swathe through the gathered nobility. *The genie is at last out of the bottle,* he thought. *The fight for Edward's throne is about to begin.*

Abbeville, France
27 October 1464

Georges Havart looked around the table. Gathered with him were Pierre de Brézé, Admiral Jean de Montauban, Marshall Rouault, and King Louis' Lieutenant General: Charles de Melun.

'Gentlemen,' Georges Havart began. 'Our King has become an embarrassment to his court. I have never seen him so obsessed regarding the marriage between our two countries. He clings to any rumour that drifts into court, and all his hopes of subduing Brittany and Burgundy rest with the Earl of Warwick.'

'I fear the worst,' said Marshall Rouault. 'Warwick's ambassadors should have been here days ago to arrange the details of the marriage. I am coming to the conclusion that all Warwick promised will not be fulfilled.'

Admiral Jean de Montauban stood up and paced the room, his hands clasped behind his back. 'There are rumours circulating in the channel ports, carried on the lips of English sailors that King Edward has secretly married for love, and with each English ship that docks, the rumour swells.'

'I pray it is unfounded,' replied Georges Havart, 'for Louis desperately desires this marriage and alliance with England.'

The door opened and Etienne de Loup slipped in, his lizard eyes flickering around. 'I have the answers to your questions,' he whispered. 'The Duke of Brittany's vice-chancellor, a man named Rouville, was intercepted last night as he slipped back into France from England, disguised as a friar. I have extracted from him the intrigues of his mission in England.'

Etienne de Loup licked his lips in satisfaction as he remembered his night's work, and continued. 'The Duke of Brittany has promised every assistance for King Edward to re-conquer Normandy, and Edward has allied himself with Brittany to make war on our own King.'

Gasps of disbelief went around the table.

'And the marriage?' blurted out Georges Havart.

'There will be no marriage,' whispered Etienne de Loup, hoarsely. 'That bastard, Edward, has married a widow called Elizabeth Grey.'

Oaths of incredulity filled the room.

'Her mother,' continued Etienne de Loup, 'is the Duchess of Bedford, formally known as Jacquetta of Luxembourg. In England it is said she bewitched King Edward into marrying her daughter.'

'What do you mean, "bewitched"?' questioned Charles de Melun.

Etienne de Loup sat down and made himself comfortable. 'The woman is cousin to the King of Hungary. When she was young, she spent time in the Principality of Wallachia, which is part of Romania. As you know, Hungary and Romania were allies, and together held back the spread of the Turkish Ottoman Empire. The ruler of Wallachia was Vlad III, known as Vlad the Impaler – a great general and a great sorcerer. He was known for the cruel way he treated his enemies and his subjects. It is believed Jacquetta fell in love with this tyrant, and while she was there he taught her his sorcery of the black arts.'

Etienne de Loup smiled, showing off his sharpened, yellow teeth. 'Of course, it is all rumour and superstition,' he said, with a shrug of his shoulders. He rose slowly from his chair. 'My main concern is that she is closely related to the court of Burgundy and I fear will use her influence, be it sorcery or not, to align King Edward with them.'

'Then King Louis' dream of a marriage between France and England is finished,' sighed Georges Havart. 'The reality of civil war is now inevitable.' He rose wearily from his chair, and shaking his head, sadly, he said, 'Come, my friends, we must tell our King to prepare for bloodshed, for that is what lies ahead for our beloved France.'

Part Two

Four years later: 1469–1473

Chapter 9

All for Love

Château Koeur-la-Petite, Lorraine, France
2 August 1469

Margaret of Anjou stood by the window watching her son, Edward, the Prince of Wales, now aged sixteen, practise with pike and sword on the lawn below. Two of her retainers, Sir William Vaux and Sir Robert Whittingham, were both target and teacher to him. The two men had married ladies of her household when she had been Queen in England and now they were part of her trusted inner circle at her small court in France along with the exiled Bishop of St Asaph, who cared for their souls, and Sir Edmund Hampden, who cared for their finances. Margaret looked on with pride, as her son weaved and ducked below her. After the failed attempt on Warwick's life four years ago, and the anguish of Simon's execution, her son had been her only source of pleasure. She had watched him grow from a young boy, to a handsome intelligent young man.

'The boy is becoming skilful,' said a voice, soft with age. 'He will make a fine king.'

Margaret turned, and looked at the old man sitting behind her. She smiled at him. Sir John Fortescue was her chief advisor – he had been her husband's chancellor in the great days of the royal court, and had been loyal to her throughout her exile. He had reached the great age of seventy years, and loved her as a father loved a daughter.

Margaret left the scene at the window and sat down beside Sir John. Taking his hand gently, she looked into his old, fading, blue eyes. 'We will have no talk of kings,' she said. 'Edward will inherit all he needs from my father, then he will marry, have many children, and live a contented life devoted to the arts.'

Sir John smiled. 'Your son is no soft artisan; he is a brave young champion and you, my little Margarita, will not stop him from having his battles. Fighting flows in his blood, although, I don't know where his courage and daring comes from; certainly not from his father,' he said, raising an enquiring eyebrow.

Margaret blushed slightly, and then looked towards the window.

Sir John gently pulled her chin around towards him; he could see the sorrow in her.

Margaret saw the concern in Sir John's eyes and gently squeezed his hand with affection.

'I have news from Doctor Morton,' Sir John said, brightly.

Interest replaced the sadness in Margaret.

'It concerns Warwick. Do you remember when King Edward announced he was already married?'

'Yes,' Margaret giggled. 'Oh, how we laughed when we heard the news of his humiliation.'

'And you recall that Warwick slunk back to his estates to sulk, and plot his revenge,' continued Sir John. 'Well, over the last few years, he and King Edward have been at loggerheads, plotting and sub-plotting against one another, but Warwick's revenge has now started in earnest.

'Doctor Morton reports that King Edward's brother, George, the Duke of Clarence, has secretly married Warwick's eldest daughter, Isabel, at Calais even though Edward had forbidden the union. They have formulated uprisings in the north of England and in Kent, which I presume will lead to open rebellion. The most chilling news is that they captured Lord Rivers, the father of Edward's Queen. Warwick, true to his promise, hacked his head off. River's son, John, was also taken, so Warwick chopped his head off for good measure.'

Margaret rose from her chair, walked to the window, and studied her son. *If Warwick could, he would chop his head off too*, she thought, with a shudder. 'So, the Duchess of Bedford has lost her husband and a son, and her daughter, Queen Elizabeth, has lost a father and brother.'

'Aye,' replied Sir John. 'Warwick has certainly stirred up a hornets' nest.'

Margaret returned to her chair. 'So, Warwick intends to replace Edward on the throne with the brother, George?'

Sir John nodded, 'and his daughter, Isabel, as queen.'

Margaret rose from her chair and paced the room, anger filling her voice. 'Has this barbarian no conscience?' she cried. 'He tumbled poor, feeble Henry from his throne and when he was finally captured in sixty-five, paraded him through the streets of London on a donkey with his feet tied to his stirrups and a straw hat jammed on his head.' Her voice sank to a sad whisper. 'He made a mockery of my poor husband who now awaits his fate in that grim Tower...' Raising her fists tight in anger, she cried, 'Then, he places Edward on the throne and when he loses control of him, decides to replace him with his weak-willed brother, George. The man must have been spawned by the Devil and delivered from Hell. He is a cruel savage who feeds only on the domination of all around him.'

Sir John, his arms outstretched, moved to calm Margaret. 'He has not replaced King Edward yet,' he said, softly. 'Remember, the man is no poor feeble Henry.'

The knock was so loud, it stopped their conversation dead. Margaret and Sir John stood quietly as the anger within the room faded away. Margaret closed her eyes and cleared her head. She heard Sir John call 'Enter'.

Lady Whittingham entered the room, closely followed by Lady Vaux.

Margaret smiled. 'Ladies, what warrants our attention so urgently?'

'There is a gentleman arrived,' said Lady Whittingham, breathlessly.

Lady Vaux brought her hands up to either side of her face and shaking her head she cried, 'My Lady, his face is so severely scarred, tis hard to make out his features; we should send him away, you should not have to countenance him.'

Lady Whittingham made for the door. 'I will go...'

Sir John raised his hand. 'Ladies, stop. I feel there is something you have not told us.'

'We do not want our Queen upset,' blurted out Lady Vaux, as her companion moved closer to the door. ''Tis best he goes.'

Margaret rose from her chair. Her two ladies-in-waiting moved closer together. 'Who is this gentleman?' she asked softly.

'He calls himself Captain Malortie,' whispered Lady Vaux.

'And why is he here?' asked Margaret.

The two women stood, wringing their hands.

Lady Whittingham stepped forward. 'He says he has a message from Pierre de Brézé.'

Margaret slowly lowered herself down on to her chair, her face turning white. Lady Vaux rushed to kneel by her side.

Margaret looked at Sir John. 'How can this be?' she stammered. 'My dear Pierre was killed at the Battle of Montlhéry, four years ago. Does this man speak with ghosts?'

'Well, tis best we ask him,' said Sir John, firmly. 'Fetch him in.'

Captain Malortie strode into the room. His long, worn-out, riding boots were caked with the summer dust of the wheat fields; his uniform faded and threadbare.

Margaret could just make out, under the dirt, small patches of Pierre de Brézé's colours on his uniform. He stood tall and proud and when he raised his face to her, she did not cry out or gasp. Her two ladies-in-waiting moved quickly behind her chair, like young girls hiding behind their mother's skirt.

Margaret studied the man's face. The lower half of his nose was missing, and his right eye drooped downwards. The sword-cut responsible had left a scarred white furrow from the top of his head to the bottom of his jaw. His mouth was drawn down on the right, where another scar cut across the first one making an 'X' across his butchered face.

Captain Malortie spoke. 'I am sorry to appear before you, your Highness. If my news was unimportant I would not trouble you to look upon my features.'

Margaret was surprised; his voice was young and firm, attractive to the ear. 'How old are you, captain?' she asked.

'Twenty-six years, last month,' came the reply.

Margaret's heart went out to him. 'My poor boy,' she whispered. Turning to her ladies, she said, 'Fetch a chair for our guest, and bring wine.'

Lady Vaux passed a goblet of wine to the captain, her arm at full stretch as though he had some contagious disease.

'My ladies have told me you have a message from Pierre?' questioned Margaret, 'and as he has been dead these last four years, this makes a puzzle in my mind.'

Captain Malortie took the goblet and sat down. 'I fought alongside Pierre. I was there when our great Seneschal of Normandy fell.'

Margaret's hand shot to her mouth. 'You were with him when he died?' she whispered.

'Aye, we fought side by side.'

Margaret lowered her hand. 'Then, you must tell me everything.'

Captain Malortie raised his goblet to his lips and drank slowly, and then making himself comfortable, he began. 'The date was 16 July 1465. On that morning of the Battle of Montlhéry, a council of war was called by King Louis. The King announced that Pierre would lead the advance guard – a great honour – and would position himself on the right flank. The King would hold the centre, or its correct name, "the centre battle", and his uncle, the Count of Maine, would hold the left. Then, the King gave a quick no-nonsense speech that soldiers on the eve of battle wish to hear.'

'What did he say?' asked Margaret;

'He said that although we were outnumbered two to one, they had no men of worth in their ranks, their cause was unjust, and we had God on our side. Also, they were traitors to France, the King, and to the memory of Joan of Arc.' Captain Malortie scratched his head. 'There was more, but my injuries make it lost to me.'

'Continue with your story,' said Sir John. 'I think we have the gist of his words.'

'Pierre, I, and the other captains, marshalled our troops and moved up along the northern ridge of Montlhéry – a great northern slope sweeping down on to a plain a mile across. As the ground swept up on the other side, we could see the Burgundian host spread out along its heights. Archers stood behind sharpened stakes, the proudest knights of Flanders, Hainault, Picardy, and Artois, stood with their armour shimmering in the morning sun, their standards and banners fluttering in the breeze. The colours of gold and red, blue and silver, black and violet filled our eyes – oh, it was a sight to see,' sighed Captain Malortie. He paused and drank the last of his wine.

'More wine for our brave captain,' ordered Sir John.

Lady Vaux scampered off to refill the captain's goblet, praying that she would not miss too much of his story.

'And so, there we all waited,' continued the captain. 'They lined up on their side and we on ours; Pierre, the great Seneschal of Normandy, and his forces, to the right; Marshall Armagnac and Écorcheur Salazar stood in front of the King's forces in the centre, and the Count of Maine on the left. The sun shone mercilessly on our polished armour, the wind whipped up powdery dust from the plain. Men stood with no water for hours; the enemy was unsure of itself, but we had to wait in the heat for them to make the first move.'

'Why?' asked Margaret, softly.

'Well, our force was made up mostly of cavalry, so a full-frontal assault on their defensive positions would have been suicide.' Captain Malortie paused and drank from his refilled cup.

'Slowly,' he said, 'the Burgundy infantry began to march across the plain towards us. We watched as they struggled through the rich, yellow corn, and heavy vine fields, then our trumpets sounded out across the plain. Their advancing troops stopped, hesitant in their tracks, and then Pierre gave the signal. Our squadrons began moving slowly down the slope, with our lances swung down, and the sun rippling off their deadly points. We spurred our horses faster, galloping straight for the centre of the advancing army.

'The Burgundy cavalry raced to engage us, their foot soldiers were trampled between us, and then our two forces clattered together, hacking, and thrusting. Pierre rode on alone into the centre of the enemy. I tried to follow him, your Highness,' said the captain, anguish in his voice, 'but the enemy swallowed him in a wall of steel. I saw a sword thrust though him, and then I myself fell. My wounds,' he said, 'testify to the truth.' He stared into his wine, lost in his thoughts.

All eyes in the room stared at him, not a breath was taken.

Slowly, Margaret brought her mind back from the battle. 'So, you do not know what happened next?' she asked.

'Well, I know that we had ripped a hole in the enemies' lines, thrown them into confusion and our grateful King took full advantage. The day was his.'

'And yourself?' asked Sir John.

'I was left for dead. Some peasants, who were burying the dead, found me. They tended my wounds as best they could, and then sold me to the enemy for a few pieces of silver. They then asked a ransom for me which our King Louis had to pay, but I had to wait four long years for my freedom. Our King was still fighting for his kingdom so had more on his mind than me.'

'Aye, the crown on his head was his first concern,' said Sir John.

Margaret sat back in her chair and studied the young captain. She took in his threadbare uniform, his lank and dirty hair, the tiredness that hung on him as a cloak. 'Tell me,' she said, 'have you travelled here straight from your release?'

The young captain nodded, 'Aye, your Highness.'

'And where do you go from here?' she asked.

'I do not know,' he replied, sadly. 'With this,' he said, pointing to his face, 'I do not think I will be welcome anywhere.'

Margaret's eyes filled with compassion. 'For your courage, you are welcome here,' she said, softly. 'My small court would be the richer for your presence.'

'It would be an honour to serve you as our brave Pierre de Brézé once did,' the captain replied.

'Please, continue,' broke in Sir John. 'What is this message you talk of?'

Captain Malortie rose from his chair and stood before them. 'On the eve of the battle, along with his other captains, I dined with Pierre. We drank, as soldiers do, to death or glory for the coming day. When he dismissed us, he asked me to stay behind. He talked of a secret he held, concerning you, my Lady.'

Margaret stiffened in her chair but remained silent.

'Pierre had said he was honouring me with his trust and if he died on the morrow then I must deliver this message to you and alas, as you know, on the morrow he did die, but because of my captivity it has taken me four long years to carry out his wishes.'

Sir John looked anxiously at Margaret. 'Pray, continue,' he urged.

'You will all remember the daring attempt on Warwick's life at Rouen in sixty-four. All the conspirators were caught and brutally executed by Etienne de Loup.'

Margaret's hands gripped the arms of her chair. Her two ladies knelt with concern at either side of her.

Sir John saw tears forming in Margaret's eyes. He felt his temper rising. It had taken his Queen a long time to come to terms with Simon's death, even longer for her to smile again. 'Enough!' he cried, 'you are distressing our Lady.'

Captain Malortie stepped back, holding his hand up. 'The message I promised to deliver is that one man was spared execution, and only spared on Pierre's insistence with King Louis.'

Within the room, the world stopped turning for a brief moment and all eyes swung towards the captain.

'The man's name,' he said, quietly, 'was Sir Simon Langford.'

Margaret sat motionless. A tree struck by lightning could not have been ripped more asunder, so sudden and fierce was the shock she felt. Simon, still of this world, living flesh and bone – the thought of touching him, talking to him and, dare she imagine, being held by him, made her heart beat faster. Her body tingled with excitement and fear – fear that he had not survived, fear that he had died alone and forgotten.

Sir John watched the emotions ripple through Margaret. He prayed the young captain was not raising her hopes, only for them to be cruelly dashed. He knew she would never recover a second time. 'Why was Simon Langford not executed?' he asked.

Captain Malortie resumed his seat, fully aware of the depth of emotion his message had unleashed in this Lady of Anjou.

He leant forward so that his answer to Sir John's question was addressed directly to her. 'Because he was close to your heart, my Lady, Pierre managed to convince the King that Simon may have a use; a royal bargaining chip he could use at some future date. He told the King of the deep love you had for Simon, in order to save his life, believing that after the war was over, he could convince the King to release him back to you.'

'But that was four years ago,' Margaret said, her face crumbling with emotion. 'He may never have survived that long in one of Etienne de Loup's prisons.'

'Pierre said he had left money with the gaolers for his upkeep,' replied Captain Malortie, trying to offer her some hope.

'But that would have run out long ago,' Margaret cried, desperation in her voice.

Sir John saw the anguish that was filling her. He decided to end the speculation and take charge of the situation. Taking her hand, he looked into her beautiful eyes; eyes that were now brimming once again with tears. 'We must believe that Simon still lives,' he said, with firmness, 'so we must act immediately. No second must be wasted in obtaining his freedom.' He turned to the captain. 'You must tell us where he is incarcerated.'

The captain looked nervously at Sir John and Margaret. 'He is held at Conciergerie Prison,' he whispered.

Margaret rose from her chair. 'That is Etienne de Loup's personal fiefdom; no one ever leaves there alive!' she cried, as she slumped back down again.

Captain Malortie knelt before her. 'If it pleases my Lady, I will leave immediately to ask for information on him.'

Margaret reined in her emotions. Sir John looked at her with pride as her resolve stiffened.

'If Simon has survived, and pray God that he has,' Margaret said firmly, 'then it will be my voice he hears first, and my words that will comfort him.'

La Conciergerie Prison, Paris, France
1 September 1469

The man looked at the leather straps binding him to the solid, oak chair; their original light colour was stained with shades of dark brown and black. He wondered what had caused this staining until he realised the only liquid found in this chamber was blood. A moan of anguish left his lips as he struggled helplessly. He looked slowly around the chamber.

A large charcoal fire glowed from a grate positioned four feet from the floor. Long irons with wooden handles protruded from it. A selection of knives and pincers hung in racks to the left and right of the fire. It reminded him of a butcher's shop and with sudden horror, he realised their purpose.

'No God, please,' he moaned, moving his head from side to side. He looked down on his nakedness, his genitals hung down through a small hole in the middle of the seat. He looked back to the knives.

'Oh, Holy Mother,' he whimpered, as tears of fear rolled down his cheeks.

The faint sound of footsteps approaching turned his stomach. His limbs shook, and he looked wildly around the chamber, fighting desperately with his restraints. Knives, thumbscrews and fire, ropes and pincers, swirled before his eyes in a kaleidoscope of horror.

Etienne de Loup entered the room, holding a jacket in his hand. He was followed by a short, thickset man, with hands like shovels, and eyes as cold as fish.

Etienne de Loup smiled at his prisoner. 'Is this your jacket?'

The man's eyes widened with dread. A strained gurgle came from his throat.

Leaning over, Etienne de Loup gripped the man's hair. 'When I ask you a question, you will speak,' he shouted. 'Now, let me ask you again: is this your jacket?'

'Yes...yes...' the man sobbed.

Etienne de Loup stood up, and pulled out a letter that had been sewn into the lining.

The prisoner stared at it with terror. 'I will tell you everything!' he shrieked.

The thickset man pulled a red-hot poker from the fire.

'Oh, I know you will,' smiled Etienne de Loup. 'I know you will.'

Royal Palace, Hôtel Saint-Pol, Paris, France
25 September 1469

King Louis sat comfortably in a large, well-cushioned chair; flames gently flickered in the rich ornate fireplace. The room was small, and hung with rich tapestries. He thought it was an intimate room, a room where a small group of close friends would play cards or swap gossip while enjoying fine wines. He sighed as he ran his hand slowly over his forehead and he looked at the two frightened men standing in front of him. He had thought them loyal friends, but Etienne de Loup had once again proved him wrong. Looking at the two of them, he reflected on the last five years.

Since the failed alliance with his good friend, Richard Neville, the Earl of Warwick, he had worked hard to unite his kingdom. He had won the Battle of Montlhéry, withstood the great siege of Paris and signed the treaty of Saint-Maur-des-Fossés in September 1465, which had united all the princes of the realm behind him, except for Brittany and Burgundy. Then on 16 July 1468, his armies had thrust into Brittany. His royal squadrons had advanced with speed, destroying all in their way. The Duke of Brittany surrendered signing the Treaty of Ancenis, where he swore to obey the King 'for and against all' and renounced his alliance with King Edward of England and the Duke of Burgundy. His brother, Charles, Duke of Berry, had sworn his undying loyalty to him in exchange for the Province of Guienne. This had left only the Duke of Burgundy to tame, and then on 1 September 1469, Louis had signed the Treaty of Péronne, finally bringing a fragile peace to France after five long years of conflict.

'Etienne, come closer,' King Louis commanded.

Etienne de Loup scurried forward, bowing as he moved towards the king. As he stopped, his head turned towards the prisoners, his eyes glinting with pleasure, a triumphant smile revealing his sharpened teeth.

The two men shuddered and turned their heads away.

'Etienne,' began the king, 'tell my royal advisors why these two traitors are standing before us.'

Unblinking lizard eyes slowly scanned the room, settling on the two prisoners. 'Cardinal Balue, and Guillaume de Haraucourt – the Bishop of Verdun, have plotted to expose our King to great peril. They sent instructions by way of a joint letter…' Etienne de Loup held the letter up for all to see.

'The letter was found sewn into the lining of their servant's jacket; it was addressed to the Duke of Burgundy, urging him to incite the King's brother to reject the royal gift of Guienne, and then prevailing on them both to take up arms against our most royal King. These ecclesiastic plotters have confessed their intentions. They wished to rule our King and his kingdom by inciting the dukes and princes of the realm into open rebellion.' Etienne de Loup licked his lips as he looked at the two prisoners, then he shouted with rage at them. 'And for that, you two hypocritical bastards of the cloth will pay a grievous price.'

The two men fell to their knees, in terror. Etienne de Loup seemed to grow in stature before them, his lizard eyes glinting red with anger, his yellow sharpened teeth glistening with intent.

The Bishop of Verdun pleaded for forgiveness.

Cardinal Balue regained some of his composure; his small beady eyes looked around with arrogance. 'Your Majesty,' he said, turning his soft plump face towards the king. 'The Pope would refuse any proceedings against us. He would not permit us to be tried in a common court. Only he can judge us, so you must stop this stupid charade and release us into his custody.' A note of triumphant laced his words; a small sneer flitted across his opulent features as his confidence returned.

Etienne de Loup stepped forward and smashed his fist hard into the side of Cardinal Balue's face, sending him sprawling. The cardinal's eyes glazed over; his mouth opened and closed in shock as his blood dripped on to the white marble floor.

'Do not dare to look or address our King without permission, you traitorous bastard,' Etienne de Loup snarled, as he kicked the cardinal in the ribs.

Cardinal Balue screamed, and then rolled over moaning, his eyes now full of fear.

King Louis held up his hand and Etienne de Loup bowed and moved to the side. He studied the two men. He felt neither anger nor sadness for them, just weariness, and an acceptance that men could betray their loyalty to him so cheaply.

'Prisoners Balue and Haraucourt,' began King Louis, with frustration. 'Over the last five years, I have worked tirelessly to unite France. I have fought battles, signed treaties, and used diplomacy to secure my kingdom. I have not sat on some opulent throne surrounded by fawning courtiers, but have lived hard, and ruled from the saddle. During this time, you have lived in your palaces gathering wealth and mistresses while your parishioners work and starve to support you. I have turned a blind eye to your rich excesses, and your weakness for the soft delights of the flesh, for you are only men, but your plots of treason I will not ignore.' He rose from his chair, and stood looking down at the prisoners.

The royal advisors stood silently, watching the trembling priests.

'You will be taken to La Conciergerie,' announced King Louis, 'stripped of your clothes of office, and then whipped to within an inch of your miserable lives. I order that you are to work every day cleaning the latrines. You will eat humility daily as you reflect on your fall from privilege. You will dream of your past lives and pray for a sliver of the comfort that you used to know. Your sentence is ten years within Etienne's regime, after which, you will be exiled from France on your release, should you survive.' He dismissed them with a wave of his hand.

Etienne de Loup dragged the priests away to start their punishment.

Slowly, King Louis lowered himself back into his chair. He looked up at Georges Havart who was moving towards him. 'Tis a bad business, Georges; when even the clergy wish to steal my kingdom.'

'It will never happen again,' laughed Georges Havart. 'When others see those two shovelling shite for the rest of their miserable lives, they will think twice before duplicating their actions.'

Antoine de Chabannes, master of the royal household, entered the room. 'Your Majesty, you have an unexpected visitor,' he said, in clipped tones.

King Louis looked at the man who ran his household. He thought it strange, how certain traits in people's characters suited certain professions. Antoine de Chabannes, with his manner of speech, attention to detail, orderliness, and discipline, was born to run a royal palace.

'Margaret of Anjou requests to see you; it concerns a Sir Simon Langford,' continued Antoine de Chabannes, shrugging his shoulders with ignorance of the name.

King Louis and Georges Havart exchanged glances. The name instantly brought memories of the attempt on Warwick's life, five years previously.

'Where is she?' asked the king.

'She awaits in the antechamber to the throne room,' Antoine de Chabannes replied.

'Tell my cousin, I will attend her shortly. In the meantime, offer her our hospitality.'

Antoine de Chabannes bowed, and then left the room.

'I had forgotten the man existed, until De Chabannes spoke his name!' exclaimed Georges Havart.

'Are you sure that he still does exist?' replied King Louis, a perplexed look on his face. 'I know Pierre paid money for his upkeep but after he lost his life at Montlhéry…' He stopped, his face frowning in thought. 'But, I have no idea if the man is dead or alive,' he admitted.

Jean de Reilhac, the king's secretary, spoke out. 'With no money, he would have ended up in the oubliettes – the forgotten places,' he said, grimly. 'Not many survive in those dark, damp, rat infested cells. If the plague or some other disease hasn't killed him then he has probably starved to death.'

'Some men survive all that Conciergerie can throw at them,' said Georges Havart. 'Not many I admit, but a few do outwit her.'

'The question we should ask ourselves is this,' said Jean de Reilhac. 'If he has survived, what use is he to us?'

'Ah, *Jean de Cleverness*!' exclaimed King Louis, with a smile, using his secretary's nickname, 'has hit the nail on the head.'

La Conciergerie Prison, Paris, France
1 March 1470

Dawn was breaking as the clatter of hooves stopped. An ominous silence settled over the riders. Margaret of Anjou and her small party, comprising of Sir John Fortescue, Captain Malortie, and Sir Vaux, had arrived at Etienne de Loup's personal fiefdom.

Margaret looked up and shuddered. La Conciergerie Prison rose up before her, its huge towers disappearing skywards into the grey, half-light. To the right, stood Caesar Tower, named in honour of the Roman emperors; to the left, the Silver Tower, so named for its use as a royal treasure store, and in the centre, the Bonbec Tower. She quickly crossed herself, for she knew that tower housed Etienne de Loup's torture chambers where he encouraged his victims to 'sing'.

Glancing the other way, she watched the muddy brown waters of the Seine slipping silently past. She supposed there must have been many who would have willingly welcomed a quick watery death, a final icy embrace, rather than face the horrors that awaited them within the gates of La Conciergerie.

She looked down at the letter she was holding tightly in her hand. King Louis had given it to her, the royal authority she needed to enter the prison and seek out Simon. The king, though, had gently refused her request for his freedom, and she had not pursued the matter too hard fearing that he may refuse her completely. So, for now, she would pay for the best accommodation within the prison and the finest food. Simon would have the pick of everything; his freedom she would obtain later. Her eyes were drawn back to the grim forbidding walls of the prison and her stomach churned. Tears stung her eyes, and a sob forced its way from her lips.

What if he is dead? she thought. *What if…?*

A hand gripped her shoulder, and she looked up into the steady eyes of Sir John Fortescue.

'We will find him,' he said, firmly, 'but only if I have the Queen of

240

England beside me; someone with the bearing to make these gaolers jump.'

Margaret dried her eyes, and straightened her back. 'You have your Queen, sir!' she cried.

'Well then, what are we waiting for?' said Captain Malortie. 'Let us begin, for we know La Conciergerie never sleeps.'

The small door set in the great gate slowly opened. Margaret, and her companions, entered inside. The guard told them to wait just inside the gate while the senior gaoler was summoned. As they waited, the small group looked into the heart of the prison with a mixture of horror and fascination. In the old days, when the prison had been a royal residence – the *Grande Salle* – the Great Hall had been the dining area for the two thousand staff, but now small metal cages were suspended from the ceiling, no more than four feet square, with a prisoner crammed into each one.

Margaret's hand went to her mouth in dread, as she searched for signs of Simon. *The poor wretches in them can neither stand up nor lay down,* she thought.

'Only important prisoners end up in those,' said the guard, who had followed her gaze upwards. 'We sometimes let them out during the day, but at night they all hang with the stars. No escape, you see,' he said, with satisfaction.

Margaret looked on as two naked men were cut down from whipping posts, their backs ripped open and bloodied. One lay down on the floor, silent in shock; the other sobbed uncontrollably as he was rammed into one of the small iron cages. Around the base of the whipping posts, Margaret noticed the colour of the cloths that had been ripped from their fat bodies. Rich reds and mauves showed they were men of God. She looked at the guard who saw her questioning look.

'Oh… they were Cardinal Balue and the Bishop of Verdun, until they entered here. Now they're nothing,' the guard laughed, 'and in here for treason against the King.'

Three men walked towards them along the side of the Great Hall.

Margaret turned to meet them and the guard stiffened to attention. The tallest of the men, who Margaret identified as the senior gaoler, stood before her and bowed his head before speaking. 'My Lady of Anjou, what brings you to such a place as this?' His puzzled eyes examined her.

Margaret handed the man her royal Letter of Authority. She studied him as he read it. He was tall and well built; she guessed his age to be about forty years. His face looked as hard as granite. *To be the senior gaoler in La Conciergerie, his heart would have to be made of flint,* she thought.

'Fetch the book,' the man barked to one of his assistants. He handed the letter back to Margaret. 'When was this Simon Langford sent to us?' he asked.

'He was given into your care during July 1464,' replied Margaret.

The man laughed. 'That is more than five years ago, and as you can see, care is not a word that is used in a place such as this,' he said, sweeping, his arm around the Great Hall.

The assistant returned hurriedly, carrying a large book bound in black leather. Opening it, he quickly turned the pages. Finally stopping, he ran his finger down the page he had selected. 'Ah, I have him!' he exclaimed. 'Sir Simon Langford, an Englishman, imprisoned for treason, attempted murder of a royal prince. Piracy...' He paused, and gazed into the distance as he concentrated his mind. 'Ah, yes! I remember now; it was the attempt on the Earl of Warwick's life. All the other conspirators were executed – I remember a Sir Henry Billingham. For some reason, he had his tongue ripped out before he was executed.' He studied the book again. 'Yes, it's here. The King ordered this Simon Langford be detained. Pierre de Brézé paid for his upkeep until the end of 1465 then all payments ceased,' he said, as he closed the book.

'So he is still alive?' whispered Margaret.

The senior gaoler raised his hands and shrugged. 'Maybe yes, and maybe no.'

Margaret stepped towards him, her steely eyes flashing, and the senior gaoler stepped back.

'He had better be,' Margaret hissed. 'The King commanded no harm was to come to him, and the King is now very interested in his well-being, so for your sake you had better pray that he lives.'

'But, my Lady; disease, cold, even murder, there are many things that could have claimed him,' the senior gaoler protested.

'If he lives,' said Margaret, coldly, 'then so will you. If he is dead, then the King will have your head and more,' she said, looking at the other assistants.

Her words had galvanised them and more guards were gathered.

Sir John looked on; his Queen had certainly made them jump.

The senior gaoler, after a brief discussion with his men, turned to Margaret. 'Your Englishman should be on levels three or four. I will go with my men and search these cells immediately.' He turned to go.

'Stop!' shouted Margaret. 'I am coming with you.'

The senior gaoler looked horrified. 'Madam,' he spluttered, 'it will be no place for a woman. There will be sights that a lady should never look upon. I beg you to wait for our return.'

'It is not a request,' Margaret said, firmly. 'It is an order. Lead on.'

Margaret stood at the entrance to level three. The senior gaoler had been right; she had seen men with broken, tortured bodies; mad men, and dead men. Shouts and screams had filled the air, but now, deep in the bowels of the prison, a chilling silence filled the subterranean vaults, with just the occasional moan from one of the many cells that ran the length of the passageways. Candles burned in holders spaced along the walls throwing out small circles of light; darkness and shadows mixed eerily within the flickering glow. At the far end of the passageway, the senior gaoler was questioning the duty guard who sat at a small desk. Margaret saw the guard shaking his head in response.

'We shall have to check every cell,' the senior gaoler commanded.

Keys rattled, doors opened, prisoners held their hands over their eyes as the light from many candles flooded their cells. The guards went from cell to cell.

'He is not on this level,' said the senior gaoler, finally.

The guards started checking the cells on level four; Margaret followed close behind them.

'This one looks empty,' said Sir John. He saw Margaret's shoulders slump with the despair at the horror she had seen.

Tears welled up in Margaret's eyes. 'We are running out of dungeons to search,' she said, with anguish in her voice.

Sir John held his lantern high into the cell. It was wet with slime, the air dank. He shuddered at the thought of being locked inside, then, as he moved to go, a gleam of light simmered from the far side of the chamber. He swung the lamp, again. Light flickered out from what appeared to be a pile of rags in the corner.

Sir John and Margaret looked at each other, and then gingerly went forward, their lamps held high. Bending low, their eyes searched amongst the rags for the source of the light.

Suddenly, Margaret choked with emotion. There amongst the rags was the sapphire ring she had given Simon when he had left Bamburgh Castle to begin his spying mission at Middleham. It had caught the light from the lanterns. Then, the hand it was attached to, moved.

Margaret's heart seemed to stop, and she knelt down. 'Simon?' she whispered. Then her voice rising with urgency, she cried, 'Simon, my love.'

A head with long, matted hair and a face with a beard appeared. Two eyes opened, blinking into the light. Finally, they focused on Margaret, and a hoarse whisper came from lips that could not be seen. 'Marguerite...'

Chapter 10

Traitors Unmasked

Windsor Castle, England
1 March 1470

Elizabeth looked up from her embroidering and studied her husband: his face was animated and flushed. Anger pushed his eyebrows together and tightened his jaw; his hands moved passionately to emphasise his words. Gathered around him were his most trusted captains, the Duke of Norfolk, the Duke of Suffolk, Lord Howard, and Edward's most trusted friend, Lord Hastings, whose influence over her husband she detested. She knew he was still searching for evidence of witchcraft against her and her mother, but it was four years ago since they had last practised the black arts and the trail had now gone cold. He had accused them at the council meeting at Reading when her father had produced the wedding certificate that had spiked Warwick's guns. They had decided to let him get away with it then because Edward knew of their magic and they could not risk upsetting him by silencing Lord Hastings, but eventually they would have to find a way to destroy him.

My family are becoming more powerful at court as my brothers and sisters marry into the nobility, Elizabeth thought. *When I produce a male heir, my position will become even stronger, and then*, she considered, with a shiver of excitement, *Hasting's position will die. But first, the demise of Warwick has to be realised.*

Elizabeth watched as John Tiptoft – the Earl of Worcester – rose from his chair and unfurled a map across the table. The other men moved closer, each taking a piece of the edge to hold it flat. She thought John Tiptoft a strange man. In fact, two men in one: one half a brilliant scholar, the other half a sadistic bastard. He had studied at Oxford University, and then he had been Lord High Treasurer, then Lord Deputy of Ireland. He had been on a pilgrimage to the Holy Land, returning by way of Italy where he had studied for some years and was now the foremost scholar of Latin in the kingdom. On his return to England, Edward had appointed him Lord High Constable and this, Elizabeth realised, was where the sadistic half of him appeared. For the High Constable was responsible for, and presided over, the attainment, torture, and execution of traitors; it was a duty he carried out with exceptional cruelty and perverse pleasure. From the Holy Land, he brought new forms of execution. His favourite was impaling his victims by hammering sharpened stakes up through their buttocks and out through their mouths. All were disgusted, even the most common of people, but no one would dare protest such was his power. Elizabeth sometimes wondered if he also practised the black arts, for he was the closest man to the devil she had ever come across. She put down her embroidery and leaned closer to catch his words.

'The attack in Lincolnshire on the estate of Sir Thomas de Burgh – your Master of the Royal Horse – was a smokescreen; an excuse to raise men in rebellion against your royal authority,' stated John Tiptoft, in his flat unemotional voice. 'Two of the men responsible, Lord Richard Welles and Sir Thomas Dymoke, are now in custody within the tower, but Lord Welles' son – Sir Robert – is still free. The reports from our agents inform us that he is mustering a large army with the intention of marching on London to free his father and raise the Lancastrian flag over the capital.'

'That young Lancastrian hothead could not orchestrate such a large undertaking on his own,' said Lord Hastings.

'That is correct,' replied John Tiptoft. 'There are powerful men behind him.'

'I presume you mean Warwick, and my brother, George,' said Edward, coldly.

'I have evidence that points to them, in fact, all the Neville clan and even the Stanleys may be involved,' replied John Tiptoft.

'And our old foe, King Louis, will no doubt be fanning the flames,' said Edward, angrily. 'It would seem he wishes to wear my crown as well as his own.'

'It would seem that George also wishes to try it for size,' said Lord Hastings, with a sarcastic laugh. 'He is becoming a genius at stabbing you in the back.'

Edward rose from his chair in anger. 'George is a fool!' he shouted, thumping the table. 'But surely he would not plot against me.'

John Tiptoft placed his hand on Edward's shoulder. 'I am sorry, my Lord, but there is solid evidence to implicate him in this plot.'

Edward stared at him with disbelief.

'Your brother has turned traitor,' John Tiptoft whispered. 'He covets your crown.'

'How could my own brother wish me dead?' cried Edward.

'Because, Warwick leads the fool by the nose and promises him your throne,' replied John Tiptoft.

Lord Hastings sat back in his chair and looked across at Elizabeth and her mother, as they sat quietly listening to the conversation. *Edward*, he surmised, *could blame his brother, or Warwick, or even the King of France for his troubles, but those two scheming witches sitting not more than twenty feet away are the real cause of his problems.* They had used the forces of darkness to snare Edward into a secret marriage, which had made an enemy of King Louis and humiliated Warwick. Then, to rub salt in the wounds, he had signed treaties with the Duke of Burgundy for a political and military alliance and married his sister, Margaret of York, to him, thus sealing the alliance with a dynastic marriage. The marriage celebrations were the most magnificent ever seen in Europe, so by aligning himself so publicly with Burgundy, Edward had humiliated Warwick and Louis yet again. No wonder they thirsted for revenge.

Elizabeth suddenly caught Lord Hasting's stare, and smiled, thinly.

Lord Hastings knew that behind that cold smile lurked a veiled threat to remove him from Edward's circle. He realised that if he was not careful, then one day he would be going home carrying his head under his arm. John Tiptoft's voice brought him back to the conversation.

'We know that George and Warwick are behind this uprising. Although they send messages of support to you, they are in fact plotting to take your crown,' he said, matter-of-factly, 'and you, my Lord, must not let them know they are under suspicion. We must use their intrigues against them.'

Edward leant over the map. 'The leader of this rebellion is marshalling his forces there,' he said, pointing to Lincolnshire.

'That is correct,' replied John Tiptoft.

'Where are George and Warwick?' he asked, looking at John Tiptoft.

'They are in the West Country, raising men and ordinance to help quell this uprising, but in reality they will join forces with Sir Robert Welles to crush you in a surprise attack.'

Lord Hastings faced Edward across the map table. 'If Warwick's army joins with Welles' forces then the game will be up. We have to attack him before they can rendezvous.'

Edward paced around the table. 'These rebels within my kingdom have had ample time to prepare their traitorous plots, and Louis of France is also joining them in this treacherous mischief. Time is now more precious than gold; we must move swiftly.' He turned to face his loyal captains. 'We leave for Huntingdon tonight. Issue commissions of array for my royal army to muster at Stamford with all speed. We must deal with Welles before these traitors arrive to support him.'

'Your brother, Richard,' said John Tiptoft, 'would it be wise to recall him from Wales?'

Edward's face broke into a relaxed smile at the mention of his brother's name. 'Thank God, my youngest brother is as loyal to me as George is traitorous,' he said.

'He will not make the battle,' said Lord Hastings, 'but if he heads west with all speed he may intersect Warwick or George as they head north.'

'It would be wise to have his forces near,' replied Edward. 'If we have to deal with Warwick and Welles then we will be in need of them. Send a royal messenger to recall him with all speed.'

Edward then laid his hand on the centre of the map and looked at each man in turn; they laid a hand one after the other on top of his. 'Gentlemen,' he said, with excitement in his voice. 'To war and victory.'

'To war and victory!' the others cried in unison.

Elizabeth sat in the quiet of the empty room. Edward and his captains had departed to begin their preparations. She rose from her chair and walked over to the map table, her mother watching her. Elizabeth trailed her finger over the map. 'Lincolnshire,' she said. 'Are there many men in such a place?'

Jacquetta rose from her chair and joined her. 'Many men will rally to a standard if they think the crown of England is the prize. Even common yeomen will join if rich pickings are to be had.'

Elizabeth leant on the table and stared at the map. Slowly, she whispered, 'We have too much to lose to let fate decide this battle; my brothers and sisters are now married to the highest nobility in the land.'

Jacquetta placed two hands on the table and leaned across to her daughter. 'We have revenge to exact on Warwick for murdering my husband – your father.'

'And my brother – your son!' cried Elizabeth.

The two women looked at each other in silence.

'It's been a long time. Are you sure?' whispered Jacquetta.

Elizabeth felt the tingle in her stomach. She smelt the potions; she longed for the abandonment. 'Yes, I am sure,' she whispered heavily.

Jacquetta studied her daughter. 'The men will be gone shortly,' she spoke softly. 'I will make the arrangements.'

Broughton Castle, Oxfordshire
6 March 1470

Warwick watched as the server slowly filled his wine goblet; he felt his annoyance rising at the slowness of the man. A messenger from Sir Robert Welles had just been ushered into his presence and he was eager for his news. With irritation, he waved the server away. 'Go,' he barked.

The man stepped back and after a low bow, was gone.

Warwick beckoned the messenger closer. 'What news from Sir Robert?' he asked urgently, his body tensing as he awaited the answer.

'Sir Robert sends his greetings, my Lord. His army is resting at Grantham before beginning the final march on Stamford where Edward is marshalling his forces. He requests that you march your army northwards with all speed. Meanwhile, he will halt at Empingham and wait for you to move into position, then on your command, he will attack from the north, and you, from the south, in a pincer movement that will destroy Edward's army.'

Warwick's body relaxed as he sat back in his chair. *No bad news*, he thought, gratefully. Everything was going according to plan; soon he would have Edward's head on the end of a stake and George wearing a bloody crown. Isabel would be queen and the child she was carrying, if a boy, would one day be crowned king – his grandson. He smiled to himself, for then he could rule England as he pleased and if George objected then he would put his head on a spike and wear that bloody crown in his grandson's name. His plans for Europe would never be held back again and those scheming witches, Elizabeth and her mother, along with the rest of their malicious family, would wish they had never been born. Warwick's eyes narrowed as he looked at the messenger. 'Tell Sir Robert that we march north towards Peterborough, at dawn. We will be there within the week. When we are close enough to smell Edward's army, I will brief him on our battle plan.'

The messenger bowed and left.

Warwick took a leisurely drink of wine as he thought of the coming march. 'Time is against us,' he said, turning to his new son-in-law.

George, the Duke of Clarence, nodded in agreement. 'We must try and stall Edward until we are in a position to engage him,' he replied.

'I will dispatch a letter urging him to await our support; I will counsel that it would be better for our combined armies to attack the enemy than for him to risk all by striking alone,' replied Warwick.

George sighed. 'To write such a letter is a treacherous deed.

Warwick's eyes met George's and held his gaze.

'It is a dangerous game we play,' shouted Warwick, 'in our pursuit of the crown. Men and morals will be trampled beneath our feet, for when Edward finds out our true intentions there will be no forgiveness in his heart. If we lose, then our necks will feel the cold steel of the executioner's axe, so there is no going back. There will be no forgiveness or reprieve; we must destroy your brother or he will destroy us.'

Wales
6 March 1470

Spring advanced high into the hills, the retreating winter snows now clung precariously to only the highest peaks. The icy waters from the melting snow gorged the many streams that flowed quicker than arrows down the steep mountainsides, rushing with timeless repetition into the fast flowing river that snaked its way along the bottom of this Welsh valley.

Richard, Duke of Gloucester, raised his hand; the marching army behind him slowly shuddered to a halt. His scourers had found the perfect spot to rest before their final advance on Cardigan Castle. His royal army of three thousand men would have a plentiful supply of fresh water; their horses and livestock, rich grazing to feed on.

John Tunstall watched the watery red sun slip behind the mountains. The long shadows it cast chilled the evening air; fires flickered into life as the troops prepared their evening meal. The warmth of the flames would also be needed to see them through the long, cold night that lay ahead.

Looking over towards the royal tents that had been quickly erected, John watched the Hallet twins stamping their feet and rubbing their hands against the cold. They grumbled and cursed in their own indomitable way as they guarded the entrance to Richard's tent. John smiled to himself; their cursing and stamping reminded him of his prank with the snowballs all those years ago at Middleham just before he had been introduced to Richard. *Was it really seven years ago?* he thought. Already, two had passed since Richard, Francis, the twins, Friar Drynk and himself had left Middleham to join King Edward's court. The king, on their arrival, had knighted him for his bravery during their kidnap ordeal at Bamburgh, and although it had softened the blow of leaving his beloved Rose behind, he still missed her badly.

'Thomas; George!' John cried, as he approached the tent. 'Find some younger men to guard our Lord's tent. You are becoming too old; your bones, I fear, will cease all movement if you stand in this cold night air much longer.'

'Not too bleeding old to see you off,' replied Thomas, with a smile.

Richard looked up from a table strewn with maps and plans of Cardigan Castle. 'How does my army settle?' he asked.

'The men are in good spirits,' replied John, 'and, after our easy victory at Carmarthen Castle, there is talk of us being home in a few weeks.'

Richard looked down at his plans. 'That will depend on how stubborn Cardigan decides to be,' he said, thoughtfully.

'They will not fight hard,' said John. 'As we saw at Carmarthen, they may wave their swords in defiance but they only play at rebellion; they have no stomach to fight our royal army.'

'If these Welsh bastards don't fight then there will be no glory or honour on our return home,' replied Richard, with a touch of disappointment in his voice.

'That is why Edward gave you this campaign as your first command,' said a voice from the shadows. 'It is so that you may cut your teeth against a soft foe. He has also filled your ranks with many experienced men who will show their worth if the need should arise.'

Richard looked across at Francis Lovell.

'And grateful I am to my brother for his wise counsel in these matters,' replied Richard. 'I am sure we will have more opportunities to win our spurs in the coming months.'

'You talk of the gathering storm between Warwick and your brother?' asked John, a trace of anguish in his voice.

'Aye, with sadness I do,' replied Richard. 'There will be no peace in England until one has destroyed the other.' Then, shaking his head slowly, he whispered, 'How by almighty God has it come to this: cousin against cousin; brother against brother?'

'Because your brother, George, is weak-willed and easily lead,' stated John flatly. 'He is spreading false rumours that King Edward is a bastard sired by a lowly archer.'

'Heaven help us!' cried Francis. 'How a man can say such falsehoods and by saying so imply that your mother, nay, his mother as well, is an adulteress.'

'Warwick has dangled the throne in front of him,' said Richard sharply. 'He has turned my brother's doltish head, but it is Warwick who is behind these rumours; he also beheaded the Queen's father and brother without a trial. He will be forced to pay for these murders.'

'So, what of Warwick's daughter, Anne? Would not killing her father make things a trifle difficult for you if you wished to marry her?' said Francis, softly.

'Anne is clever,' replied Richard. 'She understands the ways of men who rule.'

Francis nodded slowly in agreement. 'And what of Rose?' he enquired, looking at John, whose face suddenly lit up at the mention of her name.

'We are betrothed to be married,' John said, proudly, excitement flowing in his words. 'The marriage will take place directly after this Welsh campaign ends. The countess and my mother schooled her in the ways and duties of a knight's consort after finally realising we would never be parted.'

Richard threw his arms around his old friend's shoulders, 'Tis good news!' he cried. 'True love, my friend, is a rare gift from God and should be treasured. I pray that Francis is likewise blessed when his time comes.'

John and Francis looked at Richard.

'So, are you not blessed with Anne, then?' asked John, a look of puzzlement on his face.

Richard looked down silently at the maps spread out before him. 'I love another,' he said, quietly.

Shocked, John and Francis stared at Richard.

'But you were fond of her,' blurted out John.

'Who do you love, then?' cried Francis.

Richard raised his hand for silence. 'Enough of this talk,' he said, sternly. 'We have a battle to plan. Francis, pray call for my captains to join us.'

Francis made for the entrance, only to be stopped as Thomas Hallet rushed in.

'My Lord!' cried Thomas. 'A royal messenger awaits with urgent orders from the King!'

Fotheringhay Castle, near Stamford
11 March 1470

Edward threw the letters on to the table. 'Warwick and George promise me reinforcements. They bid me meet them at Leicester in two days' time so that our armies can combine to destroy Robert Welles. Do they think me a fool to fall for such an obvious trap?'

'It is to our advantage that they do,' replied Lord Hastings. 'They have been slow in their advance northwards and need time to join with that traitor. If they think you are waiting, they will not hurry, which gives us more time to deal with Welles.'

John Tiptoft said, quietly, 'Warwick has been too complacent. His arrogance leads him to think you would still believe in his integrity, and that you have forgotten his scheming against you these last few years.'

Lord Hastings laughed. 'When he lays his head on the block, maybe it will all come back to him.'

'Talking of heads on blocks,' said John Tiptoft, 'I ordered that Welles' father be brought from the tower and marched north with us. I suggest we inform his son that unless he surrenders, we will execute his father.'

'I have a better idea,' said Edward, softly. 'Many have sought to betray me; their plots and intrigues go back to the Duke of Somerset at Hedgeley Moor in sixty-four. I pardoned him for his support of the Lancastrian cause and still he betrayed me. I have been generous in my forgiveness of my enemies but no more! The kingdom will see the punishment for those who commit treason against me and any who think of joining the rebels will know the punishment for their actions. I command that Lord Welles be beheaded before the royal army and the message we send to his son will be his father's head!'

John Tiptoft bowed, and with a smile of satisfaction on his face, departed the royal tent to organise the execution.

The Duke of Norfolk entered. 'Our scouts have found Sir Robert Welles and his army,' he boomed. 'They are but five miles off, near Empingham.'

'Excellent,' replied Edward. 'We will send this bloody message to him, and then we attack at dawn.'

Grafton Manor, Northamptonshire
11 March 1470

Elizabeth sat in the window seat of the dining hall looking out over the small but beautifully manicured gardens that had been one of her father's joys. She remembered playing happily in them as a child with her brother, and now they were both gone, murdered by that monster, Warwick. A sharp anger tightened within her. It had been an arduous journey from Windsor; her mother and two sisters, plus a few servants, were all that had travelled and, of course, a number of men-at-arms for protection. They had left the royal court on the pretext of being closer to the king but the real reason was sorcery.

'I don't like it,' said Anne, crossly. She was sitting next to Margaret at the dining table.

Elizabeth's eyes narrowed, 'And what don't you like, sister, dear?'

'I don't like what we are here for,' Anne replied. 'We are ladies of rank now. We should not be involved...' she lowered her voice to a whisper, 'in witchcraft.' For support, she looked at Margaret, who stood up defiantly.

'I am married to the Earl of Arundel. Anne is married to Viscount Bourchier. You—' Margaret said, pointing at Elizabeth, 'are married to a king, so going down to that cellar is madness.'

Elizabeth rolled her eyes to the heavens, in frustration. 'We are all tired and irritable from our long journey,' she said, in a conciliatory tone.

'Enough of this mollifying!' snapped Jacquetta, who had been sitting at the far end of the table, listening with growing impatience to their bickering. She stood up and walked slowly down, standing in front of her three daughters.

Margaret slowly lowered herself back into her chair.

'You are right,' Jacquetta said, sternly. 'You are ladies of rank. Your brothers and sisters have married well. Elizabeth is a queen. When she produces an heir, your children will be cousins to a king, but if Edward loses this battle then George will become king. If this happens, our men will be executed, along with Elizabeth, and you two will be put to work as kitchen maids – or worse, made whores for his troops – and what then of your father and brother's murderer?'

Anne and Margaret slipped lower into their chairs.

'If Edward wins, then Warwick and George are finished. Tiptoft has promised me they will not die quickly,' Jacquetta said with relish, before slamming her hand on to the dining table.

Both girls jumped; their mother lowered her face closer to them. 'Now, are we going to help Edward, and avenge your father and brother?'

Both girls nodded furiously.

The bolt on the solid oak door slid shut. Elizabeth looked around the cellar. The girl with no name stood by the black altar. The unfrocked priest and his assistant prepared themselves. There were four black chickens in the cage by the brazier; they would each have one sacrificed over their naked bodies. She felt her nakedness under her thin cloak. She felt the thrill of abandonment take hold. Oh, how she had missed it.

As her mother began chanting, a green flame flashed upwards from the fire. Elizabeth looked at her sisters, their faces now full of excitement, and felt dark powers stirring within the room.

Rebel Camp, Empingham
12 March 1470

Sir Robert Welles stared at the bloody sack that dangled from Sir Thomas de la Lande's hand. The top was tied tightly with bowstring and secured with red wax.

'The wax is stamped with the Royal Insignia,' said Sir Thomas, nervously.

'How come you by this?' whispered Sir Robert, his eyes never leaving the sack.

'A royal herald using a white flag of truce delivered it, with the message it was to be opened only by you,' replied Sir Thomas. He stepped forward and laid the sack at Sir Robert's feet.

The gentlemen and knights, who had gathered within the tent to discuss the coming battle, looked on with anxious eyes. Sir Robert knelt beside the sack; a small hunting knife trembled in his hand. Cutting the bowstring, he nervously opened it. Slowly, he peered inside. Without warning, an almighty howl left his lips as the lifeless eyes of his father's severed head stared back at him.

Battle of Losecoat Field, Empingham
13 March 1470

Edward watched the enemy struggle into their attack formations. There was a hesitance about them; their actions lacked confidence.

John Tiptoft seemed to read his thoughts. 'It would seem these sheep grazers know nothing of military matters. Look; they are milling around like the stupid animals they tend.'

Edward looked along his ranks. His army was well arrayed. His mounted knights sat with the dawn sun rippling off their armour. They looked invincible and gave confidence to all around them. His light cavalry awaited on his flanks, the tips of their fifteen-foot lances glistening. Foot soldiers stood steady in their padded jackets, pikes, axes, or short stabbing swords at the ready. All awaited the signal to attack, with discipline.

'Fire two salvos of cannon,' Edward ordered. 'Let's see if they have the stomach to fight.'

As Edward watched his artillery thunder into life, the rebels moved backwards.

'Well, I have never seen the like!' cried Lord Hastings. 'Every man jack of them has lost his valour.'

'We must seize the moment, Sire,' shouted the Duke of Norfolk. 'They are breaking ranks.'

'Send our cavalry to attack their flanks,' barked Edward, with urgency in his voice. 'Signal the infantry to charge without delay, and I command no mercy for the common soldiers – today they are all traitors.'

The royal army swooped down like a barbarous bird of prey. Edward watched in amazement as the rebels fled the field, casting aside their livery jackets and weapons in their haste to escape.

His cavalry swept in from the flanks like the hounds of hell, while his infantry raced down the hill and attacked, as his scourers cut off the rebels escape. The field soon ran crimson red.

At the end of the butchery, white corpses, slashed with blood, lay packed three deep across the meadow, their bodies mutilated; smashed heads dripping brains.

Edward saw a rebel with a leg hacked off, frantically trying to crawl away. He marvelled at the man's instinct for survival, and watched as one of his men walked slowly behind, taunting and kicking him, and then finally raising his axe to split his head in two.

His troops, full of the madness of war, screamed and shouted with joy at being alive, of surviving amongst the dead. They threw their helmets in the air, and roared at each other with life, while cutting the throats of any rebel who moved or cried for mercy.

Fotheringhay Castle, near Stamford
13 March 1470

Edward sat on his throne in the Great Hall of Fotheringhay Castle, holding a small wooden casket. To the left and right of him stood his captains and close retainers. Kneeling before him in chains, were Sir Robert Welles and his conspirators.

'I have in my hands the evidence that implicates Warwick and George in your traitorous plot,' Edward shouted, so all in the hall could hear. 'These letters were found near the body of their envoy to Sir Robert and show in damming detail their support for this rebellion.'

A murmur of astonishment went around the hall.

Edward held his hand up. 'Welles and his captains have confessed to their involvement.'

Shouts of 'Traitors!' rang out.

John Tiptoft moved to the front of the dais. 'These great rebels, the Earl of Warwick and the Duke of Clarence, are thereby under royal command attainted for treason. Their titles and lands forfeit, they will be hunted down and brought before a royal court for sentencing.'

The Great Hall erupted with shouts of 'Death to the traitors!'

Edward looked at Sir Robert Welles, who had been staring into space and mumbling to himself since they had brought him in. He was also shaking as though in terror of some terrible presence; it reminded him of his own ordeal all those years ago at Reading. He beckoned John Tiptoft to approach him.

'What is wrong with Sir Robert?' Edward whispered.

John Tiptoft leant close to the royal ear. 'It would seem he had a visitation in the night, and it has turned him quite mad, or it may be just the thought of the executioner's axe awaiting him, but for the moment, my Lord,' he said, with a shrug of his shoulders, 'it is all a mystery.'

'Bring any who witnessed this event to my private quarters, for I wish to solve this mystery,' ordered Edward.

Sir Henry Surtees sat opposite the king. Fresh bread and cheese filled his belly; a large cup of wine awaited his lips. Was it only an hour ago when he had been kneeling before him in chains? A death sentence had hovered over his head, but if he told the truth, the king had promised him a full pardon. Only, the truth was preposterous – nay, unimaginable – so would the king even believe him? If not, then he would still lose his head. He glanced up quickly; Edward sat patiently waiting. He was everything they said he was, and more, broad chested, tall, handsome – a regal man, a man born to be king.

'Sir Henry,' said Edward, quietly. 'Sip some wine and then tell me how Sir Robert turned mad.'

Recalling the events of the previous night sent a shiver down Sir Henry Surtees' spine. His hand trembled slightly, as he raised the cup to his lips.

Lord Hastings and John Tiptoft, who sat either side of the king, leaned closer to hear.

With shaking hands, Sir Henry placed the cup back on to the table and began.

'It was not the shock of finding his father's severed head that sent Sir Robert mad, although the outrage of it hit him hard. His anguish turned to anger and he swore to take the heads of those responsible. He became determined, his courage more resolute; all of us swore to exact revenge,' he said, looking guiltily at Edward, who stared back at him, unmoved by the implications of his words.

'Later that night, all the officers and men had settled. Some slumbered fitfully, others prayed for their souls, or victory; many talked quietly of past battles or loves. Every man faced the dawn and the coming battle in his own way. When I recall the events that followed, it would seem I had dreamt some terrible nightmare, but by the love of God,' he whispered, crossing himself, 'nightmare it was not.'

The three men listening sat still and silent. Tired candles threw deep flickering shadows around the room.

'There were five of us left with Sir Robert,' Sir Henry whispered, 'when a light breeze spiralled around us. I remember the candles flickering. We all looked to see where this unexpected draught had come from, when abruptly, the warmth within the tent drained away. The air became icy cold; the suddenness of it caught my breath. I sat there, my actions frozen, and then the wind came.' There was a tremor in Sir Henry Surtees' voice. 'Such a cold, icy wind, the like I have never felt before. Then, the candles extinguished one by one. In the darkness, a tirade of screeches and hideous laughter rang out, striking terror into our souls. Slowly, a cold, blue light filled the tent like wine filling a cup, then I saw – oh, by the holy Mary, it was hideous!' he cried.

Edward leant closer, his face pinched tight in concentration. 'What did you see?' he whispered tensely.

Sir Henry Surtees grasped his cup of wine and drank until it was empty. He lowered it slowly and stared into its emptiness. 'I saw creatures – demons – half appearing within this blue light, then fading away as though caught between two worlds. Their scaly bodies twisted with depravity, razor claws flashing, malevolent eyes gleaming with heinous wickedness. Then it came – slowly at first, its form part solid, part transparent. I didn't know that evil had a smell,' he said, grimly, 'but, by God, it has. When you breathe that foul air, it feels as though your innards are rotting within you.'

'What was coming?' murmured Edward, in a hushed tone.

'It was the Devil himself!' cried Sir Henry. 'He stood; finally complete, towering in front of Sir Robert, his glistening scaly body oozing evil. I was frozen with cold and fear, only my eyes had movement. I watched a silent scream appear on Sir Robert's lips, and then I saw, and then…oh, Holy Mother of God,' he whispered.

'Saw what?' demanded John Tiptoft.

Sir Henry tried to compose himself. He picked up his empty cup and held it tight to his chest. 'The Devil dangled the severed head of Sir Robert's father, by the hair. The lips on that bloodied head were moving – it was speaking! The eyes, tormented, moved within their sockets. It cried out in terror; screamed in despair!'

Horrified, the three men leant back in their chairs.

'For the love of God, what did it say?' asked Lord Hastings, his voice full of dread.

'It cried in a piteous voice that the Devil had his soul, and then it screamed at his son that the Devil would have his too, that the eternity of Hell awaited him.' Sir Henry paused; his face became still. 'I passed out then, I think, maybe through sheer terror or cold or maybe both,' he whispered, 'but when I awoke, the evil presence accompanied by swirling winds was passing from the tent out into the camp.'

'What had happened to Sir Robert?' asked Edward, trying to mask the fear in his voice.

'He was on his knees,' replied Sir Henry, 'staring at his father's now lifeless head, asking it for help. You have seen how he looks about all the time, searching for the Devil, his sanity gone.'

The three men nodded in agreement.

Sir Henry paused again; straightening his back, he tried to regain his composure. 'That evil presence pervaded our camp. It turned brave men into cowards. By morning, half of our army had slipped away and the rest, as you saw on the dawn, quickly followed.'

John Tiptoft laughed loudly, trying to hide the shock of what he had just heard. 'That's a tale well told,' he said, 'but it will not save your head.'

Edward and Lord Hastings exchanged knowing glances. Then, Edward placed his hand on John Tiptoft's arm. 'Your blood runs as cold as ours!' he exclaimed. 'I believe the man tells the truth.'

Edward rose from his throne, and walked to the table.

Sir Henry slipped from his chair on to his knees.

Edward bent low and whispered in his ear. 'I believe you have seen the serpents of Hell, for I have also experienced the dark forces.'

Sir Henry's eyes widened in shock.

Edward straightened up. 'What has been said here tonight must remain here.'

Sir Henry nodded his head vigorously.

'Then, I will grant you your pardon, and title,' said Edward, firmly. 'As for Sir Robert, when he is executed for treason tomorrow, his search for the Devil will be over.'

Edward and Lord Hastings watched John Tiptoft escort Sir Henry away to his freedom.

As their backs disappeared through the door, Lord Hastings turned to Edward, his face betraying the emotions of his thoughts. 'Your mother in-law is behind all of this,' he said, grimly. 'I thought she had stopped all this sorcery years ago, but it seems she does not trust you to win a battle on your own.'

'We have no proof of this,' declared Edward, with irritation in his voice.

'We will have, shortly,' replied Lord Hastings. 'I have planted agents in her household. They are to gather all the information I need to bring charges of witchcraft against her.'

'Before you bring any charges,' Edward whispered, 'I will need to see the evidence for myself. It is a dangerous game you play, so tread carefully, my friend. Is that understood?

Lord Hastings nodded his head in agreement, but already he had a triumphant look on his face.

Grafton Manor, Northamptonshire
13 March 1470

Elizabeth watched the back of the royal messenger until he had disappeared from sight, then she smiled to herself. A chuckle of triumph slipped from her lips, a look of conquest flitted across her features. Sir Robert Welles was defeated. Their magic had worked; his army had fled on the four winds so fast that the field was hidden under discarded livery jackets. The messenger said it was being called the Battle of Losecoat Field.

'What news of the Earl of Warwick and the Duke of Clarence?' she had asked, her body trembling with anticipation.

She rose from her chair, for it was impossible to sit still with the excitement. As she remembered his words, her eyes sparkled with delight.

'Those two traitors are on the run', he had replied. 'Attainted for treason, and with a price on their heads. On hearing of Edward's victory, their army had slipped away during the night. They had no choice but to flee.'

Now, the great Earl of Warwick, and his puppet, George, are destroyed, Elizabeth thought, with malice. *Common criminals fleeing from a death sentence.* She smiled. At last, she had secured her crown.

Chapter 11

Escape and Return

Wensley, North Yorkshire
20 March 1470

Men leaped from their beds, as sleep and fear collided. Some awoken by their women folk, others jerked awake, as the thunderous noise grew in the distance. Any weapon to hand was grasped – pitchfork, knife or hammer. Doors were secured. Nervous eyes searched vainly into the inky blackness of the night. The small hamlet of Wensley, nestled on the banks of the River Ure, waited with uneasy trepidation.

The force of fifty, horsed soldiers halted in the centre of the village. Men slipped from their saddles. Shouts of command rang out. Weapons banged on doors. 'Open in the name of the King!' bellowed rough voices. Nervous men were taken from their cottages; torches flickered on to fearful faces.

John Tunstall watched wearily, as the men were questioned. He had witnessed this scene many times over the last week. Travelling fast up through the heart of England, their scourers had sought out Warwick and the Duke of Clarence far and wide, but it would seem they had vanished. King Edward was also marching his army northwards towards the great City of York, searching for them. The whole of England was hunting for the king's enemies.

'There have been no sightings of them,' said Duke Richard, as he rode up alongside his old friend.

'Aye, it is a mystery to where they are,' replied John.

'It would seem they have disappeared into thin air,' replied Duke Richard, with tiredness in his voice.

John studied his friend's jaded face. The rigours of the Welsh campaign and the pursuit of Warwick had exhausted them all. A weary silence fell between them.

'We must leave,' said Richard, abruptly. 'There is no more to be done here, and our men require food and rest.'

John's thoughts turned to Rose. A large smile creased his face as he spurred his horse towards Middleham Castle.

Reining in his horse on top of the hill, where many years ago, before the time of William the Conqueror, the old wooden castle had stood, John looked down on to Middleham Castle as it rose majestically out of the white, frozen ground; a beacon of safety and civilisation. Safe within its great walls, he knew life would be stirring. Yesterday's fires would be prodded and coaxed back to life. Sleep would be shaken from reluctant eyes, as the aroma of warming food started to tantalise empty stomachs. He looked around him at the frozen countryside. Still held under a wintry frost, he imagined the cold, calculating eyes of hungry predators searching out, disciplined and patient, hoping to detect a scent or slight movement that would set in motion their first kill of the day, but for now, all was still. Nothing stirred across this cold bleak landscape, not even the wind.

As they swept down towards the castle, the dawn sun rose to greet them. John knew that Rose, and his mother, would have risen. Their ablutions now completed, they would soon be attending the countess, unaware of this early morning surprise. Excitement filled him, his heart felt as light as a feather as he thought of Rose and their forthcoming wedding. He dug his heels into his mount and urged his horse on.

The guards at the great gate stood aside, as they recognised Duke Richard's colours. John noted their anxious faces, their eyes cast down as he rode past them. The silence of the inner courtyard struck him immediately. He felt apprehensive as the Hallet twins slipped from their saddles.

'Something's not right,' said Thomas, his hand hovering over his sword.

All eyes turned towards the huge door of the Great Hall, as it slowly swung open. The Hallet twins drew their swords.

The Great Controller, appeared, his yellow eyes blinking into the sunlight. 'Lord, Duke Richard!' he cried. 'Sir John, Friar Drynk, and of course, you two rascals,' he said, addressing the twins. ''Tis good to see you all.'

Richard and John dismounted, leaping the steps to the Great Hall. They embraced the Great Controller, warmly.

'You have grown into fine soldiers!'

'And you never age,' smiled Richard.

'If only that were true,' the Great Controller chuckled.

'Why is the castle so quiet?' queried John, sharply. The question raced out of him with indecent haste. He knew that Rose, his mother, Anne Neville, or even the countess should have appeared by now. 'Where are—?'

The Great Controller held his hand up. A frown creased his face. Sadly, he shook his head. 'Come.' He waved his hand for them to follow him into the Great Hall.

West Country
30 March 1470

Warwick stared back at the dim, shadowy lights of Bristol. They flickered, taunting him, less than half a mile away. They turned his mood as black as the advancing night. Anger filled him. Once, he would have marched into its main square and demanded the best hospitality from its rich guilds. Aldermen, mercers, and grocers would have bowed low to him, their eyes glued to his feet in fear, never daring to look up to his face unless he addressed them, and yet, he had bypassed the city like a common criminal. His rage stayed corked. All his supporters, allies, and friends, who had lived well under his sponsorship, had melted away after the Battle of Losecoat Field – men he had promoted, financed, lent his name to, had all deserted him.

'May the bastards burn in Hell!' he shouted, with exasperation.

The Countess of Warwick laid her hand on her husband's arm. 'Richard, 'she said, softly, her calm manner appeasing his rage, 'this is not the time for anger. Edward and Richard are pursuing us like the wind; we know not who is friend or foe.' She slipped her arms around his waist and rested her head on his broad, bejewelled chest. 'The whole of England is now our enemy,' she whispered.

She is right, Warwick thought as the anger drained out of him. He had been betrayed by many, but his wife still held him dear, still loved, and supported him. He gently kissed her forehead.

The countess looked up, and smiled into his eyes. 'England may be finished with us,' she said, firmly, 'but we have not finished with England.'

Warwick wrapped his strong arms around her and held her tight. *After all that has happened*, he thought with gratitude, *she still believes in me*. He remembered the moment he had told her that Edward had defeated, nay, out-manoeuvred him, a warrant issued for his head. She had accepted their fate, and taken charge of the arrangements to head south. Ten days ago, their small party had fled from Middleham Castle.

He had lost their lands and privileges, and if caught, their lives too. *Yet, love me, she does*, he thought. He felt his resolve strengthen. He cupped her chin in his hand and raised her face towards his.

'You are right,' he said, softly. I will be back to take Edward's crown.'

The countess saw the determination in her husband's eyes, the lost pride returning. She lifted herself on to her toes, and kissed him passionately.

'At last, I have my Lord back,' she said, breathlessly.

Warwick looked around at his small and tired group. His two daughters, exhausted but uncomplaining, sat on bales of hay within the old barn where they had sought shelter for a few hours. Isabel, heavy with child, was being cared for by Lady Tunstall and young Rose. Twenty of his household men were patrolling the surrounding countryside, ready to raise the alarm should the king's forces be seen. He moved across and knelt down beside Isabel, gently taking her hand. 'How do you fare, my child?' he asked tenderly.

'I have no pain here,' she replied, softly, running her hands over her extended belly, 'but my back feels full of sharp knives.'

'She cannot continue this hard pace for much longer,' said Lady Tunstall. 'If she does, then she may lose the baby, and you may lose a daughter.'

Warwick looked anxiously at Isabel, and then at his wife. He saw the anxiety in their faces, which they had tried to conceal from him.

'George is sailing from Portsmouth with a squadron of my finest warships,' he said, gently. 'The sailors are loyal to a man; they will be waiting off Exmouth in two days' time to take us to France.' He placed his hand on his daughter's brow. 'Two more days, my little one, can you manage that?'

Isabel smiled thinly. 'I am a Neville. My place is with you and George. I would manage ten or twenty if you asked,' she said, proudly.

Rose watched with slight surprise as this tender moment unfolded between the earl and his family. She had not realised, or even imagined, that this mighty magnate cared, that he loved his wife and daughters so deeply, although sometimes she knew it took failure, or tragedy, for a man to realise that love is the most important element of his life. Her eyes fastened on Anne, who sat silent and withdrawn, sadness etched on her face. *Nothing will ease her pain*, Rose thought, sadly, *for she shares the same fate as me. As I love John, so she loves Duke Richard*. She sighed with frustration. Being torn between love and duty was a hard burden to bear. She felt a soft ache within her chest, as she thought of her precious John, and their wedding that was now abandoned – that special day filled with laughter and love, with music, dancing and feasting for all. She would have been the happiest bride in Christendom. Exasperation forced the sting of tears into her eyes, as she realised she may never see John again. *The world has gone mad – brother fighting brother; cousin killing cousin – why do men do this?* she thought, angrily. *They strut around like bejewelled peacocks, puffed up with pride; too proud to admit they are wrong.* Frustration joined her tears, and then she heard her name being called softly. Desperately trying to reign in her emotions, she looked up to see Anne patting the seat beside her.

'You are thinking of John,' Anne said, tenderly.

'As you of Duke Richard, my Lady,' whispered Rose secretly, as she sat down.

'I must put my feelings aside,' whispered Anne. 'If Richard's and Edward's forces arrest us, my father would be executed, so there is no choice in the matter. We must escape to France and pray that the future will be kind to us.'

'Duty comes before love,' said Rose, bitterly, as a feeling of despair settled on her.

'Life has placed us in this awful situation,' said Anne, with resignation. 'We are caught in the dreams of kings, so we must take comfort, and pray that God will set things right for us.'

'Yes, we must pray for his blessing, and the safety of Duke Richard and John,' whispered Rose, but as she spoke their names, her resolve suddenly weakened. Tears welled up in her eyes; a sob fell from her lips.

Anne tenderly placed her arm around Rose's shoulders. 'True love, and God, will find a way,' she said, firmly.

Exmouth, Devon
3 April 1470

Warwick had sailed, escaped on the wind.

John Tunstall sank to his knees on the curving, sandy beach, a lone gull circling above him. Storm clouds gathered on the horizon. He stared out beyond the breaking waves. Rose was gone; he closed his eyes in disbelief. She had been stolen from his life by Warwick, and taken where? What of his mother? She too had been snatched away. These women, whose love anchored his world, were gone. His actions were now powerless to change their future; so many false trails were laid. Warwick was heading for Plymouth, then Brixham, then east into Dorset, and yet all the time he had been racing for Exmouth. When they finally realised his true direction, they had assumed he was making for Exeter and the great docks, but the bastard had skirted the city and boarded his ships from this small fishing village.

Frustrated, John pummelled his fists into the sand. 'Damn Warwick!' he cried. 'Damn him!'

The rumble of thunder stopped his desperate thoughts. The first drops of rain created small craters in the sand around him. He rose, slowly and mounting his horse headed back towards the royal camp. Guilt filled him. He should have been with Richard. He had been wallowing in his own self-pity when he should have been at his duke's side. Shame reddened his face, as he dug his heels into his mount.

Darkness had fallen when John entered the royal tent. Richard was in deep conversation with his brother, King Edward. As the meeting drew to a close, Richard turned, and seeing John by the entrance, cried, 'Ah, there you are!'

'I beg pardon, your Grace,' began John.

'There is no need for words' replied Richard, cutting him off. 'A man requires solitude when his world is turned on its head.'

'But you have lost Anne,' replied John.

'Aye, but she is nothing to me, when compared to your love for Rose,'

Richard said, as he stood and placed his hands on Sir John's shoulders. 'Anne means wealth and territory, not love, but whatever the reason, we must both bear these hard knocks with fortitude, so have faith, my friend, you will see Rose and your mother again, I promise. But for the moment, we have a more pressing problem closer to home.' Putting his arm around John's shoulder, he guided him out of the tent. 'At dawn, we ride with the royal party for Windsor.'

John looked quizzically at his friend.

Richard looked around in the darkness, and then whispered, 'The Queen's mother has been accused of witchcraft.'

Royal Court, Château d'Amboise, France
6 May 1470

Georges Havart raced along the grand central gallery of the royal palace, his rich robes flapping with a life of their own.

Marshall Rouault struggled to keep pace with him. 'Georges, for God's sake, slow down,' he gasped, between laboured breaths.

'We have an urgent summons from the King,' panted Georges Havart, in reply. 'We have no time to dally.'

The small, petite figure dashed from the room into the gallery with a girlish squeal of delight on her lips. Her head turned back in search of her pursuers. Clattering into the side of Georges Havart, she sent him sprawling across the rich, thick Turkish carpet, and careering into a delicate Flemish chair, which disintegrated under the impact of his overweight body. The girl stood frozen to the spot. Hand over mouth, she stared at Georges Havart as he lay along the side of the gallery, all arms and legs, and covered in splinted wood. The girl's pursuer – a young boy, and her elder sister, Jeanne – stood in the doorway, vainly suppressing the urge to giggle.

'Georges!' cried Marshall Rouault. 'Are you all right?'

Georges Havart's hands patted his body. 'Think so,' he said, with uncertainty in his voice, then recovering his composure, shouted, 'I will have the ears cut off this person who dares to attack me!'

A woman's voice replied, 'I think not!'

Georges Havart looked up: the heavily pregnant Queen Charlotte stood in the doorway. Her sisters and household ladies gathered around her all straining to see him. 'Your Highness,' he said, as he struggled to his knees.

'I do not think the King would be too pleased if you took his daughter's ears,' she said.

Georges Havart looked to his side and saw Anne, King Louis' ten-year-old daughter, staring at him with concern in her eyes.

'Monsieur Havart,' she cried. 'I am so sorry.' Her small body tried to lift his opulent frame back on to its feet.

Marshall Rouault rushed to assist her. Between them, they succeeded in helping Georges Havart up on to his uncertain legs. Wood splinters fell to the ground as many hands brushed his garments. Stepping back from the fuss, he said, 'I feel it is only my pride that has been hurt.'

'Do you forgive me?' asked Anne, coyly.

'How could I not forgive such a pretty young face,' Georges Havart replied, diplomatically.

'Will you come and sit with us?' enquired Queen Charlotte. 'Take a moment to compose yourself, and sip a little wine. We spend so long in our own company, it would be agreeable for my ladies and myself to hear your latest news.'

'I would be well disposed to accommodate such delightful company, my Lady,' replied Georges Havart, 'but I have been summoned urgently by your husband, so must go with all speed to attend him.' He bowed graciously, and then took his leave with Marshall Rouault.

Queen Charlotte watched their backs disappear along the gallery. 'Men,' she whispered to her ladies. 'They are always busy with affairs of state, and the rare times we see them we have to bear the consequences,' she said, pointing to her swollen stomach.

'But how we love to see them,' sighed one of her ladies.

Laughter followed the two men, as they sped towards the king.

King Louis stood at the middle of the great oak table that ran half the length of the Hall of State. His hands rested on its finely polished surface, supporting his slim body, as he studied the fine writing on the parchment in front of him. Only a small furrow between his eyebrows gave a hint to the total concentration his sharp mind was applying. Slowly, he straightened up. Raising his eyes, he studied the great vaulted ceiling, the fine damask curtains, and the beautiful Italian paintings that hung around the walls. He once again studied the urgent message from the Archbishop of Narbonne, his eyes twinkling with intrigue.

Courtiers and valets stood silent, hardly daring to breathe lest they should disturb their king's concentration.

The great doors to the Hall of State banged open. The noise rippled around like a cannon shot. King Louis looked up. Annoyance flitted across his face, then his features relaxed as Georges Havart and Marshall Rouault walked towards him.

Georges Havart noted, as he bowed, that the king was finely dressed in purple and reds lined with gold, as was his custom when staying at the Château d'Amboise. It was out of respect for the Queen's court; also, it was important that his daughters always saw their father dressed richly, as befitted a king – it gave them a sense of their own worth, their place in the pecking order of France. When he left this feminine court, which overflowed with the Queen's sisters, and household ladies, he preferred simple hunting clothes, plain food, and basic accommodation. Extravagance and opulence, he spurned. His entourage, who travelled with him, grudgingly endured many an unsavoury meal and rough bed.

'Two days ago,' began King Louis, 'the fishermen of Honfleur woke up to a fleet of warships anchored off their coast. These uninvited guests were flying the *Bear and Ragged Staff* as their colours.'

'Warwick!' cried Georges Havart, with surprise.

'As you know, we have been following events in England,' continued the king, 'but always through a mist of confusion, rumour, and false reports, but now the fortunes of Richard Neville, the mighty Earl of Warwick, are as clear as a summer's day. Fortune, it would seem, has smiled kindly on King Edward, for Warwick is now a fugitive!' He slid the parchment across the table for his advisors to read.

'Is this all the information we have at present?' asked Jean de Reilhac, the king's secretary.

'Sadly, yes,' replied King Louis, 'but it is enough to concentrate our minds on how to handle these unexpected guests.'

Georges Havart was weary. It was now late into the evening. Messages had been arriving throughout the day from Honfleur, and King Louis had been firing off replies and instructions in a flurry of activity. He marvelled at how the king was still full of energy, his mind sparkling with plans and intrigues. He was not a man who would squander this opportunity that fortune now offered him.

Georges Havart settled back into his chair, and ran his mind over the events of the day. Warwick, they learned, had sailed flamboyantly into the mouth of the Seine, with a line of captured Burgundian and Breton vessels, causing huge embarrassment for King Louis, who, two years previously, had signed the Treaty of Péronne, bringing the troublesome dukes – Burgundy and Brittany – under his control.

That southern rebel, the Count of Armagnac, had been charged with treason, and had promptly fled to Spain, whilst the king's brother, Charles, was content, at last, with his new province, Guienne. France was finally at peace, and now, here was his great ally, Warwick, who after plundering the property of the two dukes, demanded open entry to the king's court. *God! The arrogance of the man*, Georges Havart thought. *Any other king would have sent him packing and secured his own kingdom, before new hostilities broke out with his nobles, but not Louis!* He felt exasperated. The king would manipulate every player in this game until he had won, and France was master of all.

William Monypeny, a native of Scotland, and now Lord of Concressault, was a close confidant of King Louis. He had been on secret missions to Warwick in the past, and had now been dispatched with Jean Bourré, another of the king's secretaries, to welcome Warwick, and order the Archbishop of Narbonne to offer him, and his ladies, accommodation as befitted his rank. The archbishop was to persuade Warwick to relinquish his prizes, and then see to it that they were returned to their rightful owners.

Messengers had been hurriedly dispatched to the two dukes, informing them that all their goods would soon be restored to them. Georges Havart knew this would not appease them and they would demand Warwick's arrest, but it would stall any actions they may plan to take for a while.

An urgent invitation had been sent to Margaret of Anjou to join King Louis at Amboise. Georges Havart knew not why, and so he sat, watched, and marvelled, as his king spun his web of intrigue.

'Georges!' shouted King Louis, who was bent over the table, reading the latest dispatch from Honfleur.

Georges Havart stumbled to his feet, his thoughts and rest, forgotten, 'Your Majesty?'

King Louis turned and looked at his old advisor. 'It is late and you are tired, my friend.'

Georges Havart started to protest, but the king held up his hand for silence. 'I need sharp minds, and yours is dulled by this late hour. Go to your bed, and I will have the best of you in the morning.'

'I will not protest, Sire,' replied Georges Havart wearily, as he made to leave.

'Oh, Georges, before you go,' said King Louis, with a sudden afterthought, 'I have one last task for you. As you know, my cousin, Margaret of Anjou, will be joining us shortly. The day after she leaves Paris, I want you to undertake a small mission for me.' King Louis turned back to his dispatches.

Georges Havart, now dismissed, left the chamber with a puzzled look on his features.

La Conciergerie Prison, Paris
12 May 1470

Margaret of Anjou sat in a small, upholstered chair beside the bed. She studied the frail face that slept before her. Six weeks ago, it had been covered in filthy hair, and putrefying sores; the body, skin and bone, wrapped in rags, close to death. She had employed the best doctors in Paris, but even then, they had nearly lost him twice. Leaning over, she took Simon's hand, her other one gently smoothing his brow.

Simon's eyes slowly opened from their slumber, their edges crinkled with a lazy smile, as he looked at her, then their focus moved to the morning sunlight that was streaming in through the window. After five years of being confined in dank darkness, it was more precious than gold. He would never become tired of looking at its golden rays.

'I have to go away,' Margaret said, softly.

Simon's eyes moved back to her face, a questioning look in them.

'King Louis has invited me to his court at Amboise.'

Simon leant up on to his elbow and placed his hand over hers. 'Why?'

'My father has also been invited, along with my brother,' she said.

Simon leant down and kissed her hand gently.

Smiling, Margaret ran her hand through his hair. 'I know not the reason for this invitation, and I wish not to burden you with thoughts of it,' she said, leaning forward and gently kissing Simon's lips.

'There must be a good reason for the King to invite you to the royal court,' he said, with a perplexed look on his face.

'Queen Charlotte is heavy with child. He may require my brother, and myself, to be godparents, or he may wish to help my father recover his crown of Naples,' Margaret said, shrugging her shoulders, 'but in all honesty, I have no real idea why we are summoned. All I know is that it gives me another opportunity to secure your release from this accursed prison.'

Simon lay back on his bed and looked around his two-roomed cell. His eyes took in the rich carpets, the fine furniture, and his new clothes.

'It is not that accursed,' he laughed.

'But you are not free – we are not free,' Margaret cried. 'I long for us to be unfettered, to walk together in the gardens at Châteaux Koeur-la-Petite, to sit by the river and watch the kingfishers; not to wake in the mornings with a start and a heart that feels encased in lead.'

Simon sat up and took her in his arms. 'I did not mean to make light of all that you have done for me. You have brought me back from the dead, put life into my broken body, and I too long for that day of freedom.'

Margaret leaned across and kissed him. They looked into each other's eyes with deep understanding, their hearts beating close, both desperately wanting the other, but their movements frozen by the coldness of La Conciergerie. 'I must go,' she whispered, breaking the spell.

Simon held her tight and embraced her again.

'I must go,' she said, huskily, as she rose unsteadily to her feet.

Simon lay back and watched her.

'The nurse will call daily,' Margaret said, as she regained her composure.

'You will write?' Simon asked.

'Every day, and when I return, it will be with a royal pardon for your freedom, so work hard on your exercises.'

'Why?'

Margaret leant down, and gently cupped Simon's chin within her hand. 'Because, you will need all your strength when I get you home,' she giggled, her eyes full of promise. She stood, and made to leave. Pausing at the cell door, she turned to look at Simon, her face radiant with the hope that filled her heart. Her look lingered on Simon's face. He smiled, blew her a kiss, and then she was gone.

The cell door slammed shut, the key turned in the lock, the jailer's footsteps faded away. Simon lay in the stillness with a contented smile on his face. After six weeks of fine food and exercise, he could feel his body responding, his strength returning.

The doctor had said that it was 'youth' that had saved him – a few years older and he would never have survived, but the doctor was wrong: it was his love for Margaret. He had never given up hope of seeing her again. The ring that she had given him had become a beacon of hope. When captured, he had slipped it into the lining of his shirt collar, and there it had stayed until Pierre de Brézé's money had run out. Then, he had been thrown into a common cell where the door was only unlocked when you were dead. In the darkness, he had retrieved the ring and worn it with pride. It had given him the will to survive, and then one day, like an angel, Margaret appeared, as though in a dream, and carried him from the darkness to the light. Now, she had gone to fight for his freedom, but what would he do with this freedom?

He snuggled down to ponder this enticing problem, when from out of nowhere dark thoughts filled his mind. Images of his mother and sisters, being thrown off their estate, destitute and starving, swirled into view; Warwick laughing at his failure, his comrades being dragged to their executions – all dead, except for him.

Sweat broke out on Simon's brow. He sat up and held his head in his shaking hands. The barriers he had so carefully constructed to keep himself sane during his solitary confinement, those barricades he had erected to hold these unwanted demons at bay, were suddenly swept away. His body shook uncontrollably, as tears of regret cascaded down his face.

The White Hart Tavern, Grafton Regis, England 12 May 1470

Twilight turned the thatched roof a ghostly grey; the early summer warmth chilled in the evening air. Within the tavern, travellers, government men, and locals, drew their coats around them.

'Suppose you're not lighting the fire then, landlord?' asked a forlorn voice, the answer already known.

'No fires from May to September,' replied the landlord as he cleared some tables. 'You know the rules.'

'Tight bastard,' grumbled a voice from the shadows.

The landlord, ignoring the abuse, stopped by a man sitting alone in the corner. 'Sorry to hear about your brother,' he said. ''Twas a strange business, him dying like that, and just when he was going to give evidence against the Queen's mother...' he lowered his voice, 'concerning that witchcraft.'

Nervous eyes, set in a pale face, turned towards him. Bloodless lips spoke. 'When they found him, the room was filled with the smell of burnt flesh. His limbs and face contorted as though he had been burnt at the stake. His body was too hot to touch, and yet there was not a mark on him.'

The landlord crossed himself and sat down. 'I hear you have been called,' he whispered.

With a trembling hand, the man with the pale face picked up his tankard and gulped at his mead. It ran from the corners of his mouth and down his chin. He did not seem to notice. 'Yes,' he said, his voice shrill with fear, 'but I have seen nothing – nothing, I tell you. I've only heard strange noises from the cellar, but that's all. John saw things – ungodly acts – but not me, I swear.'

'What of the other witnesses?' the landlord asked. 'Some must know more than you?'

'They have all disappeared.'

'Disappeared?' whispered the landlord, sharply.

The eyes in the pale face filled with fear. 'They have either gone into hiding or they have been…' He buried his face in his hands, 'Oh God…'

'Do you have your holy protection?' asked the landlord.

The man reached into the neck of his smock and showed a wooden crucifix hanging there.

The landlord rose from his seat and patted the man on the arm. 'I will get thee another drink,' he said. 'I think you need it.'

Returning, the landlord placed a full tankard on the table. The man reached forward and drank greedily.

'Slow down,' said the landlord. 'It's not a race.'

The man abruptly stopped drinking. The tankard dropped from his hand and a gurgling noise came from his throat. His eyes bulged out of their sockets; his hands clawed frantically at his throat as he desperately fought for air.

The landlord stepped back in horror as the man dropped to his knees and then fell forward. Spasms jerked his body across the floor. Nearby drinkers, their faces frozen in fear, moved quickly towards the exit door. They heard the death rattle rising up through the man's throat. His body twitched three or four times, and then was still.

Jacquetta, the Duchess of Bedford, reached into the bucket of water and retrieved the small wax figure that had been lying on the bottom. *Fire and water*, she thought, as she crushed it within her hand. *What wonderful elements they are.*

She slumped back into her chair. Creating magic tired her easily now as her old age advanced, but she still allowed herself a smile of satisfaction, as she thought of Lord Hastings and his stupid little plan to have her tried before the Privy Council for witchcraft. Well, now he had no witnesses left to testify against her. He would look most foolish standing before them, his guns spiked. She could imagine the look of thunder on the Lord Chancellor's face as he was told there was no case to bring against her. Did he really believe he could beat her? Although, she did concede, that she quite enjoyed their sparring. It made life just that little bit more interesting, even though he was no match for her, and once she became bored, well, she would enjoy killing him. She even had a special ceremony planned to send him on his way.

Baynard's Castle, London
20 May 1470

'What do you mean?' shouted Lord Hastings at his secretary.

The man bowed even lower; it was unusual for his master, normally a man of good humour, to lose his temper. 'There are no witnesses to testify,' he repeated, trying to keep his voice firm and confident.

'No witnesses?' cried Lord Hastings. 'By the Holy Mother, where are they all?'

'Some are dead by means most foul, or disappeared,' replied the secretary, shaking his head in puzzlement.

'So, we have no one to bring before the Privy Council who can corroborate these allegations of witchcraft against the Queen and her mother?'

The secretary stood silent, words now redundant in the matter.

'No witness means no investigation, and no investigation means that fat bitch has escaped me. By God, she is making a fool of me!' Lord Hastings shouted, his face turning red with anger. 'Bring me a full report on the deaths of these witnesses; I must go and inform the King.'

The secretary bowed and hurriedly left the room.

Lord Hastings lowered himself into a chair and sat quietly with his thoughts. *She has escaped me. That woman has wriggled herself free, and in doing so, has saved that scheming bitch, the Queen, and the rest of her family. Hell's teeth, to be rid of them, for the kingdom and I would sleep safer in our beds.* He heaved himself from the chair, and with a heavy heart, made his way to Edward's quarters.

'Tis good news,' said King Edward. 'The duchess has no charges to answer; the matter is now closed!'

'It is only closed because there are now no witnesses,' replied Lord Hastings, bitterly. 'And, you and I both know witchcraft was used to silence them, the power of which we have experienced ourselves.' He looked at Edward, and shook his head from side to side, in disbelief.

Edward returned his look. 'I know your concerns are real', he said, quietly, 'but I cannot have my Queen and her family put on trial, and my kingship destroyed over rumours and false charges. You have no solid evidence, so that's the end to it!'

'Only for the moment,' said Lord Hastings, grimly, 'and I warn you, these rumours will haunt your kingship until it is resolved.'

The king's mother, Cecily, entered the chamber, followed by her ladies-in-waiting, who curtsied low to Edward, showing him ample bosoms and shy fluttering eyelashes.

As Edward ran his expert eye over them to see whom he had not bedded or whom he would bed again, thoughts of witches and warlocks vanished.

'My son,' began Cecily, a ripple of irritation flitting across her face, as she waited for his attention. 'Pray, I may have a private audience with you?

'I have come to speak on behalf of John Neville, Warwick's brother,' began Cecily, once they were alone.

'I know who he is,' replied Edward, with irritation. *Does she never stop meddling?* he thought.

'It would seem you have forgotten who he is, and what he is to your crown,' continued Cecily.

It was said with a sharpness that pricked and deflated Edwards's irritation. He sank back into his chair, a resigned look on his face. *I am King to everybody else, except her*, he thought, glumly.

'John Neville is as loyal to you as your brother, Richard, is. He has won battles for you and secured your kingdom. When Warwick and George took up arms against you, he stayed true, spurning their advances and offering you his full support. No king could ask for a more loyal subject, but how did you reward him?' Cecily asked, sarcastically. 'You took away his earldom of Northumberland and gave it back to that traitorous Lancastrian, Percy family. Then, to rub salt into his wound, you make him the Marquess of Montagu, a title with no lands or money. Have you gone completely mad?' she asked.

'He is the brother of a traitor,' Edward replied, angrily.

'And so are you,' Cecily spat back. 'Warwick is only a traitor because you made him so, or your wife, and her witch of a mother did. I warned you at the time that it would rip your kingdom apart, and it did! I warn you now: if you do not reinstate John Neville as the Earl of Northumberland, you will lose your crown.'

Royal Court, Château d'Amboise, France
20 May 1470

Greyhounds and lurchers scampered around their kennels. The sun had just broken the horizon and the dogs were full of excitement for the new day.

King Louis studied them; they were a source of great satisfaction to him – he knew all their names and histories, brothers and sisters, mothers and fathers, grandparents. Their breeding was a matter of great pride to him. He had purchased the finest pedigrees from many countries, in his pursuit to breed the finest hunting dogs in the whole of Europe, and yet, he realised, as he watched them, they were only simple dogs. They remembered no yesterday, and thought of no tomorrow; all they knew was here and now. *Men*, he pondered, *remember many yesterdays and imagine their tomorrows, but rarely live for the day, never casting away their fears or dreams to savour the richness of the moment*. He stood and silently watched the dogs, vowing to live each day to the full, as though it was his last. *For one day*, he thought, with a wry smile, *it will be*.

He turned and began slowly walking back to the royal palace. Excitement filled him. Today, he determined, was a day to enjoy; every moment precious, for the stage was set. Warwick and the Duke of Clarence would arrive shortly, and then his plans would commence.

King Louis watched from the great gates of the royal castle as his mighty lords rode off to greet these exiles from England. Behind him, Queen Charlotte, who in her eighth month of pregnancy stood big with child, was surrounded, as always, by her feminine court. Conversely, he knew that the Duke of Clarence's wife, the lady Isabel, had given birth to a stillborn baby boy – Warwick's grandson – on the rough channel crossing as they had fled England. He wondered if the sight of his wife would be an upsetting reminder, to the duke and Warwick, of their recent loss, but although it might have been unfortunate, he thought, with guilty selfishness, that it would help him to implement his plans.

The rich, hazy colours in the distance slowly came into focus. The shape of men and horse emerged, lances held aloft, dazzling livery jackets worn proudly displaying his royal coat-of-arms, and in the midst of this great company, he saw his good friend and ally, Warwick. *Let the game commence*, King Louis thought, as he walked slowly out of the gate and down the hill to greet him.

The royal welcome had been magnificent. Warwick and the Duke of Clarence had listened to the honeyed words of welcome from King Louis. Food and wine had flowed in copious amounts; minstrels, acrobats, and jesters, had entertained them and now they sat in the guest chambers awaiting the French king, for a private audience.

'We must shape Louis to our enterprise with all haste.' Warwick's voice broke the silence that had been lengthening between the two men, as the evening shadows dulled the light in their chambers.

George, the Duke of Clarence stirred from his wine-induced dumbness. 'Only a fool would refuse us,' he sighed. 'When I have been crowned King, we will repay his patronage ten times over.'

'We need funds urgently,' stated Warwick, flatly. 'My soldiers and sailors require the jingle of coin in their pockets, if they are not to grow mutinous.'

'Who grows mutinous?' asked a voice softly, behind them.

Warwick jumped to his feet, his sword half out of its scabbard, as he swung round.

George heaved himself from his chair and staggered drunkenly backwards.

'I am sorry to have startled you,' said King Louis, a smile on his face. He waved them back to their seats.

'But you have appeared like magic,' said Warwick, with astonishment.

'There is no magic; only a secret passage that runs between our chambers. It will keep our meetings private, away from listening ears and prying eyes.'

King Louis sat and studied the two English men. Warwick, he knew and trusted. He was an adventurer, a man who thought, and lived, outside normal conventions, who had no regard for kings and queens or countries. *Maybe he is a time traveller*, thought King Louis, *who has arrived like a shooting star from a distant era* – certainly, his daring exploits and great adventures had lit up the whole of Europe. He turned his attentions to George, Duke of Clarence; a young man who from the state of him obviously liked his wine. He was tall, like his brother, King Edward, but not as handsome. Nature had just robbed him of perfect features: his eyes were slightly close together, his upper lip just too long, his face rounded – not the noble cheekbones of his brother. A fine countenance had been stolen by only a fraction. It was a face King Louis would not trust.

'Richard,' began the king, addressing Warwick by his first name. 'You are a man who has turned defeat into victory many times. You have enthralled all of Europe with your exploits, so tell me, what is your plan now to revive your fortunes?'

'My plan sits before you,' replied Warwick. 'With your help, I intend to make George, King of England; Edward has shown himself unfit to rule!'

'How is that?' asked King Louis.

'He taxes the common people until they cry for mercy,' Warwick replied. 'No woman is safe from his lust be they commoner or noble. He demeans his crown with his adultery, and he has married into a witches' nest.'

'Also, a lowly archer sired him,' slurred George.

'So, these rumours of the black arts are true then?' asked King Louis.

Warwick crossed himself as he nodded agreement.

King Louis looked directly at Warwick. 'This is the first time I have met the Duke of Clarence and I can see that he is a fine young prince,' he lied, 'but tell me truthfully, is the crowd shouting out his name? Are the people of England really clamouring to make him king?'

George drunkenly tried to sit upright with indignation, but his elbow slipped off the arm of his chair, and he slipped further down into the seat, spilling his wine all over his chest.

Warwick stared at King Louis, his mouth slightly open, realising this was an upset to his plans. He quickly tried to think of an answer to allay the king's fears, but before he could, George staggered to his feet.

'I am the rightful heir to the crown,' he drunkenly shouted, like a spoilt boy. 'My father, the Duke of York, was the great grandson of Edward III; royal blood runs thick and pure through my veins, Edward has no royal blood…'

Warwick stood in front of him. 'Enough, George,' he hissed.

King Louis rose from his chair and patted the duke's shoulder. 'My young Lord,' he soothed, 'you have had an arduous journey from England, and I know you are suffering greatly for the sad death of your child. You need to rest. We will continue this conversation in the morning.'

Opening the door, King Louis called for George's servants, while Warwick steered the protesting duke through, and towards his private quarters.

Once George had settled, the king, and Warwick, took the private passage to the king's quarters.

King Louis ordered wine and sweet meats and then, finally alone, the two men faced each other.

'My old friend,' began the king, 'I will not support you in placing the Duke of Clarence on the throne of England. No gold or ships will I give you to this end.'

Warwick stretched out his legs, and leant back in his chair. He stared upwards for a while. Finally, he said, 'I appreciate your honesty, but you must understand my position. George is all I have to turn this setback into a victory. King Edward is your enemy; he is aligned with Burgundy; his sister is married to the duke. It is only a matter of time before they join forces to attack you, and then Brittany will join them. You could not survive; better to have England an ally with George, than an enemy with Edward.'

King Louis picked up a sweet almond cream, which he slowly ate as his thoughts turned over what Warwick had said.

Warwick sat sipping his wine in silence, patiently awaiting an answer.

'If you succeeded in placing the crown on George's head,' said King Louis, 'what would become of Edward?

'Well, I am still fond of the lad,' replied Warwick. 'We had been friends for many years, until he married that Woodville witch.'

'Yes, that was strange,' interrupted the king. 'It has the whiff of sorcery about it; but I interrupt; pray, continue.'

'I would place Edward in the tower, until Burgundy paid a large enough ransom to send him into exile.'

'So you would have three kings in England: George newly crowned; Edward newly uncrowned; and Holy Harry to keep him company in the Tower. Mercy is a godly virtue, but a recipe for disaster. England would be torn apart. Tis better that only one king lives. However, I believe with George as king; there would still be no peace. The nobles would not accept him, replacing brother for brother would not work and the commoners would reject him for turning against his own blood. If you placed Holy Harry back on the throne, all would know that it was you who wore the crown, so neither Henry nor George as king, me thinks. None of these scenarios would bear fruit'.

'So, you will not help me to regain my position,' stated Warwick, without emotion.

King Louis rose to his feet and paced the room. He stopped by the unlit fireplace and rested his hand on the ornate mantel. 'I will help you, my old friend, for there is another way,' he said, with a mischievous glint in his eyes, 'A strategy that would unite all England behind the throne, and place you, my dear Warwick, at the heart of it.'

Warwick lent forward; the king had his full attention.

'Henry resides in the Tower. His wife resides in France, along with their son Edward, Prince of Wales, a handsome young man of sixteen.'

'But that bitch...' started Warwick.

King Louis held up his hand. 'Let me finish. Henry is fondly loved by the people of England. He stirs no conflict. His wife, Margaret of Anjou, on the other hand, divides the country. If her son were crowned King that would unite the kingdom, and the House of Lancaster would join with the House of York.'

'That cannot be,' said Warwick, with hesitation. Her son would be Lancastrian, through and through; there is no changing that.'

'Yes, but if he married a beautiful Yorkist rose, then the realm would be unified by their marriage!' cried King Louis, as he watched Warwick try to conjure up a name that would be acceptable to the marriage. He continued, 'I believe your daughter, Anne, is of child-bearing age?'

Warwick sat bolt upright.

'I am told she is graceful and fair – would it not be the perfect match? The daughter of the mighty Warwick, who is loved by all England, and the son of old King Henry, who all are fond of – no man could find injury with that!' King Louis clasped his hands behind his back, and stood tall, a small smile of triumph on his face as though awaiting tumultuous applause for his cleverness.

Warwick sat still in his chair, staring thoughtfully at King Louis. The man had opened up a tantalising plan, the simplicity of which was brilliant. How could he not have thought of it himself? Every time he had looked at Anne, it had been staring him in the face, and it placed him at the centre of power. His own daughter and a young boy king would be easy to control, and when Anne had a son, he would be secure as the grandfather to a future king. Warwick did not trust himself to move, such was the excitement within him. Behind his small hard eyes, questions and solutions ran through his busy mind, until there was only one that had no solution to it. He rose slowly from his chair and joined the king at the fireplace.

'It is an ingenious plan, my friend, in which all the pieces of the jigsaw fit perfectly together, except for one rather large piece. Margaret of Anjou hates me with a vengeance. They say, a cantankerous and spiteful woman is the Devil's best work – she would never allow her son to marry my daughter.'

King Louis' smile grew larger. He walked to the table and refilled their wine glasses. Handing one to Warwick he raised a toast. 'Margaret of Anjou's son will marry your daughter, I'll wager my kingdom on it!'

The two men clinked glasses. King Louis laughed; Warwick looked perplexed.

Candles dripped hot pallid liquid down long stalagmite icicles of wax. Men had not slept. The moon was now transparent in the fresh sharp half-light of the early morning.

King Louis and Warwick sat opposite each other at the great oak table within the Hall of State. Men of ability and ambition surrounded them. The talk was of ships and men, weapons and victuals, and the money to finance them. They worked in small groups around the hall; each one had been detailed a task to plan. When they had formulated their strategy, it was presented to King Louis and Warwick, who either accepted or rejected it. If rejected, they went back and devised a new one. Slowly, as the day wore on, the great enterprise of England took shape. Finally, King Louis rose from his chair and announced it was done.

Georges Havart watched, as King Louis and Warwick left the hall. One was the greatest schemer in Europe; the other was the greatest adventurer. *They make a formidable pair*, he thought, as he watched their backs disappear into the darkening palace.

'How did the George take the news that he had lost his crown before it had even been perched on his simple drunken head?' asked King Louis, as he watched the server approach with the first course of their private dinner.

'Not well,' replied Warwick. 'I told him he would be next in line to the throne, unless of course, young Edward and Anne had male heirs. After much cursing, he finally said that not only had he lost the crown, he would also lose many of his estates to that Bitch of Anjou's lackeys.'

'He will be lucky not to lose his head once young Edward and your daughter are crowned,' said the king, with a thin smile. 'You should remind him of that!'

'He is only a boy,' said Warwick, softly. 'Good with a sword, but no soldier. Edward, on the other hand, is a brilliant general. He has won seven straight battles; never tasted that bitter bile of defeat. We will need good fortune to defeat him.'

'The early Roman philosopher, Seneca the Younger, said, "Luck is what happens when preparation meets opportunity" and that is the key to this great enterprise: preparation. I have ordered', continued King Louis, 'that the royal purse be opened. Gold coin you shall have, to purchase whatever you need, and to pay wages to your men. I know the crown of England will not come cheap.'

Warwick had a satisfied smile on his face, as he tucked into his second course.

'Your brother, John, must be discontented?' said the king thoughtfully, as he sipped his wine. 'He has lost his earldom and authority. Edward has given him a hollow title. Is there not opportunity to exploit this rift?'

Warwick finished his mouthful of food. He picked up his wine glass and stared at its contents as he slowly swirled them around. 'My agents,' he began, 'are on their way to England with messages for my brother to join our standard. The Earl of Shrewsbury and Lord Stanley have secretly pledged their support. When the time is right, they will start a token rebellion in the north that will draw Edward northwards. We will then land unopposed in the south. The men of Kent and Devon support us. My other brother, George, the Archbishop of York, is working to swing the church behind us. I have letters signed by myself, which will be delivered on the day we land, to the mayors of the great towns and cities of the realm, reminding them of the oppressive tax demands that Edward makes on them and their citizens, rich and poor, and how these demands are destroying the realm. Under Edwards's authority, his secretive and ungodly family are now controlling the land, but we have returned to free the people and set the rightful king upon the throne. Jasper Tudor arrives here shortly; he will rally the people of Wales behind our standards. The exiled earls of Oxford and Somerset will also be arriving to swell our numbers.'

'This is indeed good news,' said King Louis, gleefully. 'England will be ripe for the plucking by the time you land.'

'When will Margaret of Anjou be arriving?' asked Warwick, trying to conceal the distaste in his voice.

'Within the next two days. So you must be away to Saint Vaast-la-Hougue, to ready your fleet and prepare your daughter, Anne, for her marriage to Edward, the young Prince of Wales.'

'It is not a task I go willing to,' sighed Warwick. 'The girl is but fifteen and has lived most of her young life in the seclusion of Middleham Castle. She knows not the way of royal courts. She has been wrenched from her secluded life, dragged headlong across England and a storm-tossed channel, to France, and now I have to tell her she is to marry a youth I have always taught her to hate. She will be bewildered and fearful. I love her dearly, and to any lover of chivalry, this would appear to be a wicked and cynical business—'

'But it is a duty that must be done,' King Louis butted in. 'It is a pledge of faith to Margaret, and remember, our children form part of our resources. They are bargaining chips to strengthen our power. Do not forget, my friend, she will be the bride to the next King of England – what greater gift can a father give his daughter?'

'I had already given that gift to her elder sister, Isabel, which I now take away. I do not know what she or her mother will make of this,' replied Warwick, 'but in truth, I will do anything that is necessary to regain my control of England. That is the hardness of it; we who rule cannot be like normal men.'

The two men ate in silence, as they digested food and thoughts alike. Finally, King Louis broke the silence.

'While you are away, I will bring Margaret of Anjou around to our way of thinking. It may take some time, but she will be brought to heel. I will also have to obtain a special dispensation from the Pope for the marriage to take place, for I believe your daughter's great grandmother, Joan Beaufort, was half-sister to Prince Edward's great grandfather, Henry IV.'

Warwick looked up with concern on his face. 'So they are related by blood!' he cried.

King Louis nodded agreement.

'Ye Gods! A holy dispensation could take months, even years, to obtain.'

'It will be done quickly,' said King Louis, with a smile. 'I have two caged cardinals in La Conciergerie prison to barter with. The Pope would like them returned to the Vatican.' Then, leaning closer to Warwick, he whispered, 'While you are away, keep George close to your side, for as you entreat your brother, John, to join you, so Edward of England will be entreating his Duke of Clarence to join him.'

Royal Court, Château d'Amboise, France
15 July 1470

Margaret of Anjou sat in the antechamber to the throne room awaiting her audience with King Louis. She felt uneasy, but she did not know why. Sitting quietly, she sought the reasons for this sense of foreboding that filled her. Their journey from Paris had been pleasurable. Along the way, they had stayed with old friends who had entertained and spoilt them. Her son, Edward, had enjoyed the adventure of it all. His charm and good looks had won him many admirers at the grand houses they had stayed at, and they had finally arrived at the royal palace in good spirits.

It was later, when she was having dinner with her father and brother, that the first seeds of uneasiness had filled her. Their conversation had been stilted, of no account, as if they were afraid of saying something that would lead the conversation down a road of secrets. They had looked at each other nervously when she had asked questions about their visit or her son's prospects with the king's daughter; their answers had been evasive. Her womanly intuition told her something was wrong, and then that morning, just after dawn, as she was watching the sun creep across the dew-laden gardens, two riders had approached, riding as though their lives depended on it. She had lost sight of them as they had neared the great gate, and although they were some way off, she had felt a stab of apprehension. She was sure they wore the insignia of the *Bear and Ragged Staff* – Warwick's colours. She had quickly dismissed the idea as too preposterous to contemplate. Her eyes had deceived her, and yet, now as she sat awaiting her audience with King Louis, it nagged at her. She felt a shiver of impending doom run down her spine.

A courtier dressed in the blue and gold uniform of the palace appeared, and asked her small entourage to form up by the great doors that led into the throne room.

'When they swing open,' he had whispered, respectfully, 'you will be announced. Enter at a slow dignified pace. Once before the dais, curtsy, or bow, and remain in that position until the King tells you to rise.'

'Margaret of Anjou, Queen of England,' announced the senior courtier, as the massive doors swung open. 'Edward, Prince of Wales,' he continued.

Margaret hesitated. She had not been called the Queen of England since her exile had begun, and those three simple words confirmed her suspicions: there was a conspiracy afoot. Once in the room, she looked up to the dais. Her cousin, King Louis, sat on his throne, a small thin smile of welcome playing across his features.

He sits, Margaret thought, *like a spider weaving his web of intrigues*. She shuddered at the sight of him, and then straightened her back. *Well, if they want the Queen of England then they shall have her*, she thought, with steely pride. Squaring her back and shoulders, she stepped forward. The gold and silver gown she wore was inlaid with pearls and precious gems; they sparkled in the morning sun that streamed through the narrow windows like condensed shafts of gold.

As she moved forward, with her son on her arm, she looked at the men surrounding the throne. She recognised Georges Havart and Marshall Rouault, King Louis's most trusted advisors. The church was represented by Jean Balue, the Bishop of Évreux. Next to him, stood Louis de Beaumont de la Forêt, who she knew to be a two-faced weasel of a councillor. On the other side of the throne, stood the king's chancellor, Guillaume Juvésnal de Ursins, and the Governor of Paris, Robert d'Estouteville – both good men. The Grand Master of the royal household, Antoine de Chabannes, Count of Dammartin, hovered in the background and finally, through their dignity, Marshall Lohéac, General Tanneguy du Chastel, and the Duke of Bourbon, added weight and significance to the assembled royal council. Margaret knew it was a formidable gathering.

She saw, with surprise, that many men were kneeling to her as she walked towards the king. It took her a second or two to realise that they were men from her past, ghosts appearing from some far away world. She slowed her pace. She was not being haunted. These were either men exiled from England, or their sons, who had supported her cause as Queen of England. Her heart warmed to them as first she recognised the new Duke of Somerset, then the Earl of Oxford, followed by the Duke of Exeter, and finally, Jasper Tudor. All bowed with a flourish before her. All brave men who had given and lost so much in the struggle to keep the crown of England upon her husband's head. She felt bewildered, though. Why were they all here? As she moved closer to King Louis, she could feel his sticky web of intrigue begin to glue itself around her. Then, she was curtsying.

King Louis rose from his throne and quickly descended the steps of the dais. Raising her up, he kissed her on both cheeks. Then, turning to the assembled court, he held her hand and bowed. She followed his lead and curtseyed. The assembled court clapped and cheered with delight; all of them oblivious to the turmoil that was filling her.

One hour later, Margaret of Anjou was sitting alone with King Louis, who had finally stopped talking. She stared at him in silence, grateful that there was only the two of them present, for what he had just said to her was utter madness, the ravings of a lunatic.

She looked around the chamber as her mind tried to unscramble his insane requests. The chamber was tastefully furnished with beautiful Chinese chairs and tables, carved, or engraved, with dragons and warriors. Elegant blue and white porcelain vases, and figurines, took pride of place. She knew the secrets of porcelain manufacture had yet to be discovered in Europe – a king's ransom awaited the man who could solve the mystery. Elegant oriental paintings adorned the walls; their simple clean brushstrokes conveyed a world of tranquillity, a world far removed from the one she lived in. Her eyes slowly returned to the king's face.

King Louis could see the anger burning deep within Margaret's eyes as she focused on him.

'You demand my son marries Warwick's daughter?' Margaret hissed.

The venom in her voice made King Louis hold his breath.

'You dare to ask me to touch Warwick's hands, those cruel hands that are covered in the blood of my loyal subjects, the hands that took the crown from Henry's head, and the hands that stole my throne. Were I in Heaven with the angels, I would still cut out his heart.'

King Louis flinched as Margaret spat the words at him with hatred. He slowly let his breath out, realising the anger within her went far deeper than he had thought. He let the silence between them lengthen, hoping it would cool her anger. 'My dear cousin,' he finally began, his voice soft and gentle. 'This is about your son. I realise your animosity runs deep, but you cannot deny the throne of England to him, and remember, madam,' he said, with sudden force, 'your husband, Henry, rots in the Tower of London. I am offering you his freedom as well.'

Margaret threw her head back and laughed mockingly. 'Henry is happier in the Tower praying at his makeshift altar than sitting on the throne of England, and I vowed long ago that I will never again set foot on that accursed island.'

'But what of your son?' cried King Louis, his voice full of passion. 'Would you deny him his birthright? He must be crowned with Anne Neville as his Queen. Imagine: a king and queen with no Yorkist or Lancastrian blood on their hands – a king who is acceptable to all.'

Margaret rose from her chair, and slammed her hands on the table in frustration. 'My son,' she shouted, 'will never be King, and while Warwick is pulling the strings of power, he would be lucky to last a year.'

King Louis sprang from his chair in frustration, his face suddenly close to hers. 'Warwick,' he snarled, 'arrives here in two days' time with his wife and daughters, and before he does, you will agree to this marriage, one way, or another,' he said threateningly, his eyes flashing with anger.

'Over my dead body,' Margaret jeered back. 'Over my dead body.'

'That dammed woman is as stubborn as a mule!' shouted King Louis to his advisors. 'She will not bend an inch to accommodate my wishes.'

Georges Havart moved quickly to pacify him. 'Her own court sits with her now,' he said. 'They are to a one behind your plan. She cannot refuse them.'

'I hope you are right,' replied the king, wearily. 'The whole enterprise rests on this dammed marriage. As we speak, Warwick is making ready his invasion fleet and now that this great undertaking is in motion, I will allow nothing to stop it.'

Margaret sat with her father, René of Anjou, and Sir John Fortescue in the Oriental room. A frustrated silence hung around them. The rest of her old court, the exiled lords and dukes, had just left them with the bitter taste of disappointment in their mouths. She had refused to comply with their wishes, although she had been understanding of their situations, and had professed her love for them all, but to return to England, she had refused.

'There was more honour amongst thieves than between the nobles of England', she had cried. 'You are welcome to go with that pirate, Warwick, place Henry back upon his throne, and regain your estates, but I will have no part of it. My hatred for this man has not been cooled by my years in France'.

They had flattered, begged, and cajoled, but her memories of Warwick's deeds had never dimmed. Her answer to them had been, 'No, no, no!'

Sir John Fortescue took Margaret's hand, and looked into her eyes. 'Come,' he said. 'We must prepare to travel home; there is no more to be said, or done, here.'

She looked up into his kindly face, and nodded her head. 'Why,' she sighed wearily, as tears formed in her eyes, 'do they not leave me in peace?'

'Because you offer them hope, and Warwick, power,' replied René of Anjou. 'You must do what is right by your conscience and your God, but remember, your son will one day wish to fulfil his destiny, and claim the throne of England, and you will not be able to stop him.'

At that moment, they heard the sounds of marching footsteps, growing louder. They rose from their chairs, exchanging worried looks. The door burst open. Armed troops of King Louis' personal guard stormed into the room and positioned themselves around the walls.

The king swept in, his face red with anger. 'You have refused men who have given their all for you!' he shouted. 'Men, whose fathers have died in your cause. You have a cold heart, Margaret of Anjou, that's if you have a heart at all. Shall we see? Bring in the prisoner!' he commanded.

A man was roughly manhandled into the room. Etienne de Loup forced him to his knees.

Margaret's hands flew to her mouth as Simon Langford looked up at her.

'Marguerite, don't—'

Simon's words were cut short as Etienne de Loup's fist smashed into his face. He slumped to the floor, bloodied and dazed.

Margaret screamed and fell to her knees beside him. 'Simon!' she cried.

King Louis circled around them like a bird of prey. 'If you do not agree to this marriage,' he hissed, with quiet malevolence, 'then this criminal, who attempted to murder the Earl of Warwick will be handed over to him for execution, but if you agree to our demands, he will be set free. It is a simple choice: life or death.'

Margaret looked up at the king with loathing in her eyes. Her father, and Sir John Fortescue, looked on with repugnance.

King Louis clapped his hands, and ushered everyone from the room. 'I will give you both some time to think on your answers,' he said, closing the door.

The City of Valognes, France
15 July 1470

Rose stood quietly in the shadows that were thrown by the low, curved roof of the main hall. The Earl of Warwick and his family were staying at a sumptuous château that formed the centre of a great vineyard estate on the outskirts of the city. After their frantic escape from England, the serenity of the locality had lifted all their spirits – until now.

All their faces were white with shock, for the earl's words had turned their world upside down. George, the Duke of Clarence, was no longer to be king, and as such, Isabel no longer queen. The pair of them had lost their futures within the blink of an eye, both now redundant in the earl's plans. George glared at Warwick with anger in his eyes. Isabel, tears running down her cheeks, stared at her younger sister, full of resentment, for Anne was now to be queen in her place. She was to marry Margaret of Anjou's young bastard son, Edward, although, now conveniently, according to her father's latest wisdom, he was no longer a bastard, but Holy Harry's rightful heir. Lord Warwick, it would seem, would marry the devil himself, to rule England.

Rose looked at Anne, who sat straight-backed and motionless, but she knew her heart must be breaking, for she was betrothed to Duke Richard. They had played together at Middleham, danced, laughed, grown fond of each other, and now her father had betrayed that love, and had sold her virginity to the French king so that he, the mighty Earl of Warwick, could strut upon the stage of England once again. Her heart went out to her. The poor girl had become her father's last hope, his final throw of the dice. She watched as Anne tried to suppress the tears that welled up in her eyes. The pain and anguish was etched with heart-rending sadness across the young girl's face. Anne was being ordered to marry a boy she had been taught to hate, ever since she had been born.

Rose felt hot anger welling up within her. The injustice against Anne made her head swim with emotion. All she could see was the earl with his small hard eyes staring at Anne, daring her to refuse. 'The Lady

Anne...' she blurted out.

Warwick turned towards her, his hard eyes seeking her out amongst the shadows, his features a mix of surprise and anger.

Rose continued. 'Is she now just a farmyard animal to be bartered and sold to the highest bidder? So, you, the mighty Earl of Warwick can uncrown one king and place the crown on another.'

All eyes in the room looked at her with a mixture of horror and fascination. Nobody moved.

Rose rushed from the shadows and threw herself at the earl's feet. 'My Lord!' she cried. 'You cannot be this cruel to your own flesh and blood. Anne loves Duke Richard, she cannot marry—'

The back of Warwick's hand caught Rose a vicious blow across the side of her face, his cluster of gold rings slicing deep cuts across her cheek. She swayed on her knees, her mind stunned. She felt warm blood running down her neck, then his other hand, curled into a tight fist, smashed into her other cheek. She felt the inside of her mouth lacerate against her teeth, and then fell back, her mouth oozing blood.

Through her spinning mind, she vaguely heard the earl shouting. She saw the glint of a dagger in his hand. She saw it being raised over her, and then, as the darkness descended, she heard in the dim distance, Anne screaming.

Royal Court, Château d'Amboise, France
15 July 1470

As the door closed, Margaret stared at Simon with disbelief.

'Simon,' she whispered, 'are you real?' She reached out and touched his blooded face; he winced in pain. 'You are in Paris, in prison, not here,' she cried. 'I came to this royal palace to seek your freedom.' She raised her hands up to the heavens. 'Oh God!' she cried. 'How you must laugh at us, we who make plans, for now my son must marry the daughter of my bitterest enemy, and I must forgive that Devil, Warwick, his crimes against me and allow his savage lips to kiss my hand in pardon. No, no, no!' she wailed. 'This cannot be, and yet if I refuse, my one true love will be executed by this same monster who wishes to be my ally.'

'Warwick? Did you just say, "Warwick"? Is the bastard here?' cried Simon, as he struggled to his feet.

Margaret helped him up. Using the sleeve of her dress, she gently wiped the blood from his face. 'He is coming here shortly,' she said, softly, 'with his daughter, to marry my son, and if I refuse, they will kill you.'

'You cannot agree to their demands,' said Simon. 'I would rather be dead than see you in that Devil's pocket. To do as he orders, because of me, is unthinkable. I—'

Margaret reached up and kissed Simon with wild hungry passion. His arms encircled her. Their longing for each other made the world disappear. 'You cannot die,' she breathed, huskily.

He ran his hands up under her skirts. He caressed her silky thighs. When his hand moved further upwards, she moaned softly.

'It has been so long,' Simon whispered, as he forced her down on to the table.

'I will give them a little longer,' said King Louis, with impatience. 'I imagine they are still getting over the shock of seeing each other. He, I would assume, must be praying that she still loves him enough to sacrifice her son for him, and she must be asking herself if she does.'

When King Louis entered the room, his patience finally exhausted, Margaret and Simon sat quietly, facing each other across the table.

'Well, madam,' the king said, sharply, 'do you have your answer? Is it to be life or death?'

Margaret looked at Simon, a satisfied smile played across her features. He sat relaxed, with a devil-may-care look on his face.

King Louis looked at them both with exasperation, his temper finally ignited. 'What in God's name are you both smirking about?' he shouted. 'This is a serious matter that affects the future of France; it is not some trivial dispute. We are not haggling over the price of wine. So, madam,' he cried, 'I will have your answer.'

Margaret rose from her chair. Like a chameleon, her demeanour changed. She grew in stature as her back straightened and her shoulders squared. She thrust her face, now proud and set with purpose, to within inches of the king's. 'We have chosen life,' she said, spitting the words at him with venom.

King Louis clapped his hands together with delight.

'But, with certain conditions,' Margaret added, with a smile of triumph.

'Conditions? Conditions?' cried the king, his hands stopping mid-clap. 'You cannot barter over his life. Marriage, he lives – no marriage, he dies. It is as simple as that.'

'Well then, he must die,' Margaret replied, nonchalantly.

King Louis stared at her. Was the woman completely mad? But then, she knew, he reasoned, that he desperately needed this marriage, so he would have to hear her out for the sake of France. He sat down at the table, and waved her to the seat opposite.

'My dear cousin,' King Louis began; a feigned look of benign patience on his face. 'I will consider your demands.'

Margaret sat down and looked at him coldly. 'What you are doing demeans your kingship.' Her voice filled with scorn. 'It is beyond contempt.'

King Louis swallowed hard, but kept his silence.

'You are blackmailing me into taking a course of action with a man I detest – a man who destroyed all that I once held dear. With all your grand designs, you will never bring back those royal days for me, so where is the profit in all of this? I have no wish to be the Queen of England, or for my son to be King. There is not one part of my body or soul that cries out for any of this, and yet, you would still force me by means most foul to help that murdering pirate, Warwick.'

'Think of it as helping France,' interrupted King Louis.

Margaret gave him a withering glance. 'Helping Warwick will be of no help to France,' she shouted, 'but I will comply with your wishes, only if I will be the one to decide when it is safe for us to return to England. I must be sure that King Edward, his brother, Duke Richard, and Warwick's brother, John Neville, are dead or exiled, then, once my son has been crowned King of England, I will be allowed to return to live in France with Simon Langford, who you will grant a full pardon to. Thirdly, you will pay me an annual income for life that befits my position as Queen Mother.'

King Louis placed his fingertips beneath his chin, his face deep in thought. Finally, he said, 'I agree to all your demands, except for the exile or death of Warwick's brother, John.'

'Then I will not agree to the marriage,' said Margaret, sharply. 'To forgive two Nevilles is asking too much, sir!' she cried.

'You do not know all the facts, madam,' replied King Louis, his voice full of appeasement. 'John Neville, now the Marquess of Montagu, has been badly treated by King Edward, and I can reveal,' he whispered, conspiratorially, 'that he has decided to join his brother's standard in his great enterprise of England.'

'Pray, tell me what that means,' said Margaret, stiffly.

'It means, my dear cousin, that Warwick will take England without a fight. The plan is, that a minor uprising in the north of England will be formulated to draw Edward away from London. He will, of course, send for Warwick's brother to help him quell this rebellion and John Neville will go along with Edward's request, until they rendezvous, then he will attack Edward's army with his superior forces. Edward and his brother, Richard, and all their close retainers, will be killed or executed immediately after the battle. No mercy will be shown. Warwick will land on the south coast, and march on London, and then you, dear lady, will set sail for England, and the coronation of your son and his wife.'

'It sounds so simple and easy,' said Margaret sarcastically. 'I am waiting for you to tell me nothing can go wrong.'

'With the great Earl of Warwick in charge, all will be well,' King Louis said, oozing confidence. 'Now, I must away to prepare for the arrival of the great man and his family, and you must prepare your son to meet his bride.' A satisfied smile creased his face, as he rose from his chair, and made for the door. When he reached it, he turned. 'Sir Simon,' he said, 'you are a lucky man to have survived so long with your reckless ways. I would advise you to think more and act less in the future. Once the marriage has taken place, and Margaret's son, Edward, has been crowned King of England, you will be given a full pardon. You will then be free to go, but until then, you are confined to the castle.'

As King Louis swept from the room, Margaret turned to Simon. 'It is a high price I am paying for your freedom,' she said, 'but I will take payment in kind for it.' She laughed.

Simon stepped forward, and taking Margaret in his arms, he kissed her passionately. 'Then, let that be the first payment,' he said, with a smile.

Chapter 12

To Risk All

Royal Court Gardens, Château d'Amboise, France 24 August 1470

Simon Langford walked slowly through the royal gardens. The August afternoon was warm and sultry; the fragrance of the summer flowers drifted lazily around him. It had been over four weeks since Margaret of Anjou had agreed to King Louis' request.

He remembered Warwick's arrival. With his demoralised family, and depleted entourage, all of them looked impoverished. Oh, how he had enjoyed seeing the bastard humbled, this once mighty lord now living on handouts from the French king.

There had been meetings, discussions, arguments, and tantrums, between Margaret, King Louis, and Warwick, but eventually, on the 22 July, King Louis had led Warwick by the hand into the Great Hall of State. There, in the presence of Margaret of Anjou, the woman Warwick hated, he had been forced to grovel on his knees before her, pleading for forgiveness.

Simon had watched from a hidden vantage point as Margaret had kept Warwick on his knees for an eternity, his humiliation for all to see. Eventually, she had raised him up before the royal court and forgiven him his crimes against her. It was all a sham. Margaret had sacrificed herself and her son to save Simon's life, and Warwick had grimly swallowed his pride, so that he could take England and place a crown on his daughter's head.

Throughout all the meetings and intrigues, King Louis had kept Simon well out of the way. But when dusk fell, there were no such restrictions. King Louis, he thought, wanted the two of them to be lovers, so that Margaret's resolve would not weaken. The king had been right: their lovemaking had been wild and passionate, but now Margaret was gone, gone with her son and her small court to Angers, along with Warwick and King Louis. Today, within the great cathedral, Anne Neville and Edward, Prince of Wales, as he was now called, would be married, and their oaths solemnised on a piece of the True Cross – the Cross of St Laud d'Angers. It was said that if you broke your oath, such was its power that you would die within a year.

Rose Thorne sat quietly, watching the lone figure in the distance. She was seated on one of the many benches that were dotted around the gardens. This particular seat had become a calm oasis for her over the last few days. Since the brutal attack by Warwick, she had been hidden from his sight while Lady Tunstall nursed her.

Her face was still swollen, and the deep cuts down one side would take many weeks to heal, but Rose knew she was lucky to be alive. She had been told that, only the Lady Anne throwing herself on top of Rose, had stopped the earl from plunging his dagger deep into her chest. Now, she came to this seat daily to enjoy the solitude, and to hide her face from the stares that followed her wherever she walked.

She saw the man in the distance, slowly coming closer. She could see he was dressed as a gentleman, but he was still too far away to distinguish his features. She was curious now, because any man of status had left with the royal parties for the wedding at Angers. She, of course, had been left behind in disgrace. Lady Tunstall had said, 'You must keep well away from Lord Warwick'. The countess had added, 'Out of sight and out of mind'. Both of them were mystified as to why Rose had done such a thing, and both of them were amazed that she was still alive – as was Rose.

But now, Rose hated the earl with a vengeance for what he was doing to his daughter, to whom Rose now owed her life. If Anne had not stopped him in his blind rage, she would be dead, although, Rose reflected, she might as well be. She was to sail with the earl's army for

314

England. Once there, she was to be stripped and flogged, and then cast out of the earl's household on to the streets, with only the rags she stood up in.

'You look so sad.'

Rose jumped, startled at the sound of the stranger's voice. She had become so lost in her thoughts that she had failed to notice his approach.

'Judging from your injuries, you must be the poor girl who incurred the wrath of that bastard, Warwick.'

Rose heard sympathy in the man's voice. Her hands clutched the sides of her face to hide her injuries.

'Rose, once your injuries have healed, you will still be the pretty girl I remember from Middleham Castle.'

Rose lowered her hands, and stared at him with a look of puzzlement. His eyes twinkled with a hidden smile. 'You have me at a disadvantage, sir,' she said, 'for I do not know you.'

The man sat down beside her. 'Forgive me for confusing you,' he smiled. 'My name, in those days, was Robert Furneys. I was a clerk in the Great Controller's office, but in reality, I spied for the Lancastrian cause, for Queen Margaret and King Henry.'

'I remember, now!' exclaimed Rose. 'You were the one who escaped. You were lucky, for I remember the executions of those poor wretched men who didn't.' She shuddered.

'Yes, I was blessed that day,' he said, quietly.

Rose's eyes widened in understanding. 'So you must be Sir Simon Langford, Margaret of Anjou's lover.' Her hands shot up to her mouth in embarrassment. 'I am so sorry. I did not mean to be rude, but you are the talk of the castle.' She giggled.

'It seems it is such a great secret,' Simon laughed, joining in her mirth, 'that the whole world knows.'

'Is it true that you tried to kill Warwick?' Rose asked, with a sudden a look of seriousness.

'Yes, that is true.'

'It is a shame you failed. The man is a monster. He is to have me return to England, whipped and cast out in disgrace.'

Simon saw the anger flash within Rose's eyes. 'I am sure it will not come to that. The Lady Warwick and her ladies will surely speak up for you, but if you are sent back, is there not anyone to help you?'

'I am betrothed to Sir John Tunstall. His mother is here with the countess. Lady Tunstall was the one who tended my wounds. Anyway, you must remember John; he serves Duke Richard, King Edward's younger brother.'

Simon did not reply. The memory of hiding in the depository all those years ago, and spying on the Great Controller as he interviewed John, flashed before him, then the words of King Louis came back to him: 'Warwick's brother will betray them all'.

Rose noticed that Simon's face had grown serious. 'And you?' she said, changing the subject. 'What will you do when you are free?'

'I will travel to England to find news of my mother and sisters. It has been too long since I saw them last.' He noticed Rose's face turning pale, and she turned away from him. 'What troubles you?' Simon asked.

'Tis nothing.'

He saw in her eyes a sudden look of pity – a look that filled his heart with dread. He wished he were somewhere else, anywhere but here, beside this young woman who looked at him with such dismay. His blood ran cold as he forced the question from his lips. 'You know of their fate?' He watched as Rose nodded her head, her beautiful eyes filling with tears of compassion.

She took Simon's hand, and looked into his eyes. 'When Warwick returned from France, all those years ago, we heard about the attempt on his life, and how the perpetrators had all been caught and executed, all except for one who was spared death by the King of France; that one survivor being you.' She looked at Simon's pale face, as he nodded agreement. 'The earl was so angry that you had escaped death, and then he also found out that you had once been a spy within his own castle. He swore that if he couldn't have your head he would take revenge on your family instead.'

Simon buried his head in his hands. His worst dreams were becoming real, and those nightmares he had held at bay for all those years were now a brutal reality.

Rose continued. 'He seized your estates, and had your mother and sisters arrested for treason. They were taken to Warwick Castle and…'

'And, what?' Simon demanded.

'Do you want to hear the truth?' Rose asked, her voice trembling.

Simon nodded, his face now pinched tight in fear.

'It was said they were stripped naked, viciously flogged, and then branded on their foreheads with the letter "T" for traitor. Afterwards, they were thrown into the deepest dungeon. I do not know…' Rose's voice faltered as she saw the look of despair in Simon's eyes. 'I do not know their fate, after that.'

'Oh, mother of God!' Simon cried. 'Have mercy on me for what I have done.' He looked around in desolation. 'As I rotted in my prison, so they in theirs, and if still alive they rot there still.' He stood, in agitation. 'If there is still hope, I must go to them…' his voice trailed off into helpless silence.

Rose tried to offer some hope. 'I am sure if John and Duke Richard asked permission, King Edward would issue you the authority to search for them.'

'Yes, yes!' Simon cried, as he grasped at this small sliver of hope, this chance of redemption; then he remembered what King Louis had said to Margaret.

Rose saw the hesitation in him, a look of uncertainty entering his eyes. She felt a stab of apprehension, and somehow, she knew. 'What do you know of John and Duke Richard?' she demanded, her voice rising with concern.

'King Louis told Margaret of Anjou, that Warwick's brother, John – Lord Montagu, has turned traitor. His orders are to kill King Edward, Duke Richard, and all their close retainers, once Warwick has set sail for England,'

Rose stared at Simon, in shock. 'This cannot be!' she cried. 'John loves King Edward, like a brother.'

'Blood, it would seem, is thicker than water,' Simon replied, grimly.

'Then we must escape, before Warwick sails and warns them of this treachery!' The urgency in Rose's voice betrayed her mounting panic.

Simon felt a sudden sense of purpose. 'You are right. We must slip away before they all return from Angers. We will head up through Brittany to the small port of Dinan – it is near St Malo – and there take ship to England.' He took Rose's hand. 'Come,' he said, with purpose. 'We must act swiftly, if we are to save the people we love.'

Royal Court, Château d'Amboise, France
26 August 1470

The rain fell from a black-grey sky. Shivering, Margaret of Anjou looked out of the royal carriage, at the wet, sodden landscape. She imagined it as a world that had never seen the sun, a world of shadows and darkness, a world that reflected the despair she felt in her heart, for after the wedding of her son, melancholy had settled on her spirit.

Opposite her, sat Sir John Fortescue, and her father, René. Her son, Edward, sat beside her. Their excited conversation was centred on the invasion of England, and what it had meant to them all. Her mind had been dulled by it. She watched the wind swirl raindrops through the cold air. It reminded her of how King Louis had sent her own life spinning out of control. He had manipulated the opportunity that Warwick had presented to him, using carrot or stick, and the main reason for all this intrigue, she understood bitterly, was to marry England and France against Burgundy in a war to the death. Now, all these lives had been turned upside down, just so that King Louis and Warwick could further their stupid grandiose plans.

At least, Warwick had departed. She would not have to look at his arrogant face again. He had left early that morning with Jasper Tudor and the Earl of Oxford, to ready his fleet for sailing.

At least, my son still sits beside me, Margaret thought happily, *while his new wife, Anne, who wears her heart on her sleeve for Duke Richard, sits with her mother's court. There must be no consummation of this marriage until they are crowned in Westminster Abbey. For, if Warwick fails against King Edward, then an annulment would be easy to obtain. There are better brides in Europe for my son, than the spawn of that Devil, Warwick,* she concluded.

The letter had been placed on her pillow. Margaret stared at the neatly folded parchment, wrapped with a red ribbon. A single red rose lay across this seemingly unwelcome guest.

Sitting on the bed, she carefully lifted the flower. She studied its beautifully formed petals, and smelt its lingering fragrance. *A rose for love*, she thought, as a single tear rolled down her cheek.

With a trembling hand, she reached out and picked up the letter with its silent message. With the page unfolded, the words that she knew would hurt her deeply, revealed themselves.

Marguerite,

I write this, my love, with a heavy heart, for fate has once again conspired to part us. I have learnt that Warwick has taken revenge on my mother and sisters. I leave in all haste for England to rescue them. I pray they are still alive.

I know you have sacrificed all for me, but my conscience cannot allow me to stay. The die is cast. Your life must now follow the treacherous path that King Louis and Warwick have forced upon you. In your heart, you know it is a path you must walk alone.

For now, my sweet angel, be strong, and never fear, I will come to you when you need me most.

Simon.

Royal Chambers, Château d'Amboise, France
27 August 1470

'Etienne?' shouted King Louis. 'For God's sake, where is he?'

Georges Havart and Marshall Rouault exchanged worried glances.

'Men have been dispatched to find him,' replied Georges Havart.

'He will be here shortly,' added Marshall Rouault, trying to reassure the king.

'By God's Bones, he had better be,' replied King Louis, straining to keep his temper under control.

Etienne de Loup rushed breathless into the room. 'Your Majesty,' he gasped.

King Louis spun round to face him. 'That bastard, Simon Langford,' he cried, 'has escaped along with a serving maid who belonged to Warwick's court!'

'I am aware of this,' replied Etienne de Loup, with raised eyebrows, 'but I am not aware that it is cause for concern. They can do us no harm.'

'No harm? No harm?' bellowed King Louis. 'The man knows that Warwick's brother is planning to ambush King Edward and his army, and that the dammed serving maid is to marry one of Duke Richard's closest lieutenants. We can guess where the pair of them are heading, and why.'

'Tell me who told them this state secret, and I will make the bastard a head shorter!' cried Etienne de Loup.

King Louis sat quietly down in his seat, and coughed. 'It was me.'

The three men stared at him. 'Pardon?' they exclaimed, in unison.

'It was me,' said King Louis, sheepishly. 'I got carried away in my discussions with that stubborn, bloody woman from Anjou; I forgot her lover was in the room.'

'I will have men pursue them down every road in France that leads to a port,' said Etienne de Loup, 'although, I think the north coast of Brittany would be their most likely destination. They only have two days' lead on us, so with luck, we should catch them.'

'If King Edward escapes from Warwick's brother, then all our plans will be in jeopardy. They must be caught!' shouted King Louis, picking up his wine glass and hurling it against the wall in frustration.

Etienne de Loup rushed from the room, whilst Georges Havart and Marshall Rouault tried to make themselves invisible.

The Bull's Head Inn, Tower Street, London
27 August 1470

The inn was unusually quiet. The cool breeze of the hot, August night kept many outside, away from the still heat of the interior.

'How long have King Edward and Duke Richard been in the Tower?' asked Friar Drynk, as he raised a flagon of ale to his lips.

The Hallet twins stared at him.

'Dogs breath, if I know,' said Thomas. 'Duke Richard and Sir John have ordered us to report to the main gates, nine of the clock, for reasons that are a mystery.'

'It's to do with Holy Harry,' whispered George.

The other two, intrigued now, stared at George, their ears hungry to know more.

George stayed silent, and stared into his tankard of ale.

Friar Drynk raised his eyes to the heavens. 'Holy Mother,' he sighed, in frustration.

'For Christ's sake, George,' hissed Thomas. 'What's to do with Holy Harry?'

George looked furtively around the inn. 'I overheard,' he whispered, 'Sir John and Duke Richard saying that Warwick, and the French, are raising an army to overthrow King Edward and place Henry back on the throne.'

'So, you're saying, that daft bastard, Warwick, now wants to uncrown Edward and re-crown Henry?' cried Thomas, in disbelief.

'Aye, but if Henry is dead, then Warwick's plans are no more,' replied George. He lowered his drink on to the table, and they all hunched forward. 'Methinks,' he whispered, 'they are deciding his fate as we speak, and it's obvious that if they decide to put Henry to death, then we will be the executioners.'

'The deed could only be discharged by the most trusted of men,' whispered Friar Drynk, nervously, 'and there's no more so than you two.'

Thomas looked at his two companions. 'Don't be so whore-sucking daft!' he cried.

'It is not nonsense,' replied George. 'If the deed is to be done, then it will be us to do it, and the friar here will see his soul to Heaven.'

'By the Holy Mary!' said Thomas, grimly; crossing himself. 'The thought of killing Holy Harry rests uneasy with me. I don't think I have the stomach for taking a King's life.'

The other two nodded in nervous agreement.

'I hear that Duke Richard has sired another bastard with that household wench, Katherine Haute,' blurted out Thomas, in an effort to take their minds off their appointment at the Tower.

'Aye, he is to be called John of Gloucester,' replied Friar Drynk. 'Methinks the Lady Anne will be most displeased when she finds out.'

'It is the way of the world,' joined in George. 'All young noblemen sire bastards. It's called "sowing their wild oats". Lady Anne will willingly have his children, for she knows they will be the only ones that count.'

'I know that is the normal way,' replied Friar Drynk, 'but I believe Lady Anne thought the love between Duke Richard and herself was somehow special; that they would save themselves for each other.'

'Well, she's chicken-brained daft,' laughed Thomas, 'if that's what she thought. She's lucky she's not marrying King Edward. God knows how many of his little bastards are roaming around.'

'Well, the Lady Anne is in France now, and who knows if she will ever return,' said Friar Drynk, with a sad shake of his head. 'And, of course, so is our sweet Rose.'

'Aye, Sir John has been most miserable since she left. Now, those two are special to each other. The separation has left him quite brokenhearted,' said George.

'It's the not bloody knowing where they are, or what they are doing,' said Thomas. 'That's what worms away inside a man. It can turn them mad in the end, and that's a fact.'

'I am told we are heading north tomorrow,' said George. 'There's talk of a rebellion brewing. Hopefully, that will take Sir John's mind off

Rose.'

'The King is taking six hundred men to rendezvous at Doncaster with Warwick's brother, John,' continued Thomas. 'He is bringing four thousand from Pontefract to help put the rebellion down.'

'Let's pray he stays loyal to King Edward,' said Friar Drynk, with a nervous laugh.

'Well, that would be handy!' cried George. 'If Warwick lands on the south coast with his army, and his brother turns traitor, then we would all be in the shite.'

'Finish your ale,' said Friar Drynk, softly. 'It must be nearly time for our appointment at the Tower. Let us pray that when dawn breaks, our conscience is clear.'

Brittany, France
29 August 1470

Simon and Rose slipped out of the royal castle during the dead of night. There was no risk in escaping, for with no royal court in residence, most of the guards were either drunk or asleep. They stole two horses from the stables situated just outside the castle gates, and vanished into the darkness.

Skirting around the city of Tours, they headed west, following the river down through the Loire valley, passing south of Angers – the city that had just witnessed the wedding of Warwick's daughter to Margaret of Anjou's son. They finally arrived at the small village of Ancenis, where for a few precious hours they rested. In the cool of the early morning, they cut up northwards towards the coast. It was as they reached the village of Bain-De-Bretagne, that they noticed dust clouds billowing up behind them.

They both stood, frozen, their hearts sinking, and stared at the great wave of dust that was swelling up into the sky. Finally, Simon broke the disbelieving silence.

'They must be riding like the wind to have caught us so quickly,' he said, shaking his head in disbelief.

'They must be picking up fresh horses along the way,' Rose said. 'We will never outrun them now.'

Simon heard the dismay in her voice. 'If we can't outrun them, then we must out-think them. We must reach the city of Rennes and find safe sanctuary while we plan a way of safely getting to Dinan.'

At Rennes, they walked their horses through the dense crowds that flowed through the great gates, and then quickly disappeared into the murky back streets that housed the criminal underbelly of the city. Here, reasoned Simon, they would be safe. The residents would rather slit the throats of King Louis' soldiers than talk with them.

Down a narrow, crumbling back alley, they found a small stabling yard, where for a few francs their horses would be fed and watered. The interior was dark and dingy, making the ramshackle building an ideal place for them to hide and rest. A small loft, where fresh hay was stored, had been built into the roof, and for a few francs more, the stableman had agreed to let them stay there for the night.

Rose busied herself, trying to even out the hay into what she hoped would pass for two beds, although she knew they would have slept on rough boards if they had to, such was their weariness.

Simon watched Rose trying to shoo the mice away. 'I will go and find us some supper, and see if I can find out how many soldiers are chasing us.' As he climbed down the rickety old ladder from the loft, he heard footsteps entering the stables. Dropping down on to the ground, he spun around, a small hunting knife now in his hand.

'No need for that, my friend,' said a man. 'My name is Jean Pierre. I am the stableman's son and I mean you no harm.'

Simon slipped the knife away.

'You are hiding from the King's men, yes?'

Simon studied Jean Pierre. He was older, maybe aged about thirty years, and tall – over six feet – with greasy, black hair. His eyes were dark brown. His nose was large, and as crooked as a witch's back – its battered shape reflected a hard life lived on the back streets of Rennes.

'King Louis' *Garde Écossaise* arrived in the city shortly after you,' said Jean Pierre. 'They are looking for a man and a woman.' He raised his arms and shrugged his shoulders. An eyebrow rose in a questioning look.

'Yes, it is us they seek,' confirmed Simon. He looked up at the loft and saw Rose looking down on him, her face filled with alarm.

Jean Pierre followed his gaze. 'Do not be afraid, little one,' he said. 'You are safe here. We have lost many men trying to keep Brittany free. There is no love for King Louis in this city, or for his stupid Scottish soldiers.'

'We need to get to Dinan and take ship for England,' said Simon.

'Why do they seek you?' asked Jean Pierre

'We have committed no crimes,' protested Rose. 'We have

information that the Earl of Warwick and King Louis are plotting to take the English throne.'

'If they succeed,' Simon continued, 'they will form a powerful alliance and then their plan is to attack Burgundy…'

'And then Brittany,' said Jean Pierre, finishing Simon's sentence.

'So, will you help us?' pleaded Rose.

'This Earl of Warwick you talk of, is he the bastard who has just stolen and plundered many of our Brittany ships?'

Rose and Simon nodded.

'And you say, if he is successful in his plans for England then he will help the French king to subdue us to make us slaves to France?'

Rose and Simon nodded again.

'Then I must help you to escape from the city, and from the *Garde Écossaise*!' cried Jean Pierre.

'Thank you, my friend,' said Simon, with relief.

'There are many soldiers here seeking you out,' continued Jean Pierre, 'but not enough to guard all the gates out of the city. Even if they had enough, I know of some secret gates that they would never find. I will guide you out of the city before dawn, but once you are past the city walls, then I am afraid you will be on your own.'

Rose lay staring at the moonlight that shone through the gaps in the old wooden walls. They formed beautiful silver and black abstract patterns that were somehow pleasing to her eye. She had been staring at them for a long time now; the worry of the coming day, and the scurrying and scratching of mice, had made sleep impossible. 'Simon, are you awake?' she whispered.

'Yes,' came the soft reply.

'Tell me about your beautiful Margaret of Anjou; why did you fall in love with her?'

'I met her on a beautiful June evening at Bamburgh Castle. She was sitting in a tall-backed chair, her face framed by the setting sun. She was the most beautiful woman I had ever seen. All the men in her court thought she was as hard as diamonds, for she ruled and acted like a king, but I could see her soft vulnerability; it made her even more exquisite. She was like an angel that had been forced to live amongst us. Inside that hard, royal veneer, I saw a lonely woman who yearned to be loved, who needed to be held and protected. She stole my heart that day and never gave it back.'

'And now you have left her with a broken heart,' whispered Rose. 'I am sorry, I should not have told you of your mother and sisters.'

'I could not stay with Marguerite knowing their fate. I would never have rested easy. You were right to tell me.'

An easy silence settled between them. Simon, his mind drawn back in time, thought warmly of his Marguerite. Rose wondered if angels could really steal people's hearts.

'You must tell me of your John,' whispered Simon.

'He is handsome and brave,' replied Rose. 'We grew up together at Middleham Castle. I was maid to his mother, Lady Tunstall. It was a cold December; the first snows of winter had arrived, and on that day, we fell in love. Our first kiss was on Christmas night as the stars shone brightly above us.'

'But why did you love him? Why did you surrender your heart to him?'

'Many qualities made me love him, but one that captured my heart was his acceptance of me, of who I am. We live in times where our birth defines who we are, but John judges the person first, and his position, second. He loves me for myself. He treats me with respect as an equal, not as a possession or a chattel to be owned. One day,' her voice rose with a passion, 'women will be equal to men and...'

The sound of footsteps entered the stable.

'Time to go, my English friends,' whispered Jean Pierre.

Simon and Rose scrambled down the ladder.

'Here, I have brought you some bread, cheese, and watered wine. Eat and drink while I put sackcloth around your horses' hooves. Silence is the key to your escape,' Jean Pierre whispered.

Soon, they were moving quietly down the dark back alleys towards the city's walls, finally arriving at a small narrow gate hidden behind some large, wild sprouting bushes. The gate was just wide and high enough to allow a horse to pass through.

As Jean Pierre removed the sackcloth from the horses' hooves, he gave directions on how to skirt safely around the walls of the town and on to the road for St Malo.

'Before you come to the village of Combourg, you will find a bridge over the River Vilaine. Cross it, turn left, and cut across country until you reach the River Rance. Follow it north; it will lead you to Dinan.'

Rose stepped forward, and on tiptoe, kissed Jean Pierre on both cheeks. 'Thank you. Thank you,' she whispered.

Jean Pierre jerked his arms back, in embarrassment. 'I do it for Brittany, yes?' he replied.

Simon clasped his shoulders. 'You do it for us too; we will never forget your bravery.'

'Good luck, my friends, and be sure to tell the English king it was Jean Pierre who saved him.' He laughed at the irony of it. 'May God favour your cause,' he finally said, before disappearing into the dark outline of the gate.

Simon and Rose walked their horses silently away from the city. Once far enough away, they mounted their horses, turned north, and skirted around to the St Malo road. The tension pounded in Simon's chest. If they could just get a mile or so along this road, they would be safely away from the danger behind them. Their horses broke into a slow trot as the city of Rennes receded into the darkness.

'We can move faster in a few moments,' called Simon, over his shoulder to Rose, who was a few yards behind him. 'We should be far enough away by then to break into a gallop without them hearing us—'

'Stop! Who goes there?' shouted a rough voice, just ahead of them.

Simon could make out the uniform of one of King Louis' *Garde Écossaise,* standing by the side of the road, several yards away. Behind him was pitched a solitary round tent, beyond which, four horses were tethered.

Rose, now alongside Simon, looked at him with urgency. 'Tis time to

330

gallop now!' she cried. She dug her heels into her mount and galloped straight for the soldier. Cursing, he fell backwards into the tent as she rode past him.

The pair of them flew along the road like arrows. Simon could hear the shouting and swearing behind him fading into the distance. He estimated they could travel about five miles before the soldiers had saddled up and started to give chase. He surmised that the four horses he had seen tethered behind the tent meant there were only four soldiers on duty, so three would pursue them while the forth would gallop the short distance back to the city of Rennes to raise the alarm.

He thought it a clever ploy to place sentries a mile along the road from Rennes. An obvious tactic had worked perfectly. They had been discovered, but luckily, not caught. They would be some way ahead of the three soldiers, and even further in front of the troops from Rennes. If they could reach the bridge that crossed the River Vilaine and turn off the road there without being seen, then the pursuing soldiers may carry on towards St Malo, thinking that was where they would be heading.

The hot dust swirled in dense clouds around them as they galloped towards Dinan. Rose could taste its dry bitterness as it forced its way through the woollen cloth that was tied tightly around her face. Her throat was as dry as a hot, stone wall; tiredness weighed her down like a heavy cloak, but she knew there would be no respite from the pursuing troops until they had reached the sea.

Simon surmised that they were only a few miles ahead of the *Garde Écossaise* as they followed the cliff path down into Dinan. As they started their descent down to the small harbour nestled on the banks of the River Rance, they could see the river open up into a wide estuary that led to the open sea and freedom. On the opposite cliffs, they noticed a large fortified round tower, its cannon overlooking the harbour.

Simon's heart was pounding as they arrived on the quay. He looked anxiously for a ship to make good their escape. It was then, that he saw the first of the *Garde Écossaise* appear on the top of the cliffs, their blue, red, and silver uniforms caught in the rising sun. He could hear distant shouts calling for their arrest.

The two of them rode up and down the harbour's edge desperately seeking a ship, but all were unloading or loading their cargoes. It seemed that none was ready to sail.

'We are trapped!' cried Rose, her voice trembling in alarm.

Simon looked frantically around. He saw, high up on the cliffs, men looking down at them from the fortified tower.

Rose moved closer to him as they watched the *Garde Écossaise* reach the bottom of the cliff.

Suddenly, a large, red-faced man, with a beard as white as sea salt, appeared beside the two of them. He stared at the advancing troops. 'You are English?' he said, in a broad Devonshire accent.

'Yes,' replied Rose and Simon, in unison.

'Well, in that case, it's time to go!' he cried, as the *Garde Écossaise* arrived at the far end of the harbour.

They all boarded a small cargo ship, carrying wine bound for Plymouth. As their pursuers rushed down the quay towards them, the crew cast off and pushed the vessel away from the harbour wall. A gap of ten feet of water opened up between them. Two of the *Garde Écossaise* sprinted down the quayside and jumped the gap, both managing to grasp and cling on to the side of the ship. One instantly swung his sword in an arc towards Rose, missing her neck by a hand's breadth.

Simon sprang forward and drove his sword into the man's chest. Blood squirted across the deck as the guard screamed and fell backwards into the sea.

The second soldier had managed to climb over the side. He lunged at Simon, who parried the blow with his sword and then rammed his hunting knife into the man's stomach. As the guard doubled over, Simon brought his knee upwards, smashing into the man's face. He staggered backwards, now semi-conscious, hitting the side of the ship.

With lightning speed, Simon gripped one of the guard's legs. Rose rushed forward and lifted the other. Together, they tipped the man over the side.

Simon breathed heavily as he and Rose stared at the group of *Garde*

Écossaise left standing on the quayside. The soldiers waved their swords. Their ginger-haired faces, wild with hate, screamed abuse.

Rose thought her heart would burst with the harrowing sight of them only yards away. The gap between them was now sixty feet.

The man with the white beard, who had since introduced himself as the captain, ordered the sails unfurled, and the cargo ship heaved forward towards the wide, open waters of the estuary, and the English Channel. He cursed the soldiers, their mothers, and all their ancestors, as the cannon from the round tower opened fire. Shot fell into the sea all around them. He steered in a zigzag as large sprays of seawater fell across the boat, soaking them all. Finally, the bombardment stopped.

Rose felt her legs start to buckle. The tension of the last few days made her head grow dizzy, and she slowly slipped down on to the deck.

Simon caught her and with the help of the captain, gently carried her below.

Pontefract Castle, West Yorkshire
16 September 1470

John Neville, the Marquess of Montagu, stared out from the royal chambers. His view from the King's Tower looked out over the inner keep and the outer baileys, towards the gathering dusk that slowly drew a grey veil over the surrounding landscape.

He wondered if he would find sleep tonight. During the day, the castle vibrated with life as his army of five thousand men prepared for tomorrow's march to Doncaster to join King Edward. He had yet to tell these brave yeomen that they would now cheer for King Henry, and cry death to King Edward. The thought of it sent a shiver through his very soul.

This old castle of towers and keeps was now silent and dark. It seemed to John that within its haunted walls, the souls of dead noblemen prowled the shadows and stalked the living. The Earl of Lancaster, beheaded here, was said to walk the battlements just before cockcrow, searching for his head. The screams of Richard II, who was hacked to death within the castle walls in 1400, could be heard on twelfth night – the anniversary of the bloody deed. The murdered enemies of John of Gaunt, Henry Bolingbroke, and Henry V, still cursed and plagued its granite walls.

When life and conversation surrounded him, John Neville felt justified in joining his brother's standard, but now alone as night drew close, he felt the ghosts of murdered kings all around, their bloody bodies sitting beside him, their dead eyes silently watching him.

'Curse you, Edward!' John raged. 'I loved you as a brother, secured your crown at Hedgeley Moor and Hexham, supported you against all others, and still you betrayed me, cast me aside with a worthless title, an income of miserable impoverishment.'

He moved to his bed, and wearily sat on the edge of it. He could hear a few of his trusted retainers in the Great Hall below, laughing and joking as the evening drew to a close. Their untroubled minds would soon find peaceful slumber. It filled John with envy, for as night crept around him, doubts filled his mind and demons taunted him. Had he agreed a pact with the devil to commit this heinous crime – this murder so foul of an anointed king? The answer, he knew, was *yes*. In despair, John Neville placed his head in his hands. Where would this path of treachery take him? He thought of his wife and children. Would he be the ruin of them all?

South Downs, near Petersfield, Hampshire
16 September 1470

The captain had taken the beautiful ruby ring that John had given Rose as a betrothal present, as payment for his rescue of them, and to change his course from Plymouth to Portsmouth, where loyalty to King Edward could be counted on.

After berthing in its calm and natural harbour by the old Roman fort at Porchester, Simon, with the last of his money, purchased two of the finest horses they could find, and then, with no respite, they had started their frantic dash to reach King Edward before Lord Montagu launched his treacherous attack.

They had heard that Edward was somewhere up north, around Doncaster, putting a small rebellion down. They knew Warwick was still in France, but of Lord Montagu, they knew not where he was. As they galloped through the sleepy villages, Rose prayed with all her heart that she would beat Warwick's brother to reach the king.

On the crest of Butser Hill, they paused before sweeping down towards the market town of Petersfield that lay on the main London to Portsmouth road. Rose knew there would be many more such towns like this to pass through in the coming days. With renewed determination, she dug her heels into her mount, for she knew every moment now counted in the race to save her sweet John's life.

Conisbrough Castle, Doncaster
27 September 1470

Lord Warwick had landed. The news spread through the camp like the wave of an onrushing tide. His name was on the lips of every soldier; this campaign in the north had been easy soldiering but the earl's reputation meant the serious business of war was now reality.

The six hundred men billeted in and around the castle prepared themselves for the coming march south. Orders were shouted crisply, men moved quicker, a harder discipline ran unseen through their ranks.

'Warwick will be heading as straight as an arrow for London and the Tower,' stated Lord Hastings.

'And that is because Holy Harry still lives,' said Duke Richard, in frustration, to King Edward. 'You should have listened to Hastings and me, when we recently argued his fate in the Tower. Warwick will wake the Lancastrians from their slumbers by freeing King Henry and using him as a figurehead to overthrow you.'

'It is no easy matter to execute a man who is an anointed King, and is held in deep affection by the common people,' replied Edward, tersely. 'While his son lives, there would be little point, for he would just replace his father as the leader of the Lancastrian cause.'

'Well, let us hope that Warwick brings the little bastard with him, for then we can deal with him and his father at the same time,' said Richard, harshly.

Silence followed Richards's cold words, his ruthlessness naked before them all.

The silence was broken by Thomas Hallet rushing into the Great Hall, his face red with excitement. 'Your Majesty; my Lords!' he cried, bowing to Edward. 'We have visitors.' Turning to John Tunstall, with a wide grin, he said, 'Rose is here! Rose is outside!'

John stared open-mouthed at Thomas, his mind trying to grasp the impossible. Finally, he blurted out, 'She is in France. She cannot be here.'

'It's true! It's true! She's here. I've seen her with my own eyes!'

Thomas hopped from foot to foot with excitement.

John bowed to the king then dashed for the door, with Thomas right behind him.

Edward, with a perplexed look, cried to his assembled retainers, 'In God's name, will somebody tell me what is going on?'

'Sir John!' shouted George Hallet, beckoning him over to the door of the keep house, his face split by the widest of grins. Not a word passed his lips as he and Thomas ushered John through the open doorway.

Coming from sunlight into shadow, John was momentarily blinded. He stood still, as his eyes adjusted to the darkness.

'John,' said a soft voice behind him.

He spun round. Rose stood just inside the door; he had walked straight past her. 'Rose, is that really you?' he cried.

As she rushed into his arms, John picked her up and swung her round with delight. She covered his face with kisses, and then his lips found hers. Tears of joy mingled with their passionate embrace. Finally, she broke free.

'Where is Lord Montagu?' she asked, her face becoming earnest.

John saw the change in her. 'How did you get here?' he asked in astonishment. 'Your clothes are ragged; your face is battered and bruised. Who did this to you?'

Rose put a finger to John's lips. 'I will tell you all of my adventures later,' she whispered as she lent up and kissed him once again.

He pulled gently away from her. 'What troubles you about Montagu?' he asked, his eyes studying the wounds on her face.

'He has turned his coat,' Rose whispered, with anxiety in her voice. 'He has joined Warwick's standard and would kill King Edward and all around him. We fled France to warn you, to save you. I pray we are not too late.'

'But this cannot be. Montagu loves the King as a brother, he would never—'

Rose cut him short. 'Sir Simon Langford helped me to escape from France. He is Margaret of Anjou's lover, and was with her when the

French king announced that Lord Montagu had been badly treated by King Edward, who had stripped his earldom from him. The Earl of Warwick used this to persuade Lord Montagu to join his standard.'

'Who is this Sir Simon Langford? Can we trust him?' John asked with a puzzled expression.

'I would swear on the Holy Cross that he tells the truth. He would not have risked his life and travelled this great distance just to tell a lie. If we do not act quickly, then Lord Montagu will kill you all!'

'Then we must take you and he to the King with all haste, for Montagu is marching his army here as we speak. If what this man says is true then we are all dead men, should Montague arrive.' John took hold of Rose's hand and stepped towards the door.

Rose pulled him back. 'There is more,' she said, quietly.

'Nothing can be as bad as this betrayal,' John said, again turning for the door.

Using both her hands, Rose pulled him back. 'Anne Neville has been forced to marry Margaret of Anjou's son, Prince Edward. They are to be crowned king and queen once Warwick has conquered England.'

'But she is promised to Duke Richard. The union is agreed; it cannot be undone!'

'It is undone, for they are married and that's the end of it,' said Rose. 'Remember, Warwick is at war with King Edward and Duke Richard, so past promises mean nothing now, and believe me, Lord Montagu is coming with all speed to kill you all.'

'What is undone?' said a voice from the doorway. 'And who is coming to kill me?'

Rose and John stared white-faced as Richard strode across the room towards them.

King Edward studied the man in front of him. Was he friend or foe? His words had certainly turned the world on its head. The news that Warwick's daughter had been forced to marry Margaret of Anjou's son, and then to be crowned Queen of England had taken him by surprise. Beautiful Anne – blameless in all things – now used with grievous injustice by her father.

Edward glanced at Richard, who sat grim-faced at the news that his intended marriage to one of England's greatest heiresses had now been erased from his future. But, the greatest shock of all was that John Neville had turned traitor. The man had been as a brother to him, a comrade-in-arms since they were boys. The words of his mother kept revolving in his head: *If you take away his earldom, he will take your crown.* Her dammed prophesy now struck him like a dagger in the chest.

'Sir Simon, as a knight of this realm you are a mystery to me and my court,' he said coldly, 'but apparently, I am told, not to Margaret of Anjou's bed…'

Faint sniggers ran around the hall.

'This makes your standing here before me a mystery. You fled with the serving girl, Rose, from King Louis' court to save our lives, and then you tell us your lover plans to place my crown on her son's head, and then my head upon a spike. I am not sure if I should reward you for your bravery, or kill you for being a traitor.'

'Your Majesty,' replied Simon, 'Margaret has no desire to be queen or to have her son crowned king. It is Warwick and King Louis who have forced this upon her.'

'How so, forced?' asked Edward, sharply.

'She agreed to all their demands to save my life,' continued Simon. 'If she had refused, Warwick would have executed me. I told her I would rather die than let that bastard have his way, but she refused. I travelled here for two reasons: one to prevent Warwick being triumphant in his plans to kill you and your close retainers. My information is genuine,' he said, earnestly, as he saw the questioning look in Edward's eyes. 'They are coming to kill you. The second reason is to seek out my mother and sisters who are imprisoned in Warwick Castle, as punishment for my actions against that bastard, Warwick.'

'You mean the small matter of being a spy within his household and then trying to kill him,' replied Edward. 'You should have thought of the consequences of your failure, for your family, before attempting it.'

Edward watched Simon lower his head, a small action that reflected his own pain. He sat back in his chair, and placing his fingertips under his chin, contemplated the man standing before him; a man filled with remorse. He was brave enough – his actions had proved that – and he believed, honest, but the question was, how could he confirm that John Neville had turned traitor?

What had been true, and confirmed by the girl, Rose, was that Anne Neville had married Margaret of Anjou's son. Also, Warwick had landed on the south coast with a large army funded by King Louis, so if that were fact, it would follow that John Neville had sided with Warwick. Edward's mother had been proved right in her prophecy and he realised now that it had been a bad error to take away John's earldom.

Edward rose from his chair. 'You are a brave knight, Sir Simon, and have suffered much for your hatred of the Earl of Warwick. If I could indulge you with more time, I would like to have heard what drove you to such loathing, but I believe what you say about Montagu's treachery, for I know now that I treated him badly. I didn't realise his humiliation ran so deep. Time is now short, for he marches on us with five thousand men seeking his revenge. For your services to us, I will issue you gold coin and a royal warrant to search for your mother and sisters within Warwick Castle – they will still be loyal to me, at least long enough for your purposes. We now leave with all haste for Holland and the Low Countries. Our numbers are too small to deal with Montagu, and with Warwick's army advancing from the south, we would be caught between the two. Tis best to retreat and fight another day.'

Edward strode from the hall. He knew the blackness of the night would be their friend as they made their way to King's Lynn, and a ship bound for Holland.

John held Rose tightly to him; her tired face snuggled hard against his chest. He could feel her heart beating softly. He would be leaving shortly with Richard for Holland. 'It will not be for long. The King will raise an army, and we will be back before Michaelmas,' he whispered.

'Can I not go with you?' Rose pleaded.

'The King is only taking his close retainers, and men who will be

341

useful to him. You, my love, are weary from your brave flight from France and your long ride from the south coast. You would not have the strength to flee the realm with us. So, while I am away, Friar Drynk will find a safe place for you to rest, to regain your strength, and for your injuries to heal. We must be brave, for we will be reunited soon enough and then with God's grace, we will marry.'

As Rose heard John's name being called, she reached up and kissed him passionately.

Church of Saint Margaret's, Westminster Abbey
27 September 1470

Elizabeth Grey stared at the gloomy building that stood at the end of the churchyard. Its massive stone walls, built to withstand a siege, towered over her small, forlorn figure. Men hurried through its great doors carrying furniture, tableware, and food – all that was needed to furnish its cramped rooms – for this building was to be her sanctuary, a place protected by God, where no man who meant her harm could enter.

Her three daughters and her mother, Jacquetta, would join her within its imposing walls, for Warwick had landed with his army of rebel soldiers, and was marching in strength straight for London. With Edward loitering up north, resistance, she knew, would be futile.

'Have you sent the abbot to see the mayor and the aldermen of the city?' asked Jacquetta. The harshness in her voice betrayed her displeasure for their present predicament.

Elizabeth, ignoring her mother's indignation, instructed two ladies-in-waiting to supervise the supplies needed for her unborn child, for she was now eight months pregnant and knew from history that she could be confined within this sanctuary for many months. Finally, she turned her cool gaze back to her mother.

'I have asked the mayor to open the city gates to Warwick and his army. If we oppose him, I do not think my sex, or being with child, would save me from the same fate that he afforded my father and brother. If we do not antagonise him, then we give him no excuse to invade this church.'

'Warwick will hold you responsible for his loss of power over Edward, and for stopping his attempts to marry his daughters to Edward's brothers. He may attempt to charge us with witchcraft, then he would have an excuse to force us out of sanctuary, and exact his revenge. If you had allowed me to practise my black arts, then he would never have made it across the channel,' Jacquetta said, with indignation.

'You forget, Mother, that after Hastings tried to bring charges of witchcraft against us, we agreed to stop calling upon the dark forces.

'But this is different,' huffed Jacquetta.

'Anyway, we have no choice now,' whispered Elizabeth. 'We cannot cast spells on consecrated ground. We can only pray for our lives and trust in God.'

'God never helped anyone,' Jacquetta sneered. 'If Warwick decides to kill us, then no amount of praying will stop him. We both know there is only one power that is real, and if we are to survive, I must find a way to use it.'

Conisbrough Castle, Doncaster
28 September 1470

The army of Lord Montagu halted one mile from Conisbrough Castle. The midday sun shone hot on their polished armour and heavy chain mail. Horses, thirsty for water, pawed the dusty road. This war machine of swords, lances, bows, and cannon, stood in belligerent silence waiting to kill King Edward.

Lord Montagu had declared that the king had forfeited their allegiance by robbing him of his earldom, and thus the means to pay their wages. His queen and her family were witches and warlocks who used their dark powers to control the kingdom for their own evil purposes. He urged them to join with Warwick, their leader of old, the greatest 'Lord of the North', to rid the country of this vipers' nest of intrigue. To a man, they had cheered him and sworn their alliance to his noble and just cause. Now, they waited on this dusty road to obey his commands.

He watched grim-faced with shame as his envoys galloped back from the castle. They had done a duty for which he had neither the courage nor the stomach. He had sent them to deceive King Edward and his brother, Richard, to lure them and their men to their deaths. He could not face them himself with such a cowardly act of betrayal.

'My Lord!' cried one of his envoys, dismounting in a cloud of dust. 'They have gone! The King and his men left with all haste, yesterday. The castle is empty. The staff say that spies from France came and warned him of our treachery.'

Lord Montagu stared at the man with undisguised relief. 'Where are they headed?' he asked, his voice calm, the tension within him gone.

'I am told they head for the coast, and Burgundy, with a small group of retainers; Edward having dispersed the rest of his men.'

'So, we do not have to kill our old comrades!' Lord Montagu cried. ''Tis sweet news for our consciences, my friends,' He threw back his head and laughed. 'That lucky bastard, Edward, has saved not only his own skin but also my remorse. Send scourers to the nearest ports along the coast. We need to know that they have indeed sailed, and from which port. When it is confirmed he has gone, we will head south to join with Warwick. For gentlemen, it would appear that the kingdom is ours without a drop of blood spilt.'

Chapter 13

Innocence Lost

Convent at Stoneleigh Abbey, Warwickshire
1 October 1470

It was early evening. Flocks of swifts soared and dived, swooping and turning on the wing faster than the eye could hold them, revelling in their swirling aerobatics as they gathered for their last meal of the day.

Simon Langford envied their freedom, their carefree existence. They were called the 'Devil's bird' because many believed that at night they turned into demons with the office of summoning witches to their assemblies, and in winter they concealed themselves under the mud of the fields, so to be nearer to hell than to heaven, but as Simon watched them, he wished he was soaring and diving with them. How exhilarating it must be. Finally, with a heavy heart, he forced his eyes away from the skies and looked to the horizon, towards Warwick Castle.

Tomorrow, he had to face the truth and the consequences of his actions. The dull ache within his chest had become sharper, his mind never free of thoughts of his family. His very soul seemed to be shrivelling within him, and yet, he still had hope. That most human response to tragedy clung to him – a small glimmer of belief burned within him.

Maybe, by some miracle, his mother and sisters were still alive; their faith in God had been absolute. They were pure of mind and soul; Jesus would not have deserted them. A gentle hand on his shoulder drew him back from his thoughts.

'I must go,' said Rose, softly, 'the nuns have made my quarters ready.'

'I pray they will keep you safe until King Edward reclaims his crown,' Simon replied.

Rose took Simon's hand; compassion filled her eyes. 'May God be with you, tomorrow,' she whispered. 'I will pray for you and your family tonight.'

'I hope it is not too late for your prayers,' said Simon, his voice shaking with emotion.

Rose hugged Simon, and then kissed him on the cheek. She turned and walked towards the convent, words now meaningless to help him.

Friar Drynk had been charged by John Tunstall to escort Rose to a place of safety. He watched as the nuns protectively ushered her into the convent that adjoined the abbey, then satisfied he had done his duty, he placed an arm around Simon's shoulder. 'Come, my young friend,' he said, as he guided him towards the abbey. 'You must try to get some rest. Tomorrow, I will accompany you to Warwick Castle. I promise; you will not be alone when you learn the fate of your family.'

'I'm not sure if the royal warrant will be accepted now, 'whispered Simon, despondently. 'Warwick has landed in the West Country, and King Edward is now exiled in Flanders.'

'But will Warwick's men know that?' replied Friar Drynk. 'News travels slowly in these parts, so with God's blessing we can bluff our way into the castle. Once in, we will rescue your mother and sisters by using good old-fashioned bribery with that purse of gold King Edward gave you; that is, if they are still...' Friar Drynk stopped himself, as he saw the pain fill Simon's eyes. 'Come,' he said, quickly changing the subject, 'we must go and sort out our quarters and later I will pray for God's help in our quest for your family.'

Warwick Castle, Warwickshire
2 October 1471

The young officer of the watch read the royal warrant, mouthing each word as though doing so confirmed their meaning. He had never seen such a document before, and felt nervous just holding it. His eyes were wide in wonder – that the King had touched the same warrant filled him with awe.

Simon could feel his heart thumping in his chest as he watched the officer. Would he know exactly where King Edward and Warwick were? Would he refuse to help them, or even have then arrested? Simon waited nervously for the officer's response.

'I've been here one year and have never seen them,' he said, holding the warrant as though it was a piece of the Holy Cross.

Friar Drynk reached out and took the warrant back. 'Well, who would have seen them?' he asked, gently.

'Why do you seek this information?' exclaimed the officer loudly, as he regained his authority. 'Is this warrant still legal? For no one knows where the King is.'

Simon looked at Friar Drynk, who nodded, signalling Simon to proceed with the cover story they had discussed on their journey to the castle.

'The King is gathering his forces in the north and is not concerned with this matter,' Simon lied. 'He may have signed the warrant, but the information we seek is for the Mayor of Northampton. When Lady Langford and her two daughters were brought here, their lands were confiscated, divided up, and given to supporters of Lord Warwick. There is now a dispute over the boundaries of this land, which threatens to spill over into bloodshed if we don't settle it.'

Friar Drynk joined in. 'We believe Lady Langford's knowledge of these lands could help us to resolve this argument.'

As Simon stood in the dungeons of Caesar's Tower, he felt the terror of the place. He could taste the overwhelming fear it held. Before him, stood the senior gaoler, a large greasy-skinned man, with no hair or teeth. His eyes had the animal cunning of the peasant classes, always looking for the weakness in a person, to exploit. They showed neither warmth nor humanity. *The eyes of a torturer*, Simon thought, and watched as the senior gaoler studied the warrant. He knew it would mean nothing, because men of his class could not read.

'Who are you?' asked the senior gaoler.

'I come from the Mayor of Northampton to find information on the land dispute which the officer of the watch told you about. It is nothing of consequence,' replied Simon, calmly, as he held out a silver penny.

With a toothless grin, the senior gaoler snatched it from Simon's hand and slipped it into his purse. 'Yes, I remember them,' he said, in a rasping voice. 'We flogged and branded them on Lord Warwick's orders. They were to be executed, although the older one – the mother – didn't last long, and died within a couple of days.'

Simon stepped back, his face as white as a shroud.

The senior gaoler stopped talking and stared suspiciously at him.

'My friend has a weak stomach,' said Friar Drynk, quickly. Then with a smile and an apologetic shake of his head, he said, 'If the mother is dead, then she cannot answer our questions, so that is the end of the matter. We thank you for your time, and will be on our way.' He grabbed Simon's arm, and tried to steer him out of the dungeons.

'Are her daughters also dead?' whispered Simon, tersely. He wiped at the beads of sweat that were forming on his forehead.

The senior gaoler let out a loud, sarcastic laugh. 'Me thinks your friend hasn't the stomach for the rest of the tale,' he said to Friar Drynk.

'Are they dead?' persisted Simon.

'The two young ones,' continued the senior gaoler, beginning to enjoy the discomfort on Simon's face, 'were very pretty and we'd never had such handsome virgins down here before, so we didn't flog 'em as hard as the old one; had other plans for them.' He paused and smiled at the memory, while drawing his sleeve across his face to wipe off some spittle that ran down his chin.

'Because we had the warrants for their executions,' he continued, 'we could do what we pleased with them; no rights you see.' He sniggered. 'They were just dead people walking, so we turned them into whores; broke 'em both in myself,' he boasted. 'They struggled like a couple of wild fillies to start with, but I soon tamed them, then I sold their favours to any man who could afford the pleasure of them. By God, there were plenty of takers. After three or four weeks, I had to carry out the earl's orders; couldn't delay it any longer. Shame, that was, it spoilt a good thing. Mind you, the night before their hanging, we had some fun with them; I think half the troops in the castle—'

The hunting knife caught the senior gaoler fast on the side of his neck, slicing deep from ear to ear. Blood sprayed in an arc as he fell to his knees, his eyes registering first surprise, then shock, and finally bulging in panic, as he fought for his breath. His hands frantically tried to stop the gushing blood.

Simon moved slowly around him, watching him suffer before finally ramming the knife hard into the back of his neck.

Friar Drynk stared with shock at the quivering figure, the knife still sticking out of his neck, blood creeping slowly out from around the body. 'Holy Jesus,' he whispered. 'You have killed the man.'

Simon stared white-faced at the dead gaoler, tears running down his face.

'By the Holy Mary, we are murderers!' cried Friar Drynk in alarm, his eyes darting around the dungeons to check they were alone. 'You stupid bastard,' he hissed. 'You have put all our necks at risk, including Rose; we must leave immediately.'

Simon stood icy cold; the red-hot rush of his uncontrolled temper had quickly cooled as the gaoler gasped his last breath. He watched, devoid of emotion as Friar Drynk struggled to conceal the body. His family was dead, and it was through his actions that they had suffered. He was their executioner. The overwhelming guilt broke his heart.

'For Christ's sake, man, help me,' hissed Friar Drynk.

The friar's words seemed to tumble out of a long tunnel into Simon's stunned mind. He moved slowly, as if his arms and legs were made of lead. He felt he was stumbling through a living nightmare.

Between them, they hid the senior gaoler's bloody body under a mound of bedding straw.

'Come', whispered Friar Drynk, manhandling Simon towards the door. 'The gaoler will be missed from his duties in no time. We must leave unseen with all haste.'

With his heart pounding in his ears, Friar Drynk led Simon silently out of the castle. They fled on horseback, leaving their bloody secret buried in the castle's dungeon.

They were an hour's ride from the castle when they brought their horses to rest. Dusk was falling, and a chill evening wind swept over the hills.

'Damn you!' cried Friar Drynk at Simon. 'You have put all our lives at risk. When they find the body, we will both be fugitives; Warwick's men will seek us out, and what of Rose? Did you not think of her? I wear monk's robes; where is the first place they will go? The abbey, that's where. They will go straight to the abbey to search for me.'

Simon stared down at his saddle. His family were dead by his actions. He might just as well have murdered them himself. His mind was full of the finality of it all. There was nothing he could do to make things right. He could not bring his family back.

Friar Drynk could see the dreadful guilt that Simon carried on his shoulders, and knew there were no words he could say that would lessen the shame. 'Rose is now your priority,' he said, softly. 'Time is short for me. I have important letters for King Edward's allies in London, and cannot risk being caught with them on my person, so I must head for London with all speed. You need to fetch Rose and take her far away from here.' He reached out and gripped Simon's arm. 'I am sorry for you, and for your mother and sisters,' he said, with compassion, 'but Rose is the one you must focus on, now. Danger must not befall her because of your hasty actions. If I had known you were going to be stupid enough to commit murder, I would have taken her to a safer place, far from that accursed castle.'

The friar's words stung Simon into replying. 'I will head for the abbey and take Rose north to her parents. They can hide her until the situation calms down.'

The faint noise of horses at full gallop made them turn and look towards the distant hills. Soldiers appeared as tiny specks, heading straight towards them.

'Hell's teeth! They have moved fast,' said Friar Drynk. 'Do you think they have seen us?'

'Hard to tell,' replied Simon, straining his eyes towards the advancing troops. 'It would be best that we split up. You head south,' he commanded, pointing towards some woods. 'I will head west. If they have seen us, it will be me they follow.'

Simon waited until Friar Drynk was swallowed up by the forest, then he turned his horse and ran at right angles across the front of the advancing soldiers. They all turned and followed him.

Stoneleigh Abbey, Warwickshire
3 October 1470

Simon was exhausted. He had spent the night playing 'hide and seek' with Warwick's men, and now, as the sun rose in the sky, he was hidden in the woods looking down on Stoneleigh Abbey. Somehow, during the night, he had managed to give them the slip, and had doubled back to the abbey to collect Rose.

He sat on his horse, motionless and silent, watching the abbey come to life. He saw a young nun struggle out from the kitchens carrying a large bowl full of food slops, which she proceeded to empty into a large iron bucket that would later be carried down to the pigpens.

He decided to wait until the nuns had finished their breakfasting. Once they were at their prayers, he would be unseen by most. It would then be easier to collect Rose, and escape to the north.

As he waited, the warmth of the sun slowly heated his back, but he felt no pleasure from it. His mind was still numbed by the terrible events at Warwick Castle. His family was dead; the message kept on hammering in his brain. It sapped his will to live. He imagined, in a never-ending cycle of thoughts, his mother, and young sisters, full of life, chattering and laughing. He lent forward, placed his head in his hands, and silently sobbed for them.

The sounds of horses and men made him look up, and his heart sank. Soldiers appeared on the road leading to the abbey. He thought they must be the ones who had been chasing him all night. He counted twenty in all. They dismounted in the grounds, and a few entered the abbey, appearing moments later with the abbot, who they then escorted to the convent.

Simon sat, waiting and watching, but he already knew what the outcome of their visit would be. He watched with dread the events unfolding before him, powerless to change them.

Rose sat in the silence of the refectory, eating her breakfast. The rows of nuns in their black habits, sitting at bare wooden tables, reminded her of crows crowded on branches.

She had been told that, only the novice nun reading the scriptures was permitted to break the calm silence of the dining hall; such were the rules of the convent. She had been there for only a day but had already discovered that the nuns were all human, with feelings and needs. There were very few saints amongst them, and although the nuns took the three vows: poverty, chastity, and obedience, it would seem that some paid little heed to them.

The convent, though, was a model of orderliness. Novice nuns carried out the laundry and the cooking, whilst others tended to the growing of vegetables, and the care of livestock. Some nuns specialised in producing wine, ale, and honey, and others practised medicine or teaching. Some loved spinning, weaving, and embroidery; the list was endless, but there was a place for all of their talents within the convent, which grew rich because of them.

Loud knocking curtailed Rose's thoughts, and all eyes turned towards the tall, beautifully carved refectory doors. She watched in silence, as they swung open. The abbot from the adjoining abbey stood in the doorway. He beckoned urgently to the prioress, who rose quickly and walked with a dignified pace to join him. They fell into an urgent whispered conversation.

The prioress looked nervously towards Rose as the conversation became more animated. Rose's heart sank. Something was wrong; she could sense it. She watched anxiously as the abbot hurried off.

The prioress turned to look at Rose, her outstretched hand beckoning. 'Rose Thorne,' she called. 'Come with me, now.'

Excited whispers surged around the refectory. The senior nuns banged their spoons on the tables and held their fingers to their lips as Rose walked nervously towards the tall doors. She could feel all the eyes in the room following her out.

Rose sat facing the prioress. A large desk separated them. The room was spacious and two smaller desks were positioned along the opposite wall, their seats empty. Rose assumed their occupants were still at their breakfasts. Shelves and bookcases lined the walls; every ledger or sheet of parchment was neatly in its place. The office was scrupulously clean. Desks and bookcases were highly polished, using bees wax from the convent's own hives; a wonderful, earthy elixir of wood, wax, and leather fragranced the air. A cheerful fire, lit to warm the early morning chill, danced and flickered at the far end of the room. Rose wished she could wrap the room around herself, with its wonderful smells and warm comforting fire, like a magic blanket, and disappear to somewhere safe and peaceful, somewhere far, far away.

'Yesterday, there was a murder committed at Warwick Castle,' explained the prioress. 'It was carried out by two men whose description matches that of the men who brought you here, so, I am afraid I have some bad news for you. The abbot has just been questioned by some of Warwick's soldiers who have been searching the surrounding countryside for these fugitives, and they have told us that your protector, King Edward, has fled the country. The Earl of Warwick now rules the kingdom and knowing of his vile temper, the abbot decided it would be prudent for the safety of the abbey, and the convent, if he revealed your presence and your connection to the two men they seek.'

'Who was murdered?' asked Rose, quietly.

'I am told it was the senior gaoler at Warwick Castle,' replied the prioress.

Rose's heart sank. She knew instantly who had killed him. Simon's family, she surmised, had not survived.

'The two men had a warrant. They were searching for a mother and her two daughters,' continued the prioress. 'But why the gaoler was killed remains a mystery. The soldiers wish to take you back to Warwick Castle, to help with their investigation into these two men, so a report can be sent to Lord Warwick who is in London.'

Rose's suspicions were confirmed and the harsh reality of the situation bore down on her. Her heart pounded, her palms were clammy. She knew why the senior gaoler had been killed, and by whom. She imagined the earl reading the report, the anger springing into his eyes as he read her name. With his ferocious temper, she could expect only brutal punishment from him, and death would be her reward.

'You promised to protect and hide me from Lord Warwick,' Rose said firmly, her voice rising in indignation. 'You accepted gold coin in payment.'

'The world has turned,' replied the prioress, soothingly. 'I cannot be party to murder; that was never part of our agreement. Lord Warwick, we have just learned, now rules. This means he holds the royal charters for the abbey and the convent. If we displease him, he could revoke them and disband these holy orders, casting us all out into poverty. There are too many of us to risk his anger, so, my child, you must go with the soldiers, answer their questions truthfully, and you will have nothing to fear.' She smiled sweetly at Rose, unaware of the turmoil filling her.

'By association, they will harm me,' cried Rose, tearfully. 'I travelled with these wanted men and—'

'Rose, you have nothing to fear,' butted in the prioress, with slight exasperation. 'You did not commit this crime...'

'But, the earl knows of me, he will show no mercy. In France, I—'

The prioress cut her off again. 'Enough,' she commanded. 'The sin of murder has come knocking on our door, so you are going with them, and that is the end of it. I will not risk all the lives of my sisters just for you.' Opening the drawer of her desk, she took out gold coin, and placed it in front of Rose. 'Here, take your coin,' she said. 'I don't know what you have been involved in, and I don't want to know, but you are leaving this convent now.'

Rose stared at the gold pieces stacked up in front of her. *At least, I will have enough to tip the executioner,* she thought, bitterly.

'We will pray for your safety, my child,' cooed the prioress, now she could see that Rose had accepted her fate. 'You must trust in God, and all will be well.' She smiled.

Rose wanted to scream at the stupidity of the prioress' words. God would offer her no protection from the earl's rage. It was all sanctimonious humbug. She was on her own, now, and realised with a sinking heart, that she would not survive on prayers alone.

Mattersey Priory, Lincolnshire
6 October 1470

Simon sat with his back against a fallen tree trunk as the weak October sun warmed his face. His horse grazed contentedly on the rich grass of the water meadow and as he watched her, he thought again of Rose.

She had been taken by four soldiers, hands bound to her saddle. They had ridden away towards Warwick Castle. He had sat there on his horse, watching, powerless to help her. The remaining troops had split up into groups of three or four and set off in different directions, obviously still looking for him. He had swung his horse around and ridden deeper into the forest, heading north, and now, he sat just downstream from Mattersey Priory.

The sun was low in the sky when he set off for the priory. He still had his purse of gold from King Edward, so he would pay to rest there overnight. As the priory had come into view, he saw that it was built on the edge of the river, surrounded by thick forest that would be teeming with game. The clear river that flowed past would provide kingly salmon, or common perch, for the monks to eat on Fridays.

Simon decided to pay the monks to say daily prayers of forgiveness for him over the deaths of his family, to ease his conscious until he could do penance for his sins. He had thought of heading further north into the desolate lowlands. There, in solitude, within a deserted crofter's cottage, living as a hermit, he would pray for forgiveness. Then, when the first icy snows of winter came, he would walk into the bleak night and let the bitter cold take his soul.

The only thing that had stopped him was his continued love for his Marguerite. Could he die without seeing her? Would she want to see him? Would she still love him? After all, he had broken her heart twice, now. And if he did seek her out, would he end up destroying her life as he had destroyed the lives of his family, and many others? *Maybe, it would be best to disappear*, he thought, *and end my life to pay for my sins.*

But before all else, he had to save Rose. The girl did not deserve the fate he had handed her. He knew the gaolers at Warwick Castle would extract all she knew, with great skill. Warwick would show her no mercy, so he had to save her. He could not bear another death on his conscience.

Westminster Palace, London
10 October 1470

The Earl of Warwick watched the backs of Jasper Tudor and Jasper's skinny young nephew, Henry, disappear out through the doorway of his private office. He silently cursed.

Young Henry's father – Edmund Tudor, the Earl of Richmond – had been killed in 1456 defending the Lancastrian cause at Carmarthen Castle in north Wales; three months before his son had been born. Now, this young pup of thirteen years had come to claim his father's titles. Warwick had sent them away, like many before them, angry and empty handed, with vague promises for the future, but how could he restore his lands and titles when they were now firmly held by the Duke of George, who would no more give them up than cut off his own hand.

What to do about George? It was as if he was diseased. At court, all the old Lancastrians avoided him like the plague, and who could blame them? He was, after all, brother to King Edward. George would never be trusted, but being married to Isabel made it difficult to clip his wings. Warwick sighed with the problem of it all. He would have to find a way to relieve George of some of his titles and lands, if he was going to win the Lancastrians round.

Since returning, in triumph, from France, Warwick had found himself slowly being hemmed in. Each avenue he went down was blocked by either mistrustful Lancastrians or resentful Yorkists. The treasury was empty. Edward was building an invasion force in Bruges, and that Bitch of Anjou, with her son, was stalling their return to England. To cap it all, King Louis was pressurising him for troops to assist in his invasion of Burgundy.

Having used up all of his energy to retake the kingdom, he felt weary. The years, he knew were mounting against him; age was dimming his strength. He had given his all for this final throw of the dice, but now the world had gone silent, and an uneasy peace had settled over the land.

The people of England waited and watched. He knew they were tired of this war, and the ever-higher taxes they had to find to pay for it. They were tired of the ever-shifting lords who ruled them, even tired of him, the mighty Earl of Warwick. He realised he was caught between two kings, and two queens, and having thumbed his nose at all of them, he had no choice now but to play the hand he had sought – for it would be the last one dealt to him. The stakes were high and his life depended on the outcome. A shiver went down his back.

England, Warwick thought, *sits quietly calm, like the lull before a storm.*

One of his clerks entered, all nervous movement and bootlicking. His comical posturing brought a smile to Warwick's face and lifted his spirits. His melancholy faded as he watched the fawning man approach, clutching sheets of parchment.

'I have the warrants, my Lord,' the clerk squeaked, in a high nervous voice. His body was bent double with his bowing and scraping; his eyes peeking out anxiously from beneath a threadbare cap as he shuffled forward and laid the documents on the earl's desk. Retreating in short jittery steps, he scurried from the room.

Warwick laughed to himself. The man had just reminded him that he still had the authority over every man in the kingdom, so he had nothing to fear.

He turned his attention to the documents before him. The first one he ran his eyes over was a Warrant of Execution for John Tiptoft – the Earl of Worcester – also Edward's enforcer, the 'butcher of England'. Warwick knew that the whole kingdom cried out for justice. As Constable of the Realm, John Tiptoft had tortured and condemned many men to death in brutal and cruel ways. He had combined a delicate sense of the arts and literature with a harsh insensitivity to human suffering. Warwick signed the warrant. John Tiptoft would have signed his, if the boot had been on the other foot. His death would please the Lancastrians, and the Yorkists – he knew – would not shed a tear for him.

The next warrant was for the attainment of Edward's queen, Elizabeth Grey, and her witch of a mother. Warwick read the list of crimes they were accused of: witchcraft, treason, adultery, theft of lands and pensions…the list continued. He paused, quill in hand. It would be prudent to exercise some caution in this matter, he realised. They had sought sanctuary in a solid fortified building and it would be difficult to winkle them out. Also, they had not held the Tower against his army, but, surprisingly, had opened the gates of London to him instead. If he moved against them, the Yorkists would be outraged but the Lancastrians currently cared little either way. He thought it would be prudent to let sleeping dogs lie. Margaret of Anjou and her son could deal with Elizabeth as they saw fit, when they arrived, and the Lancastrian position was more secure. He placed the warrant to one side, unsigned.

Picking up the final document, he sat back in his chair and studied it intently. It was a Warrant of Execution for the serving girl, Rose Thorne. As he read the charges, his mind replayed the sequence of events that had led to the warrant's existence. It had begun when she had questioned his authority over the marriage of his daughter, Anne. He knew he should have killed her then, only Anne's pleading had stopped him. In doing so, he had unleashed a chain of events that had saved King Edward's and all his close retainers' lives. He was amazed that a mere maid could have caused him so much trouble, although, he would consider pardoning her in exchange for that bastard, Simon Langford. The man had spied on him, attempted to kill him, and then helped that wench betray his plans to Edward. Rose had confessed that Simon had killed his senior gaoler in cold blood.

Warwick felt his anger rising; he should have been signing for Simon's execution. He looked at the warrant with eyes as hard as diamonds and then signed it with a ruthless flourish. *She still deserves a rough noose around her dainty neck,* he reasoned, vindictively.

Baynard's Castle, London
10 October 1470

George, the Duke of Clarence, sat glumly in front of the roaring fire nestling a cup of wine in his hands. Neither the warmth of the fire, nor the wine, lifted his spirits. His mother, Cecily, sat opposite, studying her son's tired face.

'You have backed yourself into a tight corner, my son,' she said, matter-of-factly. There was no anger or emotion in her voice; she knew that would only turn him away from her. George needed soft words. As with a naughty child, sometimes a gentle scolding was better than a big stick.

'I pray your forgiveness for what I have done,' George said, softly.

'Now...' Cecily smiled, gently, 'is that for turning traitor against your brother, Edward, or is it for supporting that Bitch of Anjou, the woman responsible for the deaths of your father and brother? Or, maybe it's for throwing in your lot with Warwick and that evil spider they call the King of France? Oh, and I nearly forgot: there is the small matter of marrying Isabel, Warwick's daughter, when it was forbidden by the royal court.'

His mother's subtle and quick reply cut into George like an assassin's blade. He stared into his cup, wishing it were an oracle that would give him the answers to his mother's jagged questions, to help him find some excuses. He sighed deeply and remained silent.

'They have disinherited your nephew, Edward's newborn son,' Cecily continued, 'who has just been born in sanctuary.' She tried to keep the sharpness out of her voice.

George sunk lower into his chair.

'You let Warwick, and Parliament, proclaim that I, your mother, had an affair with a lowly archer called Blackburn; that Edward was the result, and thus a bastard, just so you could be the next in line to the throne. How could you steep so low?'

George looked at his mother sheepishly from the corner of his eye, not daring to look straight at her.

'I have been publicly branded an adulteress. Tis a wicked act that has achieved you nothing, for Margaret of Anjou's son, Edward, is to be the new King.' Sternly waving her finger at George, she said, 'Already the Lancastrians have pushed you to the fringes of power. Even Warwick is unsure of you and keeps you at arm's length. The Yorkist supporters will never forgive you for turning your coat. Did you not realise that you are the brother of a Yorkist King? Margaret of Anjou and her court were never going to accept you, and when her son is crowned, Warwick's days will be numbered. He will be forced to flee once again to hide behind King Louis' throne, so my son...' Cecily said, with a giggle, 'you have well and truly pissed in your bed.' She threw her head back and laughed at the absurdity of men.

George sat up; dumbfounded at his mother's reaction, then with relief, he joined in with her laughter. Finally, silence settled; matters had been addressed. 'What is to be done?' he asked. 'How can I make things right?'

Cecily had a strong maternal feeling towards her wayward son. This man, who had schemed with the princes of England and France, used his sword in anger, married an earl's daughter, and commanded men by the thousand, now sat before her like a child. *Men are a strange race*, she thought.

'George; I have given birth to thirteen children, nine of them sons. One was stillborn; four died in infancy, and one died in battle with your father. I now have but three sons left and I do not wish to lose any more, so you must agree that Edward is the rightful king. He won his crown in battle, and you were foolish to think you could steal it.'

George nodded contritely.

'Richard is fiercely loyal to his brother, so sleeps with a clear conscious. You, I know, have to drink yourself into a stupor to sleep. To rid yourself of this betrayal that fills you with guilt and to find some peace of mind, you must reconcile yourself to them.'

'But, how?'

'I have a letter delivered by a Friar Drynk from Edward. He writes of forgiveness for you. He understands you were bedazzled by Warwick –

drawn like a moth to his flame. He says if you join him and Richard when they land in England, then he will forgive all your past mistakes.'

Cecily sat back, her face content. 'Now that you have singed your wings on the bright flame of kingship, I do not think I have to wait for your answer,' she said.

George smiled broadly as he realised he could redeem himself.

'The friar is waiting to take your reply, but a word of warning: you must not mention this conversation to a soul, not even to Isabel. Go back to your estates and keep your own council. When the time is right, you will be called to meet with your brothers to confirm your loyalty, and to set all your wrongs right.'

George downed his cup of wine. 'Give me quill and parchment and I will confirm my loyalty now!'

Bruges, Flanders
20 October 1470

Friar Drynk passed the letters to John Tunstall, who in turn passed them to Duke Richard, who walked the few steps to the top of the table and delivered them into the hands of his brother, King Edward.

Lord Hastings, Anthony Woodville – the second Earl Rivers, the Duke of Norfolk, and the Duke of Suffolk, Edward's most senior and faithful supporters, stood close beside him, silent and watching. A hush spread throughout the ranks of knights and gentlemen gathered within the Great Hall that had been lent to them by the Governor of Holland, Seigneur de la Gruthuyse.

Edward searched quickly through the letters, stopping only when he recognised the hand of his brother, George. Breaking the seal, he hungrily read its contents.

The silence in the hall grew heavy with anticipation.

A smile slowly formed on Edward's face, and then kicking his chair back, he jumped to his feet. Waving the letter high in the air, he cried, 'Gentlemen; my brother joins us!'

Cheering greeted this announcement and Edward held up his hand for silence.

'My loyal Lords, knights, and brave captains: when we land in England, George will be waiting with an army of four thousand men. He also says there are many rich merchants in London who wish to fund our expedition against Warwick in return for titles and rank; even the merchants of Calais wish to help us. I believe that Warwick's days are now numbered.'

More cheering resonated around the hall. Edward waited for it to subside, then with a voice full of kingly authority, he said, 'I command you to seek out two thousand fighting men to join our distinguished company, be they German mercenaries or Flemish soldiers of fortune. We need brave adventurers, swashbuckling rogues, for victory only favours the brave. Go now and find me these men to join our bold enterprise.'

Excitement rippled around the Great Hall. Men smiled and clapped each other on the back. At last, the waiting was over.

Edward sat back in his chair, a smile of satisfaction on his face. His close retainers gathered around him.

'Tis excellent news,' said Lord Hastings.

'Warwick's reign will be short-lived,' said Earl Rivers.

'That's as maybe, although, he fought as a comrade with us many times,' said the Duke of Norfolk, with a hint of regret in his voice. 'He won the day for us at St Albans, and Northampton, and fought bravely with us at Towton on that bitter Palm Sunday in sixty-one. Twenty thousand fell on that bloody snow-covered field to win you a glorious victory and a royal crown.'

Edward nodded thoughtfully at the memory.

'And now we seek his blood as he seeks ours,' continued the Duke of Norfolk. 'It will be a sad day when the noblest of England face each other across the field of battle.'

'He has made his bed, and now he has to lie on it,' said Richard, sharply. 'Your father fought against us at Towton and now, you...' he said, looking directly at Anthony Woodville. 'Fight with us. Such is the way of this war. Men change sides or turn traitor when circumstances dictate, so there will be no quarter given when we join battle with Warwick. There must be no compassion for an old comrade-in-arms. When we fight him, it will be to the death and the quicker his head sits leaden upon a spike, then the quicker Anne...' his voice trailed off, as he stared into space.

Edward rose and grasped Richard's shoulders. 'Then, Anne, what?' he asked.

Richard looked at Edward, his eyes narrowing.

John noticed the cold detachment descend over his old friend.

'Holy Harry now sits on the throne,' Richard said, with an icy voice, 'and his son will soon join him. If our invasion is successful, then you must agree neither can live.'

'This time there will be no mercy,' agreed Edward, reluctantly.

Richard looked around at Edward's inner circle as though confirming their loyalty before saying his next words. Slowly, his eyes came back to rest on Edward. 'What if Anne's marriage has been consummated?' he asked; his voice full of anger. 'What if she is carrying a child in her belly? Holy Harry's grandson, a future king and heir to the Lancastrian crown. What shall we do, then?'

Edward threw his head back and laughed.

John watched Richard's jaw tighten; his blue eyes glittered like frozen ice.

'You laugh at my distress?' Richard cried.

'No...No, dear brother, forgive me,' said Edward, apologetically. 'I wish you no ill but you are worrying about a dilemma that is wrapped in a conundrum of possibilities.'

'They are married now,' continued Richard, like a dog with a bone. 'The seed in her belly could be growing, as we speak.'

'We know not of their circumstances,' replied Edward, irritation creeping into his voice. 'She could be dead; he could be dead. We can surmise any situation you like. The marriage may not be consummated, and even if this were so, she could give birth to a girl or a stillborn. Maybe she hates him...

'The truth is, we are not to know, so you must stop this agonising and raise your spirits, for soon we head for England to reclaim my crown. Now, go and charter ships to carry our army to England. We will need food to feed them, and the ordnance of war for them to fight with. Take Hastings, and whoever else you may need to plan our embarkation; we leave from the port of Flushing.'

Richard turned to go.

John could see he was still downcast. The curvature of his back was more pronounced, as it always was when his body tightened with tension.

Richard turned back to face his brother, his question not yet answered. 'But...' he began.

'Enough!' cried Edward, angrily. 'If your worst fear turns out to be true then I promise she will not live to give birth.'

Richard smiled grimly. He had the answer to his question.

'Friar Drynk,' called Edward, as he lowered himself back into his chair. 'I would speak with you.'

Friar Drynk stepped forward, bowing low.

'You have done your duty well,' said Edward. 'You delivered my letters and brought the replies from under the nose of Warwick. I commend you for your bravery, which will be rewarded on our return to England.'

Friar Drynk bowed even lower, his face beaming with pride. 'It was an honour to serve you, Sire,' he replied, his voice confident.

Edward beckoned him closer. 'Pray, tell me, how is the Queen and my newborn son?'

'They are well, Sire. The Queen was delivered of your son on the 2 November, by her doctor Domenico de Sergio, assisted by Margery Cobbe, the midwife. He was baptised, Edward, in honour of you. Thomas Milling – the Abbot of Westminster, and Lady Scrope, were the godparents and your son, praise be to God, is strong and well.'

'Is this not excellent news?' cried Edward, his face beaming with pride as he looked around at his retainers.

'The Queen is well,' continued Friar Drynk, 'but in fear of Warwick's men. She frets for the safety of her newborn, for the Lancastrians know he is your heir.'

Edward's face became distressed. His beaming mask of assurance slipped. 'What news of Warwick?' he whispered, in a voice filled with apprehension.

Friar Drynk smiled reassuringly as he sought to put Edward's mind at rest. 'Warwick's victory was too easy. His brother, turning traitor against you, swung the scales of fortune in Warwick's favour. He won England without a battle, so he is untried in the eyes of the nobles and the clergy. The common people know his power comes from France, their most hated enemy.

'The old Lancastrians who fought against him at Towton, or St Albans, and who still carry the scars, despise him. The Yorkists who fought alongside him are perplexed at his turn of face, and now mistrust him. The whole of England sits and watches him. He must hear the intrigue against him that swirls around the halls of Westminster, for although he is old and experienced in the ways of men, he is a man of action and not a politician. He has tumbled out of his depth. It is plain that he knows not how to mend this broken kingdom that he himself broke. So, our most gracious Queen is safe, for Warwick cannot repair the damage he has done to himself, or act in any way that upsets the delicate status quo of the warring factions around him.'

Edward rose from his chair.

Friar Drynk bowed even lower.

'Stand up, friar,' commanded Edward. 'You have spoken well, and have banished my fears with your excellent assessment of the situation in England. It would seem I have a holy man with a sharp political brain. I will keep you close, for I will need your wise council in the days ahead.'

John Tunstall watched Friar Drynk take his leave of the King, and walk towards him. He had known from the friar's hesitant demeanour as he approached that he carried distressing news. His stomach turned over, and an intuition told him that Rose was in danger. A sharp pain filled John's chest, as Friar Drynk cleared his throat and looked at him with sympathy.

Warwick Castle, Warwickshire
1 November 1470

The bitter cold November night hung crisp and brittle in the winter sky.

Rose pulled the threadbare blanket tightly up to her chin. The brazier that warmed the gaoler's office seemed an endless distance away; its glow weakly flickered and danced amongst the shadows of her cell. Sometimes, fleetingly, she even felt the illusion of its heat, but she knew its warmth died on the cold, damp walls of her dungeon. She shivered as the guard gently rang the midnight bell, its muffled note signalling the changing of the sentries,

Curling into a tight ball, Rose hugged the blanket closer around herself. She knew sleep would never come to her tired eyes. The sounding of the bell meant just six hours to dawn; six hours of life, and then her stilled heart and lifeless eyes would greet the dawn sun as she dangled on the end of the executioner's rope.

She pulled the blanket over her head, erecting an imaginary barrier against reality as she prayed for a moment of respite from the turmoil within her. Desperately, she tried to stop her mind running through the events that had brought her to this wretchedness. The face of loved ones that she would never see again filled her with despair. She could not stop the tears falling from her eyes.

When she had arrived at the castle, she had been questioned by the senior officer. She had told him nothing; acting like a scatterbrained girl, but he had seen right through her lies and had handed her over to the new senior gaoler who had still to prove himself. He had accepted the challenge with relish. That was when the beating started: first, just slaps to the face and threats of hot pokers being pushed into her orifices, then later, thin willow canes had beaten the soles of her feet, ripping and shredding the skin apart. The pain had been unbearable. She had told them everything: the flight from France, warning King Edward of Lord Montagu's treachery, Simon's mother – and sisters, and why she thought he had killed the senior gaoler. It had all come tumbling out.

Once they were satisfied with her story, they had sent their report off to the Earl of Warwick, in London. His reply had been a warrant for her execution.

The day the warrant arrived had been worse than all the pain they had inflicted on her, for that night, they had brutally raped her. Heavy sobs heaved from her chest as she remembered the three guards who had entered her cell, drunkenly jeering that a convicted felon awaiting the gallows had no rights.

'It would be a shame to let a young girl die a virgin,' they had taunted. Their cruel laughter mingled with her screams as they slapped her face and pulled roughly at her clothes. Their faces leered close; their stinking breath covered her face, their rough hands mauling her naked body. She had prayed for death as they spent their lust in her, and now, in a few hours, death awaited her, and sweet John, whose love filled his eyes, would never feel her loving kiss again. Those tender moments she had imagined they would share together would never be theirs; her dreams were now dust.

'Rose...'

The voice Rose heard was gentle – feminine.

'We mean you no harm; we come to offer you comfort.'

The soft voice settled on her as she froze under the blanket, her body rigid with fear.

'Rose, my child, we would talk with you.'

The door of her cell was securely locked, with only her inside, but she could sense that somebody was close. She felt the blanket being pulled away. Scurrying backwards on her haunches, she hit the cell wall. Its jagged flints dug sharply into her back. Her heart thumped. She held her breath so tightly that it made her head swim.

Slowly, Rose forced her eyes open. Her hands flew to her mouth in astonishment. Before her, stood three beautiful figures dressed in brilliant, white gowns edged with gold. She marvelled at their splendour. They radiated a luminous light that filled her dark and dingy cell. She became calm as a sensation of tranquillity filled her. All the horrors of the past week just slipped away. She raised herself up on to her knees her eyes wide in wonder.

'Are you angels?' she whispered, in awe.

'No, my child, we are not, but we bathe in their splendour,' said the figure in the centre of the trio. 'We have suffered here within these walls, as you have suffered.'

Rose sat upright, recognition swift and absolute on her face.

'You are Simon's mother and sisters!' she cried, in shock.

The figures moved closer, forming a wall of golden light around her, their faces radiating love.

'Why have you come back to this place of your suffering?' Rose asked.

The spirit of Simon's mother moved closer and knelt on the floor. 'Take comfort, Rose, we come to bring you hope. Your future holds many things. You will live long, and love will fill your heart.'

'I have been defiled and raped – I have no future,' Rose cried, in despair. ''Tis better I die.' She wrapped her arms around herself. 'It is too late to save me, for I am dishonoured. I have lost what cannot be replaced. My sweet John will turn his heart against me. I could never suffer to see him look at me with just pity in his eyes.'

'His love is too strong to be broken,' said the spirit of one of Simon's sisters. 'Your destinies are bound together.'

'You must keep this hope alive,' said the other spirit sister.

As Rose bathed in their light, she prayed it was not a dream. 'Are you real or just phantoms?'

'We are real, sweet Rose,' spoke the spirit of Simon's mother. The dawn will prove it to you. We have a message for Simon; you must take it to him.'

'But I am to die, shortly,' cried Rose, 'and it is through his actions.'

'It was through Warwick's actions that you suffer, my little one, not Simon's. He meant no harm to befall any of us. He carried us all in his heart. It is Warwick who will pay before God for our suffering.'

The golden spectres rose gently up into the air, their brilliance slowly fading.

'Tell Simon, we do not hold him to account for our suffering. Tell him he must continue his quest against Warwick if he is to find redemption.'

'But, will he believe me?' cried Rose.

'When he sees the golden pendant, he will believe,'

'Where will I find him?' she shouted.

'You will find him, Rose; you will find him...'

Rose stared transfixed into the cold darkness of her cell as the vision faded away. She felt uncertain. Was she going mad? Did she just dream these celestial visions?

The harsh reality of her situation returned as she heard the guards stirring. Rose shivered as the dawn light silently crept in through the narrow slit high up on her dungeon wall. Low, rough voices invaded her cell. Heavy footsteps sounded down the passageway as the guards banged and rattled cell doors to wake the prisoners. She listened with rising panic as with an inevitable certainty they advanced towards her. With each step, her death came closer. She felt small and alone.

Rising on to her knees, Rose prayed for the courage to face her death with dignity. Holding her palms together, she looked up as the first rays of the dawn sun burst through the narrow window of her cell. A dazzling shaft of light, like an arrow, hit the floor. Rose looked down. There amongst the dirt and grime, lay a beautiful golden pendant, only two feet from her knees. She stared in disbelief as its purity shone out from amongst the filth of her cell. She caught her breath; it had not been a dream.

As Rose heard keys jangling in the passageway beyond her cell door, she snatched the pendant from the floor, and dropped it down the front of her bodice, just as she heard the cell door being unlocked.

The door swung open. Three guards entered the cell.

'It's time,' said one, as he took her wrist and gently spun her around.

Before Rose had time to think, her hands were bound tightly behind her back.

Another guard stepped in front of her, his face leering cruelly close. She shrank away as she recognised him as one of her rapists, but he reached out and grasped the top of her bodice, licking his lips as he pulled her closer, his fingers slipping down and roughly brushing her breasts.

'Such a waste,' he said, his voice thick with lust. 'Me thinks if I am quick, I will have ye again while you are still warm.' His other hand slipped under her dress.

Rose clamped her knees tight together, and spat with all her might on to the guard's face. Spittle hung from his nose and eyelids; it ran down his cheek and over his lips.

The guard stepped back in shock. 'You little bitch!' he screamed, his fist rising to strike her. The other two guards manhandled him away towards the door. He fought to push through them but they held him fast. 'Enough!' shouted one. 'Give the girl some dignity to face her death.'

'I will give her dignity,' shouted the guard, as he struggled to attack her. 'I will—'

He froze as the point of a sword pricked the back of his neck.

'You will what?' asked a voice, its rich ton and strength of command, instantly recognisable. The guards bowed low as armed soldiers entered the cell and Thomas, the Great Controller, swept in. 'Well?' he bellowed.

The two guards moved away from the one they were restraining.

'I meant no harm, sir,' pleaded the guard. 'It was just a bit of horseplay.'

'He was going to rape me, again,' sobbed Rose, as she slipped, exhausted, to her knees.

The Great Controller's yellow eyes flashed with anger. 'Take that animal,' he bellowed at the two guards, making them jump with fright, 'and put him in a cell, with the door locked until I order otherwise. Then, go and tell the executioner to stand down. There will be no hanging today; but first, untie the girl.'

Rose sat in a large room that overlooked the inner keep of the castle. It was comfortably furnished; tapestries adorned the walls, large rugs covered the floor. An iron brazier glowing with charcoal kept the early winter cold at bay.

Earlier, she had scrubbed herself clean in a large, wooden tub of hot water. Afterwards, she had massaged light lavender oil into her dry and chapped skin. She had applied herbal ointment gently to the soles of her feet to ease the pain and swelling. Now, she sat clean and fresh, her thick hair fell softly around her shoulders. The face the world saw now was calm, but inside she was filled with despair; her heart was dead. No amount of washing would cleanse her now.

There was a knock at the door.

'Come,' Rose said.

A servant entered, with food and drink. He placed it on a table and without speaking, left the room. He was about to close the door when the Great Controller strode in. He studied Rose and shut the door. The spirited girl so full of life, who he had known at Middleham, had gone. The person before him was a shadow of her former self. He sighed with sympathy for her, realising that the innocence of youth, and the purity of young love, were never enough to shield her from the harsher evils of men who rule.

'Take food and wine,' he said, gently.

Rose shook her head, and stared at the floor.

'The three guards who violated you have confessed to their crimes.' Eyes that reflected their despair looked at him, and he saw the anger flash within them. 'Their crimes are great and many,' he continued, 'so I have given them a choice: one must hang, the second must be blinded, and the third, castrated, and his hands cut off. They must choose amongst themselves who receives which punishment. They have until dawn to decide, and then the sentences will be carried out. It will be an unpleasant night for them.'

'Tis only what they deserve,' Rose hissed with venom. Slowly, her anger dimmed. 'I am grateful for your rescue, sir.'

'You must thank Simon Langford for that,' he replied. 'Tis a brave act for him to come back to Middleham where I knew him as Robert Furneys, a Lancastrian spy, and offer his life for yours. I always knew our paths would cross again one day but I didn't expect, with all the saints in Heaven, it to involve you, Rose.'

She looked up at him. Simon had not deserted her, then? A flicker of understanding crossed her face.

'He told me,' pressed on the Great Controller, now that he had her attention, 'of your brave adventure in France, the fate of his family at the hands of Warwick, the killing of the gaoler and his subsequent fears for you.'

'Where is he now?'

The Great Controller sighed. 'I sent him away. There was no need to punish him further for his actions, he had done that well enough himself, and...I am getting older and the world has turned since those days. He carries his punishment within his conscience, and it will punish him every day he greets the dawn.'

'What of you, sir,' Rose asked. 'Lord Warwick sent a warrant for my execution. Will you not be in danger for defying his authority? Why have you come all this way to save me?'

The Great Controller leant forward, as though he wished to impart some great secret. 'I am responsible for all of the earl's castles, so I travel frequently between them to check that they are running smoothly, check the accounts, and so forth.

'I was intending to visit here before Simon Langford told me of your bravery in escaping from France, but also, and more importantly, that you saved the King's life – not only his life, but that of his brother, Duke Richard, and all their close retainers, many of whom I know and love.'

The Great Controller looked at Rose, his eyes glinting with hidden knowledge. 'In the world of men who rule,' he began, 'they can deal for themselves a good hand or a bad hand. I have to steer a course through their treacherous waters to maintain order; maintain, if you like, the thin veneer of civilisation, so the common people can go about their business, feed themselves and their families. If I do not, then chaos would reign, and we would return to the dark ages. So, I have to make decisions, and in you instance, it was to save you.

'The reason was simple: Warwick has overstretched himself. I supported his actions to rid us of mad King Henry and place Edward on the throne – a man born to be a king – but to reverse this, even with the help of the French, is madness, a gamble for power that will not succeed.

377

My spies tell me that King Edward is preparing his army in Flanders with the backing of the mighty Duke of Burgundy, and when he lands in England, Warwick will be no match for him. Warwick is surrounded with treachery and will not survive.'

Rose began to nibble on some sweetmeats, then, pausing to sip some wine, her eyes caught the Great Controller's.

He noticed with satisfaction the interest on her face. 'So, young Rose,' he continued, 'when I received from London, notification that a warrant had been issued for your execution, and at the same time received a visit from Simon Langford who told me of your bravery, I had to decide what horse to back.'

If I had chosen Warwick then you would have died, he thought, guiltily.

'I chose King Edward,' he said, brightly. 'I could not allow you to die. You had effectively saved him, his brother, and countless others from certain death.

'Firstly, I surmise that we will never see Warwick again. Secondly, I did not want to be responsible for your death, and thirdly, I will now be in King Edward's, and Duke Richard's, good books for saving your life. You will be reunited with John when he returns, so it is an excellent outcome for all of us.'

Tears began to fall from Rose's eyes. 'John will never see me again.' She cried with heartbreaking grief. 'How could I ask him to love me now? Those men have stolen my happiness. I will disappear before he finds me.'

The Great Controller looked at Rose, with sympathy. 'We will leave for Middleham in the morning, after the sentences have been carried out,' he said, gently. 'Do not make any decisions until we are away from here and safely back at Middleham.'

Rose shook her head. 'My decision is made,' she said, with finality. 'John will never set eyes on me again.'

Chapter 14

Who Will Win?

Royal Court, Compiègne, Burgundy Border
14 February 1471

'Where is Lord Warwick?' shouted King Louis at his advisors. 'He should have landed in Calais by now. He promised me an army for my financial backing in his taking Edward's crown. I only declared war on Burgundy because he pledged ten thousand men to support my cause. Now, my army is massed on Burgundy's borders, and I still wait like a nervous bride for him to arrive.

'And why is Margaret of Anjou still in Honfleur?' he cried, his face turning red with rage. 'Should she not be in England, her son crowned King? Has all my planning and scheming been in vain? Did the earl's words come cheaply to him, his promises hollow? Has he made a fool of me?'

'No...No, Sire,' replied Georges Havart. 'The earl has promised our envoys that he will see you shortly with his great army, but he needs Margaret of Anjou, and her son, to hold the kingdom while he comes to your aid.'

King Louis noted the slight scepticism in Georges Havart's voice.

'As for Margaret of Anjou,' Georges Havart continued, 'she hesitates to cross the channel. Her spies have reported that the Duke of Clarence now plots against Warwick. The old Yorkist followers are refusing to embrace the Lancastrian cause, and the Lancastrians do not trust them or Warwick. England is now a hotbed of intrigue and treachery, and finally, King Edward is raising a fleet with the backing of Burgundy to return to England and reclaim his crown.'

'The truth is, your Majesty,' joined in Antoine de Chabannes, the Grand Master of France, 'that Margaret blames you for this state of affairs. If you had waited for Warwick to secure England before sending her across the channel with a French army at her back, all would be well, and her son crowned King. Instead, she claims you were over eager to declare war on the Duke of Burgundy by showing your hand too quickly. You left him no choice but to support Edward and his planned invasion. She is afraid that if successful, Warwick will soon be fighting for his very existence against the greatest warrior in Europe, and that is why she hesitates.'

'My good Lords,' began King Louis, his voice now calm, his face the picture of diplomacy. 'As you know, I am wary of war. I spurn and distrust it, but by moving fast to crush Burgundy, we would have stopped Edward's invasion plans. Warwick should have understood this simple strategy: by sending me his army, we could have guaranteed Warwick's rule in England and mine in France, but now Burgundy may well invade France, and Edward, England, likewise. We are running out of time. The situation is grave. If Warwick does not come soon then I fear great misfortune awaits us.'

'I will send a detachment of your Scots Guards,' announced Georges Havart, 'to place that woman from Anjou and her son on a ship, and send them to Warwick, immediately.'

'If Edward lands in England then I fear the game will be up for all of us,' said King Louis wearily.

Church of Saint Margaret's, Westminster Abbey 24 March 1471

Queen Elizabeth sat in the silence of her sanctuary, suckling baby Edward, named in honour of his father, the king. He had lived his short five months in this cold, gloomy building of crosses and graves, but Elizabeth was thankful for its protection against Warwick.

Her three young daughters were in a side room with Lady Scrope, who was instructing them in the intricacies of needlework.

Elizabeth treasured these moments of quiet solitude; holding her baby at her breast was a special moment. Looking down at him, she wondered if he would ever see his father or even be crowned Prince of Wales. His little hand held tightly on to her finger. His rosebud lips now sucking slowly as he closed his eyes with contentment. Her heart filled with tenderness for him.

Looking around at the thick solid walls of their sanctuary, she prayed they would keep safe for a while longer, for outside, Warwick's men still walked about their business. From messages smuggled inside to her, she had learnt, with much gladness, that ten days ago, King Edward had landed at Ravenspur, a small port near Hull, and was marching at speed, south, with an army of three thousand men. At the same time, Warwick had left London and was marching north towards Coventry to marshal his forces. She knew that only one of them would survive this final mighty clash.

The sound of running footsteps and calls from her mother pulled Elizabeth out of her reverie. As Jacquetta approached, red-faced and with laboured breath, Elizabeth held a finger to her lips. Her mother stopped, and seeing the baby, nodded, as she slowly caught her breath. Elizabeth placed her son in his cot as her mother quietly settled herself into a large well-upholstered chair, sighing with the pleasure of resting her tired legs.

'My old friend, Margaret of Anjou, is about to sail from France to grace us with her presence,' Jacquetta whispered.

'How do you know that?' questioned Elizabeth, sharply.

Her mother cocked her head to one side and raised an eyebrow.

Elizabeth stared at her in disbelief. 'Where have you learnt this?' she hissed. 'It cannot be here, on holy ground.'

A sly smile crossed Jacquetta's face. 'Warwick has left London. The streets are safer now, and dressed as a merchant's wife I can travel at will. I have friends and places...' she paused as Elizabeth's eyes widened with anger, 'to practise my art,' she concluded, quickly.

'But mother...' Elizabeth snapped, making the baby jump, 'you promised; no more sorcery.'

'Tis too important to ignore,' Jacquetta retorted. 'The Earl of Devon and the Duke of Somerset are already raising troops to fight Edward. With Margaret's royal presence, many more will join their standard. They must be stopped from uniting with Warwick's forces. Edward can defeat one or the other but not both united together.'

Elizabeth knelt down beside the cot and looked with concern at her baby. 'If my boy is to become a prince, then Margaret must be delayed.' Her eyes met her mother's unwavering gaze. 'Have you magic strong enough?'

Jacquetta nodded. 'It is time that is short, so this must be done without delay.'

Elizabeth looked at her son. 'Go and work your spells; keep that Bitch of Anjou in France where she belongs,' she finally said.

Egglestone Abbey, North Yorkshire
26 March 1471

Rose reined in her horse beside the river. The small detachment of troops that the Great Controller had provided for her protection moved up alongside her.

In the gathering dusk, a half-mile upstream, stood the abbey, which, Rose had been informed, had been built on the banks of the River Tees almost four hundred years before. The gently rolling hills that surrounded the abbey still showed the scars of the old quarry workings where the stone had been cut to build it.

'Tis best we move on,' said the masters-at-arms, 'while we still have the light.'

Rose dug her heels into her mount and set her horse to canter.

It had been a short journey from Middleham to Egglestone but it had given Rose time to reflect on the past few weeks. After her ordeal at Warwick Castle, coming home to Middleham Castle had helped to calm her mind. The Great Controller, in a further kindness, had arranged for her family to visit and stay at the castle. For days, she had talked and cried with her mother and sisters about her suffering. She had felt the strong arms of her father, holding her as she had sobbed on his shoulder. It was love from her family that had saved her from madness – they had been food for her soul – and although she could never wash away the horrors of the past, they had slowly dimmed to a place in her mind where she could close a door on them, and find a sense of peace. After many weeks, she had felt strong enough to perform the quest that the spirits had asked her: to seek out Simon.

As they neared the abbey, the soft lilt of evening song greeted them, its natural cadence lifting and falling in a gentle rhythm that praised the glory of God.

The monk who greeted them wore a pure white habit, the monks being known locally as the 'white canons'.

'We come from Middleham Castle, and seek Sir Simon Langford,' said the master-at-arms. 'We were told he rests here.'

The monk's sharp eyes studied the group, but he did not reply.

'We mean him no harm,' said Rose, sensing the monk's suspicion. 'If you ask him, he will know of me.'

'Why do you think he is here?' replied the monk.

'Barnard Castle is but half a mile from here,' said the master-at-arms. 'They reported to the Great Controller at Middleham that he was found near to death in the snow on Cotherstone Moor and brought here. Do not deny it,' he barked, with growing annoyance.

The monk looked around with hesitation.

The master-at-arms slid from his saddle. With his hand resting on the hilt of his sword, he advanced towards the monk.

Deciding that prudence was better than valour, the monk stepped to one side and waved them through the great door of the abbey. 'If you come in peace, you are welcome,' he said to Rose, nervously, as the master-at-arms brushed him aside.

Rose followed the monk through the cloisters. The moon was casting silver shadows as the evening air turned cold. She shivered, and pulled her cloak tightly around herself.

The monk stopped and opened a door that led into a small, dark passageway. Light shone out through gaps in another door at the far end of the passage. Arriving there, the monk knocked once and entered.

Rose stopped, apprehensive of her emotions towards the man who had caused her so much pain. Slowly, she eased herself through the doorway, and a face with long, wild hair turned to look at her. Their eyes locked.

'Simon!' Rose exclaimed.

'Rose!' Simon gasped, in shock.

The monk slipped from the room.

Rose and Simon listened in silence to the sound of the monk's retreating steps and then Simon pulled out a chair from under a small writing desk. Offering it to Rose, he sat down opposite her, on the edge of his bed.

'I am sorry for your arrest by Warwick's men,' Simon, finally said, breaking the silence. 'Did they treat you well at the castle?'

'How do you think they treated me?' Rose snapped. She saw the dismay enter Simon's eyes. 'I was beaten, raped, and sentenced to death.' Her voice was cold and dispassionate.

'Forgive me,' Simon whispered. 'As the Lord is my witness, I meant you no harm.' He rose from his bed and paced the room in agitation. 'I have left death behind me at every turn of the card!' he cried. 'When I escaped from Middleham Castle, all those years ago, the other spies were executed. At the attempt on Warwick's life at Rouen, every man who took part was put to death, except for me. My mother and sisters died because of my actions, and now you too have suffered. Who will be next? Marguerite is coming to England with her son; are they to be killed because of me? I walked out into the snow,' he said, softly, burying his head in his hands. 'I wished for eternal sleep, to be free of this burden I carry; this nightmare that haunts me.'

'It was God's will that you were found,' said Rose, 'for life has not finished with you yet.'

Simon's hands slipped from his face; his eyes hardened. 'Aye, but I have finished with life.'

'It was not you who signed the death warrants on all those people,' Rose said, quietly. 'Warwick killed your family, not you. Believe me when I say they do not hold you to account for their deaths.'

Simon cocked his head to one side and looked at Rose, quizzically. 'You cannot speak for my family.'

'The spies, and the men who took part in the plot to kill Warwick, knew the risks; their own actions caused their deaths. Your mother and sisters hold him responsible for their suffering and deaths.'

Perplexed, Simon stared at Rose. 'How do you know of what they think?'

'The night before my execution, your mother and sisters came to me; three beautiful spirits bathed by the light of the angels. They said that, for you to find redemption, you must continue your quest against Warwick until he is dead, not to torture yourself over their deaths. Their love is with you now and always.'

385

'Did you not dream this vision?' Simon mocked. 'Could not your fate in the morning have played tricks on your mind?'

Rose slipped the cloak from her shoulders and unclasping a gold chain from around her neck, she held up the gold pendant. 'They said to give you this as proof of what I say.'

Simon gasped with wonder at the sight of the necklace in Rose's hand. 'That belonged to my mother,' he whispered, in awe.

Chapter 15

The Battle of Barnet

Barnet, Hertfordshire
13 April 1471

It was early evening as they advanced towards the small town of Barnet.

John Tunstall rode with Duke Richard and the royal host, with banners and ensigns flying above them. Behind, followed the royal army. Lines of men wore leather jerkins or brigandines with assorted kettle hats or sallets upon their heads, some shiny new, others rusty with age – hand-me-downs from fathers or grandfathers who had fought in battles long ago. Daggers hung from studded leather belts; pikes, bows, swords or axes, were carried. Shouts of good-natured insults flew up and down the lines between the different lords' liverymen, the steady beat of metal on metal, sounding out to the rhythm of their marching.

Scourers and mounted knights rode protectively out on their flanks, while officers cantered up and down the lines cursing and encouraging the slowest, sometimes stopping to confer or issue more orders. Heavy wagons and artillery carts brought up the rear. The cacophony of a great marching army resonated out into the gathering dusk.

As they approached the town from the south, the advanced guard could see the fires of Warwick's army flickering out, encamped along a low ridge to the north of the town.

'Keep the army to the south of the town,' commanded King Edward, as they settled into an inn that was now his headquarters. 'Issue orders to our captains,' he continued, 'that the men must rest where they stop. No one will be billeted in the town; there will be no warm comfort tonight. Two hours before dawn, we will advance on foot in complete silence, and creep to within spitting distance of Warwick's army. He believes in his cannon; he will fire on us before first light. The closer we are to him, the safer our men will be. Warn them that any man who makes a noise and alerts them to our presence will not see the dawn.'

'What is to be the order of battle?' asked Richard, his cool, blue eyes holding Edward in his gaze.

'You will lead the right flank.'

Richard's eyes crinkled into a smile of satisfaction.

'Hastings will take the left, and I will hold the centre.'

George, the Duke of Clarence, jumped to his feet. 'And me?' he asked, with discord in his voice.

'You will hold the centre with me,' replied Edward. 'The troops you brought will form our reserve.'

George stepped forward and made to speak, but then thought better of it. His words stuck in his throat. With his face turning crimson, he slowly sat back down.

John Tunstall knew that George had no command. Edward did not trust him to stay true to his banner and so wished to keep him close at all times. All the others in the room knew this too, but not one face betrayed it.

Earl of Warwick's Encampment, Barnet
13 April 1471

'What news do you bring?' barked Warwick at the messenger who had been ushered into his presence.

Nervous, the man bowed and held out a letter. 'It is from the French king,' he said, with humility.

Warwick grunted as he ripped it open. Lord Montagu, the Earl of Oxford, the Duke of Exeter, and other close retainers, watched as Warwick read the contents.

'King Louis has made a temporary truce with the Duke of Burgundy,' he said. 'It would seem the door of France is slowly closing on me.'

'It is no reflection on you,' cried Lord Montagu, with false cheer. He knew how much the friendship of King Louis mattered to his brother, but also how circumstances had conspired to prevent him helping the French king as promised. 'It means Louis cannot defeat Burgundy without you, the greatest General in Europe.'

'Me thinks that Louis has lost faith in me, that my promises were empty words,' Warwick said, with a faraway look in his eyes, his dreams of being the Prince of Holland and Zeeland now slipping away. He clapped his hands as though to frighten away these pensive thoughts. 'Gentlemen,' he barked, 'as you know, the Earl of Devon and the Duke of Somerset, have abandoned us. They have turned back towards the west. They have sent news that they go to welcome that Bitch of Anjou and her son, who land at Weymouth, tomorrow. It would seem they would rather fight under her banner than mine.'

'Old Lancastrians would rather fight with old Lancastrians,' said Lord Montagu, stating the obvious.

'So it would seem, for where is Jasper Tudor and his frightened little nephew, Henry? Should they not also be here with their promised four thousand men?' cried Warwick, his frustration boiling over. 'And then there's that turncoat, George, my own son in-law who has deserted me and joined his brother's banner. Ye Gods! That's three armies gone that would have swelled our ranks and given us an assuaged victory tomorrow.'

'But we still outnumber them,' said the Earl of Oxford, firmly. 'Our twelve thousand against their eight – and we have many cannon while they have none.'

'Aye,' said Warwick, 'but Edward's men will fight into the jaws of Hell for him. Ours do not fight for me. My ranks are filled with Lancastrians and Yorkists who will be fighting side by side but are still mistrustful of each other. Some fight for the Bitch of Anjou, and some would rather be fighting for Edward.' He threw a knowing look at his brother. 'But none fight for me. I do not have their hearts.'

Silence settled within the tent. They all knew that Warwick spoke the truth, and none had an answer to raise his spirits without it sounding false.

Finally, the Duke of Exeter's voice broke the silence. 'What you say is right, my Lord. We cannot disagree, for truth deflects all false arguments but there is one simple truth in that our men will fight for us: their captains, and we – your captains – fight loyally for you.'

'Aye, you are right,' boomed Warwick, with sudden confidence. 'It is now too late to dwell on this subject. If we win, tomorrow, they will take me to their bosoms as though I am their brother, so away to your men and tell them we will win. In years to come, they will stand proud. They will say we were there when the last of the Plantagenets fell.'

John Tunstall's feet sank into the wet, sodden earth as he walked silently up the gentle hill towards Warwick's army. A slight mist had begun to form across the ground, and a wet chill hung in the air. He was walking with Richard and Francis, with their men tramping silently behind them, their weapons wrapped in muslin cloth to muffle the clink of metal on metal. From the enemy line, they could see the flickering of campfires as they drew nearer. Finally, they stopped.

'This will be close enough,' whispered Richard. 'We will form our line here.'

A messenger arrived from King Edward. 'Your Grace,' he said, 'the

King is forming his troops to your left, and he requests your presence while the hour is still early.'

'I will come shortly,' Richard replied. 'John, Francis, see that the men are formed up in good order. They are to keep their harness on and their weapons ready. Tell the bowmen to keep their strings dry and post good sentries. Tell the men not to wander off, or make a noise that would alert the enemy to our presence. They know the penalty if they do.'

John had finished posting the sentinels while Francis had checked the men on the line. He now sat alone, resting his back against an old, fallen tree trunk that lay slightly forward of his men. He looked across, towards the enemy's lines. He was so close, he could hear them talking. He wondered what Warwick was thinking, having fought as a Yorkist all his life.

To be over there with the Lancastrians, he must feel as welcome as a fox in a chicken coop, John mused.

He gazed back along his own lines. All was quiet. His mind drifted back to the day they had landed near the Humber…they had marched unopposed down through the heart of England, their numbers swelling daily, and caught Warwick hiding behind the walls of Coventry. Three times, King Edward had demanded battle with him, and three times, Warwick had refused. Edward had ridden up and down outside the city walls in full harness, taunting him, but still Warwick had refused. Edward had laughed and shouted, 'It would seem the hunted are now doing the hunting', and then they had left for Warwick Castle to join with the Duke of Clarence, and his army.

It was at the castle that John had learnt of Rose's imprisonment. He felt a sharp pain in his chest as he remembered the moment he had heard of her ordeal. He had followed her trail from her arrest at the convent, to the dungeons of Warwick Castle. Her beatings and rape had unfolded with horror before him, and then her rescue by the Great Controller.

The journey from the castle to London, to free Edward's wife from her sanctuary at Westminster Abbey, had been a journey of bleak sorrow for John as he sought to come to terms with what had happened to Rose.

He had wanted to ride with all haste for Middleham Castle, but his duty to Richard had stopped him. As they marched out of London, up Watling Street and on to the Great North Road, his heart had lifted. Every mile that passed brought him closer to the Earl of Warwick, and now, at last, in a few hours, he would have his revenge, or die in the attempt...

The sharp crack of cannon made John jump. The hot fizz of air over his head, and then the thump as the ball hit the ground, focused his mind.

He hurried back down the slope towards his men. He could hear their oaths and curses as they lay on their stomachs with their hands over their heads. More sharp explosions rang out. The air was alive with cannon balls, shrieking through the night sky. The ground shook with the noise of thunder as scores of cannon fired in unison.

The men waited, their bodies tensed in fear, for the shot to land amongst them, smashing and ripping their muscle and bone to pieces. Their faces turned white with panic. Some pushed their knuckles into their mouths to stifle their screams, as again they tensed and waited, pushing themselves down into the soft earth, trying to burrow into it, wishing the ground would swallow them.

John silently thanked God that no one had screamed out and given their position away. 'Tis good news, lads,' he said, softly. 'We are so close to their lines, their shot is landing well behind us. Keep silent and all will be well.'

Frightened faces and nervous eyes relaxed into wry smiles. 'God bless King Edward for moving us so close,' someone murmured.

'Aye, God bless the King,' joined in a chorus of quiet voices. The words rippled repeatedly down the line.

Warwick stood alone at the entrance of his tent in full battle armour. He looked on as his cannon thundered into life; flame and smoke spitting from their mouths.

Lord Montagu, the Earl of Oxford, and the Duke of Exeter, were forming their men up into battle positions. Orders were sharp, discipline hard, as they steeled themselves for the coming battle.

Warwick had agreed with his brother's request that they fight on foot like the common soldier. It would give them extra heart, he had argued, because they could not flee on horseback if the battle turned. Warwick had arranged for their horses taken to the rear. *But to flee to where?* he had pondered.

King Louis had cast him off. That Bitch of Anjou would welcome him like the plague. Even this hotchpotch of an army he commanded wished he were on the other side, so they could kill him.

During the night, he had realised he was not a king, like Edward or Louis, who commanded loyalty through their royal position as a right given by God. He had tried to grasp this magical quality but like sand, it always slipped through his fingers. He knew now he could not command men's hearts, for he was not a king, but was it wrong of him to have reached for the stars? To have dreamt of such things? He felt a sense of defiance building inside of him.

By God, it is better to have reached for the stars and failed than never to have tried at all, Warwick reasoned. And what of his dreams? They were life itself. For, if men did not dream, then they had never lived. He felt his old anger returning and it steeled his resolve. He swore that if he won the coming battle, he would take the crown of England for his own. *To Hell with King Henry, that Bitch of Anjou, and her son – to Hell with all of them.*

Warwick strode from his tent, alive with purpose. 'Sound the trumpets!' he barked, his eyes shining with excitement. 'Let us go to death or glory!'

John Tunstall stood in front of a wall of men, fully encased within his armour. He was already hot; sweat streamed down his back. Richard stood to his left, Francis to his right. Behind them, the front rank slowly pushed forward under the increasing pressure from the men behind. The fog was growing thicker by the second.

'It will be more like blind man's bluff, than fighting a battle,' shouted some old soldier behind him.

Trumpets sounded out the advance. John heard the swish of arrows from their archers as volley after volley was unleashed blindly into the thick, white fog. Then, the lines of men were moving forward. They started to move faster. Men were shouting, some screaming out battle cries now they were running at full tilt.

Out of the fog loomed a wall of steel. John brought his sword down from over the back of his shoulder in a strike that he had practised all his life. The young soldier running towards him screamed as the blade cut deep between his shoulder and neck, blood spurting high into the air.

Battle of Barnet, Hertfordshire
14 April 1471, Easter Sunday

A dense fog hung over the field like a funeral veil. Nature hid, from innocent eyes, the barbaric acts of savagery being committed in the pursuit of absolute power.

The morning dew that covered the field in a watery sheen would normally shimmer in the early morning sun, giving the illusion of concealed diamonds sparkling out from beneath blades of grass, but today this lush meadow ran red with blood; nature's soft silence shattered by the reverberations of a bloody and brutal battle.

Twenty thousand men embroiled in lethal hand-to-hand combat, the harsh metallic clash of weapons, frantic shouts, and the agonised screams of the maimed or dying, echoed out from this white shroud of death. The sheer volume and spectacle of horror made speech and compassion impossible.

John Fletcher, arrow-maker to the Duke of Exeter, had no need to speak. He was sitting triumphantly astride a fallen knight whose main battle weapon lay just out of reach. He was defenceless, his helmet pushed upwards until the eye slits were now level with his forehead. He was blind within it.

John Fletcher raised his rondel dagger with its slender fifteen-inch blade specifically designed for penetrating gaps in armour, and aimed it at the thin line of flesh now exposed between the helmet and the knight's breastplate. He licked his lips as he touched the fine Italian armour and greedily wondered how much coin he would receive for it. With this rich bounty, he would buy his young wife gifts of silks and spices. He imagined, with lust, how she would thank him. Her soft breasts and generous mouth filled his thoughts. He placed the tip of the dagger into the gap and lightly pricked the naked flesh. He was going to enjoy inflicting this pain, enjoy watching the agonising spasm of death that would result. He wanted this knight to feel his death coming. 'Are you ready to die, you Yorkist bastard?' he screamed.

Abruptly, John Fletcher stopped shouting. His mind snapped back into focus as his stomach flipped. He knew he had just committed the cardinal sin for a soldier in battle: he had hesitated. A curse of terror left his lips as he saw, out of the corner of his right eye, the curved blade of a razor-sharp Falchion sword cutting through the mist with a violence of purpose towards his neck. The sounds of battle were suddenly silent. The knight beneath him, sensing swiftly rising fear, stopped struggling.

John Fletcher, in a frozen moment, was bound to this knight, his body rigid. Out of the corner of his left eye, he saw the sword disappearing away from him back into the mist. Still sitting astride the knight, he wondered how this Grim Reaper's blade had missed him. Had God performed a miracle or was it some clever illusion? Then, slowly, his head toppled forward, parting in blood-soaked savagery from his neck. As the darkness of death filled John Fletcher's eyes, he realised, to his horror, there had been no miracle or illusion.

John Tunstall lowered his sword and looked at the red mist in front of him. He had seen it before at beheadings. Once the victim's heart stopped beating, minute droplets of blood hung suspended in the air, forming a shimmering translucent red mist; a dance of death being performed over the headless corpse. It amazed him how something so delicately eye-catching could be created from an act of such violence. He kicked the body off the knight and with great strength pulled his old friend, Francis, from the mud.

Francis raised his visor and smiled, weakly. 'The bastard was just about to surrender.'

John had no time to reply, as men wearing Warwick's colours burst through the mist.

Upon seeing two fully armed knights, they turned tail, back into the fog, except for three young brothers: farmer's sons, who saw rich pickings and glory in slaying them. Their father's rudimentary lessons in fighting had taught them how to trip a knight with their pikes and then finish him with their daggers.

The biggest boy rushed towards John, his blue eyes shining with excitement, a look of triumph already on his face.

John knew from the boy's rash lunge that he handled a plough better than a pike. The move to trip him was ill shaped. Lifting his foot in a move he had practised a thousand times, and holding his sword in both hands, he pirouetted in a tight circle. Spinning with lightning speed, he brought his sword up in a fast sweeping motion just above the boy's hip bone, and then saw the look of surprise on the boy's face.

The boy's last terrified and confused thought as the coldness of death grasped him was that of his father saying that knights on foot were slow and clumsy. The blade sliced through his midriff, cutting him clean in half.

Francis dispatched the second boy, who had hesitated at the sight of his brother's bloody death.

The third boy dropped his pike and fled back into the fog, now a cowardly harbinger to their father.

The messenger reached Warwick at the rear, and the young knight burst through the fog with Lord Montagu's name upon his lips.

'My Lord...your brother begs more troops. The men protecting our right flank under the Earl of Oxford have disappeared into the fog. Our lines were not aligned with the enemy's, and in the confusion, his men have disappeared, chasing phantoms into thin air. The Yorkists have now swung around and are attacking our exposed flank. We cannot hold them for much longer.'

'Damn Oxford!' cried Warwick. 'Exeter has already drained my reserves in his fight with Gloucester; we have none left to send.' He looked with dismay towards his loyal retainers.

'We must bolster your brother's line ourselves; rally his men and restore order if we are to win!' cried one of the retainers.

'Aye, we must hold the line until Oxford returns,' shouted Warwick, with false belief, for he doubted he would ever see him again.

Warwick knew victory was slipping away. For the first time in his life, he felt totally alone, just himself within his own skin. No one could help him; he had no more grand schemes or plots left to turn events to his advantage. There was nothing left to pull out of the fire. Edward was winning and the game was finally up.

'Exeter is down!' a rough voice shouted, from the fog.

'Exeter is slain!' cried another.

A man appeared, blood flowing from a deep gash on his arm. Warwick took a step back in alarm.

'Tis finished!' the man cried. 'Our Lord Exeter is dead!' Then, with eyes wild with panic, he disappeared back into the mist.

Warwick looked on in stunned silence, towards his brother's line, just as the early morning sun burst through the fog.

In the distance, he saw a tall, dashing figure dressed in shining armour, the sun gleaming off the golden crown upon his head. He watched with dismay as King Edward, mounted on a beautiful white horse, his banners flying before him, smashed with all his might into the centre of his brother's wavering lines, driving with all his force towards Lord Montagu's Pennant. With horror, Warwick saw it fall.

John Tunstall scanned the battlefield as the sun finally drove off the morning fog, and saw, with relief, Richard standing under his battle standard, axe in hand, fighting with his natural rhythm and strength, showing no quarter or mercy. He motioned to Francis to follow him.

The bedlam and noise of battle sounded out all around them. Piles of disfigured corpses crowded their vision. The fighting was at close quarters – brutal and bloody.

John felt the sweat streaming from every pore in his body. His blood felt on fire; his sword arm, numb. He had to find respite soon, for he knew battle fatigue was setting in.

Moving towards Richard's standard, John saw the enemy was starting to thin out, slowly moving away. They knew the carnage two fully trained knights could inflict, but this was something much more momentous. He realised, with elation, that the enemy's stomach for the fight was deserting them; it was as if some unknown force had swept across the battlefield like a plague. He prayed that this was that gathering moment when the battle finally turned in their favour.

***

The Lancastrian army had sensed an unseen force. It had sucked the courage from their bodies and filled their hearts with despair. Their hopeless clamour of resistance was growing weaker. Their frightened eyes flicked all around, seeing, as though for the first time, this bloody field that surrounded them.

Hearts pounding, bodies sweating, the cold taste of fear filled them, and then a silent irreversible order whispered into all their ears, for slowly, in unison, they started retreating. Their backwards steps, slow at first, became quicker. Finally, dropping their weapons, they turned and ran in blind terror, their courage gone. Deserted by their God, the Lancastrian army was in full flight.

The beautiful green English countryside spread out before them. The same fertile land that proud tenant farmers, yeomen, and shepherds had tilled, grazed, and nurtured to feed their families was now their enemy, a hunting ground for the chasing Yorkist army. Many knew that they would be dead by the morning, buried beneath the wet, bloodied mud.

John and Francis arrived beside Richard's standard in time to watch the fleeing Lancastrian army. Removing their helmets, they let the cool air refresh their sweat-stained faces.

'Tis sweet relief from the hellish heat of battle,' said Francis, as he took a cup of cool, watered wine from a young squire. He drank thirstily.

Orders were now being shouted. A sense of urgency filled the air.

John knew they must unleash the cavalry and seize this opportunity to finish the enemy. Excitement was starting to build within him. Now, it would be like the old days he had heard so much about, before the battle of Agincourt where the English longbow had made full-frontal cavalry charges suicidal, but this fleeing army was a different proposition. He watched with growing impatience as the squires removed their horses' battle armour to make them more fleet of foot. He knew the king's scourers were already awaiting the signal to charge. These mounted men-at-arms who normally protected the flanks of the foot soldiers when marching, became lightly armoured cavalry. In battle, they were fast, ruthless, and would terrorise a fleeing army.

Richard saw the frustration in John's eyes. 'Patience,' he said. 'The enemy cannot escape its fate. They are exhausted and in complete disarray. We will catch them as swiftly as the falcon catches the hare.'

With banners flying, and bugles sounding out in victory, King Edward, with a large force of retainers, rode across the battlefield towards them. Reining in his horse, he leaned down and clasped his brother's hand, his eyes shining bright with the elation of triumph. 'The day is ours!' he cried, with elation. 'My army fought with fearless courage. Warwick is vanquished!'

'Our victory will not be complete if he escapes to fight another day,' replied Richard, with cold logic.

Edward studied his younger brother, knowing he was right. Warwick had cut himself adrift and could not be saved from his fate. With Richard's cool gaze never leaving his face, he finally uttered the words that would have been unthinkable only a short time ago. 'Warwick must not leave this field alive!' he cried, to his assembled cavalry.

Richard gave a self-satisfied smile. Warwick was going to pay for what he had done to the Lady Anne, and to all his future plans. 'Twenty gold coin to the man who slays him,' he shouted, with vengeance in his voice.

Edward raised his sword high into the air and roared with jubilant triumph. 'With the help of almighty God, we simple soldiers have won a great battle; it is now time to finish this day in glorious victory!'

The assembled cavalry raised their weapons in salute to their king, and then with trumpets sounding, one thousand mounted men-at-arms, knights, and nobles, set loose, knowing that their thundering noise would strike fear into the fleeing army.

John was filled with excitement. This was his first, full cavalry charge. He had ridden in skirmishes and minor engagements with Richard, in Wales, but never in full battle order. He had trained and dreamt of this moment since he was a small boy and now it was real. Mounted on a fine horse, wind in his face, sword in hand, he was at last a worthy knight. He knew his father would be proud, watching over him. This moment would be a jewel in his memory, for this was what he was born to do, and this is what he lived for.

As he galloped over the fields towards the fleeing army, he thought of Rose. Scanning the horizon, he looked for Warwick. *It is time for the bastard to pay for what he has done to her,* he affirmed.

The old foot soldiers left behind to guard the battle standards, watched with knowing eyes as the cavalry hunted down their prey. They would shortly start stripping the corpses that lay around them, searching for gold or coin. They knew that the rules of survival for a fleeing soldier were simple: if he was within one mile of the cavalry, he was dead; two miles, he had a fifty-fifty chance; three miles, he would survive. The light and fleet of foot lived, the wounded, fattest, or oldest, died. It was the ancient law of nature – survival of the fittest.

Richard Neville, the mighty Earl of Warwick, finally admitted to himself that the battle was lost. He watched as his men-at-arms broke ranks and fled the field like rabbits before the fox. Also fleeing, were the farmers and yeomen, normally solid and strong, but now reduced to a terror-stricken rabble. He knew more would perish in this rout than had died in the battle. Death held no glory for the losers.

His heart became heavy with grief as he recalled his younger brother, John, the Marquess of Montagu, being overwhelmed and cut down. Warwick knew that despite joining his cause, John's heart had always been with Edward. He had fought as a Lancastrian because Warwick had deemed it so, and now his brother was dead, killed for a cause he did not believe in.

A great weariness came over him. This last great effort for supremacy had left him exhausted, and his advancing years weighed heavily.

Am I not the maker of kings, he thought, *the mightiest Lord in the land? How have the men that I cultivated – nay, nurtured – within my own household, who I then promoted to the highest ranks in the land, brought me to my knees?*

A sharp anger filled him. A small spark of defiance started to glow within him, stiffening his resolve. The Bitch of Anjou was landing at

Weymouth. If he could reach her, then he could still triumph over Edward and his brothers. *These three sons of York will live to regret opposing me. This battle may be lost, but I can still win the war and avenge my brother's death.*

He gathered his thoughts. Around him was a small band of loyal and trusted retainers who were waiting for his order to retreat. He knew they could hear the dull pounding of the advancing cavalry in the distance. Their faces stained with sweat, blood, and mud, and they watched him with uneasy eyes.

'We must make for the horses,' said Sir James Metcalfe, with a calmness that betrayed no fear, 'or stand and fight.'

Warwick smiled ruefully at the challenge, and then with one last resolve, he swung into action and gave the order to retreat.

They started running to the rear. The ground was soft and wet, and Warwick's body, now past the invincible glow of youth, struggled across the open ground, his heavy armour sapping his strength. He felt only shame as he lumbered clumsily along, shame at this ignominious retreat. He stopped to gather his breath and noticing his young squires leading their horses towards them, he pulled off his helmet to saviour the cool air. 'With God's good grace, we will disappoint Edward's cavalry!' he cried.

His men cheered and redoubled their efforts to outrun the charging tide of horses behind them.

Warwick's spirits rose. He would, against all the odds, live to extract his revenge on those sons of York. He felt the elation flowing through his veins...then it changed. A sudden uneasiness filled him, turning his stomach. Why had his squires stopped moving?

The Earl of Warwick's squire realised the situation was desperate. He and the other young attendants were on the brow of a small hill, moving towards their retreating lords, when he saw in the distance the advancing Yorkist cavalry. Quickly calculating the distance between them, the squire realised with a sinking heart that the odds were against them – the earl had left his retreat too late.

The squire brought Warwick's horse to rest at his side, and the other squires did likewise with their mounts. They turned their frightened eyes towards him. As the most senior amongst them, his eighteenth birthday was only weeks away. Some of the younger boys had only just seen their fourteenth. He could see that they were full of fear, and some had tears in their eyes. This timid little army stood in silence.

The great warhorses stood proudly beside them, dressed in their shining armour; the bright, coloured patterns of their master's standards embroidered on their blankets. Silver bells hung from their armoured reins. They stood perfectly still; just the occasional flick of a tail or the twitch of an ear was all that moved as they waited with discipline for their next orders.

The squires were dressed in their thick, padded livery jackets, and heavy woollen breeches; their only weapon was a small dagger hanging from their belts. They were never expected to fight; only to serve their masters. Before the battle, they had been full of mischief and high spirits, playing pranks on each other and receiving the occasional slap from their betters for their devilment. They had listened to the old soldiers' tales of courage and bravery in battles past. They all thought today was going to be a glorious victory and nothing had prepared them for the bloody reality of war. They had watched it all unfold before them: the cannon, the archers, and the full-frontal assaults. The sights had shocked their senses. Some had wet themselves with fright, whilst others called out softly for their mothers.

The Earl of Warwick's squire knew it was a lost cause. He was not going to throw his life, or their lives, away. He addressed them quickly, urgency in his voice. 'If we continue, we will be put to the sword by the Yorkist cavalry, for it is too late to save our masters, although we are duty bound to try.' He paused as their eyes widened in fear. 'Or, we could retreat and save ourselves,' he said, quickly, trying to lessen the shame of even uttering them. 'The choice is a simple one: we must choose between life and death.'

Frightened heads could only stare back at him, their voices frozen with fear.

'Raise your hand, if it is to be retreat.'

Hands shot into the air.

'Then, mount!'

The senior squire's order jerked the boys into action, their young bodies moving quicker, relieved at their deliverance. They were no longer concerned with Yorkist or Lancastrian causes, lords or masters. They would have signed their souls to the devil to survive. Now, they had their lives back, they began to swiftly ride away.

The Earl of Warwick's squire stopped on the brow of the hill and looked back. He watched as Warwick and his men stood frozen, staring after him. He felt the shame for deserting them burn into his soul, and then made his escape.

Warwick and his retainers stared with disbelief as their only hope of escape disappeared into the distance. He was stunned that these lowly dogs would even dare to be disloyal to him, but he knew his eyes were not lying. In these final moments, even his young squire was betraying him. The realisation cut into him like a knife – they had been abandoned to their fate. The ground now shook with the sound of the advancing cavalry.

Warwick knew their time had run out. This was the day; this was the moment they would face their deaths. They turned to face the oncoming enemy; this small band of brothers, now abandoned, formed a defiant straight line. Warwick moved along it quickly, gripping each man's hand in a silent farewell. No words were spoken – no words were needed. They had spent a lifetime fighting together. He remembered the adventures, battles, intrigues, and plotting, and of course, the women...what a time they'd had. If he was going to die, he could not have chosen better company.

His men raised their swords in salute, and the anger in Warwick's eyes softened, replaced with pride. He checked his armour for one last time, and then threw his helmet aside. He wanted the sun on his face when he died. He walked forward, away from his men, sword drawn, to face the oncoming cavalry.

Warwick did not hear the horse that bore down on him from the rear, its sounds hidden by the thunder of the advancing cavalry. It caught him unawares; such was the swiftness of it. The rider's mace caught him hard on his right shoulder, and he spun forward, smashing into the ground. He knew his shoulder was broken, his sword arm now useless. He saw his comrades rushing to protect him, but they were overrun by the first wave of cavalry. He saw his attacker spin his horse around and slip from the saddle. Warwick looked up into a face cold with hatred – a face surrounded by wild hair. In the far reaches of his mind, the man's features registered.

'Who are you?' Warwick hissed, between teeth clenched in pain.

The man gripped Warwick's hair, yanked his head back and ran a razor-edged, hunting knife across his throat. 'My name is Sir Simon Langford, and this is for my mother and sisters,' he said with venom.

Warwick felt warm blood gushing down his throat. He opened his mouth to shout defiance at this bastard whose life he had sought for so many years, but no sound came out.

Simon pushed the hunting knife hard into Warwick's open mouth, ramming it with all his might through the back of his head, pinning it to the ground. 'And that is for my father!' he cried. Years of anger finally flowed from him as Warwick's blood flowed free.

Warwick felt the pain ebbing away. The world grew distant, the noise of the battle fainter. He knew his earthly time was over; how short it now seemed. Events from his life rushed through his mind in a kaleidoscope of memories, until a dam of ominous guilt burst within him. All the men he had executed, tortured, and butchered for his grand designs, flashed before him. He desperately tried to shut them out, but their faces, frozen in terror, kept looming up before him. There were too many to stop. His body felt leaden and cold as though already buried in the damp, dark earth. He heard his brother's voice weakly calling his name, as though trying to save him from some untold terror. Then, it became weaker and faded away. Fear gripped him like a vice. There was no escape; he was falling, tumbling over and over down a long black tunnel. Screams of torment rang out in the distance.

The once mighty Earl of Warwick started to pray frantically as the screams became louder, finally filling his whole soul with terror.

It was early evening. Two swallows swooped low overhead, a small vanguard heralding an early summer. The sun slipped below the horizon; its last rays gently pushed down by the advancing night. The day's bloody business lying on the blood-soaked fields would soon lay hidden under a shroud of darkness.

Duke Richard and John Tunstall were standing quietly, just inside the entrance of a tent. In its sombre interior, four large candles burned, their brightness flickering out from each corner. In the centre, lay the bodies of John Milewater, Thomas Parr, and Thomas Huddleston. They rested on a low trestle table. At the head of the table, a large wooden crucifix inlaid with gold and precious jewels softly shimmered in the dancing candlelight.

Five monks knelt around the bodies, each representing the five wounds of Christ. They were dressed in dark, heavy habits, the hoods pulled up over their heads hiding their features as they quietly intoned prayers for the souls of the dead men.

Richard and John took one last look at the scene inside the tent, and satisfied all was well, stepped outside into the cool evening air where the tranquil calm of the tent was broken by the sights and sounds that greeted them. Spread out before them was the camp of a great, victorious royal army. They heard shouts of laughter and joy rippling around, reflecting their great victory. Then a hushed silence of mourning descended for comrades lost. These sounds of great sadness and joy swept around the camp as darkness fell.

'John, and the two Toms were good men,' said John, softly. 'I remember their bravery when they helped rescue us from Bamburgh Castle.'

'Aye, they have served me loyally, all my life,' replied Richard. 'They were both father and brother to me, and today in the heat of battle, they laid down their lives to protect me. I will build a chapel to honour them. Prayers will be said every day for their souls to rest in paradise and walk with the angels.'

Both men stood in silence as their thoughts wandered over the events of the day.

'Damn Warwick!' cried John, sharply. 'If he had accepted the pardon offered by King Edward at Coventry it would never have come to this bloody battle.'

'Well, at least George saw sense. It was good to have him reconciled to us.'

'But for how long?' replied John, with bitterness. 'He's a snake in the grass, that brother of yours. Edward will need to keep him on a short leash. It seems the more he drinks, the worse he becomes.'

Richard studied his old friend. Under the thick tangle of black hair, crystal-blue eyes looked back at him. Above the full lips was a proud Norman nose – a sign of royal blood. John's was a face he had known since childhood. He had a good soul and Richard valued his loyalty and friendship above all else. 'I know you have no time for my brother, and I also take no joy from his company. His many betrayals over the past few years have hardened our heart against him, but I believe it is better to have him pissing out of our tent than pissing into it.'

'You are right,' said John. 'But mark my words; he will eventually gather enough rope to hang himself and I wager his drinking will be his downfall.'

As they stood in the gathering darkness, Richard quietly quoted from the writer, Chastellain:

'It is not surprising that it has come to this, for princes are men and their affairs are high and perilous, their natures subject to many passions, such as hatred, greed and envy, their hearts a veritable dwelling place of these evils, and it is all because of their pride in reigning'.

'They are true words,' agreed John. 'Warwick's body is a testament to them, and it is a lesson George would do well to heed, or one day, he will suffer the same fate.'

A cold wind whipped across the ground. Both men shivered at the sudden chill. The night was moonless, with no cloud. The stars sparkled with intense brightness as they crowded the black sky.

John looked up at them, and Richard followed his gaze.

'Some say that each star is a soul waiting to enter Heaven,' said Richard.

'Well, if that's true,' replied John, 'then plenty have been added today.'

'It was Simon Langford who killed Warwick,' said Richard.

'I know. I arrived at Warwick's body as Simon rode away.'

'You did not challenge him?'

John heard the surprise in Richards's voice. 'No, I did not. He killed the man we both wanted dead.'

'There were many men who would gladly have killed Warwick, if they'd had the chance. I only asked if you had challenged him because of what he did to Rose.'

'I would talk with her first before taking any action. Do not forget: Warwick killed the whole of Simon's family. The man was driven by hatred and vengeance, but meant no harm to her.'

'Then what of you?' enquired Richard. 'Will you still marry her? She has been violated and will not come to your bed a virgin.'

John looked up at the heavens. The question caused his heart to ache. The solid rock that their love had been built on was now gone replaced with the shifting sands of uncertainty. 'I will always love her,' he said, quietly, 'but will I marry her? Only when I find her, will I know the answer to that. But, what of the Lady Anne?' questioned John. 'If her marriage has been consummated, will you still marry her?'

'If she is not with child, then, yes, I would marry her, but you are jumping the gun, my old friend. Remember, her bastard husband still lives; she is still his wife.'

'Supposing she is widowed in the near future?' said John, still wanting to hear the answer to his question.

'Well, yes, I would marry her, if she is not with child, but I do not know if she would willingly marry me, now. It is a few years since we last set eyes on each other, and I now carry this curse upon my back,'

Richard said, sadly, as he flexed his shoulder blades. 'Now her father is dead, she will inherit half of his estates, and I badly need those estates to compete with George. So, willing, or unwilling, I will marry her. She may not bring her virginity to the marriage bed, but she would bring me the wealth and lands as befits my position.'

'So, you would not marry her if she had no wealth to bring to the marriage?'

Richard laughed at the naivety of the question. 'I do not love Anne as you love Rose. I have already fathered a boy and girl with Katherine Haute, the woman I love, and who loves me despite my affliction. Sadly, I can never marry her because of her lowly rank, so Anne would be my wife as custom dictates. It would be a marriage of convenience for both of us. She will do her duty and provide me with male heirs, and I will do mine by giving her the high status and security she requires.'

'But were you not upset on hearing of her marriage?'

'I was angry, because she was mine. She belonged to me, promised by her father. There are few women I can marry within the nobility that reflect my royal status, and even fewer that I like, but if I did not marry her, it would not break my heart.'

'So if she is with child, she will die on your orders, and if not, she will live, married to you, but blissfully unaware that you would have killed her?'

Richard let out a long sigh. 'John, I am not as other men. I am the brother of a king and as such am bound by matters of state. I must put king and the country above all else. You must understand that I am fond of Anne and wish her no harm, but she cannot give birth to the heir of the Lancastrian throne. Imagine the great grandson of Henry V, alive and well; the country would never be at peace. Therefore, to put an end to these bloody civil wars, and secure my brother's throne, she would have to be sacrificed. The world is a hard place, and we have to make hard decisions. It is the price we pay for our noble birth.'

'I am sorry, I did not mean to offend,' apologised John. 'Sometimes, I speak from the heart, and not the head.'

Richard smiled. 'There is no offence taken. It is good when you speak so true. It gives me thought for my conscience, but come, we must attend to our duties. I am meeting with Edward and the council. Margaret of Anjou has landed at Weymouth, and although we won a great victory today, there is still much to do.'

They clasped each other, both glad the other had survived the day.

'I will check on the men,' said John, 'and then I meet with Francis. We have an appointment with a few bottles of wine.'

'I look forward to joining you, later,' replied Richard, as they parted to attend to their duties.

Chapter 16

The End Game

Cerne Abbey, Dorset, England
15 April 1471

Margaret of Anjou wandered through the abbey gardens in solitary silence. For the first time in weeks, she enjoyed the sensation of solid earth beneath her feet, although, she wished it was the firm soil of France, and not the shifting sands of England that she walked on.

In Honfleur, on the orders of King Louis, Marshall Lohéac, and his Scots Guards, had forced Margaret on to a ship with her small court, to be dispatched across the channel with all haste. For many months before this, she had worked tirelessly to stall the crossing, for she knew England was still unsafe, with Edward and Warwick stalking each other, and she was desperate to await the outcome of their final battle, for if Warwick lost, then the enterprise of England would be finished.

Even then, fate had held them back, for as they set sail, a huge storm had blown up and driven them back to seek the safety of the harbour. There, for two long windswept weeks, they had ridden out the tempest. Many of the crew had said it was witches' work, such was the severity and length of it, but finally, it abated, and now, after an absence of eight years, Margaret was back in this accursed land.

Her mind filled with thoughts of Simon. It was because of him she was back in this land of madmen. She wondered where he was, and if she would ever see him again. A shiver of dread passed through her body as she wondered if he was still alive.

Oh, God, she thought. *Love is such a curse. Life would be so simple and straightforward without it, but how my heart would sing to see him.*

The sounds of footsteps caught her ears and she turned to see thirty or more soldiers striding from the abbey towards her. At their head was Edmund Beaufort, the 4th Duke of Somerset, and his younger brother, John, the Marquess of Dorset. Also with them, was John Courtenay, the Earl of Devon. Margaret's son hurried along with them.

She knew they had news of Warwick and King Edward. She stood perfectly still and appraised them as they approached. She thought it strange that men on their own were usually calm and rational, but the thirty men approaching her had a swaggering menace about them, with their swords and daggers swinging from their belts. She sensed an aggression simmering from their midst. Maybe, she reasoned, it was the powerful smell of sweat and leather, which caused this veneer of belligerence, or perhaps it was just something that men did when gathered in numbers; like wolves, or wild dogs, they became a pack.

If I did not know these men, I would be fearful, she thought. *But, I do know them; I am their Queen.*

The nobles bowed with a flourish; their men dropped to one knee.

'Do I march for London as Queen of England to celebrate Warwick's triumph or do I take ship to France with all haste?' Margaret asked; her voice firm and clear so all could hear her.

'Warwick is dead,' stated Edmund Beaufort, with undisguised delight.

A ripple of elation passed through Margaret's body. At last, the monster was slain; his wings finally turned to stone. The man who had forced the crown from her head was now dead. She looked at Edmund's smiling face. 'Your father and brother served me well, and have now been avenged.'

'Aye, they can rest in peace, but I cannot,' Edmund Beaufort replied. 'Not until we have returned the kingdom back to its rightful rulers.'

Margaret suppressed the laughter that tried to well up from her throat, although her eyes could not disguise her amusement. 'Me thinks France beckons with all haste,' she said. 'We will not defeat Edward, for the crown of England now sits firmly upon his handsome head. As you can see, I have with me only a small court, which comprises of Lord

Wenlock – who is over seventy; Doctor Morton – who is over fifty and not in the best of health, and Sir John Fortescue – who is a wonder at eighty years old. Also, my son of seventeen years and his wife, two ladies-in-waiting and their husbands, and you three: nobles with little experience of war, and currently, with only thirty men between you. So, forgive me for stating the obvious,' she said, suppressing a giggle, 'but I fear we are not equipped to defeat Edward's victorious army of thousands of well trained and battle-hardened troops.'

'Madam, we must head with all speed down through the West Country,' said Edmund Beaufort, earnestly. 'The ancient Lancastrian names of Beaufort and Courteney – noble names that stretch back through the generations – will rally men to our standard. We will head for Exeter, Bath, and Bristol, gathering troops as we go. Jasper Tudor has sent word from Wales that he will join us with a large army. Edward will be no match for us.'

'If you and that will-of-the-wisp, Jasper Tudor, had joined with Warwick at Barnet, then Edward would be no more,' Margaret shouted at them. 'You were fools to let such an opportunity slip through your fingers. Remember the saying "Divide and conquer"? Well, you have done that to yourselves. How Edward must be laughing at your stupidity. If you had supported Warwick, then I would now be heading to London to crown my son King of England, but by leaving him to stand alone you have destroyed any chance we had of winning the crown back.'

'Mother!' cried Prince Edward, his eyes shining with excitement. 'If you return to France, it will be alone, for I head to Exeter to raise an army and reclaim my rightful throne.'

All eyes turned to Margaret as she stood silently studying her son. She saw the fire that burned in his eyes. She had seen the same in Simon's eyes when he had left her to attack Warwick, all those years ago. Now, her son had the madness, consumed with dreams of being a king. She knew nothing would calm his passion but she could not leave him to his fate. She would go with him and try, over the coming days, to change his mind. Fate was once again forcing her down a road she did not wish

413

to travel.

With icy bitterness, Margaret said, 'You had better go and inform your wife that her father is dead. Without him, her use to us is over. This child of Warwick is unwanted baggage. Thankfully, the marriage was never consummated, so it will be easy to obtain an annulment. There are plenty of princesses in Europe who will sit better as Queen of England, and I certainly do not wish to have grandchildren who carry the blood of Warwick in their veins.'

Prince Edward looked fleetingly at his feet, and then sheepishly at his mother, his face slowly turning bright red.

Margaret knew in an instant the reason why and her eyes widened in angry disbelief.

Ellerton Priory, Yorkshire Dales
24 April 1471

Rose watched the grey mist on the surface of the river silently fanning out. It covered the surrounding Dales beneath with a great, white, misty lake, filling the ditches and hollows, hugging the cold earth with its wet touch, as though trying to smother the beauty of God's creation. In the watery half-light of the dawn, it gave the illusion of standing on a cloud, just as she imagined the saints and angels must stand as they watched out over the world.

'Come on,' huffed Sister Mary as she waddled along.

Rose thought Sister Mary's little legs moved surprisingly quickly for someone of such ample proportions.

'Not only must we see to the sheep,' Sister Mary urged, 'but because Sister Agnes is sick, we also have the goats to attend to, and we still have to be back for vespers or we will miss breakfast.'

Rose smiled at the slight panic in Sister Mary's breathless voice, for she had learnt that the good sister never ever missed a meal, snack, or drink.

Rose had joined this Cistercian Order on her return from seeing Simon at Egglestone Abbey. It was a small convent comprising of some fifty nuns, not too far from Middleham Castle, and her family. She had been accepted as a novice nun, at last finding peace under the loving cloak of God.

Sister Mary had told Rose that the order had been formed during the reign of Henry II. The poor king had ordered the murder of his own archbishop, Thomas Becket, and had then spent the rest of his life praying for forgiveness, whilst being punished by God, who turned his four sons against him, one by one. Even to this day, a prayer was said daily for his soul.

Rose made her way to the pens. The lambing season had started and all the ewes in their small flock had produced healthy lambs. They had been put in the pens overnight to keep them safe from predators. She swung the gates open to let the sheep out into the pastures, and watched the newborn lambs run unsteadily beside their mothers; the sight left Rose feeling empty inside, for she had now chosen a childless life. Thoughts of John and what should have been flooded into her. Once again, tears welled in her eyes.

'Rose!' shouted Sister Mary, as she strode towards her. 'Drive 'em up to the higher pasture. There's good grazing there and they will produce better milk for their young ones.'

Rose nodded, fighting back the tears.

'What's wrong?' asked Sister Mary, as she came closer.

''Tis nothing,' Rose whispered.

'You were thinking of him, weren't you?'

Rose nodded.

'Oh, Rose,' said Sister Mary, as she placed her arm gently around Rose's shoulder. 'You cannot carry this guilt and pain forever. The men who raped you have been punished; it was not you who committed this crime. You are innocent in the eyes of God, innocent in the eyes of the world, and innocent in the eyes of the man who loves you.'

Rose nodded, and took a deep breath. 'You are right,' she said, as a fragile smile creased her face. 'I do not mean to be so weak.'

'It is not weakness, but mark my words, Sir John will come looking for you, and he will love you just the same as he always did.'

'He will never see me again!' Rose cried. 'I would rather die than feel his pity.'

'Time will tell...' said Sister Mary, quietly. 'Time will tell...'

As they arrived at the convent, Rose could see a horse silhouetted in the stillness of the morning mist. She could see the steam rising from its flanks; it had been ridden hard. Her heart fluttered in alarm, her pace slowed.

Sister Mary, sensing Rose's apprehension, slowed with her. ''Tis nothing to concern us,' she said.

'Could be my John,' Rose whispered, her eyes searching around, frantically.

The sound of footsteps came from within the entrance hall. They grew louder. The great doors swung open and Rose turned to flee, but Sister Mary held her firm.

The shape of a man stood in the gloom of the doorway.

Rose looked with consternation towards the looming figure as she struggled to break free of Sister Mary's vice-like grip.

'Rose, you have nothing to fear,' said the figure, as he came towards her.

Sodbury Hill, Gloucestershire
2 May 1471

He walked slowly through a peaceful wood. Shafts of sunlight fractured the calm shade. Birds, feeding their young, swooped low, protecting their nests. Rose walked beside him, her delicate hand gently holding his. She was smiling, her beautiful eyes sparkling, her eyelashes fluttering as she talked excitedly about their future. As they passed a fallen tree trunk, she pushed him against it. Frantically trying to keep his balance, he clawed at thin air, and then he fell to the ground, his legs hanging over the trunk. Rose raced away, running through the forest, her laughter following in her wake. With feigned anger, he chased after her. Finally, exhausted, she stopped; her back against a tree. He placed his hands either side of her shoulders. His heart pounded. She reached up, and pulled him to her. They kissed…

'Sir John…' the words were distant. 'Sir John…' the voice was louder, urgent.

John Tunstall turned away, but hands shook him. He concentrated his mind to stay asleep, to stay with Rose, but she was lost to him. His dream evaporated and he woke to see his squire's face close to his.

'In the name of God!' John shouted. 'No sooner do I find sleep than you take it away from me.'

'You are urgently required in the King's tent,' replied the squire, with an aggrieved air. 'Duke Richard has sent word that he will meet you there.'

John placed his hand on the squire's shoulder. 'I did not mean to sound harsh, but sleep around here is as rare as a unicorn's turd.' He stifled a yawn.

As he entered the royal tent, John noted that it would be a couple of hours until the cock crowed. Candles shone brightly, bathing the interior in a golden hue. The warmth within made the tiredness he felt even harder to control. Stifling another yawn, he watched as King Edward paced around the table in frustration, the heads of his captains swivelling from left to right.

'I have been deceived,' Edward growled. 'Our Duke of Somerset has melted away into the night.'

'I would wager he is racing for Gloucester,' said Lord Hastings. 'There is a bridge there that crosses the Severn.'

Edward stopped his prowling, a look of comprehension filling his eyes. He stared at Lord Hastings. 'So, you think he plans to join with Jasper Tudor.' His eyes widened in sudden understanding. 'My God,' he whispered. 'If he succeeds…'

'Then, when we close for battle they will outnumber us two to one,' finished Lord Hastings.

'Then, he must not succeed,' stated Richard, calmly.

All eyes turned towards him as he rose from his chair and looked around the table. When he spoke, his voice carried authority.

'The Mayor of Gloucester – Sir Richard Beauchamp – is Yorkist to the core, so will be loyal to our cause. A royal warrant should be sent, telling him that on no account must Margaret of Anjou, and her army enter the town and cross the river. The gates are to be firmly closed.'

'The messenger must leave immediately,' urged Edward, his frustration gone and replaced with excitement. 'Our army must be roused and marching within the hour if we are to catch them.'

Richard beckoned to John.

John mounted his horse and placed the royal warrant safe within his tunic. The Hallet twins, also mounted, moved up alongside John.

'It is a dangerous mission,' said Richard. 'You must avoid their army at all costs, so take the high road through Nailsworth and on to Stroud. Our scourers tell us they have taken the low road to Berkeley Castle, so with luck, you will have no contact with them. When you arrive at Gloucester, hand the warrant to the mayor and then help him organise their defences. We will follow on, a day behind you.' He reached up and clasped John's hand. 'It is vital,' he commanded, 'that you secure those gates.'

John smiled and nodded towards the twins. 'We both know these two could hold the gates of Gloucester alone.' Digging his heels into his mount, he cried, 'See you in two days' time, my Lord!'

Richard watched them race like the wind, away from the royal camp.

City of Gloucester
3 May 1471

Margaret of Anjou stood on the top of Coney Hill looking down upon the entrance to the city of Gloucester, its massive oak gates shut and barred. Her spirits sank. She looked around her at the faces staring silently towards the city. Her heart went out to her son, still just a boy, with no experience of campaigning, just a figurehead in this risky enterprise. Standing next to him was Anne, who now had the hollow title of Princess of Wales.

Edmund Beaufort, his brother, John; Hugh and John Courtenay, all stood as though turned to stone, their faces grim. This terrible setback had knocked the wind from their sails.

Lord Wenlock and Sir John Langstother joined them.

Lord Wenlock bowed. 'My Lady, the city is well organised in its defence. It would take a month of Sundays to breach them.'

Margaret threw an icy look at Edmund Beaufort, and then at John Courtenay. 'Well, gentlemen, you have brought us to this situation, so what are your plans now?'

Edmund Beaufort stepped forward. 'We will march for Tewkesbury with all haste. A small ford there crosses the river. I will send word to Jasper to meet us there with his army.'

Margaret knew he spoke the words with false confidence, for they all knew Jasper Tudor had disappeared at the very moment they needed him – the man was a coward, and would betray them.

Lord Wenlock butted in, putting all their thoughts into words. 'We must think of France, my Lady. We have had no word from Jasper Tudor. He betrayed Warwick and I believe he will do the same to us. Edward and his brothers are but a few hours behind us and our men are exhausted. We must flee, if the House of Lancaster is to survive.'

Edmund Beaufort knew that Lord Wenlock spoke the truth – they all did – but his pride, like his brother and father before him, overcame the hopelessness of the situation.

'There will be no fleeing,' Edmund Beaufort shouted, his bravado returning. 'I, and the others, have spent long years in exile, and we have had our bellies full of it. We will head for Tewkesbury, where with Jasper Tudor, or no Jasper Tudor, we will stand and fight.'

Margaret looked at her son. She saw in his eyes that he had lost hope in this enterprise. She knew he was no fool – without Jasper Tudor, they were doomed. *Still*, she thought, *he is only young. He would never admit to the truth, for he would lose face with his captains.* He was caught like a fish in a net. There would be no fleeing with her to France, but if she went with them to Tewkesbury, she would have another day to make him change his mind, or find a plan to save him. It was worth the gamble.

'Come,' urged Lord Wenlock, 'we can be in Bristol in two days, and from there take ship to France, and safety.'

Margaret saw the hate that filled Edmund Beaufort's and his companion's eyes. As they glared at Lord Wenlock, their hands slipped down to their swords.

Margaret stepped between them. 'We march to Tewkesbury with all haste. Once there, the decision to fight, or not, will be made.'

John Tunstall and the Hallet twins looked out from the battlements of Gloucester's great gatehouse as the Lancastrian army moved off.

'Well, that's them well stuffed,' said George, with a knowing laugh.

'They thinks they be marching for Tewkesbury,' said Thomas, 'but it will be more like Hell when King Edward and Duke Richard catch 'em.'

John knew they were right. He turned away and cast his eyes over the soft, rolling hills of the Vale of Berkeley, looking into the distance for a faint dust cloud that would herald the arrival of Edward and his army.

As he gazed at the peaceful countryside, his thoughts turned to Rose, again. A deep longing caught him by surprise. Where was she? Was she safe? The pain in his chest thumped like a hammer. *One more battle,* he vowed, *and then I will seek her out.*

Ellerton Priory, Yorkshire Dales
3 May 1471

As Rose watched the young, spring lambs discover their new world, her thoughts returned to that day two weeks ago when the horseman had arrived. She recalled how she had tried to flee, thinking it was her John coming to find her. She remembered the shame that had filled her, and Sister Mary's strong hands holding her firm...

The man had stood before her, his long, tousled hair framing his face like a wild storm. She remembered his words: 'Rose, you have nothing to fear'.

Simon Langford had held his arms out, a smile softening his features. She had run to him. He had held her tightly and whispered the words that had set her free: 'Warwick is dead'.

That morning, he had told of the great battle that had taken place at Barnet, and how he had found Warwick standing alone with his captains.

'I have avenged the deaths of my mother and sisters, and all the others who died at the hands of that monster', Simon had said.

Rose remembered the look of sadness that had swept across his face as he confessed his heart was still heavy with guilt. Killing Warwick had not set him free of his demons. He told her he was going to travel to the uplands to pray alone and find salvation in God's words.

She had watched him ride slowly away. Staring after him, she had prayed he would find redemption. For herself, calmness had settled upon her. John had survived the battle, for Simon had seen him just after slaying Warwick. Now that the monster was finally no more she had felt a feeling of elation, as though a curtain had been drawn back, letting the sunlight back into the darkness that had surrounded her for so long.

As she stood watching the young lambs, Rose dared to think of a future with John – the spirits had told her they would meet again. The thought filled her equally with hope, and dread.

Sister Mary called her. As Rose turned to go, her steps felt lighter, and a smile played upon her face. She did not know what the future held, but her heart was beating with hope, for finally, at last, she felt alive.

Tewkesbury Abbey, Tewkesbury
3 May 1471

The day had been long and hot. Margaret of Anjou, with her daughter in-law, the Princess Anne, had ridden on horseback the thirty-six miles from Gloucester to Tewkesbury Abbey at the front of her son's army.

The men had suffered agonies of thirst, and all the time high up on the Cotswolds, like a circling eagle, King Edward and his army had shadowed them relentlessly, matching them stride for stride.

Entering the abbey brought them cool relief from the hot, May sun. Margaret's ladies-in-waiting, Lady Vaux and Lady Whittingham, along with old Sir John Fortescue sat quiet and still in the shadow of the cloisters, too tired and weary to help organise their quarters.

Margaret watched, amazed, as Anne took charge of the situation.

'Your Highness,' Anne said, as she approached with the abbot. 'May I introduce, Brother John Streynsham, the abbot.'

The abbot bowed low.

Margaret was pleased with the respect he showed, and waved him upright. 'We are grateful for your hospitality,' she said. The man was growing old, perhaps in his late fifties. His face was lined and worn. She considered that the huge responsibilities of the abbey were taking their toll on him, but his eyes were sharp and bright – laughter lines formed around them. She could see he had enjoyed a good life in the service of God. 'You two seem to know each other,' she said looking at the abbot, and then to Anne.

'Aye, my Lady,' said Brother John. 'Anne's aunt, Cecily Neville, the Duchess of Warwick, is buried in the large chapel she built here in 1438, and the Countess of Warwick – Lady Anne's mother – is also a loyal supporter of the abbey.'

Margaret noted that his voice was soft, but firm. The abbot was a man who was used to giving orders and having them obeyed. She turned her attention to Anne.

'I have stayed here many times,' Anne volunteered, before Margaret could speak. 'My family has always had close ties with the abbey.'

Margaret felt the glimmer of an idea forming. 'Anne, as you know the abbey so well, please take our ladies-in-waiting and arrange our accommodation. I would speak with the abbot in private.'

When they were alone, Margaret and the abbot sat down. She studied him with an expression of benevolence, for here was the man who could save her son. 'My dear abbot,' she began, 'tomorrow, our army will join in battle against King Edward.'

Brother John nodded.

'You may not be aware,' Margaret continued, 'but we will struggle to win this battle.'

Brother John was taken aback by this frankness. 'Surely, it will be God who decides the outcome,' he said, gently.

'If only that were true,' Margaret sighed. 'Edward commands a battle-hardened army. We, on the other hand, have inexperienced soldiers led by the Duke of Somerset, who like his brother and father before him, is hot-headed when he should be calm, and tactically lacking when he should be inspired. If we had Jasper Tudor here we would be equal to Edward, but the dog is not here, so tomorrow, the House of Lancaster will, I believe, be defeated.'

'So, why do you stand and fight if the outcome is already decided?' asked Brother John. 'Could you not disperse your army and take ship for France?'

'My son, Edward, has always believed he would win his kingdom back with his courage and his sword, and tomorrow is his day of reckoning. Even though he has doubts now, that Jasper Tudor has betrayed us, there is still some silly romantic notion within him that says he cannot desert his men.'

'So what's to be done?' asked Brother John. 'You are obviously telling me this for a reason.'

'Tomorrow, when the battle turns, I have arranged with certain captains – Lord Wenlock being one – that they are to safely escort my son from the battlefield. They are experienced enough to know when that time will be. Then, they will bring him here, where I now ask you to give him sanctuary, to hide him from King Edward's men until it is safe for him to take ship to France.'

Brother John sat in silence as he digested this request. He knew, if he agreed, it would put his life and his brother monks' lives in danger. 'It is a dangerous thing you ask,' he whispered. 'You ask many to risk great danger to save one.'

Margaret moved closer to him, her voice conspiratorial. 'Only a few would know,' she whispered. She saw the abbot was unsure of what to do, but he had not dismissed her out of hand, so she played her last card; she knew he was fond of Anne. 'If my son dies, then so will his wife, the Princess Anne.'

'Anne is but a girl!' Brother John cried. 'She has no say in any of this conflict.'

'She is pregnant with my son's child,' Margaret whispered.

Brother John stared into Margaret's eyes. His mouth opened slightly as he realised what this would mean.

'Yes,' said Margaret, as she saw the abbot working out the implications. 'If my son dies, then they could not let her live with the new heir to the Lancastrian throne growing in her belly. They would hunt her down and kill her.'

Anne listened to the arguments that filled the room. Raised voices fired angry words around her. She watched the Edmund Beaufort, the Duke of Somerset, thump the arm of his chair in frustration; Margaret, sitting straight-backed, her arm outstretched, accusing him of leading his men to their deaths. The Earl of Devon jumped from his chair, shouting his support for the duke. Lord Wenlock wrung his hands nervously as he offered his loyalty to Margaret.

Anne looked at her husband, who sat silently gazing into the fire, lit to keep the damp air that flowed off the River Avon at bay. He had not shown his support for the duke and his captains, who were going to stand their ground and fight. Neither had he joined his mother's cause, whose supporters argued that they disperse their army tonight, under the cover of darkness, and then take ship for France.

Anne felt anger that he had been forced into this situation. She had grown fond of Edward, and now loved him. They had been forced to marry to satisfy her father's and King Louis' pursuit of power, and although she had tried not to like Edward, she had found him handsome and charming. They shared a bed as husband and wife, but he had not forced himself upon her. It was only after she had learnt that Duke Richard had sired two children with a lowborn wench that her interest in Edward had blossomed, and although he did not know it, he had helped mend her broken heart.

She remembered the first time they had made love. He had been tender and thoughtful. With each eager thrust of his young body, her love for Richard had faded away. After that first night, they had become insatiable young lovers, craving each other's body. Sometimes, she felt ashamed of her lustfulness, but she could not stop herself. She craved the excitement of their naked intimacy.

Anne stood up and went to join Edward by the fire. He looked into her eyes as her hand sought his. There was gentleness in his look and she wished they were back in France, safe from all this madness.

Edward sat for a while and then gently squeezed Anne's hand as though it was some sort of secret sign. He stood up and stepped into the centre of the room. The swiftness and intent of his movement stopped the heated arguments between the opposing parties. All eyes stared at him.

'There has been enough talking,' Edward said, his voice firm. 'We have an army of brave men camped outside with captains, dukes, and a prince to lead them, so tomorrow, we stand and fight, and may God grant us victory.'

There was a murmur of approval.

'Somerset, we leave at three of the clock to prepare our army. Until then, I wish you good night and advise you all to get some rest, for it will be a hard day tomorrow.'

Margaret sat silently, watching her son as he left the chamber, with Anne following closely behind him.

Edmund Beaufort, and his captains, rose from their chairs, and gallantly bid her good night. He left, trying to hide the look of triumph on his face.

As they were leaving, Margaret beckoned Lord Wenlock to stay. Once alone, she quietly whispered instructions to him.

Edmund Beaufort, standing silently outside the room, watched with mounting anger at their secret conspiring.

Chapter 17

Battle of Tewkesbury

Tewkesbury, Gloucestershire
4 May 1471

The great guns of King Edwards's army: *Dijon, Messenger, Fowler of the Tower, Newcastle,* and *London,* thundered out across the dawn sky.

John Tunstall felt the ground tremble. He looked out across the battlefield towards the enemy. They had, against their backs, the River Tirle. To their right, he could just see the town of Tewkesbury emerging through the dawn light, its great abbey beginning to dominate the skyline.

He felt sorry for the men who opposed them. This ragtag Lancastrian army only stood to fight because they were too tired to run any more. They knew that King Edward had never lost a campaign, so the physical battle was already won. He heard the whoosh of arrows join the heavy thump of the artillery.

He looked down the lines of the King's well-disciplined army. Lord Hastings was commanding the right flank, Edward – the centre, and Richard – the left.

The trumpets to advance rang out. The butterflies in John's stomach disappeared. He stepped forward with Richard and their men, advancing towards the enemy.

Lord Wenlock sat upon his battle horse surveying the advancing Yorkist army. He crossed himself and thanked the Lord that he had survived their frightening rain of cannon ball and arrow. He watched with disbelief as the hot-headed Edmund Beaufort, stung into action by the Yorkist bombardment, abandoned his solid defensive position and started moving his troops towards the enemy. *The man is a fool,* Lord Wenlock thought. *With him in charge, we will be easy pickings.*

Edward, Prince of Wales, sat beside Lord Wenlock, watching King Edward's army struggle through the thick hedges and waterlogged ditches, towards them.

A messenger arrived from Edmund Beaufort. 'You are to advance with all speed and attack them before they make solid ground,' he cried.

Lord Wenlock drew his sword. 'I will order the advance,' he replied, calmly, as though discussing the weather.

Prince Edward made to draw his sword, but Lord Wenlock pushed it across him.

'There will be no advancing yet,' Lord Wenlock whispered. 'Only if Somerset breaks the flank of Edward's army, will we advance.'

They watched as Edmund Beaufort and his men started their outflanking manoeuvre. It was then that Lord Wenlock and Prince Edward saw the two hundred Yorkist scourers hidden in a small copse not far from the duke's left flank. It was a trap set by Richard of Gloucester, and there was nothing they could do to stop it. They watched in horror as the Yorkist cavalry charged at the duke, catching him completely by surprise, and then, Richards' troops turned to attack him on his right flank. Caught on both sides, the Lancastrians went down like corn before the scythe.

Men began to flee, and Edmund Beaufort, realising all was lost, broke free, and raced towards Lord Wenlock.

Lord Wenlock waited for him to arrive, his helmet still held by his squire, his reins still slack in his hands. 'Get ready to signal the retreat, for Somerset has lost us the battle, as I knew he would,' he said, with a wry smile. 'It is time to implement your mother's plan and seek the safety of France.'

As the duke thundered up, Lord Wenlock winked at Prince Edward, and then turned to greet the duke.

Edmund Beaufort stood up in his stirrups, and brought his battleaxe down with all his might on to Lord Wenlock's head, cutting his brain in half. Lord Wenlock's eyes rolled up into his head; the wry smile frozen, as he tumbled from his horse.

'That traitorous bastard has betrayed me!' roared Edmund Beaufort.

Seeing the duke slay their leader, Lord Wenlock's men dropped their weapons, and fled the field.

John Tunstall looked at the fleeing army as they raced towards the river. He knew there would be no escape for them.

Evesham Abbey, Worcester
7 May 1471

Margaret of Anjou knelt before the high altar. To her left, knelt Anne; to her right, Lady Vaux and Lady Whittingham.

Her three companions were praying for the safe return of their husbands, who they had last seen three days ago, preparing for the coming battle.

Margaret prayed for her son, and that Lord Wenlock had escorted him from the battle to the safety of the abbey. She knew that all of her group were exhausted, not knowing if their men were alive or dead.

The abbot placed his hand gently on each of their heads in turn and said a prayer for the safe return of their loved ones, whilst monks on either side of the great altar sang gently in support of them.

Margaret knew this ceremony was pointless because the battle had taken place before they had arrived at Evesham. Their men were either dead, or alive, but it was all they knew to do, and it stopped them going mad with the uncertainty of it all. She rose from the great altar, and followed by her small court, walked slowly through the Chancery and out into the morning sun. She screwed her eyes up against its brightness, and as they slowly adjusted, she heard footsteps approaching. They were solid and regular, not the soft sound of monks walking.

She turned with apprehension to see who approached. Her stomach turned over, for there, stood Sir William Stanley, one of her most hated enemies. She supposed that he had been sent on King Edward's orders to tell them the battle was lost.

Sir William stood gloating in front of her, a triumphant smile fixed upon his weasel face.

Margaret's three companions gathered round her, clinging desperately to each other.

'I have three widows and a childless mother before me!' he cried, with mocking laughter. 'Your son, and your husbands, ran before they had even fought. They have paid the price for their cowardice and—'

Margaret, her eyes flashing as hard as diamonds, launched herself at Sir William. Like a tiger, she was upon him, her nails ripping down his face.

He fell back on to the stone pathway, the shock of her frenzied attack freezing his actions.

A young Yorkist knight, who had seen more than enough death and mutilation over the past days, stepped forward and dragged her off. A man-at-arms held the point of his sword at her throat.

Sir William slowly stood up, blood streaming from his wounds.

'You thought you could drain the spirit out of me,' Margaret hissed with venom, her eyes blazing with hate.

Sir William stepped back from her.

'You delight in the death of my son, and our husbands, you serpent of the Devil. You are the lowly dog of the underworld; you will never bring me to my knees.' Then, throwing her hand out, her long finger pointing directly at him, she cried, 'I curse you, your sons, and all your generations to come. May you all die of hideous causes, and may the world bring sorrow to all your doors.'

Sir William pulled his sword from its scabbard and pointed it at Margaret. 'Stop your foul cursing,' he shouted, 'or I will silence your tongue for ever!'

Margaret lunged forward at him, but the young knight held her firmly. 'You put no fear in me, you murderous dog!' she shouted back.

Sir William drew back his sword and thrust it forward. Lady Whittingham threw herself in front of Margaret, and the sword blade buried deep in her chest. With a scream, she fell dying.

The young knight released Margaret and drew his sword against Sir William. 'Have you not seen enough killing?' he shouted. 'God will show you no mercy for this foul deed.'

Sir William, his sword dripping with blood, his face white, hurried from the scene as monks came running from the abbey

'You will burn in Hell for this wicked act!' screamed Margaret at his departing back.

Lady Whittingham, with a dark red stain spreading across her chest, lay with her head resting in Anne's lap.

Margaret knelt beside them, and gently took Lady Whittingham's hand.

The abbot joined her. 'I have sent for the senior healer,' he said, softly.

Margaret looked at him, knowing from the look in his eyes that it was hopeless.

Lady Whittingham moved her head slowly to look at her mistress. She smiled, weakly. 'I will join my husband in death,' she whispered. 'I would be with him in Heaven than live without him on earth.' A shudder racked her body and then her heart was still.

Margaret looked down and saw her gentle smile, frozen forever. Her lifeless eyes stared up at her. The abbot leaned forward, and gently closed them.

They sat in the abbot's house, their faces wet with tears. Their men folk were dead, and the horror of Lady Whittingham's murder filled their minds. An elderly monk handed them each a goblet of strong wine and gently tried to soothe their sorrow.

The young knight entered the room and seeing their wretched state made to leave.

'I would have you stay,' said Margaret. 'I wish to know the events of the battle.'

He turned and walked slowly towards her. Anne and Lady Vaux gathered round, clutching each other's hands for comfort.

'There was no battle,' he said. 'Somerset saw to that.'

'I knew he would be our undoing,' said Margaret, bitterly.

'On the morning of the battle, your army was defending a strong defensive position. We knew the battle would be hard. There were ditches and hedges in front of us that would slow our advance, and then we would have had to battle uphill to reach your positions. To our complete disbelief, Somerset abandoned his defensive line, and led his men to attack the Duke of Gloucester's right flank, but Gloucester had secretly hidden a force of cavalry in a small copse further to his right, and they attacked. Caught between them and Gloucester's troops, Somerset's men were slaughtered, but he somehow escaped and galloped towards Lord Wenlock and the Prince Edward. He killed Lord Wenlock with a single blow to his head. It was the signal for the entire Lancastrian army to take flight.'

'Do you know the fate of my son?' asked Margaret, softly.

'Yes, my Lady, not all of your army fled the field. Your son, along with Sir William Vaux, Sir Robert Whittingham, and a small band of brave and loyal men, stood their ground and fought bravely for your cause, but it was hopeless and they were overwhelmed.'

'Did you show no mercy when our brave men were surrounded?'

'King Edward had commanded there were to be no prisoners taken.'

Margaret stared at the knight for a long time. Finally, she asked, 'How did my son die?'

'He died bravely. He was the last Lancastrian standing. It was a noble and brave end. Richard, Duke of Gloucester delivered the fatal blow. You should all take pride that your men died bravely. King Edward treated their bodies with respect. They lie in Tewkesbury Abbey awaiting a Christian burial.'

'And what of Somerset, and his companions? What was the fate of those cowards who abandoned our men to die?' asked Lady Vaux, with disgust.

'They fled to Tewkesbury Abbey where they sought sanctuary, but Richard of Gloucester dragged them all out. He tried them for treason and sentenced them all to death. They were beheaded in the market place at Tewkesbury the next day.'

The three women sat still and silent, staring at the young knight as though in a daze.

Margaret broke the silence. 'So, Richard, the Duke of Gloucester, was determined to remove all who had a claim on my husband's throne?'

'Yes. He said there would be no peace until all the royal blood of the Lancastrian line had been spilled on to the earth.'

Margaret of Anjou, Anne, and Lady Vaux, sat on thick hay in the back of a simple cart, as though they were peasant girls away to the harvest. There were two cavalrymen bringing up the rear, and two ahead.

The three of them sat in shocked silence at the deaths of their men folk, and the murder of Lady Whittingham. Her body, still warm, lay wrapped amongst the hay. They travelled back to Tewkesbury, taking her to be buried alongside her husband. The warm May wind had dried their tears, leaving fragile lines of grief upon their faces.

Margaret moved closer to Anne. 'We must talk of the future,' Margaret whispered, gently taking Anne's hand. 'I have lost a son, and you are now a widow.'

Anne nodded and placed a hand on to her slightly swollen stomach. 'But, I carry my husband's child,' she said.

'Yes, you carry his child, and my grandchild, but if King Edward and his brothers discover this, then you will not live. He could not take the chance of it being a boy and so the true heir to the throne.'

Anne nodded again, and then her eyes flashed with defiance. 'They have killed my father and my husband,' she whispered, 'but they will never take the life of my unborn child. I swear this on the Holy Cross of our Lord.'

'So, we must have a plan,' said Margaret, with quiet determination, 'a plan that will hide the pregnancy. I believe that once we are back at Tewkesbury, King Edward will take me into his custody. He will either kill me, or imprison me, but whatever the outcome, I will not be able to help you.'

Anne's hand flew to her mouth. 'Please, do not leave me to face this alone.'

'We will have no choice in the matter, but what is important is that you find sanctuary, somewhere for you to carry your full term in safety. If we are to outwit Edward and his brothers then you must follow my instructions.'

Anne looked into Margaret's eyes. 'If it saves my child, I will do whatever you say.'

'Good,' replied Margaret. 'We know that when we arrive at Tewkesbury, I will be detained, but once you are in his presence, you will ask permission to bury your husband with honour, within the abbey, and to remain there to mourn for him and your father as custom dictates. Also, request to bury Lady Whittingham alongside her husband. They cannot refuse such an honourable request. Lady Vaux will then seek out a safe sanctuary for your term with the help of the abbot, whom I know to be loyal to you and your family.'

'But what of Duke Richard?' said Anne, in frustration. 'He will not know I am pregnant so will still want to marry me, not for love, I know, but for the inheritance from my father. He will want my lands and wealth for himself.'

Margaret considered this. 'You must send him away by telling him that you will not marry the man who helped kill your father and who killed your husband. Tell him that you will need time. Tell him you will let him know when your heart has eased. Do not refuse outright; if you give him hope he will leave you alone. Once the child is born, you can then follow your conscience, for you are a widow of great wealth and do not have to answer to any man. If you are delivered of a boy, promise me you will send him to France for safety. My father will help you. Lady Vaux knows my father's court well, but the boy must never be in England. Promise me this.'

'I will do, or say, whatever is needed to protect my baby,' said Anne, defiantly. 'But, I will never marry, or forgive Duke Richard for what he has done to me and my family.'

The smell told them they were nearing Tewkesbury. The sweet, sour, aroma of death wafted towards them. They held their lace handkerchiefs to their mouths, and then they saw the first quartered bodies stuck up on poles on either side of the road leading into the town.

Anne and Lady Vaux huddled down into the side of the cart, their bodies retching in horror. Margaret stood and looked out across the battlefield. She had led her own army many times and had seen the aftermath of warfare. She saw the mass graves being dug, the bloodied and broken bodies being thrown into them, and she knew as they were buried, so too finally, was the Lancastrian cause.

Then, she saw the heads, seventeen in all, stuck on sharpened poles at the end of the line of quartered bodies, like a grand finale of horror. She saw the Duke of Somerset's, and then the Earl of Devon's, his eyes wide in terror, his tongue sticking out, frozen in his death scream like some hideous gargoyle. Next, she saw the severed head of young James Gower, her son's sword bearer. A gasp of surprise left her lips; that they would behead someone so young.

God! Their revenge runs deep, she thought. And then she felt the panic rising within her. *Was her son here, too?* 'Please spare me that sight,' she whispered.

When they had passed, Margaret breathed a sigh of relief; the young knight had told her the truth.

The Black Bear Inn, Tewkesbury
10 May 1471

John Tunstall studied Margaret of Anjou, this queen of poor mad Henry. Some said that the news of her son's death had broken her spirit, that the great warrior queen had finally been humbled. Looking at her, he knew this was not true, for she stood tall and proud before her captors. He marvelled at her beauty, and could now understand why Simon Langford had given his all for her love.

King Edward sat upright and alert in a huge high-backed chair. He was dressed in chain mail and leather, his metal gauntlets tossed casually on to a table beside him. He looked every inch the warrior king. He studied Margaret; beside her stood Anne, and Lady Vaux.

The royal court had heard about the terrible death of Lady Whittingham. Sir William Stanley had said that it was an unfortunate accident when defending himself from that Bitch of Anjou's attack. However, Edward had shown his displeasure that one of his knights should kill an innocent woman. He had Sir William exiled from court and sent back to his estates in the north, in disgrace, to await further punishment.

Duke Richard stood to the left of Edward; George, Duke of Clarence, stood on the right. Lord Hastings stood to one side with Earl Rivers.

The room was bare and airless. Sunlight shone through narrow windows high up on the walls. In these thin shafts of golden light, John saw dust motes suspended in mid-air. He felt the sweat run down his back. He looked at Anne and thought about how they had both grown up together at Middleham. He remembered how they had played as children. Just over a year ago, she had been safe and secure at her father's court, but now the world had changed. Forced to flee to France, she was then ordered to marry the son of her father's greatest enemy. Now, her father was dead, her husband was dead, and her mother in sanctuary within Beaulieu Abbey. He could see she was no longer that little girl he once knew. She had grown into a woman; her body had filled out into womanly curves. Her fair skin and blue eyes gave her a beauty that turned men's heads, and she stood like her mother-in-law, straight and proud, with her father's royal blood flowing through her veins.

Edward stood and walked towards Anne. He took both her hands in his and smiled. 'Lady Anne, it has been a long time since I saw you last.'

'It was at Warwick Castle, many years ago,' she replied, coldly. 'You went hunting with my father.'

Releasing her hands, Edward said, 'Sadly, much has changed since then, but I have no quarrel with you for your father's crimes, so I grant you a royal pardon, which also includes Lady Vaux, for I have no quarrel with her, either.'

Anne looked at him, her face showing no emotion. 'Thank you, my Lord.'

John noticed that her words lacked warmth.

Edward continued. 'Now that you have no male relation to look after you, I have decided to make my brother, George, your legal guardian and—'

Richard stepped forward. 'Forgive me, brother, but I am better placed to fulfil that duty—'

'I will not hear of it,' George butted in. 'She will come with me and be under her sister's protection within my household.'

John saw an icy calmness descend over Richard; an air of ruthlessness he had seen many times before.

'She will come with me,' Richard whispered with venom, at George. 'She was betrothed to me by Warwick, and she is still betrothed to me now, and by God, I will marry her!'

'You do not love her,' sneered George. 'You want her lands, her wealth. You already have a woman who bears you children – what is the wench's name?' He looked at Anne, unable to keep the look of glee from his face. 'Katherine Haute; that's her name!' he cried.

'Enough!' cried Anne. 'I am not some animal to be bartered over. I am not some little orphan in need of protection. My mother still lives, although you seem to have forgotten this, for you are fighting over her lands already.'

Looking icily at Richard, she said, 'Do not presume that I would marry the man who killed my husband in cold blood.'

Richard stared hard at the floor, and John could see the cold anger building within him.

'And, what of you?' Anne shouted at George, as tears formed in her eyes. 'You fled to France with my father; you married my sister, and plotted to steal your brother's throne. First, you betrayed him, and then you betrayed us. I would rather go to Hell than live in your house!' she cried. 'No man will ever trust you again. Wherever you go, they will whisper about you. They will watch you out of the corners of their eyes and distrust your every word.'

'Enough of this!' cried Edward, in exasperation. 'Anne, you must have a guardian to protect you.'

'My Lord, I am now a widow, and as such, under the laws of the land, require no one to hold authority over me. I am free to make my own way in the world without hindrance from any man. You would agree that this is so?'

Edward nodded, in reluctant agreement.

'So I will stay at the abbey and bury my husband with honour. I shall supervise the internment of Lady Whittingham and her husband, and then I will mourn and say prayers for my father who was slain by you three sons of York.'

'It was in open battle that your father died,' said Edward, irritated. 'It was he who caused that battle in a bid to steal my crown.'

'It was her lover that killed your father,' said George, pointing his finger at Margaret, his voice triumphant. 'Sir Simon Langford, a man who shared your mother-in-law's bed, delivered the fatal blow.'

There was a brief, shocked silence, broken by a simple question from Richard.

'Are you with child?' he asked, his voice cold and hard.

The question caught Anne off guard. She turned and stared at Richard, the revelation about Margaret's lover killing her father had clouded her mind. Her hand went instinctively to her stomach. The three sons of York were staring intently at her, and a threatening silence filled the room. She suddenly felt afraid.

'The marriage was never consummated,' said Margaret, her voice strong and firm. 'I would never allow it. Warwick was my hated enemy. Do you believe I would allow our Lancastrian blood to be tainted by this girl?' she said, pointing at Anne with disdain. 'This spawn of the Devil?'

'So, she is still a virgin?' questioned Richard, as he stared unblinking at Anne.

John saw his eyes taking in her beauty, a glimmer of desire growing in them.

'Yes, the Yorkist bitch is still a virgin.' Margaret spat the words out, with contempt.

Anne silently thanked Margaret for saving her with her harsh, calculated words. It had allowed her time to compose herself, and she too had seen the look of desire in Richard's eyes. 'May I take my leave for the abbey?' she asked, looking at him from beneath her long eyelashes, her voice soft and girlish.

Richard stepped towards her. 'I will accompany you, if my brother agrees.'

'I would ask that Sir John accompany me, instead,' said Anne. 'Much has happened between you and I, and it would be best that we do not see each other until my heart is healed.'

Richard stepped back. 'You are right, my Lady. Time is needed, but do you give me hope?'

Anne half smiled at him. It was a seductive smile. She saw the desire grow within him; she had him hooked like a fish. 'Yes, my Lord,' she whispered, although the thought of him naked in bed with her, with his crooked back, turned her stomach.

John, leading Anne by the hand, walked her slowly from the room. Lady Vaux followed.

Anne's heart pounded as she entered Tewkesbury Abbey. She had eluded Richard and his brothers' questioning, and now, she was safe – safe within its sanctuary. A feeling of relief swept over her, her great secret would be secure here, at least, for now.

Looking up at the great stone pillars and the beautiful stained-glass windows, she let the peace of this holy place calm her soul.

She looked at John. It had been many years since she had last seen him – how he had changed. She remembered the laughing young boy of their childhood. Memories of their time together at Middleham Castle flooded back to her and she felt a pang of sadness that those carefree days were now gone, forever. Young John was now Sir John, and with his change from boy to man, he had become even more handsome with his black hair and crystal-blue eyes. She could see why Rose loved him so.

'It is so good to see you,' Anne cried, wrapping her arms around him and hugging him tight. 'Oh, John, you remind me of happier times, of long hot summers playing in the woods, and crisp white winters full of snowballs and mulled wine.'

'But, now we are no longer children,' John replied, his arms returning her hug. 'We are in the real world of men, politics, and war.'

'Yes,' Anne sighed, sadly. 'Our innocence is gone, and I know that the games we play now are for real, but don't you just sometimes long for the old days when all was well in the world?'

John threw his head back and laughed. 'We did have some wonderful times!'

Do you remember,' Anne asked, 'when you came from secretly meeting Rose, to my mother's chambers with your guilt exposed by the stable straw clinging to your backside?'

John smiled at the memory. 'I remember that night; it was the night I think you and Richard grew fond of each other.'

Anne drew away from him and pursed her lips, thinly. 'That was long ago,' she said, coldly. 'He now has a wench who shares his bed and bears his bastards. All know she is wife to him but for a ring of gold.'

'And all know he can never marry her. Only someone of your rank can he wed. He thinks very fondly of you, Anne, and wishes you no harm.'

'He thinks very fondly of my estates!' she cried 'Also, his back has grown pitifully crooked since I saw him last. If he were the last man on earth, I would never marry him.'

'Do not antagonise him. If he thinks all is lost between you both, he will be cold and ruthless to get what he wants.'

Without thinking, Anne's hands went instinctively to her stomach. She could feel its slightly swollen tightness – the first signs of her precious baby. She noticed John's eyes following her hands and quickly moved them away. His eyes returned to hers, a look of comprehension in them. A small gasp of fear left her mouth and tears formed in her eyes.

'You are not the virgin widow that Margaret says you are,' John whispered. Anne's silence confirmed his suspicions. He stared at her for what seemed hours, his mind stunned by the revelation that she was pregnant. He saw her on the scaffold, her head on the block, the axe raised and glinting in the early morning sunlight, Richard's raised hand, and then the axe falling…

Lady Vaux, who had been quiet, spoke up. 'No one knows of this,' she whispered, trying to stem the tremor in her voice.

'They will kill you if they find you are with child,' John blurted out, in shock. 'Richard has already convinced his brothers that old King Henry must die on their return to London. Edward and George do not have the stomach to kill an anointed king, but Richard has no such qualms. If he knows you are carrying Henry's grandchild, well…' his words trailed off, as he suddenly realised the predicament.

'Will you tell him?' asked Anne, her eyes never leaving John's face.

He looked at Anne, and then at Lady Vaux. 'He…he is my Lord. I have sworn loyalty to him, and you know we have been companions since childhood.'

'And so have we,' said Anne, softly. 'You have been the brother I never had.' As Anne watched John, she could see his mind groping for the answer to his dilemma: to whom should he show his loyalty?

'I could see you were quite taken with the Lady Anne,' laughed Edward, 'and it is easy to see why. She is now a woman of real beauty, not the skinny young girl you last saw.'

445

'It is not often that one can see the cold Duke of Gloucester melting under the spell of a woman,' said George, as he joined in with his brother's laughter.

Richard allowed himself a smile. 'As you know, it is not the woman I marry, but her estates. That she is beautiful is a bonus, however, I still say the doctor should check her virginity. We cannot believe what Margaret of Anjou says. If she is not a virgin, then she may be pregnant with the heir to the Lancastrian throne.'

'And what then?' said Edward. 'Do we chop her head off, too?'

'I will marry her, so I would have control of her lands, and then execute her,' said Richard.

The hardness in his voice made his brothers shudder.

'No more of this talk,' said Edward. 'There has been enough bloodshed over the last few months. We have already killed her father, and uncle, plus her husband. You will know when you see her again if she is with child.'

'Talking of that arrogant bitch from Anjou; what's to be done with her?' asked George.

'We will take her back to London with us,' replied Edward. 'Let's see if a dungeon in the Tower can drain the arrogance out of her.'

'Holy Harry must be dealt with,' said Richard. 'We have news that the Bastard of Fauconberg, Warwick's cousin, is sailing up the Thames with his fleet to attack the Tower and free him. Harry will always be a rallying point for the Lancastrian cause.'

'Fauconberg is the Neville's last throw of the dice,' replied Edward. 'He will not succeed. London has closed her gates to him, and he has no support from the people.'

'Richard is right,' joined in George. 'Fauconberg, in trying to free Henry, has signed his death warrant and although he will fail, others will try. Your crown will not sit easy on your head while Henry lives.'

'But he is an anointed king,' said Edward, irritation creeping into his voice. 'It would be a crime against God to kill him.' He looked around the room for support. 'Hastings,' he barked, 'you are being very quiet on this matter; it not like you to lose your tongue.'

Lord Hastings pushed himself away from the wall he had been leaning against and walked slowly into the centre of the room. 'Edward, you are my King and friend,' he said. 'As my King, I would say to you that England cannot have two anointed kings. One must die for peace to reign, and as my friend, I say, if you wish to be king then you must make decisions that are made for the good of the realm, but maybe not for your soul.'

'Friar Drynk – what would the voice of God say?' asked Edward.

'He would say that it is better for one to die than thousands. Did he not sacrifice his own son for the good of mankind? You must sacrifice Henry for the good of the realm.'

'The people will never know the truth,' whispered Richard. 'We will say he died of shock on hearing the news of his son's death. The people will mourn him, for they held him with affection in their hearts, but will love you for bringing peace to the realm.'

Edward nodded. 'You have all argued well for Henry's death.' He looked around at them all. 'So, this terrible deed will rest with every one of you.' He paused, his eyes resting on Richard. 'As you are the Constable of England, it is your duty to carry it out.'

Richard half smiled, a look of triumph fleeting on his features. 'The kingdom needs a king, not a monk,' he said, flatly. 'The deed will be done.'

The early morning sun was lightly brushing the fields with golden hues as it broke the chill of the air.

John and Richard brought their horses to a stop on a hill that overlooked the royal army.

'How was Anne when you left her?' asked Richard.

They watched the army break camp and prepare for the march back to London.

'She is weary, sad, and confused. Her life has been turned upside down many times over this last year. She needs time to rest and come to terms with all that has happened.'

'Did she mention me?' asked Richard.

'Yes, we talked about the happy times we all shared at Middleham.'

'I mean, now. How does she talk of me now?' He studied John's face as he awaited the answer.

John stared back at his companion and friend. He knew Richard could be cold and ruthless when events dictated, but to John he was always loyal and true. He took a deep breath. His stomach lurched, for he had never lied to him in all the time they had been together, but he could not condemn Anne to death. This great matter was between Richard and his brothers; it was not for him to judge who should die within their royal world. 'She is still fond of you,' he lied. 'You must give her time. I believe if you are patient, you could win her again.'

Richard smiled, broadly. 'It would be good to have a willing bride, rather than one who has to be dragged to the altar. I will give her plenty of time to come round to the idea of our marriage, but at the end of the day, she will be my wife, be it willing, or not.'

There was a silence between them as the question of Anne filled both their thoughts.

'What of your plans?' Richard asked. 'Do you not have someone you wish to see? Somebody called...what was it now...? Dandelion...? Buttercup...?'

'Rose,' replied John, with a look of bemusement. He saw a sly smile appearing on Richard's face.

Grinning broadly, John said, 'With your permission, I will leave today.'

'Go!' laughed Richard, slapping John on the back. 'Find her, and don't come back until you have married her. Take the Hallet twins with you for company and protection. I will join you later at Middleham Castle, for we have business on the Scottish border this summer.'

Tower of London
21 May 1471

In the distance, through the gathering dusk, lights flickered out.

Margaret of Anjou saw them through tired eyes, their appealing charm mesmerising her, beckoning her, although she knew they held only danger.

She was weary. In the old days, these distant lights from the great Tower meant warmth and safety; a comfortable bed and food. She shivered, not against the chilled evening air, but with fear, for a cold damp dungeon awaited her, and then maybe a short step to the scaffold.

For her, the journey from Tewkesbury to London had been long and arduous, but for King Edward, she noted, it had been a journey of triumphant progress.

The villagers and townsfolk had come out to cheer him on his way, and to stare at her, the vanquished queen. Some had tried to throw rotten fruit or vegetables at her, but had been chased off by her guards and although Edward had decreed that she be shown the appropriate respect for a person of royal blood, she realised she was now a figure of ridicule to be despised and tormented. There was no honour for a defeated queen.

As she approached the outer gate of the Tower with Duke Richard, Lord Lovell, Earl Rivers, and their retainers, she saw the guards stiffen to attention. They passed through the next gatehouse into the inner ward, where they finally stopped. Yeomen of the Tower held their horses steady as they dismounted.

Margaret looked up at the great, white tower that dominated the castle. Its walls looked cold and hard in the evening twilight. The smooth Caen stone, imported from France that provided the detail in the facing of the towers, made her think fleetingly of her home near Lorraine, and then of Simon.

Her spirit lifted as she thought of him and then her heart sank; it was her attempt to save Simon that had brought her to this humiliation. She looked into the dark entrances to the towers, where many had entered, but few came out.

She could see the royal chambers where she had stayed as queen. She remembered how she had ordered the walls to be whitewashed and then decorated with frescos of beautiful flowers. She wondered if they were still the same.

Her thoughts of happier times vanished as suddenly two yeomen guards took hold of her and escorted her towards Beauchamp Tower. Their rough hands dug painfully into her arms as they dragged her brutally across the yard. She stifled a cry of anguish as the cold dark entrance loomed before her. She looked back to see Duke Richard and his two companions, being led by the constable towards the Bloody Tower, where she knew her husband, Henry, was imprisoned.

The cell door slammed shut behind her. Margaret heard the guards walking away, laughing, and sniggering at what they would do if they had been locked in the cell with her.

She looked around at her spartan surroundings. In the gloom, on the far side of the cell, she could see a straw pallet; near to it, stood a small table, and two rough chairs. A small, barred window looked out across the inner ward. She walked across to it and saw directly opposite, the Bloody Tower.

Looking up, she could see candles burning brightly within one of the rooms. She reasoned it must have been Henry's room, as he had always lit candles at his holy altar, where he prayed for hours every day.

It had been seven years ago when she had left him, for France, and she never thought she would see him alive again, yet, there he was, only yards away from her. She stared, fascinated, at the enlarged shadows the candles reflected on to the walls, when she saw a shadowy arm raise up, a sword held within its hand. Her fascination turned to horror as the hand plunged down; her blood turned cold as she heard a loud shrill scream of terror.

The realisation of what was happening hit Margaret like a thunderbolt. 'They are killing Henry!' she cried, into the darkness. She saw the shadowy arm rise for a second time, but this time, the second shrill scream was cut short.

Margaret stood transfixed with horror, her breath coming in short gasping spasms.

The door to the Bloody Tower crashed open, and the figure of Duke Richard stumbled out, his face reflected sheet-white by the rising moon, a bloody sword in his hand. Lord Lovell and Earl Rivers quickly followed. All three mounted their horses and raced away.

Looking back up to the room, Margaret could see only one stationary shadow – they had left the constable to clean up their murderous actions. She walked across to a chair and slowly sat down, resting her forearms on the table. She lowered her head and silently wept for poor harmless Henry. Then, great sobs welled up for her beautiful son. She had hidden her grief well since her capture; they would never see her weaken, but now alone, the gates of her despair opened.

Margaret of Anjou's grief flowed in a torrent of tears. She was alone, and defeated.

Chapter 18

Love Triumphs

Middleham Castle, North Yorkshire
23 May 1471

Rose watched the sun slowly disappear over the horizon. She had decided to sit and enjoy its waning splendour, and not to move until she saw the first star of the night.

Her thoughts turned to the changes in her life. It felt right to be back at Middleham Castle. She reasoned it was where she belonged. The slow, tedious life of a novice nun was not for her. Sister Mary and the Mother Superior had gently steered her away from taking her vows, and finally, she had agreed with them. Their wonderful kindness had shown her that the world was still merciful and compassionate, and they had explained to her that she could never take her vows and marry Jesus because her heart still belonged to John.

The experience of Ellerton Priory had been good for her spirit. The dreadful ordeal she had suffered at Warwick Castle was still raw and still haunted her dreams, but since she had heard of the Earl of Warwick's death, it had become easier to bear. Justice had been done. The earl, she prayed, was now supping with all the devils of hell.

She was sitting in Lady Tunstall's old rooms. The Great Controller had said she could stay there while they waited for news on the outcome of the battle between King Edward and Margaret of Anjou. So, while they waited, Rose had started preparing the rooms for Lady Tunstall's return. It was known she had arrived back in England, but where she was still remained a mystery.

John Tunstall, and the Hallet twins, approached the castle, weary from their long hours in the saddle. They were covered in sweat, and dirt from the hot, dry dust of the early summer roads.

It had taken five days of hard riding to get from Tewkesbury to Middleham. Now, at last, the castle stood before them. Its great granite walls were bathed in moonlight that scattered huge shadows across the ground around its base. The hour was late as they approached, and lights appeared above the Great Keep.

'Who goes there?' demanded a voice.

'Sir John Tunstall and the Hallet twins on the King's business,' John replied.

They sat patiently on their tired horses, listening to the urgent shouts from behind the walls of the Great Keep. While they waited, John glanced up at the stars that filled the vastness of the heavens. It occurred to him that Rose was lost in the vastness of the north. Would he ever find her?

A small door in the great gate swung open, and a huge tree of a man eased himself through the narrow opening. Raising himself to his full height, he stepped towards them. 'Is that you, young John?' he asked, and then seeing the twins, 'and you George and Thomas?'

John slipped from his horse, and stepped towards the master-at-arms. 'Aye, it is us!' he cried.

Two huge hands held his shoulders in a vice-like grip. 'Welcome home, Sir John. Welcome home,' cried the master-at-arms, with excitement in his voice.

A few moments later, they were all seated in the guardroom just inside the Great Keep. The master-at-arms had ordered the kitchens to be opened, and bread and cold meats brought for their new guests. He had also sent word to the Great Controller that Sir John and the Hallet twins had arrived with news of King Edward's victory at Tewkesbury.

'A lot has happened since that day you threw those snowballs at the twins,' laughed the master-at-arms.

John smiled at the memory. Was it really over eight years ago? It was also, he remembered, the day he had fallen in love with Rose.

'Aye, and he has proved his courage many times on the field of battle since then,' said George.

'You have grown from a young boy to a man, in these last eight years. I wish that I could have been with you,' said the master-at-arms. 'As you know, I fought alongside your father many times, but, alas, I am too old and slow to fight in open battle now.'

'No slower than those two,' replied John, nodding in the direction of the twins.

They smiled broadly at the affectionate insult, secure in the respect they knew John had for them.

The Great Controller burst into the guardroom, his yellow eyes flashing with excitement. ''Tis good to see you all,' he said, his eyes scanning their faces. 'Now, tell me, what news from Tewkesbury?'

'A great victory for our King Edward and Richard,' replied John. 'The Lancastrian cause is finished. Somerset and Prince Edward are slain, and Margaret of Anjou is held in the Tower.'

The Great Controller sat down. 'This is wonderful news,' he said, making himself comfortable. 'Pray tell me how the battle was won.'

Between mouthfuls of cold meat, bread, and sweet pastries, John and the Hallet twins told the story of the campaign, and that Duke Richard was now the master of Middleham Castle.

Turning to the master-at-arms, the Great Controller said, 'It is time to remove Warwick's *Bear and Ragged Staff* from all areas of the castle and replace it with the insignia of Duke Richard's *White Boar*.' He looked at the weary faces around him. 'Forgive me for talking so much,' he said. 'I know the hour is late, and you must be weary from your journey. I have made hot water available, so wash, and then get some sleep. We will talk more at length tomorrow.' He rose from his chair and prepared to take his leave, beckoning to John to follow.

John and the Great Controller stood alone in the shadow of the Great Keep.

'Have you come to seek out Rose?' asked the Great Controller.

'Aye,' replied John. 'I will travel north at first light to find her; I will not return until I do.'

The Great Controller placed his hand on John's shoulder and gently turned him around until he faced the inner keep of the castle. Pointing up to the battlements, he said, 'There is no need to travel north in the morning. Do you see the lights shining out from your old quarters?'

John nodded.

'Rose is nearer than you could ever imagine,' he whispered. With a wink and a smile, the Great Controller disappeared into the night.

All else within the castle was in darkness; John's heart began to beat faster.

It was close to midnight. John stood silently at the foot of the steps – the steps he and Rose had raced down so many times, in what seemed a lifetime ago.

He had washed the sweat and dirt from his body, and beaten the dust from his clothes as best he could. He looked up the steps as they spiralled into the darkness. Slowly, he started to climb. As he made his ascent, his earlier weariness vanished, replaced with an intense energy. Reaching the door, anticipation coursed through his veins. He leaned against the wall and tried to gather his thoughts. There was only the door's thickness between him and Rose.

He knocked twice. His knuckles, white with tension, were poised in mid-air as he listened for any sound. He heard a slight rustle of movement, and his body filled with emotion. Throwing the door open, he stepped into the room.

Rose stood beside a tall, oak bench. A half-embroidered cushion cover hung loosely in her hands. She stared at John, her eyes wide with surprise.

John stood motionless, his eyes taking in Rose's simple, turquoise cotton dress, edged with ribbon. A ring of blue beads circled the crown of her head. Her thick brown hair tumbled around her pretty face and shoulders. He watched as tears of joy filled her beautiful eyes.

'John?' Rose whispered. Her legs started to buckle. She dropped the cushion cover and reached out with an unsteady hand for support.

John caught her as she started to fall. His strong arms curled around her waist.

Rose circled her arms around John's neck, and their lips met in a kiss, then, slipping her hands away, Rose pushed John from her, releasing him for their embrace.

They stood, a few feet apart, staring at each other, their breathing quick and shallow.

'I have something to tell,' Rose said. 'Once I have told you, your love for me will never be the same.' A great sob welled up from her chest. 'Oh, John, I love you so much, it hurts,' she cried, as tears rolled down her cheeks, 'but I have to tell you the shameful truth.'

John placed a finger gently against her lips. 'I know of what you are about to say,' he said. 'Edward met his brother, George, for their reconciliation at Warwick Castle, and while I was there I was told of your terrible ordeal.' He looked into Rose's eyes and saw the pain that filled them. 'Oh, Rose, my darling, I have been fearful of this moment ever since I learnt of your suffering, not knowing where you were, living each day wondering if we would ever be together again, but you must believe me,' he said earnestly, his eyes filling with tears. 'I love you with all my heart. You must not carry this shame. You have done nothing wrong.'

He dropped his hands to her waist and pulled her closer to him. 'You could do me no greater honour than by becoming my wife,' he said, finally, as the tears rolled down his cheeks.

Rose's face broke out into a fragile smile. She slipped her arms around John's neck and kissed him. 'I love you as life itself,' she whispered softly as her tears mingled with his.

Scooping her up into his arms, John carried her towards the bedroom.

Through the darkness of sleep, John could hear the sounds of men and horses. He tried to make sense of these jumbled dreamlike thoughts. Were they preparing for battle, or just breaking camp? Why had his squire not woken him? A gentle hand touched his shoulder; soft lips kissed his cheek.

'Are you awake?'

John opened his eyes to see Rose lean down to kiss him again. A surge of joy shot through his body. He was not under canvas on some godforsaken field, preparing for battle, but here at Middleham Castle, in his old rooms, with Rose lying beside him. He sat upright, smiling, as the night before flooded back to him.

'That grin of yours couldn't get any bigger,' Rose laughed.

John lent over and kissed her. 'We must marry before the week is out,' he whispered, excitedly. He saw the look of love in Rose's eyes as he took her in his arms. 'I swear we will not be parted until you are my wife.'

Joy filled Rose's heart – the three spirits had been right.

Amiens Cathedral, France
1 June 1471

King Louis knelt in the towering Cathedral of Amiens, praying for news of Warwick and Margaret of Anjou. For weeks, he had listened to rumours and gossip about their fates, and the longer he waited, the worse the situation seemed.

He finished his prayers and rose from his knees. Turning from the altar, he looked down the centre aisle towards the great doors at the end of the knave. There, he saw gathered, a deputation of his closest advisors. He noted they all looked dejected.

'You have news of Warwick?' King Louis asked, with a sinking heart.

Georges Havart stepped forward, nervously. 'Our grand designs with Warwick are finished, your Majesty,' he said, quietly. 'He fell in battle on 14 April at a place called Barnet.'

'And Margaret, and her son, what news of them?' asked the king, his voice full of disappointment.

'She is captured, and her son slain. The Yorkists are victorious. Edward once again rules England.'

'Margaret was taken to the Tower of London, and her husband put to death on her arrival,' whispered Etienne de Loup, hoarsely.

King Louis brushed past them, his face full of anger. Stepping out of the cathedral, he walked briskly towards his Scots Guards who were tending his horse, his posse of advisors rushing to keep up with him. He suddenly stopped.

'Our grand designs with Warwick, and Margaret of Anjou, have reached a dismal end,' he cried, with frustration. 'Our dealings with that man have brought us only sorrow. Come, we must plan on how to deal with Charles of Burgundy, and Francis of Brittany, for they will be renewing their triangular alliance with King Edward against us. They will be strengthened by this turn of events, while we are weakened.'

'We must use guile and subterfuge to play for time against these adversaries who grow arrogant against us,' said Georges Havart.

'Yes, you are right',' said King Louis, a sudden sense of purpose in his voice. 'We will use our wits to divide them. We are, I think, somewhat more adroit than they are at these diplomatic games. Summon the Milanese ambassador, Sforza de Bettini, and the Spanish ambassador – we have much to discuss.' With his mind now fully focused on the future, Warwick and Margaret of Anjou were now forgotten – consigned to history.

Tewkesbury Abbey, Gloucestershire
5 December 1471

John Tunstall could see the ruthless anger in Richard's eyes, as he glared across the table at John Streynsham, the Abbot of Tewkesbury. He felt sorry for the man, whose grey and lined face reflected his terrible dilemma. To answer Richard's question would condemn the person he sought so urgently to death.

'Where is Lady Anne?' barked Richard, again. 'She was left in your keeping, last May, and now you deny all knowledge as to where she is.' He thumped the table in frustration.

The abbot flinched. 'I – I told you, my Lord,' he stammered. 'She left with Lady Vaux and a few servants shortly after they buried their husbands. I do not know where they went, or their whereabouts, now.'

'You lie,' snarled Richard. He stared at the abbot with contempt in his eyes. 'You lie to me in this house of God, you hypocritical bastard. Do you take me for a fool?'

'No – no, my Lord,' flustered the abbot.

Richard stood up. 'You have until the morning to tell me where she is. If you do not, then you and your monks will suffer my wrath. Men of God you may be, but you are still just men to me.' He leant forward across the table, bringing his face closer to the abbot. 'I dragged Somerset and his followers from the holy sanctuary of your cathedral and had them executed, so do not think you and your monks are safe within its walls.' He straightened up to his full height, the threat hanging in the air between them.

The monks in attendance stared white with fear at Richard as he stood with his hunched back, and his face contorted with anger. He could have looked as though he was the devil himself.

The Black Bear Inn, Tewkesbury
5 December 1471

It had been snowing softly when they left the abbey. Snowflakes as large as goose feathers drifted gently down to settle on the frost-hardened ground. The warmth from the roaring fire in their lodgings was a welcome luxury as they stared out of the window, hypnotised by the falling snow.

John's mind returned to the warmth of the summer and his marriage to Rose. They had been wonderful carefree weeks, until Richard's arrival at Middleham Castle, when he had reviewed his new estates. Mustering his men, they had left to campaign against the Scottish raiders who were causing so much trouble for the English farmers just south of the border. John had again seen Rose, briefly, when they had stopped at the castle, on their way to London to see King Edward and confirm Richard's marriage to Anne. Now, they were back at Tewkesbury, seeking her out.

Francis Lovell entered the room, brushing the snowflakes from his shoulders. 'We will not be going far tomorrow if this keeps up,' he stated, matter-of-factly.

'If we find the whereabouts of Lady Anne, then we will go to her, snow or no snow,' replied Richard.

'I'm not sure the abbot knew where she was,' said John. 'He seemed very timid – frightened even. If he did know, then I'm sure he would have told us.'

'Oh, he knows, all right,' said Richard. 'He may appear timid, but that's part of his act. I think he has courage; you don't become an abbot by being timid. But the real question is, why would he hide her from us? What doesn't he want us to know or find out?'

'There is only one thing it can be,' said Francis.

John and Richard stared at Francis, both with a bemused, questioning look.

'She has gone back to France,' Francis continued. 'I think, she probably met somebody there who she fell in love with, and now she is free, she has gone back to marry him.'

'What evidence tells you this?' questioned Richard.

'Well, she is very beautiful, and we all know what those amorous Frenchmen are like. They dress and strut like peacocks. One is sure to have turned her head.'

'I wish you were right,' laughed Richard, at his friend's fanciful theory. Then, his face turned serious. 'If my suspicions are true, then I think it may have been her husband, Prince Edward, who turned her head. I will get to the bottom of this mystery, if it's the last thing I do.'

John felt a hot wave of guilt sweep over him.

There was a sharp knock on the door. One of their senior men-at-arms stood in the doorway.

'Sorry to trouble you, my Lord, but we have a monk here who says he must speak with you on a matter of urgency.'

Richard looked quizzically at his two companions, and then beckoned to the monk.

The man entered the room, his head bent low; the hood on his habit pulled up, and covering his features. The snow that clung to him quickly melted, forming little puddles of water around his feet.

'Stand by the fire and warm yourself,' said Richard, kindly.

The monk moved closer to the fire.

'I am intrigued by your presence,' continued Richard. 'Tell me, what brings you here?'

'I know where she is,' the monk whispered. 'If I tell, will you leave the abbey, and the monks, in peace?'

'You have my word,' answered Richard, his eyes glinting with excitement.

'She was taken to Hailes Manor,' the monk replied, quietly. 'It is near to the village of Winchcombe. The manor house belongs to Hailes Abbey; it is a day's ride from here,'

John's heart sank. Anne had been betrayed by a cowardly monk; her death warrant signed by a man of God.

'Hailes Abbey,' repeated Richard. 'Was that not founded many years ago by monks from Beaulieu Abbey?'

'Yes, my Lord,' replied the monk. 'It was founded by Richard, Earl of Cornwall, the younger brother of Henry III, around the year 1246, using monks from Beaulieu Abbey.'

'Do the two abbeys still have close ties?' asked Richard.

'Very close, my Lord.'

Richard rose from his chair and walked to the window. He stared out at the falling snow. 'Anne's mother is being held at Beaulieu Abbey, on the orders of King Edward,' he said, quietly, as though talking to himself, 'so messages must pass weekly – even daily – between the two abbeys. Anne is in one and her mother in the other...' his voice trailed off. He turned back round to face the others in the room. 'You will show us the way to Hailes Manor' he barked at the monk.

'I do not wish to be involved, my Lord,' the monk replied. 'I have risked enough already.'

'You have risked nothing but your conscience,' said Richard, dismissively. 'For if I'm not mistaken, the assistant abbot was wearing the same ring I now see on your finger. Have you decided to betray your abbot, so you may take his place?'

The monk's hesitant nod confirmed his agreement.

'Well, if we find the Lady Anne, I will gladly make you the Abbot of Tewkesbury,' said Richard. 'But first, you will lead me to her.' The sudden harshness in his voice brokered no refusal. He turned to the others. 'Raise the men,' he ordered. 'We ride for Hailes Manor, immediately.'

'Tonight?' cried Francis, incredulously, as he looked out at the deepening snow.

'Yes, tonight,' replied Richard. 'We have not a moment to lose.'

Hailes Manor, Gloucestershire
6 December 1471

The pale dawn light revealed an icy landscape. Anne held her newborn son tight against her chest. She looked down at him to check he was wrapped well against the cold draughts that often slipped silently into the room. He was just two weeks old, and she had named him Edward, after his father.

She moved towards the window and held him up so that he could look out at the falling snow. She watched his eyes blink and widen at the whiteness of his first snowfall. Anne smiled and kissed Edward on his forehead. It was then that she saw the four horsemen moving slowly towards the manor.

Her stomach tightened with fear. Who would be coming in this weather? She moved closer towards the window and stared at the approaching figures.

The door behind her opened. She turned around, her face white with worry. Lady Vaux, and a wet-nurse entered.

'There are men approaching,' said Lady Vaux. 'Move away from the window.'

The urgency in Lady Vaux's voice made Anne step back quickly into the shadows of the room.

Lady Vaux rushed to the window and stood silently looking at the approaching figures. 'Go and find Sister Mary,' she ordered, 'and prepare the secret room.' She glanced round at the wet-nurse, who nodded and left.

'Who can it be?' asked Anne.

'I don't know, but they must have urgent business to travel in these conditions,' replied Lady Vaux. She turned back to the window and watched the approaching men. She saw their horses were struggling through the deep snow. It would be a while before they reached the manor house. She breathed a sigh of relief. 'You must take the baby to Sister Mary, while I check there is no evidence that would make them suspicious.'

Anne nodded and hurried from the room.

Lady Vaux gathered up the baby's belongings to hide them away. She stood clutching them nervously, as she watched the advancing horsemen. Slowly, her hands relaxed. Her stomach stopped churning, as she recognised the leading horseman. It was Abbot John. She watched as he and his companions slowly fought their way through the snow towards them. *What is so urgent to make them undertake such a hazardous journey on such a terrible night?* she wondered. Her stomach started churning again.

The abbot and his three companions huddled around the fire, slowly easing the bitter cold from their bodies. Their thick woollen habits were frozen white. It had been a hard journey, and all were still too numb with cold to speak. Lady Vaux busied herself supplying hot drinks and food.

Anne entered the room. She stopped and took in the scene, her face full of concern.

The abbot turned from the fire to face her. 'My Lady,' he whispered, as he tried to rub warmth into his hands. 'I have distressing news: Richard, Duke of Gloucester, has arrived at Tewkesbury, and is searching for you.'

Anne's hand shot to her mouth. 'Then we must leave!' she cried, her face suddenly filled with worry. Glancing out of the window, she saw the freezing landscape, the snow swirling in the bitter wind. Her body slumped in despair. 'We are trapped,' she whispered, her eyes darting around the room with mounting panic.

'The young prince must be taken to the docks at Gloucester, and then by ship to France. I have brought some good men with me who will assist in getting him there safely but they must go today; there is no time to be lost. Duke Richard is not to be underestimated.'

Anne stared at the abbot but his words seemed far away. She was thinking of Margaret, who had brought her only beloved son, Edward, back to reclaim the Lancastrian throne, and now he was dead. That could not happen to her own son. The abbot was right; her beautiful baby boy had to be taken to the safety of France.

'If we are going to brave the snow and escape, then we should be organising ourselves,' she cried. 'Lady Vaux, Sister Mary, come with me. We must wrap our baby prince up well against this weather.'

Hailes Manor became a hive of activity. The abbot had given them little time to prepare for their escape. Two nuns and two wet-nurses quickly gathered food and drink for the journey, and all the warm clothes and blankets they could find.

Anne busied herself issuing instructions and helping here and there, but her heart was heavy. She acted bravely, but tears were never far from her eyes.

Finally, they all stood in the large entrance hall ready to face the cold. The three monks who had arrived with the abbot had gone to bring the horses from the stables. Anne held her baby close, now fearful for his future, whilst Lady Vaux reassured her that all would be well. The abbot also whispered words of comfort. She heard the horses outside, and clutching her son tighter to her chest, she silently said a prayer for his safety.

Suddenly, the great door flew open and an icy wind blew, swirling snowflakes around the hall.

Anne let out a gasp of horror, for framed in the doorway, sword in hand, stood Duke Richard.

He strode into the hall. To Anne, his great fur cloak flowed out around him like a beast from hell. As he approached, she saw the blood dripping from his sword. She shrunk back in terror against the wall.

The abbot raised his hands protectively and moved quickly in front of Anne. Richard, without a word, ran him through with his sword; the move executed with vicious brutality. The abbot let out a short grunt of surprise and crumpled, dying, to the floor.

Anne screamed with fear as she wrapped her arms protectively around her son.

Richard glared malevolently at the baby, his sword hovering over him.He pulled his arm back to strike. Instinctively, Anne turned her back, and hunched over to protect the child. Her eyes tightly shut with fear as she waited the fatal blow, but then she sensed, rather than felt, a body move between her and Richard.

'Enough, my Lord, you must stop this bloodshed!'

Anne recognised the sound of John's voice. She held her breath, praying for a miracle.

The silence in the room hung in the air as though it was suspended in time itself. Nothing moved. All eyes were frozen, unblinking, staring at Richard.

Slowly, he lowered his sword, the rage within him gradually fading. He looked at John, who stood between him and Anne, and gave a wry smile. 'You're a brave man,' he said, as his composure returned.

It was mid-afternoon. The December light was slowly greying and the wind had gone. A silent stillness hung over the soft white landscape.

John was just finishing his rounds, checking that the thirty-five soldiers they had brought with them had eaten, and had warm billets to sleep in. Satisfied all was well, and that the guard rosters had been organised, he headed for Anne's room. He needed to speak with her before he talked with Richard. He had left him with Francis, who had instructions to keep Richard calm and entertained until John got back.

The two soldiers who stood guarding the door stepped aside. John knocked. There was a rustle of movement, and the door slowly opened. Lady Vaux peeked out at him, and smiled, opening the door wider and ushering him in.

Anne was sitting in a high-backed chair, close to a small struggling fire that smelt of wet wood. She looked up and greeted John with a weak smile.

John knelt beside her. Her face looked tired and fragile. He looked into her sad eyes.

'Oh, John,' she sighed, 'sweet John; you saved us from that monster's sword and I thank you with all my heart.' She brushed the hair from his eyes and stared deeply into them. 'Does he still want our blood?'

John moved to the chair opposite her and leant forward, his face close

467

to hers. 'We both know the implications your son brought into the world when he was born, so you understand why the Yorkists would want him dead?' he stated. 'Edward's crown will never sit easy on his noble head if word got out that there was a grandson of Holy Harry waiting to reclaim it.'

Anne wrapped her arms around herself and sat back in her chair, her eyes wide with dread. 'So we are doomed?' she whispered.

'There is only one way to save your son,' John said.

Anne reached out and gripped John's arm. 'I will do anything!' she cried.

'You will have to sacrifice yourself, your feelings, and your dreams.'

Anne's eyes searched John's face, trying to grasp what he meant by these words.

'You must marry Richard,' John said, gently knowing the effect his words would have on her.

Anne's hand flew to her mouth, her face registering shock. 'Marry him,' she blurted out. 'Marry that hunchback from Hell who would kill my son? Never...'

'It is the only bargain you can make to save him,' John said, forcefully.

Anne sat back in the chair, her eyes smouldering with indignation, and waited.

'Richard's key objective is to take control of your, and also your mother's, estates,' John continued. 'He needs them desperately to compete with his brother, George, who, being married to your sister, has already inherited the Warwick estates in the Midlands and the south of England. George is now making a claim on your estates in the north of England and Wales by petitioning Edward and stating that you forfeited them by your marriage to Prince Edward. That means if Richard fails to take control of them, and George's claim is upheld, then it will make him the most powerful magnate in the land and Richard, the poorest. So, to be on equal terms, Richard must marry you.'

'So, you believe he would trade my son's life to achieve his aims?' Anne asked, with disbelief.

'Yes, I believe he will.'

Anne covered her eyes, and shook her head sadly. 'This man and his brothers have killed my father, my uncle, and my husband, and you now say I have to marry him?' She looked across the room to where her baby was sleeping; tears crept into her eyes. 'I have no choice,' she cried, as her eyes lingered on him. 'I will have to harden my heart, and make my peace with him as best I can.'

John saw the grim resolution on her face, and took her hand. 'You may be a woman, but you have the courage of your father,' he said, gently, and then rose from his chair. 'I must go and persuade Richard to allow your son the safety of France in exchange for your hand in marriage. Lady Vaux can take the young prince to Margaret's family where you can be assured he will be secure and loved. England will never know of his existence.' He turned for the door.

Anne rose from her chair. 'John,' she called.

John stopped and turned to her.

She stepped towards him and took hold of both his hands. 'Thank you,' she whispered, as she leant up on to her toes and kissed him lightly on the cheek. 'You are truly the brother I never had.'

John blushed slightly as he smiled down on her.

'You must forgive me,' Anne continued. 'I have not asked after Rose?' She looked at him, enquiringly.

'We were married shortly after the Battle of Tewkesbury, on the 1 June,' John replied, with a proud grin, 'and she is now with child. I hope to return, God willing, for the birth in April.'

Anne smiled at hearing his good news. 'I will pray that all will be well when the baby comes,' she said.

John lent down and returned her kiss. He left her then, to be comforted by Lady Vaux, while making the most of the short time she had left with her son.

'It is a bargain made in Hell,' said John to Richard. 'Anne has no choice but to marry you to save her son, which will give you possession of her lands, but the price you both must pay is to suffer a loveless marriage.'

Richards's eyes glinted with satisfaction. 'Love has nothing to do with marriage,' he replied, cynically. 'It is all about position and wealth. Love is a bonus that may happen to a few. Tell her I will only agree to the terms of this contract if she agrees to consummate the marriage and provide me with an heir. Our child must have our pure royal blood in his veins.'

John stared at Richard, his mind racing as he thought of what was being asked of Anne.

'You must make her understand that this is expected,' said Richard, forcefully. He waited for John to nod his agreement. 'If she agrees,' he continued, 'then her son will be taken to France and from this day forward we will deny all knowledge of him. The abbot and his three monks are dead, and deserve to be for their traitorous action in hiding him from us. The assistant abbot will take care of their burials, and inform his brother monks of some reason for their deaths. The nuns are sworn to secrecy, to protect their convent from my wrath should they speak of it, and the wet-nurses will go with Lady Vaux to France never to return, on pain of death.'

Francis stood up, threw more wood on to the fire, and then slowly resumed his seat.

The three of them, sat in a semi-circle around it, silently watching the flames lick around the new logs.

'Do you wish me to escort Lady Vaux to Gloucester docks, tomorrow?' said Francis, breaking the silence.

'Yes,' replied Richard. 'Take ten men at dawn and escort them on to the first ship bound for France. As you are now to be responsible for the task, you must ensure that the baby is no longer called, "baby prince" or "royal prince". All reference to his royal birth will cease forthwith, and he will now be the common son of a wet-nurse, should any ask.'

'What are your plans for the Lady Anne once her son has gone?' asked John.

'You, my old friend, are also to take ten men at dawn, and escort her to Beaulieu Abbey where you will make arrangements to take her and her mother back to Middleham Castle. Also, I believe your mother, Lady

Tunstall is with her, as always, her loyal companion, so you will, at last, be reunited,' he said, smiling at John.

John felt a ripple of excitement at the thought of finally seeing his mother.

'I will travel to London,' continued Richard, 'to meet with Edward and ask his permission to marry Anne. He, of course, knows nothing of her child and, God willing, will never know. Also, because we are both brother and sister in-law, and first cousins, we will need a special dispensation from the church to make the marriage legal. I will see the archbishop and put that in his good hands to arrange. Once all this is done, I will return to Middleham.'

John rose reluctantly from the warmth of the fire. 'I will go and inform the Lady Anne of the arrangements for tomorrow and organise the men for the dawn start,' he said, with a heavy heart.

Middleham Castle, North Yorkshire
15 March 1472

Rose sat quietly, brushing Anne's hair. It had grown so long in the last year that it now reached down to her waist. She began braiding long strands and fixing them in an intricate pattern around the crown on her head. This was the day of Anne's wedding to Richard. It had been arranged for midday, and the atmosphere in the room was one of sad resignation.

Rose shifted her weight. Now eight months pregnant, she found that if she sat too long in the same position, the baby pushed on her back, or side, making her uncomfortable.

Anne turned around and gently placed her hands on Rose's stomach. A soft smile broke across her face, as she felt the baby kick. 'That's a boy, if I'm not mistaken,' she said, with a knowing look.

Rose gently took Anne's hands. 'Have you any news from France?' she asked, earnestly.

Anne shook her head. 'It is over three months since my baby was taken and I still have no news.' Her hand covered her mouth as she forced herself not to cry. 'I have no one to help me, either,' she whispered, dejectedly. 'Duke Richard has forbidden all mention of him. It is as if he was never born.'

Rose could see the despair in Anne's eyes. She longed to help, and then an idea formed in her mind. There was a rumour that Margaret of Anjou was being released back to France.

'Do not despair,' Rose said. 'I think I may be able to arrange for regular news of your baby to come from France.'

'How?' Anne cried, her eyes searching Rose's face.

'You must trust me,' replied Rose.

There was a soft knock on the door. One of Anne's ladies-in-waiting opened it a few inches. Rose heard John's voice. 'It is time,' he said.

Anne gripped Rose's hand tighter, her eyes filling with tears.

'It is for the best,' encouraged Rose. 'You have saved your baby's life by doing this.'

Anne nodded in agreement. 'I will take strength from his memory,' she said as she swallowed her tears, and then as though she was cladding her body with invisible armour against the forthcoming ordeal, she said, with steely conviction, 'I am the daughter of the great Earl of Warwick, a Neville, and never again will I show such weakness.' She rose from her seat and walked slowly from the room. With each step, her determination grew stronger. She would show only fortitude in the dark days ahead.

Rose turned to John, who lay beside her in their bed, and blessed her good fortune. She kissed him lightly on the lips.

He smiled at her. 'And what was that for?' he asked.

'We are blessed to have our love,' she said, as she snuggled up to him, knowing that Anne had gone to the matrimonial bed with clear eyes, and her head held high. No one would have known of her inner feeling towards the bridegroom. 'I keep thinking of poor Anne. She will never know such tender love with Duke Richard.'

'She has played her hand as best she can,' John replied.

'But she has no news of her baby son, and that is too much for any woman to bear; a loveless marriage, and a son who is all but dead to her.'

'There is nothing I fear we can do to help her,' said John, sadly.

'There is something we can do,' hinted Rose, and she sat up. 'You must go and seek out Simon Langford.'

'Simon Langford?' repeated John, with a puzzled look.

Chapter 19

New Beginnings

City of London
20 May 1472

Margaret of Anjou glanced back as she rode slowly away from the great Tower of London. She shuddered at the evil within. Death and pain stalked daily within its shadowy archways and foul dungeons. Turning her face away, she crossed herself and thanked the Lord for her safe deliverance.

It was said that all prisoners who escaped the Tower take a legacy that they carry for the rest of their lives. Margaret knew hers was the white face of Duke Richard, with his bloodied sword. It would haunt her dreams, forever.

She had been told that Henry's body had been taken to the church of St Paul's, where it had been publicly displayed to the people of London as proof of his death. Under the cover of darkness, his body had been spirited away over the black waters of the Thames to that cheerless village of Chertsey, where, without ceremony, the sons of York had secretly buried the evidence of their crime.

Alice de la Pole, the Duchess of Suffolk, and old friend to Margaret, moved up beside her. 'No more dark thoughts,' she said, her face breaking out into a smile. 'You are free of that terrible place. Tomorrow, you will arrive at Ewelme Manor, and,' she added, with a mischievous look, 'I have organised a small celebration for your freedom.'

Margaret returned her friend's smile. She had known Alice for twenty-seven years. Alice and her husband had brought her from France to marry King Henry in the April of 1445, and they had remained close ever since. Alice, now in her sixty-eighth year, had always been like a mother to her.

'Thank you for petitioning the King to have me released into your care,' said Margaret. 'If I had been much longer in that damp and dark place I fear my health would have been broken.'

'Well, now you will have gardens to walk in, and our estates to ride with horse, and hunt with falcon,' replied Alice. 'While we get some colour back into your cheeks we will petition the King of France to finance your freedom.'

'How much does King Edward demand for me?'

'Fifty-thousand crowns,' replied Alice, 'but he will agree to ten thousand a year spread over five years, if, of course, you agree to sign away your claim to the English throne.'

Margaret threw her head back and laughed. It was the first time Alice had heard her laugh since she had first visited her in the Tower over a year ago.

'I will willingly sign it away,' Margaret said. 'Not being Queen of England is no loss to me, and I believe will be of no loss to the English. Show me the contract, and I will sign it.'

'That will be the easy part,' said Alice, thoughtfully. 'The stumbling block will be convincing King Louis to pay the ransom demanded.'

'Louis will find a way, if it is to his advantage,' said Margaret. 'He will make sure he gets value for money before he agrees to pay, although, the outcome, again, is of no interest to me. Sadly, there is nothing in England or in France for me to live for. Since my son's death my heart has been cold.'

Margaret spoke with such melancholy that it brought a lump to Alice's throat.

They followed the River Thames out of London stopping over at Slough, Maidenhead, and Henley. From there, they had headed north-west into Oxfordshire where they had halted to rest the horses on Gansdown Hill.

Alice pointed out the tall turrets of Ewelme Manor, which were just visible to the eye on the distant horizon. 'We are nearly home, my Lady

Queen.'

Margaret smiled at the affectionate term. 'Lady Queen' was how Alice used to address her in private, when she had been lady-in-waiting. It somehow reaffirmed the strong bond between them that had been forged on that rough channel crossing all those years ago, when she had accompanied her as a young bride to England.

The turrets of Ewelme Manor were now dominating the skyline as they rode through the grand estate towards them. They were only decorative, Margaret knew. Since the invention of cannon, castles had become obsolete and the rich were now building opulent red-bricked houses full of comfort and rich furnishings. The march of time had rendered useless the huge, cold, draughty castles of the past.

Margaret breathed in the sweet fresh air. It was late spring, and summer was just beginning to claim its allotted time. Carpets of bluebells spread out over the floors of the oak and beech woodlands. The white and yellow flowers of the wild strawberry shone bright and glossy in the afternoon sunlight. Amongst the clovers of the short grasslands, yellow 'lady's fingers' grew plentiful, and the meadows were filled with buttercups. Nature was renewing itself. Young fledglings were learning to fly, lambs and calves to walk.

Margaret willed herself to be happy, but although her eyes saw beauty, her heart was still heavy. She sighed; would she never break free from this heavy cloak of sadness that she wore?

Ewelme Manor, Oxfordshire
24 May 1472

Margaret's arrival at the manor house had gladdened her heart. She had walked the beautiful galleries of the house, and marvelled at the craftsmanship of its new stone fireplaces, rich tapestries, and paintings that adorned the walls. After the Tower, it was a welcome retreat of comfort and peace.

Her rooms were sumptuously furnished with furniture from Italy and Spain, with thick North African rugs covering the floor. Her bed was a joy to behold, after the hard pallet she had endured within her cell.

Alice had presented her with a wardrobe of new dresses and undergarments – her old worn dresses that held the dirt of the Tower were taken away and burnt. Alice had also found two of her old attendants – Petronilla and Mary – to wait on Margaret.

Margaret felt comforted to have faces she knew and people she could trust, around her. Alice had thought of everything to make her stay comfortable.

At first, King Edward had wanted Margaret imprisoned two miles further along the road at Wallingford Castle. Alice's husband was the constable there, and he had told Margaret that it had been the home to other royal ladies in days gone by: Isabella, wife of Edward II, had lived there. The widow of the Black Prince – Joan, Countess of Kent – had lived and died there. Catherine of France, and even Margaret's husband, as a boy, had stayed there. For Margaret, its cold empty turrets would have been as bad as the Tower. Fortunately, Alice had persuaded the King to let Margaret be held under house arrest at her estate.

After bathing, Margaret dressed for the small celebration that Alice had organised. She chose a simple, white, linen dress that flowed gently out from her hips to her feet. The top of the dress was oversewn with beautiful ivory silk that tightened in at her waist, and covered the sleeves. Down the front was a double line of pearls. The simple style of the dress showed off Margaret's natural beauty and slim figure; it pleased her.

Her ladies-in-waiting brushed and pleated her fine, blonde hair, and finished it by pinning a ring of wild summer flowers around the top.

Alice entered the room and gasped with delight. 'You look beautiful!' she cried. 'Where is that waif from the Tower?'

Margaret smiled as she stepped forward and hugged Alice. 'With praise to you, she has gone.'

'Come,' said Alice, softly. 'We have time for a walk in the gardens before the feast.'

The sun was waning as they walked. Margaret felt the coolness of the evening air through her simple linen dress. The freedom and space of the gardens delighted her as she looked up at the big cloudless sky above. It seemed to stretch forever into the distance. *How different*, she mused, *from the small square patch I used to glimpse at from my cell in the Tower.*

They walked arm in arm past the beautifully sculptured conifers, and the small tightly cut hedges that gave the garden its shape.

'How are you feeling, my Lady Queen?' asked Alice.

'I feel light-headed as though in a dream; as if detached, like watching someone else, and scared I will wake up soon and be back in my cell.'

Alice squeezed Margaret's arm. 'It is real, my Lady Queen.'

'Then, I feel wonderful, and sad, all at the same time, if that is possible,' replied Margaret.

'That will change.'

Margaret saw a smile appear around Alice's eyes.

'You are still young,' continued Alice. 'God will not desert you.'

They walked slowly on in silence, until Alice stopped. 'I have forgotten an important detail for tonight's feast!' she cried. 'Carry on down to the end of this path. The garden ends there but the view across the valley is beautiful; you must go and see it. I will come back shortly to escort you into the Great Hall for our celebration.' She turned, and hurried away.

Margaret looked after her, puzzled, and then carried on slowly towards the end of the path, happy to have a few moments alone.

She was so deep in thought, she did not see the figure that stepped out from the hedges and trees, and who stood, watching her approach. She sensed, more than saw that someone was there. She stopped and slowly raised her eyes.

The setting sun was behind him, casting a shadow over his features. When she saw his wild blonde hair blowing gently in the breeze, her heart started beating faster. She saw his stance – it made her gasp: one leg straight, the other slightly bent with the shoe turned out. She knew then, without a doubt.

'Simon?' she cried. 'Simon?'

They rushed towards each other, their eyes never leaving the other's face. Then, feet away, they stopped as though an invisible wall stood between them.

Tears slowly rolled down Margaret's cheeks; her ears hummed with the beating of her heart, and then she was in Simon's arms, holding him tight as though her life depended on it.

'I said I would come when you needed me.' Simon's voice was thick with emotion.

Margaret looked up at him; her tears mingled with his, as they embraced. Their bodies clung to each other as they both felt their empty hearts fill with joy. It seemed an eternity before they relaxed. They stepped slightly away from each other, their eyes hungrily studying the other.

Margaret spoke first. 'It is nearly two years since you left me at Château d'Amboise,' she said, her eyes flashing with hurt, 'and I have endured too much because of you.'

'I had to go,' Simon said, softly. 'I was told the fate of my mother and sisters.'

'And did you find them?'

'No. Warwick had them killed.'

Margaret's eyes softened with compassion. She moved closer into Simon's arms, and rested her head on his shoulder. 'I lost my sweet son at Tewkesbury,' she whispered. 'He was shown no mercy, and killed by that monster, Richard of Gloucester. I was taken to the Tower of London, and on my first night there, under cover of darkness, Richard came and murdered poor Henry as he prayed. The man is more ruthless than the Devil.'

There was a silence between them. Finally, Margaret said, 'We are all that each other has left in this world; we must never be parted again.'

Simon lifted her chin and kissed her, tenderly. 'You have more than just me,' he said, with a broad smile.

Margaret stepped back, and studied his face. 'Anne?' was all she said.

'You have a grandson called Edward, after his father. He is safe in France with Lady Vaux, at your father's court.'

Margaret reached up and kissed Simon, passionately. Tears of joy formed in her eyes.

Hurwell Manor, Tunstall Estate, Darlington
14 December 1473

John Tunstall awoke with a start. He had been dreaming of the day he had been detailed, by the Great Controller, to become Duke Richard's companion.

Lying in the darkness, he could feel the warmth of Rose sleeping beside him. He snuggled deeper under the bedclothes enjoying this time before dawn, before having to face the cold of the winter morning.

It was ten years ago to the day that he had attended his interview with the Great Controller. His mind rolled back over those years: Richard arriving at Middleham Castle as a young boy...now he was master of it, and married to Warwick's daughter, Anne. She had given him a son, but now kept her own household, and rarely saw Richard, who travelled the north much of the time on official business, and who also had mistresses, and bastard children, to keep him occupied.

Jacquetta of Luxembourg – the Queen's mother – had suddenly died in May the previous year. She had been called a witch, but no one had found the proof, although Lord Hastings had tried hard enough.

Margaret of Anjou had returned to live in France with Simon Langford and her grandson. They sent letters secretly to Rose, telling her of his progress. Rose would pass on the news to Anne, who was forever grateful.

King Louis still schemed and plotted his way around Europe, but now left King Edward in peace, at least for the time being, although once Burgundy was brought to heel, John mused, that might all change.

What of George, Duke of Clarence? His drinking was becoming uncontrollable. John knew there would be trouble ahead with him, one day.

Rose stirred gently beside him.

And what of me? John pondered, as he lay in the warmth of the bed. *I have my love close beside me. My son of eighteen months is growing healthy and strong. The Hallet twins live and work on the estate, and are very much part of the family.* They had both married silk-women from York, so had, at last, been domesticated.

My mother resides happily at Middleham Castle in her old rooms, although she visits us here to see her grandson; she is still the faithful companion to Lady Warwick, now the earl's widow.

After the last ten years of battles, intrigues, and betrayals, life had finally settled down. Every one of the players was either dead, or in their rightful place, and King Edward was secure on his throne.

May peace reign for many a long year throughout this green and pleasant land, John thought, before turning over. Putting his arm around Rose's waist, he gently pulled her closer…

AUTHOR'S NOTE

Richard, the Duke of Gloucester (later Richard III), was the youngest brother of Edward IV. Being the youngest was not deemed important enough to have his early life chronicled by the writers of the day. All that is known about him was, that aged ten, he was taken to Flanders by his mother, when fleeing from the advancing army of Margaret of Anjou. Margaret had just slain Richard's father, the Duke of York, and his older brother, Edmund, the Earl of Rutland, at the battle of Wakefield.

Richard, as a young boy, appears once again in the chronicles of 1463, where it was written that he was sent to Middleham Castle as a ward of the Earl of Warwick, to be taught the rudiments of knightly conduct. Therefore, the early years of Richard's life are sketchy.

His time at Middleham Castle coincides with the last year of the Lancastrian resistance led by Queen Margaret of Anjou.

In the book, I have him kidnapped by the Lancastrians who are clutching at any means possible to stave off their imminent defeat. This episode is complete fiction, but the reasoning behind it is that when the Earl of Warwick advanced up through the north-west, hammering the last nail into the coffin of the Lancastrian cause, he allowed the great fortresses of Alnwick and Dunstanburgh to surrender peacefully. He pardoned all the men within, as was the custom in those days – the less damage to a castle the better. In the case of Bamburgh Castle, no such pardon was forthcoming. Warwick shipped cannon all the way from London to smash the walls of this great fortress to pieces No mercy was shown to the garrison. It was the only castle to receive such violent treatment throughout the whole of the period called the 'War of the Roses', and the question is: why?

My theory is that something had happened concerning the officers, or men, of the occupying garrison, and my fictitious answer is that they had kidnapped Richard, a royal prince – the youngest brother of their hated enemy, King Edward, and a ward under the personal protection of the Earl of Warwick; hence, the level of force used against them.

Margaret of Anjou: Dates, locations, and battles are historically correct, although, a few dates have been changed slightly to allow the story to flow. To solve some of the mysteries that surround her, I have introduced a fictional lover, named Simon Langford.

Margaret left Bamburgh Castle shortly before Warwick smashes down its walls. She abandons her husband, Henry VI, and flees to France. Why? For sixteen years, she had ruled and fought for his crown, and then, suddenly, she gives up her royal world.

My reason for introducing Simon Langford is that she realises the game is up. The Yorkists have won, and after sixteen hard years of ruling as a woman in a man's world, she is exhausted.

Simon offers her a new world, a new life away from her sexless marriage to Henry. She was still a beautiful young woman at this time; she could have taken Henry with her to France, but chose not to, despite knowing that she would never return to England. She could have crossed the border into Scotland, and continued the fight from there, but again, chose not to.

Later in the book, Simon is used by Louis XI to force Margaret to return to England against her will.

In the history books, there is always a question mark as to why Margaret allowed her son, the Prince Edward, to marry the daughter of her most hated enemy – the Earl of Warwick. Margaret loathed Warwick with a vengeance. He had destroyed all that she held dear, and had taken the crown of England from her head, so why did she agree to the marriage? I surmise that Louis XI held something over her – something he could blackmail or threaten her with. We may never know the true answer, but holding her lover's life to ransom, I believe, would have been a good reason to force her to agree to all that King Louis asked of her.

Edward IV: Much is known about Edward. His life was well documented. Handsome and clever, every inch a king, it was his marriage to the widow, Elizabeth Grey, who was reported to be six years older than he was, and already with two young sons, that still mystifies historians today.

He should have married Isabella of Castile, uniting England with Spain, or the Bona of Savoy – the younger sister of the Queen of France – uniting England with France, or even Mary of Guelders, the widowed Queen of Scotland; thus bringing peace between the two countries. Instead, he secretly marries the widow of Sir John Grey, a Lancastrian knight, who had been killed fighting against the Yorkists at the battle of St Albans.

Edward then allows the Earl of Warwick to go to the court of King Louis XI to negotiate a marriage for him that will unite the French and English courts, even though he is secretly married to Elizabeth Grey. Maybe, he thought he could annul the marriage once he had grown tired of her, or have her secretly disappear. We will never know.

We do know that at a great meeting of the nobles at Reading, just as Warwick is to announce the name of Edward's French bride, Edward blurts out that he is already married, sending Warwick and himself on a path to civil war. Why did he do it?

It is well documented that, Elizabeth Grey's mother, Jacquetta – the Duchess of Bedford – dabbled in witchcraft throughout her life. She was even attainted to appear before Parliament to answer charges of sorcery. On her death, in 1472, small leaden figures were supposedly found amongst her possessions. All this may be hearsay and rumour, but I have used these connections to the black arts to explain why Edward acted as he did – he was bewitched into doing so.

The Earl of Warwick: All dates and battles within the book are correct. The only fictional account is the attempt on his life at Rouen. This is pure fiction. Although, a man as powerful and ruthless as he, I feel sure, would have attracted many plots against him.

The date of his death at the Battle of Barnet is correct, but how he died is open to question. There are many differing accounts as to the manner of his demise, whether it was on horseback or foot. All agree that he was fleeing the field. I have him on foot; if he had mounted a horse, I am sure he would have escaped.

Lady Anne Neville, Warwick's younger daughter: All dates are correct. Not many facts are known about Anne's life. Was she strong or weak? Nothing about her physical appearance survives, but the great historical mystery that surrounds Anne is the question: where was she for the ten months after the Battle of Tewkesbury?

Her husband of six months, and Margaret of Anjou's son: Prince Edward, was dead, slain by Richard of Gloucester at the Battle of Tewkesbury. Her father, the Earl of Warwick, was now dead, so she had become an extremely rich widow having inherited half of his estates.

The accepted story seems to be that Richards's brother, George – the Duke of Clarence – kept her as a ward or prisoner to stop Richard marrying her and taking control of her lands. George wanted them for himself, and the story goes that he kept her hidden, working as a kitchen maid for ten months, before she was discovered and rescued by Richard – sounds like Cinderella! She was the daughter of the greatest noble in the land; she would have been used to complete luxury, servants, and fine foods. The thought of her slaving away in a hot kitchen does tend to stretch the imagination.

Being a very rich widow, under English law at the time, she had to answer to no one. She was independent. I surmise that she was pregnant. She was young, healthy, and married for six months to a young and healthy husband. Her disappearance for ten months, in 1471, to have the baby, makes perfect sense. She had to keep the birth secret, because, if a boy, he would be the heir to the Lancastrian throne, and a major threat to King Edward and his brothers.

I will state that I can find no documentation to prove she was pregnant, or had a child, so my account of this is purely fictional.

David Saunders

Website: http://www.thedreamsofkings.com
Email: thedreamsofkings@gmail.com

7312854R00274

Printed in Great Britain
by Amazon.co.uk, Ltd.,
Marston Gate.